PRAISE FOR *A DIVI*

"In a writing style reminiscent of Tes spins **a breathtaking tale** based on t   ...., ..v v osepn and his wife Asenath. This story inspired me with its authentic characters that leapt off the page with their struggles, triumphs, and resilient faith. Romance, suspense, intrigue, and a beautiful message of forgiveness make this a story readers won't be able to put down!"

~ Heidi Chiavaroli
Carol Award-winning author of *The Orchard House* and *Hope Beyond the Waves*

"Ifueko Ogbomo has penned *A Divine Romance* that will resonate in our hearts well past the last page. Though the story of Joseph is known, Ms. Ogbomo used historical romance to layer in the gaps in a way that puts the reader in a Biblical setting and brings his story to life. Her use of poems, stunning imagery, and the love of a God who chases after the one will endear her to lovers of Christian fiction."

~ Toni Shiloh
Christy Award-winning author of *In Search of a Prince*

"I initially thought I would read the first few pages of *A Divine Romance* just to satisfy my curiosity about this biblical fiction debut. Well, one page turned to twenty, twenty to fifty, fifty to a hundred, and before I knew it, by late that same night I finished the book! Ifueko Ogbomo captures the drama of the biblical epic of Genesis and evokes a sense of beauty with colorful imagery and vivid descriptions of the ancient world in *A Divine Romance*. **Gifted storytelling** brings an intricate cast of characters to life and portrays the greatest kind of love there is: the healing love that comes from God."

~ Jenna Van Mourik
author of *Jerusalem's Daughter;* host of *Biblical Fiction Buffs*

"Ifueko Ogbomo has brought her effortless eloquence and spellbinding storytelling to **an unforgettable masterpiece of historical fiction**. I read *A Divine Romance* with unexpected

i

intensity. Admittedly, I found moments when tears burned my eyes and other times when its vivid scenes so consumed my thoughts, that with childlike excitement I could hardly wait to answer the question, "What next?" *A Divine Romance* is an extraordinary debut. Ifueko seamlessly and uniquely ushers us into an exciting and intriguing world of fascinating biblical characters and facts, intertwined with a very creative and imaginative fictional world of suspense, filled with love, hope, betrayal, and so much more. With such vivid imagery one easily sees in this biblical romance a riveting film begging to be produced."

~ Rev. Nims Obunge MBE DL
Deputy Lieutenant to His Majesty's Lord Lieutenant for Greater London

"*A Divine Romance* is **captivating, beautifully written, and gripping**. The plot is well executed. The characters are amazing. I can only imagine the amount of research Ifueko put into crafting this inspiring story. Biblical fiction is my favorite sub-genre of Christian fiction, and I have about three authors I trust to keep me fed. Ifueko Ogbomo is on her way to taking the fourth place. A really beautiful debut."

~ Ebosereme Aifuobhokhan
Christian fiction book reviewer and influencer; host of *Batya's Bits blog*

A Divine Romance

A Divine Romance

A NOVEL

IFUEKO OGBOMO

INSPIROLOGOS
PUBLISHING

To my Eternal Lover

***

I live, as you love
Breathe, for breath you give
I am, as you are, 'I AM'
Free, for you forgive

A READER'S GUIDE FOR *A DIVINE ROMANCE*

Ifueko Ogbomo invites you to discover:

ANCIENT EGYPTIAN CITIES, DEITIES, FASHIONS, & NAMES

MAP OF ANCIENT EGYPT

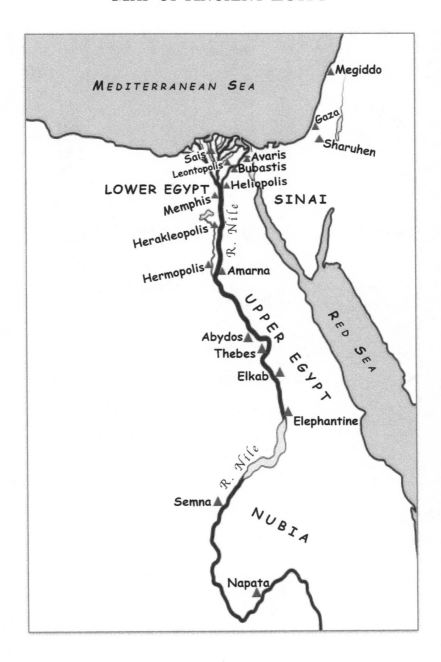

DEITIES OF ANCIENT EGYPT

(The table below lists Egyptian gods referenced in *A Divine Romance*)

RA

ISIS

OSIRIS

HORUS

Name of god	Territory/Expertise of god
Hapi	Nile | Annual flooding of the Nile
Horus	Sky | Kingship
Isis (sister/wife of Osiris)	Life | Fertility | Childbirth | Magic
Osiris	The afterlife | The dead | Resurrection
Ra (or Re)	Sun | Universal creation | Life
Set (brother of Osiris)	War | Chaos | Storms

Fashions of Ancient Egypt

Kalasiris - Ankle-length, formfitting, linen sheath dress with one or two shoulder straps. Worn by women.

Nemes - Striped head cloth, covering the entire head, with two large flaps (lappets) hanging down behind the ears and in front of both shoulders. Worn by Pharaoh.

Shendyt - Short men's skirt, gathered at the front, typically covering from the waist to just above the knees.

Usekh - Necklace or broad collar covering the shoulders, typically with gold clasps, sometimes featuring a long, waist-length stem. Made from colored stone beads, metal, or flowers. Worn by women, men, and gods.

Makeup was worn by both sexes. Black kohl eyeliner made from galena, red lip color made with ochre, and blue or green eyeshadow fashioned from crushed malachite.

Usually barefoot, people wore leather sandals on special occasions. Except the priests, who wore papyrus sandals.

Children under the age of six did not wear clothing, but they did wear jewelry: anklets, bracelets, and *usekhs*.

NAMES OF CHARACTERS IN *A DIVINE ROMANCE*

*Fictional characters bear interpretive Ancient Egyptian names,
except for one or two with Hebrew names (underlined).
Uppercase names are biblical.*

NAME	MEANING	CHARACTER
Akhenaten	Effective for Aton—a sun god	Pharaoh of Egypt
Akhom	Falcon / Eagle	Step brother of Pharaoh
Aneksi	She belongs to me	45th wife of Pharaoh
ASENATH	Gift of the sun god	Daughter of Potiphera
Bakenranef	Servant of his name	Royal treasurer
Basmat	Fragrance	Nurse of Joseph's sons
Benerib	Sweet of heart	Daughter of Neferubity/ Potiphar
EPHRAIM	Fruitful	Joseph & Asenath's 2nd son
Haankhes	May she live	Tsillah's cousin
Heqaib	He who controls his heart	Na'eemah's nephew/ adopted son
Idu	Boy	Asenath's distant relative
Inyotef	He who his father brought	Heqaib's son | Meriiti's twin
JOSEPH	Savior	Vizier of Egypt (also called Zaphnath-Paaneah)
MANASSEH	Causing to forget	Joseph & Asenath's firstborn
Mayet	Cat	Teacher of seductive arts

NAME	MEANING	CHARACTER
Meresankh	She loves life	Heqaib's daughter
Meriiti	Beloved of the father	Heqaib's son | Inyotef's twin
Merit	Beloved	Asenath's handmaiden
Metjen	The leader	Overseer of Pharaoh's wives
<u>**Miriam**</u>	Sea of bitterness	Mother of Merit
Na'eemah	Mother	Asenath's mother figure (Her late mother's handmaiden)
Narmer	Raging catfish	Asenath's instructor of musical instruments
Nebemakhet	Lord at the horizon	Second captain, king's guard
Neferubity	The beauty of the king of lower Egypt	Nubian princess; Daughter of Panehesy
Neheb	He who belongs to the plow	Deputy overseer of Pharaoh's wives | Metjen's right hand
Panehesy	The Nubian	King of Nubia
Patareshness	The land rejoices in her	39th wife of Pharaoh
Pehernefer	At his end there is good	Pharaoh's chief butler
Perneb	Lord of his house	Steward of Joseph's house
POTIPHAR	He whom Ra gave	Captain of the king's guard
POTIPHERA	Meaning unknown	High Priest of Heliopolis | Father of Asenath
Sahure	He who is close to Ra	Priest | Satiah's twin brother

NAME	MEANING	CHARACTER
Satiah	Daughter of the moon	Priestess | Asenath's childhood best friend | Twin sister of Sahure
Semat	The companion	Asenath's chief handmaiden
Senbi	To be healthy	Warden of King's Prison
Senenmut	Mother's brother	Chief royal scribe
Tsillah	Shadow	Asenath's handmaiden
Wadjenes	Fresh of tongue	Steward of Joseph's house
Wehemmesu	Rebirth	Pharaoh's chief baker
Wenennefer	The one who continues to be perfect	Priest; Father of Satiah and Sahure
ZAPHNATH-PAANEAH	Revealer of secrets or Savior of the world	Vizier of Egypt (also called Joseph)

RELATIVES OF JOSEPH/ZAPHNATH-PAANEAH

NAME (HEBREW)	CHARACTER	IN RELATION TO JOSEPH
Abraham	Jacob's grandfather	Great-grandfather
Asher	Jacob's 8th son	Step brother
Benjamin	Jacob's 12th son | Rachel's son	Brother
Dan	Jacob's 5th son	Step brother
Gad	Jacob's 7th son	Step brother
Isaac	Jacob's father	Grandfather
Issachar	Jacob's 9th son	Step brother
Jacob/Israel	Patriarch of Israel	Father
Judah	Jacob's 4th son	Step brother
Laban	Jacob's uncle	Great-uncle
Leah	Jacob's first wife | Rachel's older sister	Step mother
Levi	Jacob's 3rd son	Step brother
Naphtali	Jacob's 6th son	Step brother
Rachel	Jacob's second wife	Mother
Rebecca	Wife of Isaac	Grandmother
Sarah	Abraham's wife	Great-grandmother
Reuben	Jacob's 1st son	Step brother
Simeon	Jacob's 2nd son	Step brother
Zebulun	Jacob's 10th son	Step brother

PROLOGUE

Love not
Harden your heart
For love is but a yoke
Carved by the gods to enslave all
Mortals

***

White.
It was the most beautifully bittersweet, unwanted yet beloved gift she had ever been bestowed. Fashioned from a fabric the purest of hues, she deemed it the loveliest raiment in all existence and one worthy of a queen. At least it was in her innocent eyes. Grasping two fistfuls of its pleated skirt, she buried her oval face in the delicate cloth, wanting to revive the unique scent of the garment's rightful owner. But it was long gone.

It was not supposed to be gone. Just like she was not supposed to be resting in her luxurious chambers in the middle of the day, especially one so fair-weathered as today. But then again, she had not expected the rite of passage into womanhood to feel like a hive of angry bees stinging her belly from within. Mercifully, she was beginning to feel like her body belonged to her once more, for it was all she could do the past three days to sit in bed, sipping spicy vegetable soup and nibbling on freshly baked bread. Well, that and daydream.

Sighing, she leaned back onto her plush pillows, gently pulling the garment upward and laying her cheek on its delicate fabric. Closing her eyes, she let her mind wander back to the day she first beheld a familiar feminine form adorned in this stunning *kalasiris*.

1

ONE YEAR EARLIER

The evening air was chilly, so a robust fire was burning from the heart of the lavish indoor garden in the center of her family's extravagant villa. Sprawled out on an intricately woven mat, as close as possible to the fire, she was enjoying its warmth while practicing hieratic script on papyrus. This was but a prelude in anticipation of the imminent arrival of her best friend, which she was looking forward to, because any ten-year-old daughter of nobility would testify that daydreaming about love and marriage was twice as much fun with a partner in fantasy. She had just penned a difficult hieroglyph flawlessly when she caught wind of a familiar, cherished scent. Raising her head to find its source, she let out a gasp of delight that echoed across the garden. The slender, bronze-skinned, raven-haired beauty that sauntered toward her sparkled in jewels from her head to her ankles, but her brilliant-white, one-shouldered *kalasiris*, fitted her form to perfection, its bejeweled belt enhancing her waistline.

"Blessings of the evening, my little sun," the approaching lady of the house said with a cheerful wave. Neglecting to return the greeting, the wide-eyed little girl dropped her ink-laden reed pen, leaped to her feet, and in five swift strides, closed the distance between both females.

"Mother, you look like a goddess! Where are you going?" she asked, circling her mother in awed admiration.

Mother's laugh burst forth like the sound of a brief melody. "Your eyes are affected by affection, my little sun!"

"What does that mean?"

"It means you cannot see my flaws because you look at me through a veil of love. And to answer your question, I am going to a wedding."

"A wedding!" The girl yelled, clapping her hands in excitement. "Will it be a big one?"

"Yes! There will be many guests as the bride hails from an enormous family. Her mother had twelve children!"

"When I grow up, I want to have a big family," she said, spreading her slender arms wide, "with hundreds of children!"

"Hundreds?! My little sun, that is not a family, it is a VILLAGE! And after you birth your first child, I have no doubt you will change your mind."

"Never!" the determined child said, shaking her head from side to side as her thick chestnut curls bounced. "I WILL have a village, Mother! And a big wedding feast—at the palace!"

"The palace? In that case, you will have to marry Pharaoh, lord of Egypt—long may he live!"

The girl paused as twin furrows appeared on her flawless, brown-skinned brow. "But, Mother, does he not already have a wife?"

"He has many! And he will marry even more."

"Then I do not wish to marry him. I want to be my husband's only wife—like you are."

Raising her bracelet-bearing arms in surrender, Mother replied, "Then you had better be content to have a smaller wedding here at home. Better a small wedding to be the only wife than a royal wedding to be one of many wives. Would you not agree?"

"Yes, Mother," the daughter meekly agreed, "But may I still wear a beautiful wedding dress?"

"For the queen of a village? Only the most beautiful wedding *kalasiris!*"

"And jewels!" she yelled with renewed vigor, pumping her fist skyward.

"The rarest in all the land!" Mother said, her outstretched arm encompassing the garden in a graceful gesture.

"And I want my husband to love me as much as Father loves you!"

Mother paused, a sad expression crossing her dark eyes for the briefest moment. In a voice just above a whisper, she said, "By the mercy of Isis, he will love you much more."

The girl felt her mother's lips brush the crown of her curly head, and then she looked up into her mother's shiny eyes. They locked smiles for a moment. Then Mother broke the silence with a swift shake of her stylish head. "Now, a wedding awaits me. Does the queen of the village grant me permission to go?"

"Yes! You may go," she said with head held high and right arm extended in a dramatic wave.

Giving an exaggerated bow, Mother responded, "Your servant is most grateful, Your Magnificence."

Laughing, the happy child threw her arms around her mother's waist, reveling in the sweet scent of her fragrance. Long after her mother departed, she was fantasizing about owning such a goddess-worthy gown.

THE PRESENT

She opened her eyes and looked at the white *kalasiris*: the only gift she owned she had been allowed to select herself. It was but three months ago that Na'eemah—her mother's chief handmaiden—had given her the painful pleasure of keeping just one of her late mother's garments. There had been no doubt in her recently bereft mind about her choice. With trembling hands, she had latched on to the stunning *kalasiris*. In that moment, her fantasy from the day she first saw it became a bitter reality.

Even now, the gods permitting, she would instantly trade the regal raiment to have but a moment with its previous owner. In lieu of that, being able to call the garment her own would have to suffice. Until the day she could *make* it her own. She was eleven and still too small for the lovely attire. If she could make herself grow up faster just to have it fit her sooner, she would.

She fingered the fine fabric, admiring how its white color contrasted her sun-kissed skin, and speculated to what future occasion she might wear it.

A special temple festival.

Her best friend, Satiah's wedding.

Perhaps even her own betrothal ceremony—to Sahure. Assuming Satiah had her way, and the best friends became sisters by marriage. Though she was not exactly sure how a ceremony between herself and Satiah's twin brother would unfold—he was always red-faced and tongue-tied in her presence. She giggled at the thought of him trying to nod his way through the ceremonial questions, and her bold best friend yelling out the answers from behind the nearest pillar.

Shuffling herself out of her lavish ebony bed, she gingerly picked up the *kalasiris*, and draped it over her brown shoulder such that its skirt fell to her bare feet. Taking a few steps forward, she imagined herself walking down the center of a grandiose hall.

If I am half as elegant as Mother was, the eyes of every man shall be on me. But my eyes shall only rest on one man: my groom. She pictured herself standing tall, front and center of a magnificent chamber, as the priest performing the ceremony began: "Radiances, Reverences, Eminences, and people of Heliopolis, you are wel—"

"Come, my sunshine, your father calls," a familiar female voice from outside her chamber said, interrupting her daydream.

Father is home! Spinning around and laying the beloved garment back on her bed, she bounded past Na'eemah's plump, womanly figure, and raced towards her father's wing.

I wonder what he brought me, she thought with excitement, her waning abdominal discomforts forgotten. She did not know why he was home, but one thing was certain: if her father had returned earlier than scheduled, today was a special day.

Servants raised opulent curtains as she sped from a spacious hallway into a grand antechamber, in a most ungraceful manner. Once before the doors to her father's receiving chamber, she stopped and took a few calming breaths. Then, stepping inside, she paused at the door frame and looked at him, awaiting his invitation.

He was reclining on his favorite, one-armed sofa. Sitting up, he lifted a welcoming hand toward her.

"Come, gift of Ra."

"Life, prosperity, and health, to you, Father," she said, dipping her head in a bow and then entering gracefully.

Smiling, he returned the greeting, "Life, prosperity, and health, to you, daughter. I see your lessons are going well."

"Yes, Father," she said, warmed by his rare praise. He seemed almost cheerful today—more like his old self.

Patting the soft cushion beside him, her father said, "Come, sit. I have something for you."

Eager, she sat and raised her face toward his. "What is it, Father?"

"This," he answered, holding a sheer, small, white fabric.

What is that? She thought, trying to practice her lesson on *listening more than one speaks.*

"Na'eemah tells me you are having your first bleeding."

Why would she tell Father that?! Too mortified to answer, she merely nodded.

"Therefore, you are now a woman. It is time you know you are no ordinary woman . . . Your mother would have been better suited to explain this . . ." Father's eyes grew distant for a moment, even as her own heart tightened.

"I miss Mother." She whispered, but Father did not seem to hear her. Shaking his head, his eyes focused on her once more.

"From the first moment you opened your eyes in this world, we knew you were a gift from Ra himself. Yours is no ordinary life— you have a divine destiny."

"I do not understand, Father."

"Patience, daughter, your father still speaks."

She gave an apologetic dip of her head as he continued.

"The gods have destined you to bring honor upon this house, and the eternal favor of Pharaoh, lord of Egypt—long may he live. For no later than the dawning of your eighteenth year of life, you shall become a royal bride. Your husband shall be a pure-blooded royal, chosen by the lord of Egypt."

I will not get to choose my husband?

"I pray Ra, who has given you such unmatched beauty, sees fit to make you the wife of Pharaoh himself."

Wife of Pharaoh? Her heart skipped a beat. *Mother said Pharaoh has many wives!*

Oblivious to her rising anxiety, her father went on. "Henceforth, you are to be preserved from prying eyes. No man but your husband shall see your face." He picked up the sheer fabric and reached his arms toward her face.

No one shall see my face anymore? The thought was alarming. Before she could stop herself, she raised both hands, shielding herself. "I do not want my face hidden!"

"It is not about what you want, but what is right. Unworthy eyes must not behold the face of Ra's gift. You are a woman now; comport yourself as such!" Her father tried to hold her head in place with one hand while using the other to veil the bottom half of her face. It was proving to be a herculean task, as the frightened girl was squirming with all of her might.

"Sit still, child!" her father hissed.

She felt like she was suffocating. *Why do the gods hate me? They took Mother away. Will they also let Father make me invisible? No. I will NOT be invisible!* Forgetting every lesson on propriety and protocol, she did the only thing that came to mind: she opened her mouth and bit down hard.

Her father let out a sound like a wounded animal as he abruptly released her. "The curses of Ra!" He yelled, his plump, fair face suffusing with crimson. "Have you gone mad?"

She leaped off the sofa, blazing eyes aimed right at his. "I hate you! I wish it was you who died instead of Mother!"

He moved so swiftly she did not see it coming. The sound of his open, bejeweled palm colliding with her soft cheek echoed like a solitary thunderclap. She fell backwards onto the floor. Five fingers of fire began spreading up the right side of her face as a lone tear streamed down it. The slap shocked even more than it stung— Father had never struck her before. His re-approaching hands sent waves of panic rushing through her petite frame and she cowered. But the second slap she feared did not follow.

She heard silence, followed by her father's long, weary sigh. When she looked up at him, his face bore a strange look.

"Come, gift of Ra. One cannot hide from one's fate."

As she rose on shaky legs, the truth soured her stomach like a rotten pomegranate: there was to be no fighting her father or fate.

She approached him with her head lowered in defeat.

He lifted her face toward his, but she kept her eyes averted from his. Tenderly drying her now wet cheeks with the offensive article, he used it to conceal the bottom half of her face. "One day, you will thank me for this," he said. Then he rose and strode out of his chamber without a backward glance.

She lowered her head and let the tears fall. She did not realize anyone else was there until she felt soft, fleshy arms envelop her.

"My sunshine, do not cry." Na'eemah comforted. "Your father is only doing what is best. You are the gift of Ra. When your time comes, you will be the envy of all royal wives—"

"No! I do NOT wish to be a royal wife!"

"Bite your tongue! Ra must not hear you speak so! It is your destiny."

"No. I do not want . . . I do not want them anymoooore!" she wailed.

"Them? Calm yourself, child. You are losing reason."

The tears poured down her veiled face as sobs shook her frail frame.

"I . . . I do not want . . . I only want Mother!" She crumbled to the floor and gave rein to her renewed, intensified sense of grief. She wanted to tell Na'eemah, but she could not speak past the guttural groans gushing from her throbbing throat. Not that it mattered. Na'eemah would not understand. Only Mother could, for only Mother had known.

The wedding *kalasiris*.

The grand feast.

The village of a family.

She no longer wanted them. They no longer mattered—she was now invisible. *If no man can see me, how could any ever love me? Even Father does not love me anymore.*

She could not have been more wrong about today.

It was not a special day.

It was a sad, bad one—a black day.

Were the gods inclined to grant her desires above Father's, she would make but one, four-word request of them: *Take me to Mother*.

PART I:

VEILED

Colors of sunrise
Splashed across earth and sky. Lo!
A glimpse of heaven

***

SIX YEARS LATER

Shimmering.

The waters of the Nile were golden with the reflection of the sun. The clear sky was brightest of blue hues. It was the perfect day for a leisurely boat ride. A rather tall, large oarsman stood at the helm of the cedar canoe in which she sat. Her father was seated in the crevice before her, the only other passenger on their small water vessel. He had his back to her, and he seemed quite intent on studying the man rowing their boat. She was wondering whether to break the silence with an inquiry about their destination, or a comment about the wonderful weather, when something strange caught her eye.

The oarsman had dropped his rather thick, long, single oar and lifted both his hands skyward. As if on cue, the sky grew overcast. Strong winds streamed in from the east and began rocking their sea vessel. She grabbed on to the sides of the small catamaran, desperately trying to stay in her seat, as her father fell out of his, landing on his knees.

"Father!" she yelled, alarmed. He made no response. *Why is he silent? Is he injured?* She tried to rise and was immediately knocked to the floor of the wind-tossed craft. Maintaining a grip on one side of the boat, she slowly began shuffling her way toward her father hoping to come to his aid. Much to her surprise, the boatman seemed perfectly in control of his stance.

"Oarsman! Come. Help my father!"

The enormous man approached. Not bothering to look at him, she kept her eyes on her father. He was rocking back and forth on his knees as if bowing. She had just reached his side, and was trying to stretch one hand out to assist him, when the oarsman towered over her.

"It is not your father who needs help," he said, in an amused, eery voice.

Utterly stunned that any servant would dare question her instruction, especially one so obviously urgent, she snapped her head up. "How dare you—"

The sight of his fearsome face paralyzed her. His eyes were a burning yellow and filled with hunger, and his head resembled that of a horse. But it was his large, pointed teeth grinning at her that sent chills racing down her spine. *"By the mercy of Ra!"* she whispered fearfully.

"I will show you the mercy of Ra!" he said sinisterly, reaching down and grabbing her neck.

She felt her throat closing in and her air supply cutting off. He lifted her off her feet as effortlessly as one would pick a stray thread off a cloak. She tried to kick him with her legs, but it felt like she was kicking against copper. His ensuing laughter chilled her blood. She attempted turning her head to look at her father. He had turned and was looking up at her. *Help me, Father!* She screamed on the inside, the words unable to push their way past the death grip on her neck. Through her blurring vision she made out her father's features more closely, and any hope she had of him saving her shriveled up and died. His lips were sealed shut and his arms were bound in front of him.

With tears streaming down his face, he continued bowing, silently pleading with the one who was presently draining the life out of her. She felt her limbs grow numb, and the image of her father distorted as her life ebbed. Suddenly, she felt the vice-like grip on her neck loosen. She gasped in a gulp of air and felt her senses return for the briefest of moments. Just long enough to feel herself being swung through the air in a circular motion.

"Fare thee well!" yelled the frightening steerer of their boat as he opened his arm and released her. The splash her plunge created assaulted her ears. Her next gasp for air filled her lungs with icy waters. Coughing and spluttering, she tried to swim, but it was as though watery hands beneath her worked in tandem with the coppery ones above her. While the latter pushed her, the former pulled. She felt herself sink lower and lower until there was neither fight nor breath left in her. Nothing remained but black, chilly silence. It was so cold, it started to feel warm. But then the warmth grew, and a brightness seemed to surround her. As though being pulled up by invisible arms, she began to rise, faster and higher, until she broke through the water's surface, gasping and flailing her arms wildly.

She was still panting and tossing when she realized she was actually in a very different, much safer location. Familiar carvings were etched into the ceiling above her, and beneath her were the softest, most expensive bed sheets in the land. Knowing she had been dreaming did not immediately translate to the calming of her alarmed senses. Her heart was racing and her hands were shaking. She was drenched. Flinging the covers off her sweat-soaked skin, she swung her legs over the side of her high bed.

By the life of Pharaoh, what does this dream signify?

She had not the faintest idea, but the sinking feeling in her stomach told her it boded no good. Experience had proven that her dreams were self-fulfilling prophecies of doom. The first time she'd had such an unsettling dream was the day before Osiris ushered her mother into the afterlife. The last time was the morning of the black day. Until now.

She still felt like she was suffocating. *I need air!* Lightly rubbing a hand over her throat, she looked around her chamber. Judging by the dimness both within and outside its latticed window, the day had not yet dawned, but she did not care. This would not be the first time she had escaped to her place of comfort without the help of sunlight. She slipped her feet into the papyrus sandals at her bedside. Just beside her cot stood an intricately carved small cedar table. She reached for the veil that lay on it, pausing a handbreadth from it. Although it was now like her second skin, it seemed unappealing after her vivid dream.

13

It is still dark anyway. I can do without it for now. Rising, she fastened it to a fold in her sleeping tunic. *My cloak.* Feeling her way around the room, she took her cloak down from its usual resting place and wrapped it around herself, then stealthily made her way out of her chambers, not wanting to awaken the snoring handmaiden nearby. She needed neither assistance nor interference for this excursion, merely stealth and speed.

***

She did not know what it was like to dwell in an immortal paradise, but surely, the serenity of this elevated place was comparable. Lifting her oval face skyward, she closed her eyes and began taking in deep, calming breaths. Her brief but brisk excursion out of her luxurious home had been worth the few scratches it had earned her. This was the one place where she could rid herself of the disconcerting feelings that had filled her since awakening. Dwelling on the mysterious dream would not shed light on its meaning, only fan the flames of her mounting anxiety. She was not blessed with the gift of interpreting visions of the night. Merely the curse of having them before misfortune manifested itself in her life. Were he not himself cast in her dream in an unflattering light, she might ask her father for a meaning.

Satiah might know. Her childhood best friend had been conscripted into the life of a priestess since the girl's crimson visitor showed up, one short month after her own. The separation had stolen whatever little sparks of joy might have remained in her childhood after the black day. She had been too heartbroken to make another real friend since. Seeing Satiah at the occasional temple festival was still the highlight of those ceremonies. And today was one of such. Although, there was neither a guarantee she would see Satiah nor that the priestess would have any insights about her disturbing dream. It was probably best she focused her efforts at Temple today on beseeching the gods to blow away whatever ill wind was coming. Until then, she would make the most of this moment of serenity and liberty.

A gentle breeze rustled through her waist-length hair, causing curls to envelop her slender frame. She speculated if the resulting soft, tingly feeling might resemble a lover's caress.

Not that I will ever know that pleasure; I will be eighteen in less than a year. The thought was unnerving. The age that inspired celebration for most noble young women inspired dread in her. Like a never-ending plague, the memory of the black day past stained her present. She rued the day of her veiling like the visit of an armed bandit. It had robbed her of two irreplaceable things: faith in her father's love and hope of finding true love. Feeling a familiar sorrow wrap itself around her heart, she shook her head. *Stop these miserable musings; you came here to forget.*

Shutting her eyes more tightly, she drew her mind back from images of her foreboding future to sounds in her present, pleasant surroundings.

The melodic chirping of a bird in a branch nearby.

The whispers and whistles of the wind whipping through the leaves.

Sensing the faint light of dawn suddenly intensifying, she opened her eyes and involuntarily caught her breath. There was something mesmerizing about the bronze, orange, and yellow hues of a new dawn. The seamless blend of colors never ceased to amaze. Each was distinct, yet together they formed one spectacularly luminous shade.

Horus is indeed a celestial artist without a human rival to paint such multicolored magnificence every morning. Adding to their awe-inspiring quality was the fact that even though each dawn broke at about the same time daily, no two dawns were exactly alike. The one thing they had in common was that each, including the one she now gazed upon, was breathtaking. A slow smile spread across her unveiled face.

Here, where heaven kissed earth, was her favorite place to be.

Here, looking down and drinking in the scintillating scenery of the city of Heliopolis, or looking up and soaking in the splendor of the stunning sunrise.

Here, nestled in the thick branches of the largest tree that sat at the top of the highest mound, in the fields at the end of a weathered path, emerging from an almost imperceptible gap in the fence surrounding the luxurious residence she called home.

Here, suspended between ground and sky, she was free. Free to be anyone—that is, anyone else.

Up here, she was not a sacred gift from the sun god.

She was not a mysterious curiosity—the favorite subject of citywide gossip.

She was not a rare prize desired by men and envied by women.

Not the motherless daughter of the high priest.

Not a friendless virgin hidden beneath a fragile veil.

Up here, she was just a seventeen-year-old girl called A—

"My lady!"

A bright, female voice interrupted her reverie. Her chief handmaiden was the only one who knew her secret haven. If Semat was here, the house was stirring. And it would be bustling in no time—as was typical of all festival mornings. Once back in her home, she would have to make haste. Sighing, she closed her eyes for a moment longer, not wanting to leave the soothing stillness of this sweet moment. Reopening her eyes, she drew her veil from the folds of her garment and fastened it across the bottom half of her face in one fluid motion.

Beginning her swift, well-rehearsed descent from her treasured tree was always akin to climbing down from the heavens to the earth. Her seven handmaidens would undoubtedly describe her predestined, predictable life as pampered. But with each passing day, hers seemed more like a life sentence than a life—and the fact that her prison had bars made of gold did not make it any less suffocating.

Once more upon solid ground, she faced her most trusted handmaiden.

"Blessings of the morn, my lady," Semat said, bowing her head.

"And to you, Semat. Were you seen?"

"No, my lady. Most were yet to rise when I noticed your absence."

"Good. Let us return as discreetly as we each came."

"Is . . . Is all well today, my lady?"

The question of the hour. "It remains to be seen what the day will bring."

"Naught but the mercy of Ra," her handmaiden said confidently, turning toward their villa.

Any other morning and she would have affirmed Semat's statement with the words, '*So be it.*' But this morning, she caressed her throat and silently swallowed the lump seemingly swelling therein.

2

Three suns rise each day
One at dawn. The others:
As you open your eyes

***

Arresting.

The twain amber windows to her soul stared back at her from a burnished bronze mirror. They were her gift, and her curse. Their yellowish-golden color striking against her sun-kissed complexion, they drew admiring glances and the occasional bold compliments from strangers. Ironically, they had invited teasing from childhood playmates, making her wish for ebony eyes. As well as straight, dark hair, like her mother's. She still wished the gods had bestowed brown eyes upon her at birth, but for a much more significant reason than escaping careless childhood tongues. Had she not been born with eyes reminiscent of two suns, she would not have been branded 'The gift of Ra.' Her life would have taken a path completely different from the one it was taking.

"Is my lady not pleased with her attire?" Semat inquired.

The young mistress let her boldly lined eyes take in the rest of her reflection. Her tall, slender figure was flattered by a light, linen *kalasiris*. The formfitting, cap-sleeved sheath dress boasted a belt that accentuated her tiny waist. Precious stones sparkled from the broad *usekh* that adorned her long neck. Fashioned in traditional style, the elaborate necklace covered her shoulders and extended down to just above her bust. Broad, beaded bracelets circled her dainty wrists, papyrus sandals laced her slim feet, and a gold anklet decorated her right ankle. The veil that fell from the bridge of her

19

pointed nose across her high cheekbones was fashioned from a sheer, white fabric. Extending past her chin, it hid uniquely shaped, full, pink lips presently rouged with ochre.

Turning from side to side, she could find no fault in the attire, but many in herself.

Limbs too long . . . bust too large . . . lips too full . . .

"You grow more beautiful every day, Asenath."

Turning away from the mirror, she flashed a brilliant smile at the olive-skinned, full-figured older lady who had just sauntered into her lavish chamber. "Your eyes are affected by affection, Na'eemah."

"That is a fault I have no desire to correct," Na'eemah responded, her small, brown eyes misty.

Turning back to the mirror, Asenath ordered, "My wig, Semat."

As her handmaiden hastened to retrieve the raven-haired, bejeweled ceremonial accessory, she turned to one of her six secondary handmaidens. Indicating her thick hair, she said, "A few more strokes through, Merit, and then braid it." Picking up a wide-toothed comb, the shy maiden set to work. Asenath might not be able to darken her eyes, but she would ensure every strand of her chestnut curls was tucked beneath the fringed wig that women customarily wore for formal occasions.

"You fret needlessly, my sunshine. Even in a dress fashioned from stalks of wheat, you would still be the most beautiful woman there."

"Would you like me to change into such a dress?" Asenath said, wiggling her eyebrows.

"The mercy of Ra! What would your father say?"

As Asenath giggled at Na'eemah's widened eyes, Semat returned with a long, dark wig accessorized with gold trinkets. Asenath lowered her head slightly so her handmaiden could crown it, keeping her gaze on the mirror. Her reflection now boasted straight, dark hair. *Perfect.* Spinning around to face Na'eemah, she gave a gracefully exaggerated bow. "The gift of Ra is ready."

"Excellent. Your carriage awaits. The daughter of the high priest cannot be late to Temple!"

"Late?" Asenath gasped in feigned shock. "Ra would surely turn the sun black in his fury!"

"You jest, but he just might!" Na'eemah said, wagging a plump finger at her. "Lest I forget, I made a special batch of honey cakes for your father. I used your mother's recipe. Merit will carry them along. Asenath, do not forget to deliver them; they are his favorite."

"Certainly. But are you not joining us today?"

"I fear there is already a festival underway in here," Na'eemah said, pointing at her temple. "This throbbing is surely the beating of a thousand miniature drums!"

"The mercy of Isis, Na'eemah, why did you say nothing until now? I should stay and make you a healing balm."

"You shall do no such thing. Moreover, I have a feeling I might make a better recovery with my own recipe."

Asenath gasped. "If that is the thanks I get, I shall take my skills elsewhere!"

"Yes, to the house of the gods! Now go!"

Asenath leaned in to kiss Na'eemah's forehead and whispered, "Please, rest. I do not know what I should ever do without you." The comforting feel of the motherly woman's soft hand cradling her veiled cheek for the briefest of moments drew a smile. Even though Na'eemah said nothing, her misty-eyed silence spoke volumes. Turning away, Asenath took two steps towards her door.

"Your shawl, my lady," Semat said, holding out a light, pleated fabric.

As Asenath halted, the dark-haired, doe-eyed maiden wrapped the shawl about her broad shoulders. It had a twofold benefit: to hide her feminine frame from lustful eyes and to shield her skin from the scorching Egyptian sun.

"Thank you, Semat."

"For the love of Ra, put those long legs of yours to use!" Na'eemah urged, waving Asenath toward the polished wooden door of her room. The dark brown shade of the door matched that of her expertly designed cedar bed and the shelving on the left wall of her chamber.

"Right away, commander Na'eemah!" Asenath said, marching across the dark, gleaming tiles on the floor of her otherwise white, pristine quarters. Hearing the motherly woman's deep, throaty chuckle made her smile.

Strolling briskly down the spacious hallways of her apartment within the women's quarters, she headed for the courtyard. On days when she was in a haste, she did not appreciate the vastness of her father's palatial villa. Evidence of his affluence and high-ranking status in Egyptian society, the imposing rectangular residence boasted four sections, each accessible from a hallway leading to and from the central courtyard. The north section possessed extensive guest quarters, while the east had their largest chamber—for festivals and feasts. In the west wing stood her father's favorite feature: a mini temple with a prayer room and a scriptorium featuring his handwritten copies of the sacred texts. The south sections held their living quarters: the women's quarters facing the sunrise and the men's quarters facing the sunset. And just behind those, outside the main house, sat both the servants' quarters and the spacious stables. Her favorite section of the main house was not within it, but atop it: the sturdy, flat roof. Not only ideal for meditating and sunbathing, it was the next best hideout when she needed some time alone and could not leave the premises.

Thanks to her mother's impeccable taste, their impressive villa was decorated in the most exquisite wooden furnishings. Murals artistically displaying heroic feats of various gods and goddesses were strategically located on the walls of every chamber. Asenath had received many a theological speech as a child, standing before those images. Her parents had been equally passionate about educating her childish mind with the antics of Egypt's immortals. Where her father's accounting of such feats had been factual, her mother's had been poetic. Strolling past a beautifully carved statue of Isis, one such maternal tale from happier days past came to mind.

"Love is a powerful force, my little sun. As is hate; but love always wins. I tell you, a woman will do almost anything for a man she loves. We are inherently inclined to take after our beloved goddess, Isis. She was the wife of the mighty Osiris. His brother, Set, hated him and was jealous of him, so he killed Osiris. But do you know what Isis did?"

"What, Mother?" she recalled asking, ever eager to hear another exciting tale.

Just as eager to tell her story, her mother responded, "She used her magic powers to resurrect him. Then they had a son, Horus, who grew up to defeat Set and restore order back to the kingdom."

Thanks to the proficiency of her instructors, Asenath now knew her mother had carefully omitted the gory details of that legend. Incestuous matrimony, brutal sibling dismemberment, and posthumous impregnation were just a few of the shocking specifics that her sacred lessons had brought to light. Even though Isis had been her most admired deity as a child, somehow, her being the epitome of love now seemed somewhat incredible. Nonetheless, Asenath still offered her most fervent daily private prayer to the goddess, since she was the deity that possessed the magical power to alter fate. As for her mother's many fantastic fables past, whether they held truth was now doubtful, but at the time they first graced her childish ears, the heroes and heroines were as real to her as the lights dancing in her mother's animated eyes.

Meandering through the well-lit courtyard that housed their indoor garden, she glanced at the life-size stone sculpture of Ra that sat in the heart of the flowery enclosure. Even though it was the largest, the sacred sculpture was just another one of several statues of deities that graced the magnificent abode she called home. It was only natural that the patron god of Heliopolis should hold a place of honor in the home of the city's high priest. But today, the half horse, half man statue reminded her of her dream and revived the nagging premonition that had since settled itself in the pit of her belly.

She hoped she had not offended the sun god. Lost in a train of foreboding thoughts, she barely registered exiting the villa, or the subsequent horse-drawn wagon ride. It seemed mere moments had passed when she felt a gentle nudge on her shoulder.

"We have arrived, my lady," Semat said. "Shall we descend?"

For better or worse. Asenath thought, nodding in response.

Bearers assisted them both out of the wagon, and Asenath glanced around the monumental mansion of the gods. Within moments, her six secondary maidens had positioned themselves, three on each side of her. Semat stood before her, a questioning look on her face. At Asenath's affirmative nod, Semat spun around and began leading their impressive octet. This was the formal fashion in which Asenath typically made her entrance into Temple, and it ensured people gave the proper respect and distance due the daughter of the high priest. It also attracted glances of both admiration and envy as easily as a flame drew moths. Asenath was therefore not unaccustomed to being the center of attention whenever she made a peregrination to the main sanctuary.

Temple is crawling with worshippers today, she observed, trying to avoid eye contact with the people staring at her, as her entourage made its way forward. *Not that it should come as a surprise; we are commemorating the festival of the new moon after all.* Deliberately shifting the focus of her gaze to her ostentatious surroundings, she was reminded of the majesty of the masterpiece that was the Temple of Ra. Even though it was all too familiar, she could not deny the vast stone structure was statuesque in every way. Spanning hundreds of acres, it housed numerous estates—her father's villa inclusive—which were grouped into a hundred villages. Merely looking around from a singular vantage point on the ground, it was hard to grasp that it also boasted nine dozen orchards, three ships, four workshops, and employed over twelve thousand workers. And every one of them, the overseers of the estates—lesser priests, scribes, and soldiers—reported to the high priest, her father, Potiphera.

Walking quickly through the open outer court, she could not help but notice large numbers of men and women with offerings of cattle and coins waiting to present their tokens to members of the priesthood and make their prayer requests. Nor could she ignore the mouth-watering aromas emanating from the bounty of food nearby, including freshly baked bread and honey cakes. Not lost among those scents was a distinct smell coming from what was undoubtedly a massive number of amphorae containing freshly brewed beer.

No festival would be complete without an abundance of food and intoxicating drinks! She thought, smiling to herself.

Once they entered the main sanctuary, the scent of the incense burning in multiple censers permeated her nostrils, even as the sound of lively music filled her ears. When they finally arrived in her designated seating area, her handmaidens lifted the sheer, white strips of fabric that demarcated it, and she gracefully lowered herself onto one of the comfortable cushions and waited for the ceremony to begin.

Moments later, the gong sounded, and the music ceased, signaling the approach of the high priest. Looking and walking as dignified as always, Potiphera stepped out from behind the velvet curtains that fell from the tall, arched ceilings all the way to the polished bronze floor. The light of the torch he carried reflected off his completely bald head. As he stepped forward on white papyrus sandals, his long, one-shouldered, white linen robe flowed loosely around his tall, heavyset frame, except where a thin, white belt around his broad waistline held it in place.

Asenath heard the soothing sound of a rattling *sistrumsa* spread across the sanctuary. It was reminiscent of a breeze blowing through papyrus reeds. Taking their windy cue, the priests behind the curtain began to hum a familiar chant. Potiphera proceeded up a flight of seven steps leading up to the stone altar at the center of the smoky sanctuary. As he placed his small torch into a massive bronze censer to set its flammable oils ablaze, light flooded the sanctuary.

Now illuminated was the intimidating bronze statue that stood behind the brightly burning censer. It had the body of a man and the head of a falcon, upon which sat a sun disk inside a cobra. The statue wore a white linen *shendyt*—a knee-length, wrap-around skirt—and a belt tricolored red, blue, and green. Accessorized with a grand *usekh*, bracelets, and anklets, it held a scepter in its right hand, and an *ankh* cross in its left.

Carrying out the next step in his priestly duties, Potiphera assumed a kneeling position before the statue with his head bowed to the ground. Every priest and priestess present simulated the same posture where they stood. The high priest lifted his head and both arms and began the prayer chant, and the other members of the priesthood echoed each phrase: "O great Ra, giver of life . . . Supreme ruler of sky, earth, and underworld . . . God of the sun and provider of order . . . Maker of pharaohs and kings . . . The mighty creator who fashioned man from the drops of your tears and sweat . . . Look upon your humble servants in favor this day . . ."

Favor? Asenath questioned silently. *The favor of Ra orchestrated my loveless life. If I am to take my dream at face value, the mercy of Ra will only orchestrate my dreadful death. Should I really be begging Ra for mercy or favor?* . . . If her Father could hear her blasphemous thoughts, he would surely rend his priestly garments—after he sacrificed her as a burned offering. *Never mind Father, what if Ra can hear my thoughts?* Alarmed, she instantly refocused on her father's chant.

"O Ra, find us among those who honor you . . . Those who worship you at your rising, and lament at your setting . . . Receive our offerings, for we are naught but your cattle . . ."

Her father's call and response petition was drawing to a close when Asenath's keen eye caught a strange movement at the entrance to the sanctuary. Two armed guards stood there. Noting the deep-blue *shendyts* wrapped around their loins, and the broad gold collars on their otherwise bare shoulders, her eyes widened.

Palace guards! Here? Not being of the priestly tribe, they could not enter the holy chamber. Their very presence at the entrance during a ceremony was a bold move.

She caught Semat's ever-attentive eye and inclined her head in the guards' direction. Semat followed her gaze and arched a brown eyebrow as a priest appeared, seemingly out of thin air, to receive the unexpected visitors. What seemed to be a heated conversation ensued, but the priest stepped out and Asenath could not see the trio any longer.

I wonder what that was about!

Just as her father concluded the chant and rose, the priest reentered the sanctuary looking quite flustered and began briskly making his way toward the altar. Rising from her knees, Asenath observed him with the intensity of a hawk watching a chick. Upon arriving at his destination, he peeped out from behind the pristine curtains but waited for Potiphera to descend the steps. Then he bowed and leaned toward the high priest, as though whispering in his ear. Immediately, Potiphera strode out of sight behind the curtain, and the lesser priest took his place on the stone altar to announce the next phase of the ceremony.

A swap of priests mid-ceremony? Something is wrong. Asenath's curiosity attained new heights. In as low a voice as possible, she instructed the dutiful handmaiden kneeling at her side. "Semat, get as close to the entrance as possible and discreetly find out what you can. Go!"

As Semat rose to do her mistresses' bidding, Asenath seated herself once more, while trying to sight her father. Her efforts were rewarded a few moments later, when she saw him step out of a previously concealed door beside the main entrance. A young priest escorted him. Potiphera exchanged words with the guards for a few moments. Then he turned to speak to the young priest and was still doing so when he pointed directly at Asenath's enclave. The priest bowed and then headed in her direction. Asenath saw Semat intercept him and they spoke briefly, then both headed in her direction.

She was tingling with suspense at this point. She had not spoken to him in years, but the tall, fair, masculine figure that now stood behind the curtain of her enclosure was a familiar one.

Semat lifted the drapery and peered in with a silent question, and Asenath nodded eagerly. Then her handmaiden announced the visitor, as protocol demanded. "Sahure, son of Wenennefer, priest of Ra." Stepping aside so he could enter, Semat further declared, "Asenath, daughter of Potiphera, high priest of Heliopolis."

Sahure entered and bowed his shaved head slightly. "My lady . . ." When his eyes met hers, his long face turned a shade only slightly less intense than a tomato's. "His Reverence Potiphera . . . I mean, your father . . . I beg your pardon . . ." He cleared his throat nervously.

Asenath was grateful for the veil that hid her smile. He was taller and more manly now, but Satiah's twin brother had not otherwise changed from the blushing, stammering boy she remembered. "Be at ease, Sahure," she said.

Sahure dipped his head slightly before proceeding. "His Reverence has implored that I personally inform you that his presence has been requested at the palace by Pharaoh, lord of Egypt—long may he live. He departs at once and cannot feast with you. He will send word at his earliest convenience."

A palatial summons! Asenath was simultaneously shocked and intrigued by this news. Biting her tongue to keep from barraging him with a host of questions for which he probably had no answers, she looked him in the eye. "You have my thanks."

He bowed and turned to leave, but she called out, "Sahure!"

When he turned around, she asked, "How is Satiah?"

"My twin is more overbearing than ever, for she is with child again," he said with a broad smile.

Smiling back, she said, "Please convey to her my warmest greetings."

"Certainly."

As Sahure walked away, Asenath's eyes lingered appreciatively on his strapping figure. Her mind, however, was racing.

Attendance at a palatial gathering was planned. Any such summons would typically come during one of her father's four months off Temple duty. *What in the name of Ra could be important enough to warrant the high priest leaving Temple in the middle of a ceremony? Why would Pharaoh need him so urgently? Does this have something to do with my dream? Will this voyage to the palace bode favorably or otherwise for Father?*

She wanted answers, and she knew where to get them. Everyone who was anyone knew the best gossip in all of Egypt happened at the palace, and was swiftly spread through the extensive grapevine that servants of nobility shared. Thankfully, she knew someone who had connections within it. Someone who would be all too eager to exercise some lesser-used skills in unearthing insights as to the reason for her father's summons.

'Tis time to put my chief revealer of palatial secrets to work.

3

Juicy
Sweet secrets spilled
Morsel after morsel
Each sparking a hunger for more
Gossip

***

Meditative.

That was the state in which the suspense-filled Asenath presently pretended to be. Seated on a plush animal skin on the floor of the women's guest chamber, she wore a loose, sleeveless, white *kalasiris* with a fringed sash tied around her hips. Hair tied up and away from her unveiled face, she had her legs crossed and arms outstretched, palms facing up, with the tips of each thumb and index finger held together.

"Power," said the woman seated in similar fashion, directly across from Asenath, her kohl-lined green eyes as piercing as they were unblinking. Punctuating her words with subtle movements of various parts of her lithe, bejeweled body, she continued, "You must learn to wield it through every fiber of your being while remaining seemingly helpless to the untrained eye."

Maintaining her facade of composure, Asenath silently nodded at the renowned mistress of movement and the seductive arts. Mayet had been a greatly lauded, widely traveled dancer in her youth. Now older, she remained in her home city of Heliopolis, training the daughters of nobles, as well as the best temple dancers. Potiphera had employed her to school his beloved daughter in the mastery of sensuality and dance. It was just one of the many educational endeavors in place to prepare Asenath for her unavoidable destiny.

"Every move must be graceful and deliberate . . ." Mayet continued, her motion almost hypnotic. "Executed correctly, they empower you to intoxicate a man until he yields to your every whim, as dough does to a baker's hands." The dark-haired, fair-skinned woman may be advanced in years, but she moved with the stealth of her ever-present feline companion, who was presently perched beside her, staring at Asenath with eyes as green as his owner's.

Silently mirroring her instructor's every move, Asenath tried not to cough. The pungency of Mayet's perfume was only surpassed by the irritating quality of her voice. Listening to her was akin to hearing a hyena in heat.

Focus on her words, not her tone.

"Remember, you are a woman . . ."

Unfortunately. Why Mayet stated the obvious with such pride, Asenath could not understand. The men had the final say; in humanity and, it appeared, even in deity. After all, it was Ra who had decided her fate, and as often as she appealed to Isis, the goddess who held the power to change fate, her prayer was yet to be answered.

"The force of your feminine charms is irresistible," Mayet continued, her rouged lips pushed forward in an almost permanent pout. "It lies in every curve of your body . . . in every stride of your gait . . . every pose of your form . . . every flutter of your lashes. Asenath, you can speak volumes with the slightest arch of one brow, the subtlest purse of your lips, and the softest whisper of a sigh. Now breathe in and out."

Resisting the urge to murmur, Asenath complied. *Where is Semat?* Asenath had instructed her chief handmaiden to alert her the instant her source returned from milking a cluster on the palatial grapevine. Were Na'eemah to find out about the errand of espionage, she would have a thing or two to say about Asenath exploiting her most loquacious handmaiden's natural charm to gather gossip. Tsillah, on the other hand, relished the opportunity. That, and the honey cakes Asenath had let her keep considering Potiphera's sudden absence. The delicious pastries were but a small token of the young lady's appreciation for her handmaiden's resourcefulness.

"Asenath, focus!"

"I beg your pardon, Mistress Mayet."

"Now breathe in and out again. And slower. Focus on drawing out your power from the inside . . ."

As Asenath complied with more enthusiasm, her wandering eye caught Semat's face briefly appearing between the curtains. Her pulse quickened. *Tsillah has returned with news!*

As Asenath exhaled excitedly, Mayet stood.

"Now rise. We must perfect your *Raqs Baladi*. I need to see more fluid belly rolls and more precise hip twists. Your arms must punctuate the movements of your hips and your footwork must be lighter and swifter, like this." Lifting her hands gracefully, Mayet demonstrated an arrangement of quick movements with pointed feet, made a vertical figure of eight with her torso, and ended with a fast hip shimmy.

Belly rolls will have to wait. Asenath began to rise but then bent over suddenly, clutching her belly. She groaned.

Twin creases wrinkling her otherwise flawless brow, Mayet dropped her hands. "What ails you?"

"My belly," Asenath said through clenched teeth. "It feels as though an entire nest of hornets is let loose within me."

Mayet took two steps towards Asenath. "Maybe you should lie down—"

Asenath made a heaving sound and quickly placed a hand over her mouth. "I fear the contents of my last meal may soon grace the ground before us . . ."

"By the mercy of Isis!" Mayet exclaimed, retreating swiftly. "Shall I send for a healer?"

"No!" Asenath said sharply. Catching herself, she groaned again. "Send for Semat . . . she . . . she will know what to do-oo-oo!" Hearing Asenath's retching noises, Mayet rushed toward the entrance.

"Semat?"

Appearing at once, a comical expression on her face, Semat answered, "Yes, my lady?"

"Your mistress is in distress. Tend to her! Quickly, girl!"

Her face instantly sobering, Semat rushed over. "My lady?"

"My gut aches," Asenath groaned. "We must have a word with the kitchen maidens, but first, take me to my chamber."

"Certainly, my lady," Semat said, assisting her mistress on her feet.

Asenath placed one arm around Semat's shoulders and leaned on her. She clutched her abdomen with the other arm, wailing and limping as they hobbled out of her private guest chamber. She moaned until they were out of earshot, upon which they both burst into fits of laughter.

"The mercy of Isis," Semat said, wiping joyful tears off her cheeks. "You should have seen her face when she thought your belly would eject its contents right before her eyes!"

Asenath grinned. "When it comes to the powers of deception, I believe this student has become the teacher," she said, giving an exaggerated bow.

Semat applauded with unbridled delight.

"Now, lest I perish from suspense, tell me, where is Tsillah? Does she have news?" Asenath inquired.

"She awaits in your chamber, my lady."

"To my chambers we go then, without delay!"

Not losing another moment, the women hastened into Asenath's nearby chamber.

Upon sighting her mistress, the most striking of her six secondary handmaidens, bowed in greeting.

Wasting no time on pleasantries, Asenath inquired, "What news have you, Tsillah?"

"I fear I may not have much to tell, my lady," said the ebony-skinned, slender maiden.

"Some news is better than none!"

"Certainly, my lady. You recall my mother's brother's third daughter, Haankhes, is handmaiden to the wife of one of the palace guards."

Asenath nodded eagerly.

"It turns out her mistress was to bring forth a baby two days ago. The dear lady was in such terrible pain—it being first birth and all. Haankhes said the midwife was nearly beside herself with worry. The baby was upside down and no matter how hard she

32

tried, it would not turn aright."

"And?" Asenath asked, crossing her arms and drumming the fingers of her left hand on her right elbow.

"And her mistress nearly screamed the house down. When the babe finally exited the womb, it was a boy. But he was born with one eye brown and the other blue! The midwife almost dropped him in her shock. She said the gods probably cursed him. If you ask me, I think—"

"Tsillah!" Asenath said, briefly throwing her hands up in the air, "I am sure your opinion on the inauspicious infant with mismatched eyes is insightful, but in the name of all that is sacred, will you tell me what is presently happening at the palace?"

"Forgive me, my lady," Tsillah said, briefly dipping her head, while Semat stifled a giggle.

"Forgiven!" Asenath said with a dimissory wave of her hand. "Now, the news," she urged her tall, talkative handmaiden, placing her palms together and repeatedly drumming her long fingers against each other.

"Haankhes's mistress's husband arrived home two days ago in anticipation of the baby's birth and she heard him tell his wife that it had been nearly impossible to get leave from the palace. He said Pharaoh, lord of Egypt—long may he live—has been sequestered in his judicial chambers, along with all his advisors . . ."

Intriguing!

"He also said every renowned seer, soothsayer, sorcerer, high priest, and magician in all of Egypt had been summoned to the palace. As at the time he left, there were all being held in conference within carefully guarded chambers, and no one outside knew why."

"Why, in the name of Ra, would every available Egyptian gifted with sight be summ—"

"Asenath . . ." Na'eemah heavy footsteps could easily be heard entering the chamber. She waddled in, breathless from her quickened pace. "My sunshine, are you well? Mayet said you took ill so suddenly . . ."

Asenath turned to her handmaidens and said dismissively, "That will be all, thank you." As they bowed and exited her chamber, Asenath faced Na'eemah, sheepishly. "Forgive me for worrying you needlessly. I fear I may have exercised my powers of pretense to satisfy my curiosity about Father's mysterious summons."

Na'eemah grunted. "I see you have put your chief source of palatial gossip to work again. No one was ever bitten who let sleeping mongrels lie!" she added, her sweaty brows laced with deep furrows.

"But, Na'eemah," Asenath wailed childishly, "you cannot tell me you are not yearning to find out the palatial happenings! Did you know *all* the notable high priests, soothsayers, sorcerers, seers, and magicians are there right now at Pharaoh's summons? So it is not only Father—"

"Interesting as that may be, o curious one, the wisdom of the ages deems it better to report a matter one has seen, not merely heard. Personally, if I must hear a story, I prefer it to come straight from the source. And it will be told to you thus, soon enough."

"Soon enough?" Asenath lamented, pacing back and forth. "It might be weeks before Father comes home! Even then, he is not always forthcoming with details."

"Forthcoming or not, you will get those details straight from the source, in person, the day after tomorrow."

Halting her pacing instantly, she looked at Na'eemah with widened eyes. "Father is—"

"Indeed, he is. I received word moments ago. Furthermore, he has ordered that a dinner be prepared in festival fashion, for two evenings hence."

Festival fashion? Asenath felt her heart skip a beat. That could only mean one of two things: either a special guest was being honored or a special occasion was being commemorated. She could not think of any special occasions her family should celebrate this month, so she asked the obvious question.

"Is he bringing a guest?"

"The messenger did not say. We will simply have to wait and see."

First a palatial summons for all Egyptians gifted with spiritual sight, and now a dinner in festival fashion. Why? And what does all this have to do with my dream? That unanswered question conjured up so many scenarios of hypothetical answers in

34

her overactive imagination that she knew two sleepless nights lay ahead of her. The day after tomorrow could not come quickly enough. Especially since she could not overlook the unpleasant sensation growing in the heart of her belly. It was not the false nausea conjured up to escape an unsuspecting instructor, but a very real, all too familiar, nagging premonition.

***

Two mornings later, Asenath was feeling fairly foolish, as she made her way from her formal lesson chamber to the kitchen. She was not looking forward to confessing the most recent happenings of her day to Na'eemah, but she found herself being drawn to the kitchen like a moth to a flame. It was probably because the flurry of activity within the chamber of cuisine matched that presently unfurling itself between her ears. The reason for the bustling both around and within her was the same: every available servant in the house of Potiphera was preparing for his arrival, and the mysterious dinner.

Asenath had been musing over the imminent festivity for the past two days, having concluded that her father must be honoring an unknown guest tonight. Trying to decipher the identity of that guest had caused Asenath to spend the day thus far with her head everywhere else but where it was supposed to be. Thus the present state of embarrassment in which she found herself. Strolling into the kitchen, she hovered at the entrance, wondering whether it was wise to draw the attention of the red-faced, sweaty-browed woman currently barking orders.

"By the mercy of Isis, a gentle sprinkle of parsley is sufficient. You have practically given the duck wings of parsley. 'Tis a mercy it no longer lives or it should surely take flight!"

Asenath giggled as Na'eemah set her sights and her tongue on another servant. "And you! See that freshly washed linen is draped down the feasting table. And take a censer of incense with you. Set it aflame now; the fragrance needs hours to saturate the air." The servant made the mistake of standing still. "Do you need the blast of a trumpet horn to precede your departure?"

In response, the servant merely inclined his head toward the kitchen door. Na'eemah turned around, twin furrows gracing her brow. "Asenath? What in the name of Ra are you doing here?"

Asenath understood Na'eemah's confusion. She was meant to be in her music lesson presently. Her third of the day, following social graces and healing arts. Since childhood, her father had seen to it instructors had thoroughly educated her on topics ranging from sacred rituals to palatial protocol, beauty treatments to healing spells, in addition to the basics of mathematics, science, reading, and writing. Her keen and curious mind had inspired enthusiasm in her teachers, especially in her favorite subjects: literature and languages. The results were inevitable: Asenath was now more extensively educated and well-read than even her male contemporaries. She was usually a favorite student, but today, she imagined her tutors would not be singing her praises. In her lesson on social graces, when asked to recite the twelfth maxim of Ptahhotep, which outlines how one should behave in court, she had inadvertently launched into a flawless delivery of his sixth maxim: *The proper behavior of a dinner guest*. At least she knew what protocol demanded of her tonight. She had nothing with which to console herself for the happenings in her last lesson, however, which was why she lowered her eyes and answered Na'eemah's question.

"Master Narmer had to leave suddenly, on account of a headache."

"What did you do?" she heard Na'eemah ask.

"I may have played a wrong note or two on my lyre," she said, shifting her feet.

"I see. Is that all?"

"Not exactly. Being that I caused his discomfort, I offered to apply the healing potion I had earlier today learned to make, to soothe his aching head."

"And?"

"The pain dissipated. But within moments, hives covered his forehead. Apparently very itchy ones. The more he scratched, the more they multiplied," Asenath said, stealing a glance at Na'eemah. Her mother figure held her gaze for the briefest moment of silence.

Asenath tried to defend herself. "But I loaned him my sash to tie around his offended forehead before he hastily departed."

A snort of amusement escaped Na'eemah's plump lips. "So he is scratching his way down the streets of Heliopolis as we speak?" She asked, eyes twinkling before letting a full-blown round of belly laughter break forth from her.

"It is not that amusing," Asenath said, pouting.

Unable to respond, Na'eemah merely leaned over, laughing louder, placing an arm on her knee and holding her side as the shade of her face deepened from red to crimson. Asenath could not deny the image of her otherwise dignified old instructor, itching his way from street to street was rather comical, and she began to laugh.

After minutes of laughter, Na'eemah straightened up and wiped her wet cheeks. "Thank you. I needed the comic relief. But I must get back to the matters at hand."

"What can I do?"

"You can amuse yourself until it is time for your beauty regimen. You know your father will expect nothing short of perfection from the gift of Ra at a celebratory dinner."

Asenath's morning routine had been altered today, to include a lengthier meditation on the rooftop, with chants and prayers, and an omission of her beauty routine which was now scheduled for late afternoon. Both alterations were to ensure she was at her calmest and looked her best for tonight's feast. Her septet of maidens would ensure she was flawless. As for remaining calm, she needed to find something to occupy her mind until then.

"Very well, Na'eemah. Amuse myself I will."

"Writing, or reading?"

"Neither. I hear the call of the outdoors."

"Ensure you return with no scratches."

"Not a one," Asenath promised, turning and heading toward the door. "I am looking forward to what the servants dish out tonight, that is, those of them that survive the afternoon with you."

Retrieving an intricately carved bow and a set of six copper-tipped arrows from a low ebony table, Asenath exited the villa and made her way to their extensive outdoor gardens. Her typical target, a thick-stemmed oak tree, stood at the far end of the garden. Selecting an arrow, she loaded her bow. Stretching its waxed string out, she steadied her right arm using her right cheek. When she released the arrow, it hit the center of a worn ring on the tree's stem. Her second arrow split the first in half.

Not bad for a girl. Letting a self-satisfied smile grace her lips, she recalled the accidental discovery of her archery skills. A distant relative of her father's had brought his son to spend a brief part of the hunting season with her family. The boy, Idu, was a little older than she was. Idu's father had insisted he undertake archery lessons. This had led to both fathers and Idu spending significant time in the garden. The young Asenath, not wanting to lose a moment of her father's attention, had asked if she could also play with the bow and arrows. She remembered the surprised looks on the men's faces, but what roused a fire in her, was Idu's condescending comment: *"Girls cannot shoot."*

Asenath had fired back immediately. *"Says the boy who has not so much as grazed his target in the last ten tries."*

His face turning the shade of an over-ripened tomato, the plump lad had scoffed. *"If you can hit the tree, I will not only give you my honey cakes, I will stand on my head while you eat them!"*

Asenath had pleaded with her father, who yielded and showed her how to wield the bow and arrows. Much to Idu's dismay, it turned out his female competition had a powerful arm and a keen eye. She may have missed the ring, but she did hit the tree on her first attempt. Then she'd spent the next several minutes trying not to choke on honey cakes while watching Idu's pathetic but hilarious attempts to stand on his large, flushed head. Her passion for archery had been born that day. And it had never waned since.

Savoring the sweet memory of her first sporting victory, she loaded her third arrow and sought a tougher target. A pheasant landed on a branch very high in the tree, and she took aim. As the arrow struck the branch directly below the bird, it took flight.

"Well, I was looking forward to roast pheasant for dinner, but with your aim, I think I will have to make do with lentil stew."

She smiled at the sound of the familiar, rumbling voice and turned around. Towering as tall and muscular as ever, a mischievous grin on his fair, freckled face, was Na'eemah's nephew, Heqaib. As a boy, bandits had raided the villa in which his parents served and orphaned him. Na'eemah had raised her brother's only child as her own. Having spent his youth in their household, he was the closest thing to a brother that Asenath had. He had left two years ago to be trained in the military, and now served officially as head of the temple soldiers, and unofficially as her father's chief personal guard and confidant.

"Careful, Heqaib, or I might aim for that chip on your left shoulder and deliberately fall several inches below the mark."

Honey-brown eyes widening, Heqaib gripped his heart, groaned, and fell to the ground, absolutely still.

"I see you have given up on growing up," Asenath said, shaking her head in response to his theatrics.

He propped himself on his left elbow and flashed a warm smile. "Naturally. How else could I hold on to my boyish charm?" he asked, wiggling bushy, auburn brows, the only evidence of hair on his shiny head.

"Delusional, are we? Or is that an overflow of wine talking?"

Heqaib leaped to his feet, chuckling. "Only the radiance of your eyes outweighs the sharpness of your tongue."

"Yet the sharpness of mine is no match for the smoothness of yours."

Stroking his double chin as though deep in thought, he said, "Who am I not to use the silver tongue with which the gods saw fit to grace me?"

Asenath rolled her eyes. "Surely they are beside themselves with pride! Well, are you going to use your divine endowment to enlighten me on tonight's mystery guest, or have you taken a vow of silence?"

Heqaib lifted a large hand to his face and pressed his thin, pink lips together using his right thumb and index finger.

Asenath sighed. "Like mother, like son. Alas, I am left to the mercy of my father. Where is he?"

"Refreshing himself from the long journey. Mother said to tell you, you dine at sunset."

"Do you not mean *we* dine?"

"Indeed, I do not. This dinner is strictly by invitation, and I fear I am not invited."

Asenath arched an eyebrow. "Interesting. In that case, I think I hear the baths beckoning me." She started heading toward the house, but paused and turned back to him. Indicating her bow and arrows, she said, "I would leave these, but I think you might hit more targets with your charm than you ever could with your aim."

Heqaib dropped his chiseled jaw for a moment. Smiling, he shook his bald head from side to side. Asenath tossed her hair over her bare shoulder and sauntered away. Yet with every step she took, her heart picked up pace. Now that she was moments away from filling in the missing pieces of a mysterious puzzle, she found herself in possession of an unexpected nervousness.

4

A bright sky darkens
A silent wind screams
Alas. A fear has formed flesh.

***

Setting.

The sun had just begun to wane when she entered the feasting chamber. With the curtains drawn open over its large windows, it was beautifully lit. The yellow, orange, and red hues of the sunset added a natural effulgence to the lights of the many ornate oil lamps interspersed across the room. Every corner held evidence that the staff had labored all day.

Since her father typically arrived at events earlier than scheduled, it did not surprise Asenath to find her father already seated, lounge-style, on his luxurious, one-armed sofa. She was, however, very surprised that no other guest was present.

"There she is," he said, stretching out a bejeweled arm. "The one in whom I am well pleased. Come!"

Someone is in good spirits. Relieved, she strode toward her father; her leather-sandaled feet silent on the polished floor. Her light blue linen *kalasiris* was cinched at her slender waist with a matching sash. Its single shoulder strap held with a gold pendant that bore their family crest: a turquoise lapis lazuli stone engraved with the symbol of a glowing sun.

"You look resplendent," he said, smiling. "All the daughters of Pharaoh collectively could never outshine your beauty. Your mother would be as proud as I am."

Unusually high praise coming from a typically insouciant parent, Asenath observed appreciatively. "You are too kind, Father," she said as she greeted him with a deep bow and reverently crossed her arms together at the wrists. There was a faint sound of metal clashing as the gold bracelets on her wrists grazed each other. She felt his hand gently pat her ceremonial wig for the briefest moment. It was the faintest touch, but it symbolized approval and coming from him, it warmed her girlish heart.

"Sit and let us feast. For we have cause to celebrate!"

"I am delighted to hear that, Father. Just what are we celebrating? And where is the guest of honor?"

"As curious as your mother and even more impatient," he laughed. "All will be revealed in due course. You and I are guests enough for now. Wine!" he commanded, stretching out a goblet-laden arm. As the serving staff filled it with a rich, red wine, Asenath seated herself across from her father. The long, low table between them was hewn from acacia wood, its surface almost hidden beneath a surfeit of tantalizing delicacies. Reaching for her wine-filled goblet, she looked at her father, question unspoken. He beamed at her, raised his goblet and gave a royal toast. "Life, prosperity, and health!"

"Life, prosperity, and health!" she echoed, raising her chalice in toast.

"Be at ease, Gift of Ra; we dine alone."

Alone? Scanning the room, she realized the servants who waited on them tonight were all female. *This is turning out to be an evening of pleasant surprises,* she mused, unclasping her veil. She flashed her father an appreciative smile.

With an almost imperceptible nod, he signaled the servants, and they began dishing out the assortment of fine foods. Her father started with the freshly baked bread and slices of cheese, then proceeded to the spit-roasted duck, lentils, and vegetables. She took delicate bites of honey-roasted wild gazelle, garlic, and onions, topped off with an array of vegetables. In their typical manner, the sweets would be saved for last: honey cakes for him, and fresh dates for her. They conversed between bites.

"Tell me, have you been well?"

"Yes, Father."

"Keeping up with all your lessons?"

"Yes, Father. Numbers and Astronomy are as unappealing as ever, but literature and languages make up for them. I am learning Amharic now."

"Amharic? With your fluency in Arabic, that will be three languages. You will soon put the royal translators out of work!"

Four, if you count Merit's native tongue, Asenath thought, not daring to ask her father to add a servant's language to the list. *A daughter has to have some secrets.*

"And how are your lessons with Mayet?"

"She says my *Raqs Baladi* finally looks more like a dance and less like a seizure."

Potiphera bellowed, his broad midriff bouncing as his dark eyes disappeared into his round face. "Ra be praised for your timely improvement."

"I am glad to see you in such high spirits, Father. I imagined the worst at such a hasty summons to the palace." *Not to mention my disturbing dream.*

"You need not have worried. All is well. Indeed, all is better than well. My time at the palace was riveting. I return bearing wonderful news."

Asenath's eyebrow shot up. *He seems exceptionally excited.* "Pray tell, Father."

"I wish your mother were here on a day like today; she would know how best to deliver it."

How best? I sense a thorn in this rosy news.

"I imagine she would tell you a story . . ." he said wistfully.

"She probably would," Asenath agreed, equally reflective. "One that would have had me on the tips of my toes, no less!"

"Then, in her honor, permit me to make my humble attempt at storytelling."

Father telling me a story? This is too good to be true.

Simultaneously clearing his throat and clapping the cake crumbs off his large, olive-skinned hands, Potiphera adjusted himself more comfortably on his cushions. As he did, his blue-belted robe rose mid-calf, exposing thick, hairy legs above his normally well-manicured, sandaled feet.

Forgetting her uneasiness momentarily, Asenath smiled at the rare sight and reached for another golden-brown date. Clearly, the typically hairless high priest had been occupied with a pressing matter for the last few days.

"It was the darkest of nights," Potiphera began dramatically. "The lord of Egypt lay on the softest of linens in his royal chamber. Alas, his sleep was troubled, with not one, but two of the most mysterious dreams. In the first, a septet of fat cows emerged from the Nile, followed by another of malnourished cows. The latter proceeded to swallow their well-fed counterparts . . ."

Intriguing.

". . . And in the second, seven shriveled spikelets of wheat consumed seven plump spikelets that sprouted from the same stalk."

Pharaoh's dreams are even more mysterious than mine! Reaching for another delicious morsel, she let her father continue his tale.

"After such a troubling night, His Divine Magnificence apparently sent for the royal seer to inquire about the meaning of the dreams. Alas, the famous diviner could not interpret them. Our perturbed sovereign then sent for all the wise men and magicians in Avaris, but none could explain his visions of the night before. By nightfall, our distressed majesty had messengers dispatched with express orders to commandeer every notable soothsayer, sorcerer, priest, magician, and wise man from every city in Egypt."

So that is when Father was summoned!

"For two nights, we were all gathered before Pharaoh, lord of Egypt—long may he live. Those of us from the priesthood burned incense of balsamum day and night, beseeching the patron gods of each of our cities to grant us the elusive interpretation. Still, not one among us had any visions or gained any insights to offer.

"Our formidable ruler grew more furious by the hour. *'Perhaps your powers of perception have been dulled by an overabundance of fine dining!'* he ranted. *'I should have you all thrown into the dungeons for a time. That will sharpen your senses!'*"

Asenath's eyebrows rose toward her hairline.

"Mercifully, before he could deliver on his threats, his chief butler mustered up the courage to speak. Trembling like an ensnared antelope, he confessed he recalled a young Hebrew in the king's prison who had years ago proven his powers of divination, and would likely have the answer to the royal conundrum."

A Hebrew diviner? Doubtful.

"As you might have guessed, murmurs of doubt and disapproval filled the grand hall. Nonetheless, Pharaoh dispatched guards at once to fetch the enigmatic Hebrew. All of us at the palace stood at attention for an entire morning, anticipating his arrival."

Nobles standing in wait for a prisoner? This is quite the tale. Her curiosity peaked, and her dates forgotten, Asenath fixed an undivided gaze on her father.

"Upon the arrival of this mystical prisoner, no one could deny either his youth, or that his was a stature blessed by the gods. A more striking man I could not find within the palace. He seemed unusually fair—perhaps for want of sunshine. But if it had not been mentioned he was a prisoner, I should never have known. He walked as a man of authority and spoke the most fluent Egyptian I have ever heard from a foreigner's lips!

"Even more astounding than his elocution was his power to divine. Hardly a moment passed after he—with closed eyes— listened to His Divine Magnificence tell his mysterious dreams, before he opened his eyes and enlightened us all."

Perched on the edge of her seat, Asenath listened with rapt attention.

Potiphera took a sip of wine and continued.

"He said the two dreams had but one meaning. That god was showing Pharaoh what he was about to do."

"Which god?" Asenath asked, unable to contain her curiosity.

"A brilliant question, but the Hebrew did not say. He said that seven years of great bounty would come throughout Egypt, after which would follow seven years of severe famine."

Famine? In Egypt? Unlikely.

"He further stated that the famine would so severely deplete the land that all the plenty before it would be forgotten! Then he illuminated that the dream was repeated to His Divine Magnificence because his god had established this matter and would undoubtedly and shortly bring it to pass."

"Incredible!"

"You can say that again! By now, I was among the many in the

45

regal hall whispering the last question you asked. Still, none of us dared pose the inquiry when the lord of Egypt had not. If we were not already astonished at how astute the Hebrew's interpretation seemed, we watched in amazement as the young man proceeded to advise our sovereign without a hint of fear. In ten lifetimes, I could not forget what he said next: *'If it pleases His Divine Magnificence, let a wise and discerning man be selected and placed in charge of the land. The man shall appoint officers to collect one-fifth of all the harvest of Egypt in the seven years of plenty. The food should be gathered and grain stored in large granaries, as a reserve, to be eaten during the seven years of famine. Thus shall Pharaoh preserve his people from perishing during the years of scarcity.'*"

Bold indeed, this Hebrew, Asenath thought as her father echoed her sentiments.

"Whoever heard of such audacity from any noble not appointed to Pharaoh's advisory committee, let alone a prisoner? The flutter of a fly's wings might easily have been heard in the overwhelming hush that fell upon the great chamber."

"With good reason," she said, thinking, *He certainly does not speak like a commoner.*

"Indeed," her father agreed. "If we were surprised by his bold statement, what His Divine Magnificence did next astonished us all. Rising, he announced that there was no one such as this man who possessed the Spirit of God and therefore he, Pharaoh, was immediately appointing the Hebrew seer over all of Egypt, to do everything he had advised!"

What?

"We all watched in amazement as Pharaoh took off his signet ring and himself set it on the young man's finger. Then announced that henceforth, all of Egypt shall be governed according to the Hebrew's word, and without him, no man in this land shall lift either hand or foot!'"

"He made him vizier?" Asenath's asked, astonished.

"As surely as the sun will rise tomorrow! Within moments, the new vizier was clothed in the finest of linen robes and a gold collar placed upon his neck. And Pharaoh commanded that all must bow the knee before him! And that, Gift of Ra, is how a Hebrew prisoner became Egypt's vizier. Is that not the most incredible tale you have ever heard?"

"Without a doubt!" Asenath said, applauding elegantly. "Long live . . . what is the vizier's name, Father?"

"A detail I neglected. His Divine Magnificence announced the vizier of Egypt be known to all as Zaphnath-Paaneah."

"'*Revealer of secrets.*' Apt. In that case, long live Zaphnath-Paaneah!"

"A sentiment you do well to offer, daughter."

"Thank you, Father. And may I say, Mother would be proud of your storytelling."

"Prouder still she would be, to hear how the story concludes."

Why would Mother be proud? "Then, by all means, conclude it," she said, apprehensively.

As her father lifted his chalice to his lips, a petite servant entered carrying an ebony chest and headed toward them.

"Your timing is impeccable!" Potiphera said, drying his lips on a linen napkin. The servant lay the chest beside him, bowed, and exited.

"What is this?" Asenath inquired.

"A fitting end to an incredible tale. As a gesture of his immense favor toward the new vizier, our benevolent ruler presented him with a twofold prize. First, he was immediately paraded in grand style before the people of Avaris, all of whom bowed to the new governor of Egypt."

"A vizier deserves no less. Second?"

"He was to be given a gift of inestimable value, one befitting a powerful man, second only to the lord of Egypt. Naturally, it had to be a pure flower of the rarest beauty."

The hairs on Asenath's neck began to rise.

Springing to his feet, Potiphera said, "The question then was simple: where would Pharaoh find such an elusive bloom?"

A sinking feeling roiled in her gut.

"His Divine Magnificence assigned his brother, His Radiance Akhom, the duty of finding such a flower immediately. Having recently been blessed with an open invitation from His Radiance to present any matters that might concern His Divine Magnificence, your father saved the day. I sought a private audience and gently reminded His Radiance that such a flower had been growing, carefully preserved, within the house of his servant," Potiphera concluded, pointing at himself and bowing slightly.

It cannot be! Asenath's throat instantly became drier than a drought-plagued desert.

5

The river of fortune
Flows past skill, speed, and strength
To crown its victor

***

Trapped.

Asenath felt as though massive invisible walls were closing in on her. Unaware, her father unclasped the ebony chest and gestured toward its contents.

"Lo, a gift from Pharaoh," he said, waving his hand from the chest to her, "for the gift of Ra."

Asenath sat stunned.

"You, daughter, are tonight's honored guest."

Me? Something large and bilious wedged itself in her throat, temporarily robbing her of speech.

"Come! Your first wedding present awaits."

Wedding? Now? This news was more than a little disconcerting, and Asenath was trying and failing to act unruffled. "Surely you jest, Father."

"Jest?" he said, mildly amused. "I am as serious as he who weighs the souls of the departed on the immortal scales of justice. But I could not be more pleased with what I see before me."

"But, Father, I am barely seventeen!" Asenath squeaked, her rising emotions loosening her tongue, "I was not to be presented as a royal bride until my eighteenth birthday."

"Correction: *no later than* your eighteenth birthday. You could have been wed years ago, had Ra chosen it to be so."

"But have I not been groomed all my life to wed *royalty?*"

"You were prepared to be presented as a royal bride to whomever the lord of Egypt chooses," he reminded her. "I assure you, royalty or not, at this moment there is no one Pharaoh favors more highly than your future husband. Did I not just share that by sovereign decree neither man nor beast is to lift hand or foot but at the man's command?"

Heart thumping against her chest, she rose and paced the polished floor. "But, Father, he is a foreigner—a *Hebrew*." Pausing, she looked at him. "You yourself once told me nothing good could ever come from a Hebrew."

"Your father is not omniscient," he retorted. "Besides, he may have been born a Hebrew, but the man I saw walks and talks like any Egyptian prince."

"He was a *prisoner*. For what crimes? Did you even ask?" she said, panic causing her voice to climb in pitch.

"His past is irrelevant. He now wears Pharaoh's signet ring! What better way to secure a seat of power for our family than to join forces with the house of Egypt's vizier?"

Resuming her feverish pacing out of sheer desperation, Asenath lamented, "But he is a pagan, and I, daughter of a high priest! How could you possibly expect me to—"

"How could I not expect you to be his wife when Pharaoh has commanded it?" Potiphera interrupted, his eyes flashing. "You SHALL bring eternal favor upon the house of Potiphera. IT IS YOUR DESTINY!" he thundered, slamming his left palm on the table. The collision of his rings with the polished tabular surface echoed like an all too familiar slap. The sound froze her to the stillness of a statue.

"The matter is settled," Potiphera concluded in dark tones. "You leave at dawn!"

Dawn? Her heart skipped a beat. As much as she wanted to cry out in protest, she recalled a proverb Na'eemah had shared the day following her father's first—and only—strike against her: *An aggressive answer leads to a beating, but speak sweetly and you will be loved.*

"Forgive me, Father," she said, bowing deeply. "I . . . I do not know what came over me. You are right . . . I am truly favored of Ra . . ." Stepping quickly toward the open chest, she continued,

"And, most fortunate to receive a bridal gift from the lord of Egypt himself."

"Indeed you are," her father said, more calmly. "And what a gift."

Her eyes took in the sparkling piece of jewelry within, bittersweetly. It was one of the most intricately crafted *usekhs* she had ever seen, and just the type of jewel her mother would have loved. The necklace was solid gold and had a thick, circular collar with a pendant at its center, from which a long stem extended downwards to the wearer's waistline. The ring of gold was inscribed with Pharaoh's hieroglyphs of absolute authority. Its scarab-shaped pendant was fashioned from a chesbet stone, so the golden specks of pyrite within its primarily dark blue color would flatter her amber eyes.

"It is exquisite," she whispered.

"And well worthy of gracing one equally lovely," her father said, lifting the treasure out of its dark enclave.

Asenath turned around and gracefully swiped the tresses of her lengthy wig to expose her long neck. While her father adorned it, her mind worked frantically.

Dawn is too soon! I need more time!

Her mother once told her that in the heart of a battle, it was wisest to target the enemy's weakness with all of one's strength. *Father has never resisted a good wager.*

"There!" Potiphera said, his task complete.

He who hides his intent makes a shield for himself. Her father himself had quoted that maxim on more than one occasion. Now, she would test its truth on him. Releasing her artificial hair, she spun around and flashed what she hoped was a convincing smile. "How do I look?"

"Like royalty!" he said with a proud smile.

"Thank you, Father. It appears I must retire swiftly to prepare for my journey. Before I go, how about a game of *senet*, to close this celebratory evening?"

"A *senet* game?" Potiphera asked with a raised brow.

"Yes. With a good wager, of course . . ." she quickly punctuated, looping her arm in his.

"A wager . . ." Her father beamed. "What have you in mind?"

Fortune favors the bold, Asenath. What have you remaining to lose?

"Nothing too grave," she said, gently leading him toward the entrance of the feasting chamber. "Should I win, you permit me six weeks at home to . . . complete final preparations for such an enviable role." *And strategize my escape.*

"And should you lose?"

Isis forbid it! "I lose, I leave at dawn."

"You negotiate boldly given that you play a game of chance. Alas, Pharaoh's orders will not be left unfulfilled for so long."

As her heart sank, Asenath's shoulders drooped.

"However, I am not without feeling, so I may indulge a counter-gamble."

"I am listening."

"Should you win, you may have . . ." Pausing, he inclined his head slightly as though making a mental calculation. "Five nights. On the dawn of the sixth day, you depart with no further objections. Do you find those terms agreeable?"

Asenath stopped walking, turned, and looked him directly in the eye. "As long as I have your word, Father," she said evenly.

"I am a high priest," he said, mildly irritated. "My word is binding."

"Then we are agreed," she said, far more calmly than she felt. "Where shall we play?"

"The guest of honor decides," he said, to her surprise. Asenath analyzed quickly. Her guest chamber would afford her the most comfort, but his might leave him more relaxed. The more at ease he was, the more careless he would be. Playing in his chambers would also mandate she replace her veil, a welcome covering in present circumstances, since she wanted her emotions to remain well-hidden.

"Your receiving chamber?" She suggested.

"I have no objections."

As Potiphera strode into the hallway, Asenath swiftly refastened her veil and followed, walking in time with his leisurely gait.

This might be the last time I walk these hallways as an unmarried woman. A wave of feelings rushed over her. *Focus,*

Asenath, focus. The only thing that matters right now is winning this game. She inhaled and let out a slow breath. Repeating the action twice, she felt herself become more calm.

Upon entering his receiving room, Potiphera dispatched a brief order to a servant and made himself comfortable on a lavish couch. Another servant poured him a flagon of beer as the first returned with the *senet* board and pieces. The set had been passed down for generations of her mother's lineage, and she remembered watching her parents play using this very board.

Asenath seated herself on the opposite end of the sofa and subtly signaled that the servant lay out the elements of the game. He placed the thirty-squared board made of three rows and ten columns at the center of the couch. The hieroglyphs etched on the side of the board were facing her. Beginning with a dark piece and ending with a light one, he arranged five dark pieces and five light ones in the first row, on alternating squares called *houses*. Then he bowed and stepped aside.

Potiphera casually stretched his arms. "Let the game begin. I grant you the first move."

Surreptitiously drying her sweaty palms on the skirt of her *kalasiris* while hoping for good fortune, she threw the four double-sided paddles. They landed, showing two colored sides and two black sides.

Not a strong start, she thought, moving the first of her white pieces two houses forward. Her father threw four black sides. Smiling smugly, he moved his black piece five houses forward and tossed the paddles again. His second toss was similarly favorable.

Her pulse quickened. *'It is not he who begins well, but he who ends well that is crowned the victor.'* Recalling her mother's words slowed her racing heart.

Senet was the game of passing into the afterlife. Befitting, since life as she knew it was fading away. Worse, she was entering a royally arranged marriage with even more uncertainties than the one she had imagined and dreaded for the past six years. Shaking her head slightly to stop the anxious thoughts racing through her mind, she concentrated hard on the pieces before her.

Father and daughter were equally competitive, so the game progressed with very little banter. Each focused on becoming the first to get all five pieces off the board.

Several minutes later, with two pieces remaining on the board versus her father's one, beads of sweat broke out on Asenath's forehead. All three of their pieces were on the final row, yet to pass the house of happiness. Landing on that square was a mandatory move, for which exact tosses were required.

"Nervous, my dear?"

"No, Father," she lied.

"You need not be. The sooner you leave, the sooner you become mistress of your own powerful, opulent household."

"Yes, Father," she said monotonously.

Her next throw of the *senet* sticks moved one of her pieces three houses forward, to capture his. This resulted in them swapping places and her getting the security of having her two pieces back-to-back, right in front of the *house of happiness*. Thus, when Potiphera made the exact same toss, he could not move the three paces forward. He had to maintain his position and forfeit his turn.

You can do this, Asenath. As an afterthought came to the forefront of her mind, she looked up at her father. "Although, Father, the longer I stay, the more time I have with you."

"How sweet," Potiphera smiled. "But I have to return to temple duty at once; the royal summons interrupted me at the start of my month of service."

"True. Does this mean you will not be journeying with me to Avaris?"

"Not immediately, but I will have Heqaib escort you to your husband's home and ensure you are well received. Typically, I would follow to celebrate your wedding feast; but in these special circumstances, with our sovereign having already sanctioned the marriage, and your husband a foreigner with presumably different traditions, a feast may not occur. Feast or not, rest assured, I will be celebrating with you in your matrimonial home soon enough."

So I am to enter my husband's home publicly uncelebrated and unaccompanied by father or mother. All the more reason to delay my departure.

Asenath fervently flung the paddles. *Please, please!* One colored side, three black. *Yes!* She moved a square forward to the *house of happiness* and took another turn. This time, the sticks yielded the exact opposite results. Smiling, she moved the same piece three houses forward, to the *house of Re-Atoum*. This meant she was automatically granted yet another toss.

A frown instantly appearing on his face, Potiphera grunted.

Asenath's next throw afforded her two paces, allowing her to land her last piece on the *house of happiness*.

But now it was her father's turn again. He could still win in two moves if the paddles yielded a black-sided quartet each time.

As he cast the sticks, Asenath took a deep breath and closed her eyes. She remembered her mother telling her, "*This is a game of chance—you cannot predict the way the paddles will fall, but you control two things: your reaction to their fall, and the direction in which your pieces move. Remember, sometimes you have to take a step back to better move forward.*"

She heard him move one square forward and take another turn. She opened her eyes as the paddles were landing and her heart skipped a beat: four black sides!

Potiphera let out a curse. From its present location, moving his final piece five paces forward would land it on the dreaded *house of water*, from whence it would instantly be reversed, eleven houses backwards to the *house of rebirth*. Instead, he moved five paces backwards, landing in almost the same disadvantaged position.

Isis be praised! Heart hopeful, Asenath made her next throw. Heeding her mother's advice, and avoiding a fate similar to her father's, she moved her second piece one step backwards. This placed it on the *house of three truths*, earning her another turn that empowered her to move three paces forward, and she gratefully swept her penultimate piece off the board.

They each had one piece left—and the same tight-lipped expression on their faces. Potiphera's receiving chamber was now deathly silent.

He drained his goblet. Then he threw four colored sides and moved his last piece back onto the third row.

Observing her lone white piece sitting on the *house of happiness* in a moment that was anything but joyful, the irony was not lost on her. As she flung the quartet of sticks into the air, she offered a silent prayer. *Any god so inclined as to have mercy upon me, please grant me more time.* When the paddles landed, she only saw one dark shade. It was the sight that had made her father curse moments ago, but in her case, it was a swift, impeccably timed answer to her desperate prayer. Not bothering to execute the winning gesture, she buried her face in her hands and heaved an audible sigh of relief.

"It appears fortune favors the bold," Potiphera declared.

For now. Favored or not, this victory was bittersweet. She had won one battle, but the war against her dreaded destiny was one in which she had little hope of emerging victorious.

"Congratulations. You have earned yourself five more nights in your father's house. Use them wisely."

Asenath lifted her misty eyes to her father's dry ones. With the most sincerity she had dared to show all evening, she said, "Thank you, Father. I will."

Suddenly wistful, her father spoke gently. "Your happiness matters to me, Asenath," he said, leaning forward and patting her head. "I did my best in your mother's absence to prepare you for what you now enter. I wish she was here . . . in a way, she is. I see so much of her in you . . ." As though catching himself about to fall into a well of weakness, he sat up abruptly. "The vizier may not be Egyptian, but he is still a man. I am certain he will receive you with the greatest pleasure. Remember your lessons. Make your father proud."

Asenath nodded silently. She was too afraid any attempt at a verbal response would unleash the flood of emotions raging within her.

6

A bird. Caged no more
Wonders as it soars
Do I fly or do I dream?

***

Surreal.

Egypt's new vizier awakened to a feeling that he could hardly put in words. He lay in the softest bed he had ever felt in his thirty years of living. For the third consecutive night, he had slept like a newborn nestled in its mother's bosom. He let his eyes wander around the vast, impeccably furnished bedchamber. It was just one of many imposing rooms in the palatial residence that now belonged to him.

The speed with which his circumstances had changed from pitiable to enviable left his head spinning. Four nights ago, he had gone to sleep as a prisoner with no hope of release, surrounded by inescapable prison walls.

No home.

No family.

No name.

Yet the night following that, and every night since, he had gone to bed as vizier of all Egypt, surrounded by impregnable palace walls. His new chambers were also guarded, but these guards were there to ensure his *safety*, not his confinement. It was too great a miracle for his mind to comprehend.

If this be a dream, Lord, may I never wake.

The day was just dawning, but he could already hear the sounds of the palace stirring. Flinging his soft sheets to the side, he sat up and swung his legs over the edge of the kingly bed. His bare feet fell on a plush animal skin. The distinct clear of a throat caught his ear. Turning toward the sound, he saw the figure of a man standing at the entrance to his sleeping quarters.

"Blessings of the morn, Your Eminence," the man greeted.

"And to you, Wadjenes."

Striding into the room with an armful of raiment, his new steward announced, "Your Eminence's bath is drawn. I have taken the liberty of ensuring that this morning an assortment of Hebrew delicacies awaits in the dining chamber. Would His Eminence prefer to bathe or feast first?"

The newly emancipated man was temporarily speechless, at a loss for how to answer what seemed a simple question. *A luxurious, private bath and foods I thought never again to savor, both at my disposal. And I get to choose which I enjoy first?* He could hardly grasp his fortune. Years incarcerated in a foreign land had erased the memory of the foods he grew up eating. And a chamber in the dungeons did not afford anyone the pleasure of bath waters. *At least not typically,* he thought, as his mind wandered back to a most unexpected bath, and the moments leading up to it.

FOUR DAYS EARLIER

A scroll in one hand, the prisoner in charge of ensuring the welfare of all others, slowly made his way down a dark, narrow hallway. As the annoying hum of a fly assaulted his ear, he swatted the rolled parchment at it reflexively. Sighing, he ran his empty hand through the disheveled mass of thick, dark curls on his head. How the insufferable pests made their way into these dungeons would remain an unsolved mystery, but he knew what attracted them: the stench. He had grown accustomed to it over the years, but it inspired days of nausea when he first arrived at the intimidating, inescapable residence. Alas, what he could never become accustomed to was the thought of the rest of his life wasting away in this wretched place.

Lord have mercy. Briefly scratching his long, unkempt beard, he continued inching towards the warden's chamber, intending to submit his latest report on the prisoners' well-being. Shoulders sagging with a sorrow that stemmed from hope too long deferred, he was turning a corner in the narrow hallway when a fleshy figure forcefully collided into him.

"Mercy! Is there a fire?" he asked, trying to retrieve his fallen scroll.

"No, but you must make as much haste as if there were!" a familiarly authoritative voice answered.

"My lord Senbi! I was en route to deliver the report to you!"

"Never mind that. Other skills are required of you this fortuitous morning, and not by me, but by Pharaoh, lord of Egypt—long may he live!"

"Surely my ears deceive me, for I could have sworn you said the lord of Egypt needs *me*."

"You heard correctly!"

"What could Egypt's sovereign possibly require of anyone unfortunate enough to live in these lamentable quarters?"

"Evidently something no one in the palace can provide."

"And he presumes I can?"

"By the life of Pharaoh! Are you going to stand here questioning your good fortune or seize this rare opportunity? You have what any man in Egypt would kill for: an audience with His Divine Magnificence. Now!"

"But look at me, my lord! How dare I stand before the lord of the liberated stinking of captivity?"

Slapping him on the back, Senbi thundered, "That, my favored friend, is what the gods made baths for! Make haste! There is much to do and little time!"

Moments later, he watched as though in a trance, while the warden sharpened a pair of menacing knives. In keeping with Egyptian tastes, Senbi hastily rid him of every strand of facial hair, save that of his eyebrows. Thereafter, the newly hairless man had barely shed his filthy tunic when the merciless blow of icy waters slamming against his nearly naked body almost floored him. He inadvertently gasped at the shocking sensation.

"Quickly, do what you can with this while I retrieve a fresh tunic!" Senbi said, tossing a torn rag at the perplexed prisoner and hurrying away.

Retrieving the poor excuse for a washcloth, he attacked the layers of dirt on his feet, alas there was no ridding his fingers of their ink stains. A tunic-laden Senbi returned forthwith, thus the freezing bath was over as swiftly as it had begun.

THE PRESENT

My most fleeting bath has become my most historic. Running ink-free fingers over his bald head, he smiled at the wonder of it all. *I must remember to send a gift to Senbi. He could certainly use a new set of knives—*

"Your Eminence?" The voice of his new steward brought him out of his reverie.

Wadjenes! "Pardon me, I was lost in thought. You asked . . ."

"To know if His Eminence would prefer to feast or bathe first."

A loud rumble of from his middle answered before he could. "It appears my belly betrays my eagerness to sample cuisine from my land. I am touched you would think to afford me such a pleasure."

"I am here to ensure His Eminence's every desire is fulfilled."

"And willing to go to great lengths, I see. Surely, finding gold in a beggar's bowl is easier than securing Hebrew dishes for an Egyptian table."

The steward's mouth turned up in the faintest smile. "It was no trouble, Your Eminence. Should I have the meal brought here?"

"I shall adjoin to the feasting chamber momentarily. Allow me a moment."

"Certainly," Wadjenes responded, bowing deeply, and adding, "I shall leave these here," as he laid the clothing on a large couch, and exited.

The second most powerful man in all of Egypt looked at the royal robes, the heavy gold necklace and ceremonial wig on the couch, and the most skillfully crafted leather sandals on the floor beside them. As he reached for a robe, the sparkle from his right hand caught his eye and he paused. There upon its middle finger sat Pharaoh's signet ring: the small but mighty jewel that authorized him to rule in all matters except the throne. The words the lord of Egypt spoke when he bestowed the ring echoed in his mind: *Only in regard to this exalted throne shall I be greater than you!*

Overwhelmed by a fresh wave of awe, he fell to his knees and lifted his hands high. "Lord God, I kneel in awe of your loving-kindness and your wondrous works. The depth of your mercy is still too much for me to comprehend. I, the forgotten son of a Hebrew shepherd, now govern Egyptians. I, a condemned prisoner with no hope of release, am now free. My Lord and my God, I have not the words to express the profoundness of my gratitude. Thank you for causing me to be remembered and making the gift you gave me to bring me before Pharaoh. It is like a dream that I, who was but days ago only responsible for the well-being of criminals, now have charge of every man, woman, and child in an entire nation. Why you would choose me for such a task, I cannot understand. But I know it is an assignment too great for my strength. Forgive me, if one so tremendously blessed dares request anything at all, I ask only that you who saw fit to assign me this mission, grant me the wisdom, discernment, and grace to execute it according to your will. You who have caused me to receive favor before both the lord and the land of Egypt, grant that your face never ceases to shine upon me. For I may be able to live without the favor of men, but I would not survive a moment outside of your favor. All that is within me, thanks you for all that is around me. Thank you, O Lord, for the mercy of a day like this. May your will be done in my life, this day, and always."

Lowering his hands, he rose with a renewed sense of determination to make the most of the day. His reflection in a small mirror caused him to pause. He still found the hairless, beardless face that stared back at him strange. As unfamiliar as his new name. The one the lord of Egypt had given him, without ever asking for the one his father gave him at birth.

Lord, how do I answer a name only you, the demystifier of all mysteries, are qualified to bear?

It was a thing of wonder to imagine that strange as it was to him, his new name was familiar to all of Egypt. For the same day the lips of the lord of Egypt had first uttered it, thousands across the land had thundered it in shouts. For a moment, he closed his eyes. He could still see masses of heads bowing to him as he rode upon the very chariot of Pharaoh through a sea of humanity. He could still hear their collective voices, like the sound of massive waters falling from a mountaintop, as they chanted, *Long live Zaphnath-Paaneah!* There was but one man in the whole of Avaris that had yet to utter his new name. He opened his eyes and that man's dark brown eyes stared back at him. Then the smallest of smiles spread on his face and he whispered, "Long live Zaphnath-Paaneah."

***

The mountain of scrolls that lay before the new governor of Egypt did not seem to have shrunk much in the past two hours. Yet he had ceased to number the ones he'd already read. Reports. On trade. Building projects. Water supply. Farming. Cattle. Transportation. Security. Foreign visitors. And these were daily reports. Reviewing them was but the first task in the enormously broad array of daily duties for which, as vizier, he was now responsible.

"His Radiance, Akhom, to see His Eminence," a guard announced.

"Send him in," Zaphnath-Paaneah ordered. The half brother of Egypt's ruler had extended him quite the warm welcome and been more than gracious the past three days. Every noble bold enough to do so had mentioned the royal was a fountain of wisdom, and the wiry highborn was proving them correct.

"I see you are not one to waste any time, Zaphnath-Paaneah," Akhom said, dispensing with pleasantries.

"Not when duty calls, Your Radiance."

"I have already said, call me Akhom."

"Your Radiance is too kind. To what do I owe the pleasure of your presence, Akhom?"

"I have merely come to offer my assistance in any way." Indicating the pile of parchments on the desk, he added, "I imagine those would intimidate even the most astute of minds, at first."

"I am honored to be entrusted with the duty."

"Even so, I am well acquainted with the duties of a vizier. Your predecessor was His Divine Magnificence's and my father's cousin. A worthy man—quite a shame he passed so suddenly."

"I am sorry to hear it; If I may inquire, how did he pass?"

"In his sleep. Most astonishing to us all, since he seemed in excellent health."

"You were rather close then."

"Enough for me to be well acquainted with the demands of his duties. You have quite the task ahead of you. Do not hesitate to inform me should there be any way in which I can be of help."

"You are most gracious. Indeed, all the nobles I have had the pleasure of meeting thus far have been gracious."

Akhom grunted. "As well they should. You now hold the strings to all their purses. I believe you met all men of note at the formal introductions yesterday. Except the captain of the king's guard. A fact I find surprising. I do not believe I have ever heard of his absence from any official meeting before now."

"We are already acquainted. Though it has been many years, I know him to be a man of character; no doubt there is a good reason for his nonattendance."

"Indeed. I am sure he will report to you soon enough."

"I look forward to it." *More than you could ever know,* he silently added, wondering what it would feel like to have one he once called master bow to him. Just one more of the many strange occurrences that each new day as vizier brought.

"Very good. I trust your personal staff is satisfactory?"

"Wadjenes is proving himself an excellent steward. I foresee nothing falling out of place in his care."

"Marvelous. He came highly recommended as the best man to steward such a grand residence."

"Grand indeed. It exceeds even my wildest imaginations of comfort, except in one aspect . . ." *How do I explain a hunger for total liberty to one who has never been bound?*

"Let me guess; it is missing the presence of a woman."

"I fear I am quite accustomed to the lack of feminine presence."

"An existence I, for one, cannot fathom—sleep itself eludes me without a lady gracing my bed."

"We are not all blessed with your irresistible charm, Akhom. It has taken a royal decree to save some of us from, as you say, an unfathomable existence." He did not think his jest as comical as the royal's hearty laughter suggested.

63

"Consider yourself saved. Your bride will arrive in all of her glory in a matter of days. Her father is high priest of Heliopolis; a more worthy choice for a man with your prophetic powers, I cannot imagine."

The daughter of a priest who serves false gods. The thought was disconcerting. Oblivious to his discomfort, the royal went on.

"And an unmatched beauty, I gather. If you were not already the envy of every noble you will be, with her as your wife." Rising, Akhom smiled, "I suggest you sleep with one eye open, Zaphnath-Paaneah."

"I shall take your suggestion under advisement, Akhom."

As the impeccably dressed aristocrat exited his chamber, he leaned back in his chair and pondered.

New home. New role. New name. And I am, for all intents and purposes and by royal decree, a new husband. How can this be? The fourfold novelty was a lot for any man, and he imagined adjusting to its first three parts. But a new wife was going to require more than he might be able to give. When his childish mind had imagined the joys of becoming a husband, he had never pictured doing so without the blessing of his father; or the traditions of his fathers.

How am I to marry a woman I do not love? One who does not love me? Worse, one who does not know, let alone love the Lord? But how could I do otherwise? It would be an insult to Pharaoh—the sovereign of all Egypt and the very one who so favored him—to reject his royal bride. He could hardly find a woman who shared his faith in Egypt's palace to wed. He well knew the Egyptians despised Hebrews. His childhood aspirations toward his matrimonial home were a far cry from palatial chambers. Still, troubled thoughts danced around his mind.

How can the woman I am to call wife, the one who will raise my children, worship graven images? His father had warned him never to take a wife that could lure his heart away from God. *What then would my father say to me marrying the daughter of a high priest? What would the Lord God say to this?* "Lord, Pharaoh has given me a bride. Not one that my father would choose, not one I chose. Grant me wisdom in this matter, Lord, if it be your will. For I only wish to please you. I vow that my heart and the heart of my children, yet unborn, will worship you and you alone."

His eyes fell upon a mural of Ra etched into the wall to his right. Like the walls in his residence, those surrounding him now were strewn with images of Egyptian deities. The very air of the palace was pervaded with incense burning from censers in every conceivable corner. *They are not ashamed of their false gods. How much more should I boast in mine, the one true God?*

An idea sparked in his mind. The more he mulled over it, the larger it grew. He may not have chosen his new station or his new name, but if he was indeed free, then there was one thing he had to have full control over: his home. According to Akhom, he had but a few days before his new spouse arrived. He knew what he had to do. Pushing his chair back, he rose and headed out of his official chambers. No doubt, the lord of Egypt would find his request more than a little strange. But, if ever there was a time to present a peculiar proposal to Pharaoh, it was just after earning his highest esteem.

7

Hopeless
A twist of fate
New eyes reveal there lies
A silver lining in the clouds
Now, hope

***

Fleeting.

Four nights had flown by in a blur. This final afternoon in her childhood home, Asenath was reclining on a couch in her private chambers. A long, white cloth was loosely draped over her otherwise bare body. Beauticians were skillfully putting finishing touches to elaborate henna art on her hands and feet.

Two of her secondary handmaidens stood on each side of her, fanning her with the large traditional handwoven fans made of goose feathers. Their purpose was dual: to keep her skin cool and to help the henna ink dry faster.

Asenath stared mindlessly at the intricate design forming on the back of her right hand. Its center was a ring, representing the sun and the exquisite pattern around it spread out like rays of light. There were four similar designs, two each on her hands and feet. They only varied in the exquisite patterns that surrounded each 'sun.' It was nearly hypnotizing, watching the artisans' swift, fluid motions as the resulting art grew with each stroke. She was hoping if she focused on their work, she could still her frantic mind. But it was a vain hope, as the events of the last four days replayed themselves in an endless loop, beginning with the unfortunate dinner that catalyzed everything that followed.

Utterly distressed, Asenath had left her father's chamber and flung herself into the arms of the only person she knew truly loved her. She had wept until there were no more tears and Na'eemah had comforted until there were no more words. Exhausted from eating her fill of the bread of sorrow, she had drifted into a fitful sleep. But by the next morning, there was simply no more time for self-pity.

First, her beauty regimen had been intensified. She had soaked in the fumes of incense for hours daily until the very pores on her skin poured out the scents of iris, rose, and lemongrass. Her hair had been steeped in three liquids: milk to cleanse, berry juice to soften, and coconut oil to shine. Thereafter, the collective mass of waist-length, bouncy curls resembled the mane of a lioness. Every inch of her body had been rendered hairless using a hot honey mixture that simultaneously stung and soothed. Following her daily bath in warm goat's milk, she'd been intensely moisturized with the purest coconut oil from scalp to soles. Her impossibly smooth skin now bore a sun-kissed glow.

Second, at Potiphera's prompting, Na'eemah had ensured that a handful of Asenath's most important instructors were brought in. They had taught their last lessons, focusing on issues relevant to the new role she was entering: wife of the second most powerful man in Egypt. Mayet had seen that Asenath had stretched out every muscle until her slender frame was completely flexible. The insufferable woman had insisted that Asenath's heightened flexibility was necessary to ensure her readiness for any movement required in the near future, be it in the art of dance or the act of marriage.

At least, I shall no longer be subjected to the dual plagues of her voice and scent, Asenath thought, closing her eyes, and taking in deep, slow breaths. She heard familiar footsteps enter the chamber.

"Our work is complete, my lady," the chief artisan said.

Before Asenath could respond, she heard Na'eemah say, "Lovely! You look every bit the gift of Ra."

Do not remind me. Asenath kept both her eyes and mouth shut.

"You have done excellent work and you will be well compensated. You may leave us for now," Na'eemah said, effortlessly dismissing the artisans.

Asenath listened to shuffling sounds—no doubt the skillful handmaidens clearing up their tools. She wished she could conceal herself in one of their chests and be taken away.

"My dear, your effulgence is incomparable, even in nothing but your own skin," Na'eemah said. "That was the goal. For your adornments are merely to enhance your undeniable natural beauty. Your father has sent a gift, but I am here to present another."

Asenath lazily opened one eye to see Na'eemah's outstretched hands bearing a small linen bundle of cloth with a string elegantly tied around it. *What might this be?* Instantly curious, she opened the second eye and sat up, fastening her loose covering securely about her body. Reaching for the bundle, she paused, her perfectly arched left brow raised in an unspoken question.

Na'eemah answered with a gentle nod.

Asenath took the bundle from her mother figure's fleshy fingers and unfastened the string with one tug of a loose end. As the cloth fell open, she involuntarily sucked in a breath. *Impossible!* Lying upon the linen was a long, thin, solid gold *usekh* entrusted with an exquisite lapis lazuli stone as its pendant. The stone was engraved with the ankh symbol.

She lifted widened eyes to Na'eemah. "This is—"

"It was," Na'eemah said softly.

Staring at its simple elegance with mixed feelings, Asenath's mind traveled back to the time she last saw it.

It had been a perfect day, not too hot or too cold. Since their villa overlooked the Nile, swimming was a frequent activity. It was also a pastime she enjoyed sharing with her mother—whenever her mother was feeling well enough to swim.

Mother and daughter had been blissfully enjoying a wet, leisurely afternoon. Sprawled out on the damp, sandy shore, Asenath had been laughing at her mother's antics of sinking under water and coming up each time with her slender body stretched into a different, but equally comical pose. Every time she had surfaced, her wet, gold necklace had glistened against her bronze-skinned breast.

Suddenly a powerful wave had come and when Mother went under again, she did not resurface. Asenath had watched her mother's arms break through the surface of the river and splash about for a moment and then sink back under again. Thinking it was all part of their game, she had laughed and yelled, "Mother, another!" But there were no more hijinks.

Na'eemah had rushed into the river, screaming, "My lady! By the mercy of Hapi! My lady, please, answer me!" The distressed handmaiden had sunk beneath the waters of the Nile and resurfaced within moments, dragging her mistress's limp body to the shore. Confused and alarmed, Asenath had run toward them, only to have Na'eemah turn and scream at her: "NO! Stay back!" The frightened girl had obeyed, but kept her bulging eyes fixed on her mother's lifeless form.

Asenath still remembered her father's broken voice on the evening of that fateful day, telling her that Mother was gone, because she had taken ill again while in the Nile and its waters had been too strong for her. It was not until Asenath was much older that he had explained her mother had a rare sickness that afflicted some born with bronze skin. That ailment was why her mother had often shied away from eating sweet foods. But his explanation had come too late. Asenath's childish mind had long ago connected her mother's death with the Nile, and she had refused to set foot in its waters since. She still blamed Hapi for not preventing the fatal event, and did not join in sacrifices to the god of the Nile. As far as she was concerned, her beloved mother was sacrifice enough for him. The bitter irony that her mother died while wearing jewelry that bore the hieroglyph symbolizing life was not lost on her. How does one ever forget the day one's childhood cocoon of happiness crumbles for the first time?

I thought my eyes would never again see this necklace; yet here it is in my hands. Fingering it fondly through moistened eyes, Asenath looked up at Na'eemah.

"How did you . . . It was gone. She was gone."

"I concealed it after my lady's passing. It had been a wedding gift from her mother. I knew even then that she would want it to be the same, for you," Na'eemah said softly. Placing a hand on Asenath's bare shoulder, she continued, her voice now broken. "When you wear it, remember that you are a beloved daughter, and you will always be one."

A lone tear rolled down Asenath's cheek. "How can I possibly thank you enough? For this . . . for everything . . ."

"You can thank me by being happy, my dear girl. All I want is to see you become a happy wife and mother."

You ask a hard thing. "May Ra grant your desire," Asenath said softly.

"Now for your father's gift," Na'eemah said, rising. "Semat!"

The beckoned handmaiden lifted the curtain that led into Asenath's private sitting chamber, and in waddled a fair-skinned, dark-haired woman.

Asenath's jaw dropped.

The woman simply stood still, grinning at her.

"Surely the fumes from a surfeit of incense cause my eyes to deceive me!" Asenath said.

"Your eyes are fine; but I cannot say the same for your hospitality!" Satiah said, wagging a plump finger. Flipping her dark brown hair, she cast a backward glance. "Semat, some food and wine! And alert the musicians! This is a night of festivity!" She fastened her eyes back on her astonished friend. Rubbing the evidence of her fecundity, she added, "Surely you do not think this little thing will stop me from celebrating your last night as an unmarried woman?"

Asenath could not believe it: her spirited, good-natured, heavily pregnant childhood best friend was in her chamber. "By the mercy of Isis, Satiah . . ." she said, closing the gap between them in swift strides. The longstanding friends fell into a lengthy, teary embrace.

"So, you were planning to escape to Avaris without saying goodbye?" Satiah teased, wiping her tear-stained cheeks.

"Obviously, I have lost my mind. I am sorry," Asenath said, mirroring her friend's motions. "I have been so overwhelmed with emotions and hasty preparations. But how did you know?"

"Come now, sister," Satiah said, her green eyes twinkling. "Do you not know that deep down, your father is as soft as an over-ripened pomegranate?"

"I am . . . speechless."

"You? Speechless? A work of the gods if I ever saw one!" Satiah said, raising a hand skyward.

"Cease your mockery, Satiah!" Asenath chided, smiling. "I cannot believe you are here!"

"I would not miss it for all the gold in the temple!"

Laughing, Asenath said, "Only you could make me laugh at a time like this!"

"A time like what? You, about to become the wife of the second most powerful man in Egypt? I should think you would be bursting with excitement!"

"You think wrong. Perhaps you do not have all the details."

"No? Enlighten me then," Satiah said, making herself comfortable on Asenath's sofa and plucking a fat grape from the tray Semat laid beside her.

Seating herself cross-legged on the other end of the sofa, Asenath dismissed Semat and faced her friend. "Did you know that before Pharaoh made him vizier, he was a *prisoner*, Satiah?"

"You jest!"

"If I lie, I die! Can you imagine? I mean . . . I have been preserved for *royalty*!"

"Right you are. Although, without a doubt, his present position renders him the envy of every royal in Egypt."

"You have a point. But he is also a foreigner. A *Hebrew*, to be precise!"

"You did not tell me your interest in foreign tongues included the bedchamber," Satiah said, winking.

"Satiah!" Asenath exclaimed, her face flushing.

"What?" Satiah scoffed. "I am a married woman, and for all intents and purposes, you are too! Trust me, men are boring once you get to know them. You could do with the mystery a foreign one affords. Besides, now you have someone in your class with whom to practice your erstwhile clandestine study of the Hebrew tongue."

Asenath grunted, pensively. "Another valid point. Nevertheless, word in the palatial grapevine is that he worships only one God. How is that even possible?"

Satiah shrugged. "I see no problem there. You simply share from the multitude of deities we worship. Last time I checked, you do not even know all their names," she teased, grinning.

Asenath frowned. "Satiah, if you are going to jest about all of this . . ."

"Forgive me, sister, I merely tease. But, contrary to what you think, I do get smatterings of the royal whispers. From what I hear, he is a man of unmatched wisdom and he could not be any more handsome if he was hand-carved by the great Ra himself. So indulge me a moment, as I review. This man is wiser than a seer, more powerful than a noble, almost too handsome to be a human, and YOU were selected by the palace to be his wife. I see no cause for concern. Did it even occur to you that if he is satisfied with one god, he very well may be satisfied with one woman? Royals are not famous for monogamy."

Asenath slumped and let out a sigh. "You do not understand."

"Then help me, Asenath. Tell me, of what are you really afraid?"

"I . . . I did not want to say this . . . I mean, Mayet has mentioned in lessons that some pain is to be expected . . . the first time . . . you know . . . the wedding night."

"This baby did not put itself in here," she said, patting her protruding belly. "So you fear the pain of your first intercourse?"

"No . . . yes . . . look, I was prepared for it. Then I heard a rumor from Tsillah's sources that he was imprisoned on the accusation of rape!"

Satiah's eyebrows shot up. "Rape?!"

"Rape! Suppose he is violent? I am afraid . . ."

"Understandably so."

"Thank you!"

"On the other hand, a man can only rape a resistant woman. So, you must show him you are not only willing, but you are desirous. Better still, show him you can be dominant. Foreigner or not, he is a man. Men, I know well. My mother had seven brothers, my father, eight, and my husband has ten. They believe themselves to be in charge as heads of households. My mother taught me as a child that it is not the head, but the neck that dictates the direction in which the head turns. And we, the gentler sex, are the necks," she said, twisting her neck.

Asenath smiled. "Are we now?"

"Three whole years of a peaceful, very fruitful marriage and you dare doubt me?" she asked, pretending to be indignant.

"The heavens forbid it! Teach me, o wise one!" Asenath said with a mock bow.

"Much better!" Satiah replied with her broad nose pointed in the air. Lowering her head and sobering her expression, she continued. "Have no more fear, sister. All you need to do is set the pace from day one, and you will have him eating out of your palm."

"But how do I—"

"Here, have some wine," the expectant woman said, handing a chalice to her friend. She then shuffled forward to the edge of the couch and pushed herself up.

"What are you doing?"

"Showing you how to seduce and subdue!" Satiah answered, wiggling her eyebrows. Turning toward the door, she clapped her hands. "Semat!" The dutiful handmaiden appeared from behind the curtains immediately. "Have the musicians play the lover's dirge." As Semat bowed and exited, Satiah sashayed to the center of the room. Even with a protuberant abdomen, she effortlessly struck a seductive pose: right hip pushed out, with right hand on her waist, and left leg stretched out, bent at the knee, with her left heel raised and foot arched. She had her back to Asenath, but she flipped her long hair over her left shoulder and looked at her friend with pursed lips and a mischievous gleam in her eye. Pointing her left index finger at Asenath, she curled it toward herself and repeated the gesture, saying in a low voice, "Come here, my dear."

Asenath's legs moved seemingly of their own accord. Taking her place beside her shorter friend, she mimicked her stance.

"Perfect," Satiah said as the first notes of the popular tune wafted into the chamber. "Now pay close attention. I will show you exactly what you need to do to turn this mysterious ruler into your loyal and obedient slave. You, my dear, have one job tomorrow night: enter and conquer."

Enter and conquer. I like the sound of that. Eyes twinkling, Asenath's full lips spread into a lopsided, mischief-laden smile.

8

The loveliest dawn
Sweetly breaks but grows bitter
Innocence is lost

***

Stunning.

Such was the splendor of the sunrise three women were watching. Arm in arm, they stood on the gloriously green banks of the Nile. Papyrus trees and date palms stretched skyward from deep in the rich riverbank soils. The waters rippled as an ibis swam by. A stone's throw away from the sacred bird, causing a far greater stir in the river, was a rather large barge.

The youngest of the three women, elegantly dressed in travel attire, watched an army of servants racing back and forth, loading multiple cedar chests onto the barge. They were filled with the finest linens, jewelry, spices, and perfumes in all of Heliopolis. *A wedding gift from a father trying and failing once again to compensate for his absence.* The array of luxury-laden chests would make for an impressive bridal entrance at her husband's house. Which was exactly what her father wanted. But what else could she expect? Potiphera was not known for either subtlety or humility. Like his wedding gift, Potiphera's sea vessel was grand. Hewn from acacia wood, it required forty rowers to sail at full speed. She looked at the massive water craft that would shortly convey her away from the only home she had ever known. *He may not be here to see me off, but I have Na'eemah and Satiah beside me.*

Much to Asenath's delight, her childhood best friend had

stayed overnight. Satiah had said her husband could survive one night without her. They had spent the nighttime like they used to as little girls: curled up next to each other in her bed, talking about their dreams. Those moments were more precious to Asenath than the collection of finery her father gifted her.

Now the three women stood side by side, silently savoring their last moments together for a long time. They had said almost everything they could, and Asenath was grateful for their presence. Her ever-supportive chief handmaiden also stood nearby, but her six secondary handmaidens were already aboard.

Heqaib, who had been on the vessel ensuring everything was in order, now approached them.

"It appears it is time," Na'eemah said softly.

When he reached the pensive trio, he confirmed his mother's suspicion. "We are ready, my lady."

Asenath closed her eyes and let out a sigh. Releasing their arms, she faced the two most important women left in her life. Satiah embraced her. "I will miss you. Remember, enter and conquer!" she whispered, planting a kiss on her friend's veiled cheek.

"I too will miss you," Asenath said, squeezing her one last time before releasing her.

Turning to Na'eemah and taking in her wet cheeks, she said in a broken voice, "You promised not to cry."

"And I was foolish to do so," Na'eemah said, sniffing. "The heart that shall remain soft must not be restrained," she said. Sharing proverbs had always been her way of expressing her emotions.

Asenath wrapped her slender arms around the motherly woman's thick shoulders. "I do not know what I will do without you . . ."

Clicking her tongue dismissively, Na'eemah returned the embrace. "You do not need me anymore. You have a husband to please and a household to run. It is I who should wonder what I will do without you to look after. Surely, I will become a cantankerous old woman."

"Become?" Heqaib teased. "I thought you already were."

As Satiah giggled, Na'eemah swung one arm and swatted her son playfully. "Hush! This is no time for your jesting!"

Asenath released herself from the embrace slowly, a weak smile on her face. Looking Na'eemah in the eye, she said softly, "I do not jest when I say I will always need you, *Mother*."

"O my sunshine," Na'eemah said, hugging her one last time. "May the blessings of Ra be upon you." Releasing Asenath, she kissed her on both veiled cheeks. "Satiah and I will join your father in offering sacrifices to the gods for your safe journey." Turning to Heqaib, she said, "Come and kiss me goodbye." Heqaib hugged his mother. "Take care of her," she whispered in his ear.

"I will, Mother," he whispered back, kissing her cheek.

Asenath kept her eyes off the gigantic body of water as both Heqaib and Semat escorted her up the plank and into the barge. Mercifully, it was large enough that she could take comfort in her enclosed makeshift quarters and pretend she was on land. She would do so in a moment. For now, she turned and gave her loved ones a last wave. They waved back. As if on cue, a flock of geese took to the air above them.

She watched her father's stately villa grow smaller and smaller as they drifted further and further away from the coast. She could feel the curtain closing on her childhood. It certainly had its trials, but she realized retrospectively that except for the loss of her mother, and the black day, she had actually been happy. Now she did not know if she would ever again be able to describe herself as such.

She had known as a child that this day would come. She wondered then how she would feel now. Oddly enough, she was still wondering.

Would things have been different if Mother was still alive? Or if I was not the daughter of the high priest of Heliopolis? What if I had been born a male instead of female and could have chosen my fate? What if I had never been born at all?

Asenath sighed. *Wondering is pointless. As surely as I could not stop this day from dawning, I cannot stop my destiny from unfolding.*

One thing was certain: this journey symbolized both the end of an era and the beginning of another. One she must share with a mysterious stranger of a husband. Heart sinking, she let out a heavy sigh.

"Ten," Heqaib said. She had not noticed him watching her. "That is your tenth sigh since we left . . ."

"It is nice to know your mathematics lessons were not a waste," she said, masking her growing apprehension in sarcasm.

He smiled knowingly. "I hate to see you so downcast, my lady."

"In that case, perhaps you should stop looking at me."

"I am afraid that is a feat beyond my capabilities." She sat in stone-faced silence as he continued. "I have learned it is better to accept the inevitable than to fight it."

"Your wisdom never ceases to amaze, Heqaib."

"I am serious. He might turn out to be more charming than the finest royal, if you keep an open mind."

"I am pleased *one* of us is hopeful," she said, massaging her temples. "If you will excuse me, I need an elixir and some sleep." As she headed for closed quarters, Asenath felt a twinge of remorse. Heqaib was only trying to help, after all. But the feeling was soon drowned in the river of her despondency.

***

"My lady . . ."

Asenath heard Semat's voice as though from a distance as she slowly awakened. "Where are we?" she asked groggily. "And how long was I asleep?"

"The sun goes to sleep, my lady," Semat answered.

Sunset?! I slept all day! Either the mixture she drank to calm her nerves had been stronger than expected or she was more exhausted than she had known.

"Captain Heqaib informs we dock in Avaris soon. He asks an audience with you."

"That is a mercy at least. We will be back on land, and not a moment too soon!" Asenath said, beginning to rise. Semat assisted her up.

"Shall I bring you some refreshments, my lady? You have hardly eaten anything all day."

"Thank you, Semat. Perhaps some fruit, after I speak with Heqaib."

"Yes, my lady."

After donning her travel cloak and refastening her veil, Asenath headed for the deck. Heqaib stood stoically at the stern of the vessel. When he saw her, he beckoned with a wave. Curious, Asenath walked toward him. She reached his side and waited for a teasing remark about her having hibernated the entire journey, but there was none. "We will soon dock at the south gate of the palace. It is the only gate accessible from the river. I imagine our receiving party will then convey us around the palace to the north gate."

"Interesting," Asenath said, unenthusiastically.

Heqaib smiled. "If you are wondering why I had you surface now, I merely thought you might appreciate this view." Gesturing toward the approaching shoreline, he added, "Welcome to Avaris."

Against the backdrop of a glorious sunset, she could clearly see a magnificent city. Even from here, the palace stood out among the sea of intimidating structures. Asenath took in the awe-inspiring sight. *He knows me all too well.* "It is spectacular." Feeling guilty for her *misdirected* anger, she shifted her gaze from the brilliant landscape to the kind-hearted man now entrusted with her safety. "Forgive me, Heqaib. I apologize for being so . . ."

"Sarcastic. Self-centered. Venomous—"

"Enough!" she said, raising her hands in surrender. "Perhaps I deserve that. But the word I was looking for is *childish*. I am a woman on the eve of becoming a wife and mistress of the second most prestigious household in Egypt. I must comport myself as such." She reached out her right hand and held his left. "Thank you, Heqaib. I will treasure this moment for a long time."

"As will I," he responded, holding her gaze. Squeezing his hand briefly before releasing it, she returned her eyes to the approaching shoreline.

This is it, Asenath. Your new home.

***

A passel of servants awaited her bridal cavalcade on the bridge. The beady-eyed, aquiline-faced man in charge was of average build, but he was excellently dressed and spoke with an air of superiority.

"Blessings of the evening. I am Wadjenes, steward of the house of His Eminence Zaphnath-Paaneah, vizier of Egypt. I am instructed by His Eminence to convey the bridal party of the daughter of Potiphera, high priest of Heliopolis, to his residence."

Heqaib stepped forward. "Blessings of the evening to you, Wadjenes. I am Heqaib, captain of the temple guard of Heliopolis, chief personal guard of His Reverence Potiphera, high priest of Heliopolis. His Reverence entrusted *me* with the safety of his daughter, the gift of Ra, until such a time as she is happily settled in her new home."

"Very well," said Wadjenes stiffly. Maintaining steely gazes at each other, the men exchanged the slightest of bows.

"Our horses and wagons await below," Wadjenes said, gesturing toward the foot of the bridge. "There is a wagon for my lady and another for her maidens. My men will load your belongings into the third."

"We appreciate your gracious welcome," Heqaib responded.

Quickly clapping his hands together twice, Wadjenes commanded: "Bearers!" Four large, muscular men in blue linen *shendyts* stepped forward with a carriage. Turning to face Asenath, Wadjenes said, "They will be honored to convey my lady to the bridal wagon."

Asenath could see the carriages fairly clearly from where she stood. She had just got off a barge and was eager to have her feet on solid ground. The thought of being hoisted in the air was not appealing. Noticing her hesitation, Heqaib approached her with an unspoken question in his eyes.

"I would rather walk," she said in a hushed tone.

"Are you certain?" he asked, whispering.

Asenath nodded. "You can walk ahead of my maidens and me."

"I intend to," Heqaib said quietly but firmly. Turning toward Wadjenes, he said louder, "My lady thanks you for the carriage, but would prefer to walk this time. Please, lead the way."

"As you wish," Wadjenes said, turning swiftly and heading for the wagons. Heqaib followed him. Without needing to be told, the maidens fell into their processional formation, surrounding their mistress. As they headed off the bridge, Asenath took in the scenery.

As far as her eyes could see, there were lights so bright, she almost forgot it was night. Torches blazed from the intermittent points atop the thick, high walls that surrounded the palace. It was impossible to see anything within those walls from outside them. The narrow stretch of water below them led all the way to a large, looming gate ahead. There appeared to be military encampments on each side of the bridge, all the way up to the south gate.

She was looking skyward to her left when her eye caught a brightly lit villa in the distance. It appeared to be on a hilly area just outside the main palace walls. *The occupants must have quite a view,* she thought in passing. In a similar location, but to her right, she recognized the markings of a temple.

"My lady," Semat said, turning to her. The procession had stopped.

Realizing they had reached the wagons, Asenath said, "Ride with me."

"Yes, my lady."

Heqaib approached to assist Asenath onto the bridal carriage. "I will be on the horse next to yours. You are safe."

"Thank you," Asenath said.

He helped Semat into the carriage as well, and let their curtains fall.

Asenath sighed.

"Are you all right, my lady?" Semat asked, genuinely concerned.

"I am well, Semat. Just a little tired."

"You have had quite the day, my lady. It is to be expected."

I have had quite the week. Noticing they had begun to move, Asenath leaned her head back and closed her eyes.

Within what seemed like a few minutes, the wagon stopped. Exchanging questioning glances, the two women waited. Hearing Heqaib's voice announcing his presence at the wagon's entrance, Semat waited for a nod from her mistress before lifting the curtain.

"What is wrong?" Asenath asked.

"Nothing! We have arrived."

"Arrived? At the north gate?"

"At your new home—merely a handbreadth away from the south gate. Apparently, your illustrious husband has chosen to reside outside the double walls of the palace."

"Has he?" Asenath asked, surprised.

"Indeed, and I am curious why. But it is not my place to ask that question. Ready?" Heqaib asked, offering a hand.

"As ready as I shall ever be," she responded, taking his hand and descending from the wagon.

Asenath took in the villa's sight from its entrance, since that was where her wagon was parked. *This is the brightly lit house I saw from the docks!* Lines of servants flanked both sides of a flight of stairs leading up to an arched entryway. Wadjenes had already taken his position at the head of the staircase, awaiting his new mistress.

Turning to Heqaib, Asenath said, "Thank you. Do you return to Heliopolis tomorrow?"

"No. Your father insisted I remain until the release of your handmaidens," he responded.

Asenath smiled knowingly. Except for the chief handmaiden, all six of the others would be released to their families the morning after her marriage was consummated. "Does he fear I might refuse the vizier?"

"He simply requests that I return with the assurance of your happiness in your new home."

Asenath uttered a nonverbal sound. *Even I need that assurance.* "Then may I say I am pleased . . . to have you here, if only for a few more nights."

"The pleasure is mine, my lady," Heqaib said with a bow.

Her handmaidens were already in formation. At her instruction, Semat removed her mistress's travel cloak, revealing a strapless, formfitting, emerald *kalasiris* beneath. She was dressed like royalty, and despite her mixed emotions, she would enter her new residence accordingly.

As the virginal party of eight gracefully ascended the stairs into her new home, the welcoming servants kept their heads bowed in honor. At the head of the stairs, Wadjenes gave a curt bow to the new lady of the villa.

"His Eminence Zaphnath-Paaneah, vizier of Egypt, welcomes the daughter of Potiphera, high priest of Heliopolis, to her new home. His Eminence renders his most sincere apologies. He is not here to welcome my lady in person, as he has been detained on a palatial matter. He will return tomorrow. I remain at your service to ensure your utmost comfort this evening."

Semat turned to Asenath in inquiry, and the latter whispered in the former's ear. Then Semat relayed her mistress's response. "My lady Asenath, daughter of Potiphera, high priest of Heliopolis, accepts the apologies of His Eminence Zaphnath-Paaneah, vizier of Egypt. Due to the lengthy journey, she requests to be shown to her chambers immediately."

"With pleasure," Wadjenes said. "Please, follow me." He led the way into a luxurious house. Two servants walked ahead of him carrying oil lamps. The other servants dispersed; some to tend to the horses and others to see to refreshments for the new arrivals. Clearly a military-trained staff of servants, each knew their place and duty without question.

Asenath let her eyes roam around the long, spacious hallway through which she was led. The tiled floors were polished to gleaming perfection. The furnishings were made of the finest wood and the decor was of royal blue with gold accents. Thick blue linen curtains fell from the high ceilings. Every room they passed was exquisitely finished.

Asenath immediately noticed the absence of any statues or murals of the gods. She also observed there was no incense burning anywhere. The only scent in the air was that of the aromatic floral arrangements at the entrance of every chamber. Each bouquet sat in a small copper censer hanging from a wooden pin at the center of each door frame.

Flowers in lieu of incense? Strangely fascinating.

At the entrance to a grandiose chamber, Wadjenes paused. "Please let us know if these chambers are unsatisfactory in any way." Not waiting for a response, he bowed and took his leave.

So, these are my new quarters.

Yellow lilies hung at her door. Stepping into the antechamber, she paused and took in the decor. The rooms were elegantly furnished and very spacious—almost twice the size of her chambers in her father's house. The curtains were the palest of purple hues. A soft carpet of animal skins lay on the polished tile floor. A one-armed couch with plush violet cushions sat against a wall, which boasted large windows providing a view of well-manicured gardens.

Someone on his staff certainly has a great sense of style.

Wandering into the bedchamber, she noticed a bunch of white lilies tied with gold string lay on equally white sheets in the center of a large ebony bed.

Lovely bouquet.

"Is my lady pleased?" Semat inquired.

"'Tis not all white, but it will do. What say you, Semat?"

"It is worthy of you, my lady."

"You are too kind." Letting her hand run lazily across the soft sheets, a few thoughts drifted through her mind.

I wonder what colors Zaphnath-Paaneah prefers, assuming he even has such preferences. I suppose I should be more concerned with what he thinks of me. He let work take precedence over receiving his bride. That does not bode well; not at all.

Her father would surely be disappointed if he knew she was going to sleep a virgin for yet another night, but she was not. Whatever the morrow held, she would enjoy the comfort of one more night to answer to no one but herself.

9

The garden of honesty
Grows life from dead seed
There, rare flowers bloom

***

Summoned.

He summons me to his bedchamber like a common concubine! Asenath seethed as she and her entourage of maidens headed from her chambers to the vizier's. She had learned that despite returning home hours ago, he had remained in his private quarters all evening. He had not bothered to come out and greet her. *We have not so much as met, let alone shared a meal together, and now we are about to share a bed.* What other reason could there be for him requesting her presence in his chambers?

Semat walked ahead of her, dropping petals of red lilies—a symbol of passion—for her to walk on. Her six other maidens walked in two lines behind her. As tradition dictated, tonight they would remain within the musicians' area to dance while the marriage was being consummated.

As they turned a corner in the hallway, Asenath heard the melodious plucking of musical strings. The music was welcome because her nerves were undoubtedly as taut as the strings on the instrument being skillfully played. Spending the day in her room awaiting the vizier had been easy on her body, but hard on her mind. Semat paused and looked at her.

"What is it?"

"My lady, forgive my forwardness. I must say, you would rival any goddess in beauty. His Eminence is most fortunate."

Asenath felt her anger dissipate. Placing her hand on her chief handmaiden's shoulder, she said, "Your kindness is heart-warming, Semat."

Eyes sparkling, the faithful maiden bowed and resumed leading the procession. Asenath's flaming-red dress clung to her every curve like a second skin. The unusual garment had been designed especially for her wedding night. It hung off one shoulder and was slit at both thighs to allow room for the movement of her legs. The revealing attire was partially concealed under a white linen cloak. An intricately fashioned white veil covered the lower half of her face, leaving only her eyes showing. Outlined in kohl, their amber color shone against the blue eye shadow that enhanced her eyelids. She had declined her usual green shadows today in order to match the decor of the house. Beneath her veil lay lips rouged with red ochre mixed with the juice of berries. Her curly mane was completely concealed beneath her ceremonial wig, and that was crowned with a jewel-encrusted gold band. Her bold, bejeweled look was finished with a pair of gold bracelets, an anklet on her right ankle, and her royal wedding gift gracefully hanging from her long neck.

The closer they got to their destination, the louder the music became. Asenath felt heady. She had been breathing in the thick incense that filled her chamber for the last few hours; the same one she instructed Semat to burn specifically to appease Isis, the goddess of many desirable things, including fertility. *Perhaps the intensity of the fumes is the source of my headiness.* Alternatively, it may have resulted from her few but recent sips of the strongest wine in her bridal chests. She had indulged in the drink, hoping to calm her anxiety. She need not have bothered. Nothing but the dawning of the morrow would make this night any less intimidating.

Semat stopped walking and looked at Asenath. They stood at the entrance to the vizier's quarters and Asenath knew Semat was awaiting her command.

Asenath closed her eyes and took three deep, calming breaths. *Enter and conquer.* Opening her eyes, she nodded at Semat, who announced her:

"My lady Asenath, gift of Ra, daughter of Potiphera, high priest of Heliopolis."

The curtains parted. Asenath entered the vast chamber and the attending guards bowed and exited. She gave the room a sweeping gaze. It was simply but elegantly furnished. She was pleasantly surprised to note that, except for the wooden furniture, it was entirely decorated in white. Her gaze moved further inward, to the far left of the luxurious bed at the heart of the bedchamber. There, facing her, stood a tall, fair-skinned man with broad shoulders and a narrow waistline. The only other occupant of the chamber, he wore an elegantly fitted white linen *shendyt*, belted with a tricolored sash. His muscular chest was visible beneath his bejeweled collar; and his smooth, bald head was reminiscent of a perfectly shaped egg. But all of that paled compared to the high cheekbones, statuesque nose, and alluring, pink lips that formed his handsome face.

Zaphnath-Paaneah.

Stunned at how striking he was, Asenath's pulse involuntarily quickened.

"My lady, Asenath, I am honored to have you here," he said in an arrestingly melodious baritone.

"The honor is mine, Your Eminence," Asenath replied, bowing deeply.

"Forgive my absence yesterday. It was unplanned and unavoidable." His dark brown eyes, framed by elegantly arched, black eyebrows, were incredibly magnetic. They drew her in effortlessly.

"It is forgiven, Your Eminence," Asenath said sweetly, temporarily forgetting her anxiousness.

"You are most gracious," he said with a smile that unnerved her.

The man was so attractive, the word *'handsome'* seemed inadequate. *He is flawless.* Asenath thought, her eyes taking him in from shaved head to sandaled feet.

He gestured toward a large couch beside him. "Please, be seated. Would my lady like some wine?"

Just then, she heard the *Raqs Baladi* melody begin.

Brows furrowing, Zaphnath-Paaneah inclined his head.

Asenath's heart was slamming against her chest. In accordance with her plan to seduce and subdue, she had previously instructed her ever-efficient handmaiden to have the music begin the moment she was in his chamber.

You have entered. Now conquer! Trying to maintain a cool, confident exterior despite her pounding heart, she slowly unraveled her cloak and let it fall to the ground. Remembering Satiah's pose, she struck it, revealing almost the entirety of her slender, smooth legs through the splits in her dress. Staring directly into his almond-shaped eyes, she noticed them widen. Fluttering her long lashes and pursing her painted lips, she said in her most sultry tone, "The wine . . . can wait."

She noticed him swallow, his eyes unblinking.

Taking her cue from the music, she began dancing slowly toward him. Keeping her gaze locked on his, she executed every move with the stealth of a cat and the skill of a seasoned dancer. The music increased in volume and tempo and Asenath shimmied, twirled, and side-stepped with more energy.

Seemingly transfixed, the vizier remained rooted to his spot as Asenath advanced. She could not quite place the look in his eyes. In one swift and well-practiced move, as the melody rose to a crescendo, she twirled and dropped into a full split, right at his large, leather-sandaled feet. As the music continued more softly, she placed her palms firmly on the floor, raised her hips, and carefully drew her legs in, placing herself in a squat. Then she slowly arose into a standing position, her soft chest lightly brushing up against his chiseled torso. His intensified breathing revealed he was not oblivious to her charms, but his face slowly turned a crimson shade and he took two steps back.

Asenath frowned. She had expected him to unveil her face at this point. *Maybe he wants me to do it.* Stepping forward, she reached for the clasp on her veil. He lifted his long hand a fingerbreadth away from hers.

"No, my lady." His voice came out in a hoarse whisper, and the vein in his muscular neck was throbbing.

No? Perhaps he prefers I keep the veil on, she thought, stilling her hands. *A strange choice though not a hindrance to the task at hand.* She reached downwards for the knot on his sash. He placed his large hand on her comparably smaller one.

"Do not, please." His hands felt rough against her tender skin.

What sort of game is he playing? Trying to mask her confusion, she put on a sweet smile, hoping her eyes would reflect it. "As you wish, Your Eminence," she said, taking a step back. There was only one thing left to do. She reached up to her left shoulder and untied the single strap that held her flaming garment in place.

Right as the gown began to fall off her flawless shoulder, he yelled, "NO!" simultaneously turning around so swiftly the force almost knocked her to the ground. "My lady, I implore you, do not disrobe," he said more softly.

Shocked, she froze.

With his perfectly straight back to her, he let out a long breath. "I must excuse myself to the gardens. Please join me, after you have had a moment to . . . compose yourself. Wadjenes will show you the way." Giving a wide berth, he stepped around her without looking at her. And with nary a backward glance, he exited the chamber as though escaping the hordes of Hades.

Asenath stood there, mouth agape. Of the myriad of thoughts flooding her mind, one was most prominent: *I, Asenath, gift of Ra, have just been rejected.* It was also very clear that she would end the second night in her matrimonial home, still a virgin. Not a single one of her lessons had prepared her for this scenario. Had she lived a thousand lifetimes, she would still not have foreseen this outcome. Looking down at herself, she made two observations:

First, other than her veil and jewelry, she was naked.

Second, she was trembling. Not because she was cold, but because she was *livid.*

***

Asenath walked through a maze in the extensive gardens. She had exchanged her fiery dress for a more modest, yet still formfitting purple one. However, she donned a black veil to match her mood. Escorting her were Wadjenes, two guards, and two of her handmaidens. Indignant, she could barely take in the scenery. *Who does this Hebrew think he is, to reject the daughter of the high priest of Heliopolis?*

Exiting the maze, they approached a beautiful clearing in the center of the garden.

Wadjenes stopped. In the distance, she saw what looked like a tabular pile of stones with a fire burning in the center. Pointing in their direction, Wadjenes said, "His Eminence requests that the daughter of Potiphera approach alone from this point."

"Alone?!" Semat responded reflexively, looking to her mistress for a response.

Asenath nodded and waved a dimissory hand. It was even better that she approached alone, because she would serve this arrogant foreigner a choice piece of her mind momentarily.

Leaving the servants, she strode toward the fire. Then she saw him and paused. His strange posture took her by surprise. He was on one knee, his head bowed, facing the stones. His arms were stretched out with palms facing upwards, and his lips moved, but he made no sound.

Asenath was not sure whether to announce her presence or to remain silent. She did not have to wonder for long. He rose and turned toward her with the gentlest look in his eyes.

"You came. Thank you." Not since she looked into her mother's eyes had she seen such sincerity in anyone.

Asenath closed her eyes for a moment to regain her focus. Then she began the tirade she had rehearsed en route to the garden. "Your Eminence Zaphnath-Paaneah," she said, bowing slightly, "you requested my presence. I cannot imagine why, given the circumstances. I can only assume you have no desire for it. Surely you know I am—"

"Asenath. Gift of Ra. Daughter of Potiphera, high priest of Heliopolis. And the most stunning creature upon which my eyes have ever lain," he said with an unblinking gaze.

Taken aback, she paused. *Did he just call me stunning?*

"I must beg your pardon for my . . . behavior, earlier, my lady. I meant no slight. I shall provide what I hope is a satisfactory explanation in time, as you rightly deserve one. But if you would kindly make do with my apologies for now, and honor me with your company tonight, I would be most grateful."

Surely I misunderstand him. "My company?"

"You see . . . I would like to get to know you a little better, first. No facades, no servants, no obligations. Just a man and a woman, taking a leisurely stroll." He reached out his right hand in invitation, with his palm facing downwards. "Please?"

A stroll? This is one peculiar man. Thoroughly perplexed, Asenath reminded herself that she was the daughter of a noble, and nobility was nothing if not well-mannered. She placed her left palm on his right and they began to walk.

"What do you think of the garden?" he asked, making a sweeping gesture with his available hand.

Asenath gave a cursory glance around. "It is a garden."

If he caught her reticence, he did not let on. Unperturbed, he asked, "Have you a favorite bloom?"

"You are a diviner, so you tell me," she retorted.

The broad smile he flashed revealed an impeccable set of shiny teeth. "I see you have heard stories about me. As have I, about you. Life has taught me no echo can ever be as trustworthy as the original sound. Therefore, I would prefer to hear about the daughter of Potiphera from her radiant self."

"I see." *Handsome, charming, and spouting proverbs. Na'eemah would love him.* "You may ask what you will, on one condition."

"And that is?"

"You answer two questions first."

"You have my ears."

"What were you doing back there on your knee?"

"Honestly?"

"You said no facades, as I recall."

"Praying," he said simply.

"Praying!" she said with a surprised laugh. "To which god? I saw no statue. I smelled no incense."

"To the invisible God."

Invisible? Surely he jests; but I can play along. "And what do you call this invisible God?"

"He has no name," he shrugged.

"An invisible God with no name. Interesting." *He is out of his mind. That explains a lot.*

He laughed from his belly. It was a rich, infectious sound, and she found herself smiling ever so slightly.

"And your second question?" he asked, still smiling.

"Why have you chosen a residence here, outside the palace walls?"

"An intriguing inquiry. Viziers do typically live within the main palace walls."

"Hence my question."

"I want to come home to tranquility and a sense of freedom. With its massive walls and incessant activity, the palace can sometimes feel . . . almost . . ."

"Suffocating?" she asked.

He gave her a surprised look. "Precisely. I am very averse to that feeling."

So am I.

"I hope being housed outside the palace walls does not displease you."

"I have lived outside the palace all my life. Why should it displease me now?"

"I am delighted to hear that. We are well within the vicinity of the outer court, which houses other nobles. I simply chose a residence in its less popular southwest quadrant. Besides the serenity and sensational seaside views, there is another advantage to being here."

"And that is?. . ."

"Heightened security. The military encampment guarding the south gate is a handbreadth away, and the other residences in this area house the highest-ranking military officials."

This man is no fool. "Good to know," she said.

"Speaking of things to know," he said lightly, "may I ask my questions now?"

"Certainly. I am curious about what it is you do not already know."

"Well, first, and do not think me frivolous for asking this, but . . . your fragrance . . . it is sweet, yet unique . . . what is it?"

"You could inquire about anything and *that* is your question?"

"My first one. I thought we should start with something simple."

Fascinating. "It is a special scent made from a mixture of flowers and spices. My great-grandmother passed the recipe down. All the women in my family wear this fragrance."

"Intriguing. And does it have a name?"

"I was never told. But I call it Enigma."

"An apt moniker. Now, there is something I have been curious about since I first heard of you. Is it true that no man other than your father has ever seen your face?"

"Not since he veiled me at the age of eleven."

"Yet you would show it to me?" he asked, clearly amazed.

By the life of Pharaoh! Do I have a choice? "It is customary that a man unveil his *bride* on their wedding night," she said pointedly.

His face reddened slightly. "Of course. Forgive me," he said, shaking his head. "It is just that I feel gazing upon your face would be a rare privilege. One that should be earned by love, not granted by law."

"Love?" Asenath asked, surprised. "And what is love to you?"

"I believe there was an agreement, my lady," he said, stroking an invisible beard on his chiseled jaw. "His Eminence is asking the questions tonight."

Asenath could not stop herself from smiling. *He might be of unsound mind, but this man is definitely not boring.* "As you wish, Your Eminence. Query away!"

And query he did. He asked about her childhood, her parents, her likes and dislikes, her hopes and dreams. They must have circled the gardens multiple times, but she could not remember a single flower or plant she saw in them. Neither could she recall ever having a more delightful conversation. He posed questions that challenged her mind. His manner put doubts in her assumptions about the way men treat beautiful women. Before he escorted her to her chambers, he asked her if she would give him the pleasure of her company at dinner the next night. He did not demand it or command it. He *requested* it.

Asenath barely slept that night. She was going over the events of the past day. When she did eventually fall asleep just before dawn, it was with the astonishing realization that over the course of the past day, the feeling in the pit of her belly had metamorphosed from anxiety into anger, and then, anticipation.

10

When a young man
Has seemingly lost his mind
Alas, a fair maid
Has surely found his heart

***

Distracted.
Zaphnath-Paaneah was finding it difficult to concentrate. He sat at a large table in his formal meeting chamber at the palace. Seated to his right and left, respectively, were the second captain of the king's guard, Nebemakhet, and the royal treasurer, Bakenranef. The chief royal scribe, Senenmut, sat directly across from him. The nobles were gathered to strategize on his impending tour of the land.

Records of accounts were laid out in front of the well-fed, heavily bejeweled treasurer who had already concluded his report. They were all focused on Nebemakhet, who had hand-drawn maps of Egypt spread out before him. The astute, uniformed military official was the foremost expert on Egypt's geography.

"Your Eminence, I think it best if your tour begins here in Lower Egypt," Nebemakhet said, pointing out a location on the map, "and then proceed south to Upper Egypt. Sais is a good city for your first stop. Then journey downwards along the Nile all the way to Elephantine."

As the vizier's eyes traced the indicated route, the gentle curves of the Nile conjured up images of Asenath's figure in his mind. He inadvertently traced an index finger down the winding river and said, "Beautiful . . ."

"Your Eminence?" Nebemakhet asked, his bushy eyebrows wrinkling.

Did I say that out loud? Zaphnath-Paaneah thought, catching himself. "Beautifully brilliant strategy!" he stated, giving the confused official what he hoped was an affirming look.

"Thank you, Your Eminence," Nebemakhet said with a curious look on his angular face.

Beautifully brilliant strategy? What is wrong with me? He had spent but one evening with Asenath and already she had him, the supposedly wisest man in the land, sounding like a bumbling fool. He had been around beautiful women; since becoming vizier, they seemed to appear out of the very walls of the palace wherever he found himself. Yet none of them elicited the reactions Asenath had so effortlessly drawn from him from the moment she set foot in his chamber. The image of her curves, easily discernible beneath her red raiment and emphasized with every move she had made, was seared into his mind. Her eyes glowed like two suns and aroused in him a fiery curiosity as to what lay beneath her lovely veil. The scent of her perfume still lingered in his chamber. *Enigma. A scent as mysterious as the one who wears it.* She effortlessly occupied his mind, and he wondered if the reverse held true.

"Your Eminence?" Senenmut's raised voice roused him out of his reverie. The short, rotund scribe looked like he was waiting for an answer.

Was there a question? "Senenmut?"

Nebemakhet and Bakenranef exchanged knowing glances, while Senenmut cleared his throat. "Shall I proceed, Your Eminence?" he asked, waving a thick roll of papyrus in his hand.

The reports! Zaphnath-Paaneah realized. "Certainly!" Glancing to his left and right, he said dismissively, "Thank you, my lords; your insights have been invaluable."

As the scribe unfurled the first of many lengthy rolls of papyrus, the other two guests quickly gathered their things, glad to escape the tedious reading coming. Senenmut was indeed an exceptional scribe, but his tone could put even the most spirited sentry to sleep. Zaphnath-Paaneah watched the nobles eagerly depart and tried to rid his mind of persistent thoughts about the mesmerizing woman with whom he had spent the evening before.

He focused on the reports on Memphis, and then Bubastis, making notes for himself as he did. He was making his final note on Bubastis as Senenmut laid a second papyrus aside and picked up a third. Lifelessly, the scribe announced, "Here begins the report on Heliopolis."

Asenath's home city! Zaphnath-Paaneah sat up, his curiosity immediately aroused. *The very land that nourished such a rare flower.* Bewitching; that she was. He was not sure how much longer he could resist her charms. *Not that I desire to put up even the least resistance,* he thought, his admission taking him by surprise. If one day in her presence had weakened his resolve and driven reason from his mind, what would happen in the next few days? He shook his head briefly; as if shaking some sense back into himself. *Before you met her, you made an agreement with His Divine Magnificence; uphold it.* Bewitching or not, he would have to tell her the truth tonight. Until then, he had to focus on the work at hand. The duties of the vizier were not to be taken lightly. He knew there were nobles eager to see him fail.

Lord, give me strength to do what I must, now and tonight. And with that brief, silent prayer, he gave the droning scribe his full attention.

***

Asenath had one word for the sight below her: *Spectacular.* Having spent her first day in her new residence primarily in her chambers, anticipating her first meeting with the lord of the villa, she had decided a change was in order. Her chosen location for most of this morning's activities, the rooftop, had proven to be a feast for the senses. The sky stretched wide above her, while the palace drew her gaze westward, and the Nile, eastward. The proximity of the river had filled the air with the cawing of seagulls and the crashing of waves; not to mention an appealing scent reminiscent of rains falling on sand. Sounds and smell had both made her meditation and stretching sessions even more refreshing.

Since Zaphnath-Paaneah had no customary altars or prayer chamber, she and her septet of maidens had erected a makeshift altar to Isis and offered fervent supplications. Rather than dismiss them afterward, Asenath had them all join her for an unusual, but heartwarming, rooftop breakfast. They would be returning to their own families, as she began hers. Which would be immediately, assuming tonight held no unpleasant surprises. *Grant me insight into this mysterious man, great goddess of love.*

Asenath walked along the roof's edge, looking down at the extensive grounds beneath. She was looking forward to exploring her new home, hence sending her most trusted handmaiden to survey the territory ahead of her. Soft footsteps behind her caught her attention, and she turned.

"Well? What is the lay of the land?"

Dipping her head briefly, Semat responded, "The villa boasts four wings. The north wing houses His Eminence's chambers, and has a private entrance into the lovely gardens, which my lady has already seen."

He must really like the outdoors.

"The south wing includes the main kitchens and the servants' quarters. A path from there leads to some remarkable stables."

"Horse-riding does appeal."

"I thought it might, my lady. We are housed in the east wing, which, as you already know, connects to His Eminence's wing with that private hallway."

"Indeed. So the main entrance is in the west wing."

"Precisely. As well as formal guest chambers and a very grand feasting hall. It would be a wonderful setting for a wedding feast."

Assuming my mysterious foreigner of a husband sees fit to throw one.

"I will keep that in mind. Anything else?"

"Yes. I believe there is a chamber in the west wing my lady might find even more fascinating than the feasting hall," Semat said, eyes twinkling.

"And that is?"

"The chamber of knowledge. It is even larger than that in your father's residence."

A library larger than Father's?

"In that case, I know where I will spend tomorrow afternoon."

"And this afternoon?"

"Preparing for this evening."

"An incense soak, then?"

"An extended one. Followed by a full body massage. Perhaps we can try doing that up here today; I enjoy the warmth of the sun on freshly oiled skin."

"I believe His Eminence will enjoy the glowing results even more."

Asenath smiled. *I hope so.* Hope was all she could do at this point. She was certain of nothing with regard to Zaphnath-Paaneah.

"Speaking of His Eminence, what have you heard?"

"Nothing, my lady."

"Nothing? They know *nothing* about him?"

"They have been here less than a week. Apparently, His Eminence is at the palace all day and keeps to himself otherwise. No guests, male or female, family or otherwise, have been entertained here."

Really? "Thank you, Semat. I shall be in momentarily." As Semat bowed and walked away, Asenath wondered what manner of man she was to call a husband. *No shrines or incense? Understandable, given neither would be required to worship an invisible god. But no friends or family? Impossible. No one is an island.* He was a mortal, so he had to have parents, at least. Where were they? What was his childhood like? He was Hebrew, she knew that much. Surely he had a Hebrew name then. *What is it? Perhaps he will let me ask my questions tonight.* It seemed only fair, she had answered all of his, last night. She would prepare herself accordingly. And if she could muster the courage, she would ask what she was most curious about: the incident that earned him a chamber in the king's prisons.

***

Asenath emerged at the entrance to the vizier's villa to meet Wadjenes waiting. Per her strange spouse's request, she was dressed for an outdoor dinner. Wadjenes was not alone. Behind him stood four of the large, bare-chested bearers that had met them at the docks when she first arrived Avaris. They held an opulent carriage between them. Boasting two long, gold poles and a base of the finest cedar, its seat was covered in white linen and padded with plush, wool-stuffed cushions.

Wadjenes bowed. "His Eminence has commanded a carriage for my lady."

She nodded her assent. The bearers kneeled and bowed low so she could seat herself. Semat adjusted her mistress's thick shawl to cover the royal blue *kalasiris* beneath it. The strong quartet lifted Asenath effortlessly. With Wadjenes leading the way, they bore her toward the gardens. Semat followed at the rear, along with her handmaidens, Tsillah and Merit.

They walked in the opposite direction of the maze this time. Through a cove of trees, they arrived at a path that sloped downhill. The path ended in a clearing. There, looking every bit a prince in the purest white raiment, stood Zaphnath-Paaneah. Two white stallions were tethered close to him. Behind him, she could clearly see the Nile. A small shiver went down her spine. The bearers lowered the carriage for her dismount and the vizier stepped forward, offering a hand to assist her.

"My lady . . ."

"Shalom, Your Eminence."

She registered the delightfully surprised expression on his face. "Shalom. You speak Hebrew?"

Answering in Hebrew, she said, "Not often." Continuing in her native tongue, she added, "I have an interest in languages."

"But why would you care to learn that one? Egyptians are not partial to Hebrews."

"That may be so. But I am partial to my handmaidens. Merit's mother is Hebrew. She never knew her Egyptian father. She barely spoke our dialect when she first came to my father's house to serve. I picked up her language while she learned mine. My father heard us conversing one day and was none too pleased. But what can I say? The allure of the forbidden fruit only spurred my learning on."

"Beauty and intellect. Impressive," he said, in a tone that exhibited admiration.

"You are too kind."

Turning to the servants, he said, "You may go." Wadjenes and the bearers headed up the path. The handmaidens lingered, awaiting their mistress's command. Asenath dismissed them with an almost imperceptible wave. As they departed, she asked, eyeing the horses, "Are we riding to dinner?"

"No, I thought we might ride back afterwards."

"I see no provisions," she said, glancing around. "Am I to assume our dinner has been provided by the invisible God and shares his imperceptible nature?"

His contagious laughter echoed in the trees. Composing himself, he gestured toward the river. "Our very visible dinner awaits. Come!"

Asenath's pulse accelerated as she gingerly accepted his outstretched palm. As they walked toward the river, she noticed a large tree surrounded at its base by multiple oil lamps. A feast was laid out on white linens at the foot of the tree.

Romantic. A fire burned a little way off. There was a pile of thick cloaks laid out beside the meal. *Thoughtful, too.* Eyeing the food, she noted her favorite dishes and a few others with which she was not familiar. *He left no stone unturned.* She let him assist her into a reclined position on the cushions and accepted the cloak he offered. "Thank you."

"You are most welcome," he said, seating himself across from her similarly, leaving the array of dishes between them. His face glowed as the light from the lamps fell on it. "Is my lady warm enough?" he inquired.

"Yes, thank you."

Pouring wine into her goblet first, and his afterward, he raised his. "To your happiness, my lady."

She raised her chalice. "And yours, Your Eminence."

Knowing they would dine tonight, she had donned a suitably lengthy veil. Skillfully sweeping her goblet under it, she lifted it to her lips. The wine went down her throat warmly. She set the cup down and noticed a strange look on his face.

"That cannot be easy."

"What?"

"Having to eat with a veil in your way."

"What can I say? The longer one does it, the easier it becomes. Nonetheless, you determine how long it remains in my way."

"Indeed. And I am sorry to have extended your discomfort even a moment longer." Once again, his eyes held sincerity.

"Think nothing of it." Lightening the mood, she said, "The aromas wafting from these dishes have teased me long enough. My belly scolds."

He laughed. "We must appease it, at once."

They dug into their moonlight feast, exchanging pleasantries about the various dishes. He identified the ones unfamiliar to her. They were Hebrew delicacies and surprisingly delicious. For the most part, they ate in silence, savoring each mouthwatering morsel. Somehow, she did not find it uncomfortable. She enjoyed the sound of the breeze rustling in the trees and the feel of the cool air blowing through her hair. She knew he was watching her carefully, for every time she looked at him, her eyes met his. Realizing he had stopped eating and his gaze was unflinching, she felt compelled to speak.

"Is something wrong?"

His cheeks colored ever so slightly. "Not at all," he said, temporarily averting his eyes.

Asenath smiled, appreciating the veil that concealed her amusement from her flushed dinner companion.

11

As stars in the sky
As grains of sand. Numberless!
So your seed will be

***

Charmed.

Unless she was misreading his expression, Asenath would say Zaphnath-Paaneah seemed fascinated by her. She was wondering how best to broach the subject of his answering her yet unasked questions, when he asked one, "Tell me, do you enjoy the art of storytelling?"

Do I ever! "I have since childhood," she replied eagerly. "My mother was gifted in that art. Her gift brought me to laughter, tears, fury, and the heights of fantasy more times than I can number."

"I am well pleased to hear it. I also admire the art. My favorite story was told to me when I was but a boy. It is a tale of love unlike any I have ever heard since."

"Is it?" Asenath asked, perking up. "Do you care to share it?"

"I was hoping you would ask."

"I can never turn down a good story," she admitted.

His dark brown eyes sparkled as he began his tale. "Long ago, a young nomad fled his home. He feared the wrath of his twin brother, whom he had offended. He ended up in a strange land, and fortunately, found the house of his mother's brother. His uncle welcomed him, and the youth immediately began to work in his uncle's fields, looking after a large flock of sheep and goats. From the very moment his eyes fell upon his uncle's youngest daughter, an unquenchable love for her gripped him. She was called Rachel, and he, Jacob.

"After a month of work, his uncle asked Jacob what wages he desired. Jacob, completely besotted, told his uncle he would gladly work for seven years to have Rachel's hand in marriage. And his uncle agreed."

Asenath's perfectly groomed eyebrows leaped skyward. *Seven years of service?*

"Alas, his uncle was a crafty man. Unbeknown to him, it was against tradition for a younger daughter to marry before an elder, and Rachel's older sister, Leah, was not yet married."

This does not bode well.

"Jacob served well for the full seven years and his uncle's flocks flourished in his care. At the end of his seven-year service, a traditional Hebrew wedding took place. Which meant the bride stayed veiled during the ceremony.

Hebrew brides wear veils!

"Upon the wedding night, behold, it was Leah whom he had married. Jacob was furious!"

"As well he should!"

"Absolutely. But when he confronted his uncle, the deceptive man explained the tradition, and said Jacob could also have Rachel as a wife after he honored the bridal week with Leah. However, rather than simply let him have the woman for whom he had toiled so long, can you hazard a guess at what the uncle did?"

"Gave her to another man?"

"That would have been decidedly cruel, but he would have gained nothing. He covenant Jacob to work another seven years for Rachel."

"The effrontery! Jacob could not possibly. Could he?"

"He could and he did. He got his beloved Rachel as wife at the end of her sister's bridal week, but bound by the covenant he had made, he served seven more years in his uncle's house."

"Unbelievable!"

"Indeed. But the story does not end there. It turned out that while Leah birthed him four sons, Rachel was barren. So she gave her handmaiden to Jacob as a wife, and the maiden bore him two sons. Leah also did the same with her handmaiden, who also birthed him two additional sons. Then Leah birthed him two more sons. Thus Jacob became a father to ten sons, but none from the woman he loved."

How sad.

"Undeterred, Jacob built altars and made intercession to the invisible God on behalf of his wife. His prayers were answered! Rachel conceived and had a son; she named him Joseph. Jacob's eleventh son was Rachel's first, and only, joyful birth. Years later, she died birthing her second son."

"Tragic! And you call this a love story?"

Zaphnath-Paaneah's eyes moistened slightly, as he wistfully answered, "It is. Jacob loved Rachel all of her life. He never loved another woman like he did her. And he cherished her sons, as he had cherished her."

"Intriguing. But, I must say, a taller tale of love I have not heard. May I ask who wove this wondrous web of sentiments?"

He looked at her, his expression sobering. "It is no tall tale. I heard it straight from Rachel's mouth."

"I beg your pardon? You knew this Rachel?"

"I knew her and loved her."

"Loved her?" Asenath asked, perplexed.

"Yes. As a son loves the woman who gave him life."

Asenath's jaw dropped slightly as realization struck. "Your mother! And she died birthing . . . no. If you *heard* her tell this story, then you were . . . Joseph?"

"I *am* Joseph." The resolute look in his eyes only solidified the truth of his words.

His Hebrew name! The myriad of questions she had been keeping at bay unleashed themselves on her mind again. She voiced an easy one. "What does Joseph mean?"

"Savior," he answered with a smile.

His mother named him savior. "Do you consider yourself as such?"

His expression sobered. "No," he answered softly. "In fact, I spent the better part of my youth desperately in need of saving."

In need of saving? "From what?" Asenath inquired, noting the depth of emotion in his voice.

He paused for a moment, as though weighing his answer. Then, with a small smile, he responded, "Permit me to answer that another time, my lady. We were discussing love. If you do not mind, I would rather remain on that subject."

This man has layers. For the love of Isis, what is he hiding? She was eager to uncover whatever secrets his past held, but a lack of patience was not the quality she wanted to flaunt before a man in whose good graces she needed to be. Masking her impatience with a brilliant smile, she acquiesced. "Certainly, Your Eminence. I have heard many a true tale of exploits undertaken for love. I can honestly say none are as extraordinary as your father's. Loving your mother at first sight so passionately that he willingly worked fourteen years to earn the right to be her husband is . . . incredible!"

"If I had not heard it from my mother's lips, and seen its truth in my father's eyes every time he looked at her, I too may have thought so," he admitted. "You asked what love is to me. That level of sacrifice . . . devotion . . . affection . . . Loving someone enough to set aside your comfort for them. Beseeching God on their behalf. Staying true to them in life, in death, and beyond; that is what love is to me. That is the love I grew up dreaming of having. You will forgive me, but I can neither offer nor accept anything that falls short of that."

Asenath lowered her eyes. She was not offering that. She was offering her body, definitely, and her obedience, probably, but not her heart. Never her heart. She needed him at her beck and call, not the other way around.

Raising her eyes to his, she asked, "And is that what you offer me?"

"It is what I offer the woman I choose."

"But you did not choose me."

"No, I could not have chosen you."

"Could not?"

"I could only make you that offer on one condition."

Condition? "And that is?"

He closed his eyes and let out a breath. Opening his eyes, he looked at her. "To answer that, I fear you have to suffer another story."

The mercy of Ra! "Such cruel and unusual punishment, Your Eminence; but if you must."

He threw his head back and laughed, his handsome face becoming even more so. When he returned his eyes to hers, the light in them sparked an unfamiliar, warm feeling in the pit of her abdomen.

Rising, he offered his hand. "How about a change of scenery? I shall tell my second tale there." He gestured toward the river.

Asenath's heart leaped to her throat. "*On* the Nile?"

"Yes," he said, picking up an oil lamp. "My boat is small, but it should suffice. I think you shall enjoy the view from the water."

The view was the least of her concerns. Her heart pounded against her chest as memories of her mother's passing haunted her mind. She took a deep breath and let it out slowly.

"Is everything all right?" he asked.

Not wanting to reveal her greatest fear, or otherwise appear weak before him, she replied, "Yes. Fine!" *Asenath, you are only going on the water, not in it*, she told herself, taking his hand apprehensively. She followed him to the boat and let him help her into it. She kept her eyes on him—and off the water—as he rowed them further away from the shore. With the riverbank still in sight, he stopped and brought the oars in. Leaning back, he let his hand run through the water and sighed contentedly.

"The stars are lovely tonight, are they not?" he noted, looking skyward.

Asenath followed his gaze. "Yes." Then she looked at him. "Is His Eminence trying to evade the task at hand?"

"And incur the wrath of the sun goddess? I dare not."

Her nerves stifled her sense of humor. "Then I am listening," she said, crossing her arms over her chest.

"Look at them. Have you ever wondered what the number of the stars might be, or tried to number the ones your eyes could see?"

Asenath was not pleased to be within reach of the dark waters. "Are you telling a tale or reciting a poem?"

"Merely asking a question. Have you?"

The sooner she answered the question, the sooner he could tell his tale and they could get back on land. Waving a dimissory hand, she said, "Only a fool would embark on a mission as futile as numbering the stars, and only a sadist would order such a mission."

"In that case, the sadist would be the invisible God, and the fool would be my great-grandfather, Abram."

"I see the madness in your family goes back generations," she blurted before she could stop herself.

"And is the sharpness of your tongue also hereditary?" he retorted, smiling.

So he does possess some fire. Good. "His Eminence will have to wait and see. But please, proceed."

"Very well, my lady. Abram was seventy-five years old, married to Sarai, and she was barren."

"Madness and barrenness; your family gets more appealing by the minute."

"You have not the faintest idea," he said with a strange expression on his face. "Back to my tale. The invisible God told Abram to leave his family and his father's house and go to an unknown place that he would show him."

"And he left?"

"He left."

"His wife followed?"

"In life, in death, and beyond."

Asenath grunted. *Why am I not surprised?*

"He left because the invisible God promised Abram would not only have children, he would become a father of nations."

"I take it Sarai was much younger?"

"Only nine years younger."

"Perfect. The invisible God makes an impossible promise; how convenient. He cannot be held accountable if the promise fails. How does one catch what one cannot see? But by all means, continue, I am intrigued."

He shook his head, smiling in the most disarming way. "Many years later, Abram was content to let his most trusted servant become his heir. Until the invisible God told him to number the stars as far as he could see, and count the innumerable grains of sand on the seashore, promising that his descendants would be that many. He further vowed they would not be the offspring of Abram's servant, but the offspring of his loins. Then the invisible God changed his name from Abram to Abraham."

"Father . . . of nations?"

"Your command of Hebrew is better than I thought."

"Thank you," she said, her smile genuine.

"With the name change, every time someone said his name, they were calling Abraham into his destiny. Sarai's name was changed to Sarah."

"Princess." Asenath's rouged lips spread into a small smile, which must have been reflected in her voice and eyes, for he returned it with a broader one before continuing his tale.

"Indeed, and the princess's husband had difficulty convincing her to believe the divine promise. Sarah rationalized him into having a son by her maid, and he agreed."

"Barren, but at least *she* was sensible," Asenath said, giving him a knowing look.

He chuckled. "The story gets more intriguing. Over two decades after he first left his homeland, Abraham spied three travelers and invited them to rest and feast in his tent. Not only did they feast, one of them declared that by that same time a year from that day, Sarah would have a son. Sarah, who was baking, overheard them and laughed."

An understandable response.

"When she came out to serve her freshly baked cakes, the traveler asked why she had laughed. Shocked and embarrassed, Sarah denied it. Then he asked a question that I have asked time and again in the face of great difficulty: *Is there anything too hard for God?*"

Time and again? Imprisonment may not be the only difficulty that has plagued his life. The mystery deepens.

As if sensing her wandering thoughts, he paused and looked at the stars again.

Asenath once more became conscious of her watery surroundings. *The sooner he finishes his tale, the sooner I will be back on solid ground.* Spurring him on, she asked, "What happened next?"

"Something wonderful. True to the promise of the Lord, as prophesied by the traveler, Sarah birthed Abraham a son a year later. She was ninety, and he, ninety-nine. They named my *saba*, Isaac."

Asenath gave him a dubious look. "The first tale I could believe, but this . . . it is incredibly far-fetched."

"Absolutely. Yet, it is just as true. Our family has neither known nor served another God since. With the exception of my mother; she worshiped other gods when she first married my father. He had to put a stop to that, ridding their entire camp of all statues of deities."

What? He discarded the sacred statues? Why?

As if privy to her silent question, he said, "Because the God we serve is a jealous God. But he is also a faithful God. He demands undivided loyalty because he offers no less, even though he need not do so. He is immortal and we, mere mortals. Yet he conversed with my great-grandfather as a man would speak to his friend. It is because of his great power that my entire genealogy exists. My *saba* Issac's birth was nothing short of miraculous. And it is because of the Lord's great mercy that I live. That I lived long enough to become the revered vizier before you. He is the one who gave me both the gift to dream and the gift to interpret dreams. As for me and my children, and my children's children, we will worship no other god. Neither will I permit the worship of any other god by anyone in my household."

Certainly not his wife. Asenath felt her heart lurch. *This is no small condition. I need him to be acutely clear.* "Am I to understand that the condition upon which your . . . generous offer rests is that I pledge allegiance to this . . . invisible God?"

"And forsake all others. Yes."

Her palms were sweating. "Surely you jest."

"There are two subjects upon which I never jest: my heart, and my faith."

Asenath scoffed. "What you ask is in itself unreasonable, but of *whom* you ask it is unbelievable. My father, as you are well aware, is *high priest* of Heliopolis, dedicated to a lifetime of service at the temple of Ra. I am the gift of Ra himself! To deny Ra would be to deny my very existence; everything upon which I have built my life! What kind of arrogance would give you the audacity to make such a demand?"

He sighed. "It is not arrogance that emboldens me, my lady. It is devotion to the laws of the God to whom I owe *my* existence."

Asenath's eyes resembled two blazing suns. "Have you forgotten that I am gifted to you by Pharaoh, lord of Egypt–long may he live? Or do you mean to insult him by rejecting his gift?"

"The God who caused me to be favored in Pharaoh's sight has seen fit to keep me so favored, even in this regard."

Confound this boat! Asenath wanted to pace up and down. "I do not understand. I need you to be explicit—no stories, no parables, no poetry, no games. Tell me this instant what my fate is."

"Your fate, my lady, is yours for the choosing. Upon his naming you as my gifted bride, I humbly informed Pharaoh, lord of Egypt— long may he live—about my condition regarding the woman I would take as wife. If she could not be one of my people by birth, she must become one by faith. And, of her own free will. Furthermore," he paused and looked right into her eyes, "we must be pronounced man and wife publicly, in the sight of God and witnesses, *before* I would ever lay a hand on her."

Asenath's jaw dropped. His steely gaze left no doubt about his unflinching resolve. "You expect me to believe our sovereign ruler *agreed* to this?"

"His Divine Magnificence agreed to grant me a week with you. At the end of which, should you be unwilling to accept my condition, and should the examiners verify your purity is unsoiled, you shall be returned to the palace. You shall become as you were bred to be: the wife of Egyptian royalty. And I shall be free to choose my bride."

Asenath could feel the blood drain from her face. She had thought he would be eating out of her palm from their first night. Such irony. She was not the mistress in this game; she was the pawn.

The floodgates of anxiety flew open. If their first night was any indication of his unnatural powers of restraint, she would undoubtedly still be a virgin at the end of their marital trial week. She would be sent back to Pharaoh. Surely he would not want her for himself at that point, even if the examiners pronounced her virginity intact. Her father would never forgive her if she failed to secure what he termed *'the eternal favor of Pharaoh'* by this union. She felt hot and cold simultaneously.

This cannot be happening! This had to be a nightmare. *Is this the mercy of Ra?* She suddenly realized the air had gotten thicker and was very difficult to inhale. *My story will be the spice of palace gossip for generations to come!* She heard the labored breathing before she realized it was hers.

"My lady, are you all right?" the vizier asked, concern written all over his face.

"I . . . I want . . ." Restless, she rose on shaky legs.

The boat rocked.

"My lady, please remain seated."

"Take me . . ." She felt lightheaded. "Back . . ."

"Asenath!" she heard him yell her name. Like a marine monster, the dark water seemed to rise and wrap shockingly frigid tentacles around her. She felt a sharp pain in her head right before succumbing to utter darkness.

12

The wind
Softly calling
It whistles. Sometimes sings
Echoing the distressed soul's cry:
Freedom!

***

Beclouded.

Asenath's vision was cloudy for the first few seconds after she opened her eyes. She shut and reopened them to discover she was in her chamber at Zaphnath-Paaneah's villa. Semat sat at her bedside, cradling her bowed head in her hands.

"How long have I slept?"

"My lady!" Semat exclaimed, leaping to her feet, relief washing over her previously anxious face. "You have awakened! Ra be praised!"

"Is she awake?" A male voice asked the question. Asenath sat up immediately, involuntarily placing a hand over her unveiled nose and mouth. A poultice that had been on her forehead fell into her lap.

Semat whispered, "Have no fear, my lady. Wadjenes will not enter. He merely awaits word on your status."

Asenath lay back down, suddenly lightheaded from sitting up too quickly. She was nursing a slight headache.

Turning toward the chamber's entrance, Semat said louder, "She is awake."

"Is she well?" Wadjenes inquired.

Semat knelt beside her mistress. "How do you feel, my lady?"

Like one trampled by a chariot in the royal races. "My head aches."

"Shall I send for some tea, my lady?"

"Jasmine."

"Right away." Semat proceeded to the chamber entrance to relay her mistress's status to Wadjenes and dispatch a servant to brew jasmine tea.

"The tea will be here momentarily, my lady."

"And Wadjenes?"

"Gone to report on your status, no doubt. On strict orders from His Eminence, he has been stationed at your door since dawn."

Asenath grunted and closed her eyes, trying to process the plethora of thoughts racing through her mind. The strategy to seduce and subdue was inspired by utter ignorance of the vizier's religious devotion, and therefore, a colossal failure. She needed to devise another plan. But first, she needed to distract Semat, who was clearly bursting with gossip.

"Tell me everything that happened. Leave no detail out."

"His Eminence rushed in bearing you in his arms. You were both drenched. He said you fell in the river and fainted. I could not contain my dismay, and when he inquired, I told him you had not set foot in the Nile since your mother's passing. He seemed distressed. He said a healer had been requested and asked me to change your wet garments in the meantime, and he left that I may do so. But after he returned, he would not leave, my lady. He remained all night, even after the healer said you would awaken and all would be well." Semat said, unable to mask the admiration in her voice.

"Did he now?" Asenath asked dryly.

"Yes, my lady. In fact, he approached only after ensuring I had lightly draped a veil over you. He insisted, my lady, saying he did not deserve to gaze upon your face. Once at your bedside, he took your hand and kneeled. I saw his lips moving, but heard no words."

Guilt-induced petitions to the invisible God, no doubt. As if that will do any good! "And where is he now?"

"I am uncertain, my lady. He left just before dawn after charging me not to leave your side even for a moment. I have not seen him since. Shall I ask Wadjenes to send word that you seek him?"

"No!" Asenath yelled. *He is the last person I want to see presently.* Registering Semat's confused look, she said more gently, "I mean . . . that will not be necessary. We must not disturb the vizier. You have just said he was up all night; clearly he needs rest himself."

"Very well, my lady."

A maidservant entered bearing the requested tea. Semat poured her a cup. She watched the steam rising out of the cup for a moment, thinking. *I must have time to strategize before I see him again.* She sat up and sipped slowly and silently, relieved the tea was having the desired effect. The ache in her head began to abate. Other than fatigue, and the slight soreness on her forehead, she felt fine, physically. Still, she thought it best to maintain a facade of illness to buy herself some more time. That pretense would not be difficult; she felt sick on the inside.

I am living my nightmare! Surely he is the oarsman, and he is trying to make me incur the wrath of Ra. He must be a powerful sorcerer to have bewitched the lord of Egypt into agreeing to his utterly absurd condition. I have to get away from him. I have to escape!

The more she thought about it, the more her fears multiplied, and the more urgently she wanted to execute her plan. But if she were to do so successfully, she needed someone in her corner that was both fearless and fiercely loyal. Thankfully, the one person who fit that description was still here, awaiting the so-called assurance of her happiness. Yesterday, she had sent him word via Semat, asking that he wait a night or two longer, and promising to inform him when he could return with good news for her father. At the time, she thought consummation was imminent—once she unearthed how best to entice the vizier. Alas, thanks to his uncompromising devotion to his God, he was impossible to seduce. So, that was no longer her priority.

What a fool I was; not any more. Tossing her covering aside and swinging her legs over the edge of the bed, she looked at her concerned handmaiden. "Semat, deaf walls."

Her chief handmaiden immediately exited. Asenath knew she was scanning the hallway, and waited, her foot tapping the plush animal skin rug beneath it. Within moments, Semat returned with the assurance Asenath needed.

"We are alone, my lady."

Satisfied that no one would overhear her, Asenath rose. "Semat, look at me. You are the only one I trust who knows things have not gone as planned between the vizier and me. No one else must find out. Now, I need you to swear that regarding the events that transpire next, you will be blind, deaf, and mute."

Semat's eyes widened. "My lady—"

"Swear it, Semat!" Asenath snapped.

"By the life of Pharaoh."

"Now, disrobe. I need us to trade garments."

"But, my lady . . ."

Asenath gave her a quelling look.

"Forgive me, my lady, it is just that . . . my size . . . perhaps Tsillah's garments might be better suited?"

Asenath contemplated for a moment. Semat was shorter and thicker than she. Contrarily, Tsillah was equally slender and only slightly taller. "Right you are. Fetch two of Tsillah's garments and her travel cloak. And bring her along. Swear her to secrecy as well. Go!"

Semat bowed and made a hasty exit as Asenath began walking back and forth across the length of her chamber.

***

Amazing what a change of garments can do, Asenath thought, surveying her reflection with a sense of accomplishment. In Tsillah's white *kalasiris* and black riding cloak, she was almost unrecognizable. The only things that could give her away were her voice and her eyes. The former, she could disguise; the latter, she would simply have to hide by keeping her face lowered. Fortunately, for a handmaiden, that was expected.

"Retrieve my black veil." It was the plainest; it would do. If she left now, she could be there by sunset. Surely her story would earn her some sympathy, at the very least. She took the veil from Semat and fastened it over her nose and mouth. Satisfied, she turned around and surveyed Tsillah. Dressed in her finery, complete with a gold veil, her charming handmaiden could pass for her; as long as the talkative girl held her tongue.

"Listen carefully. I am leaving this villa for a little while. I need some time to plan . . . a surprise. Until you hear otherwise from me, you must keep my absence secret from everyone in this villa. To that end, Tsillah, as of this moment, you are the lady of the house. You are unwell and in need of copious amounts of rest. Recline in my bed. Drink tea. Keep your face veiled and your head hidden in the pillows. Most importantly, if anyone asks questions, softly mumble responses to Semat. She will know what is best to relay."

Eyes doubled, Tsillah attempted to speak. "But, my lady—"

"I will abide neither excuse nor protest," Asenath snapped. "May the mighty Ra do so to you and more if you leave this room before I return! Now, lie down!"

The scolded handmaiden hastily reclined herself on the lavish bed and turned her face away.

Asenath pulled Semat aside, whispering, "This is not our first ruse, but it may well be our last; either way, it is our most important one yet. I must not be missed. You know what to do." Asenath turned, ready to exit her chamber.

"Forgive my impertinence, my lady. But where are you going?"

"It is better if you do not know, Semat. You cannot reveal what you do not know. Have no fear; I will not be alone. Come, we will exit together as though on an errand from our mistress. Head for the servants' wing—we must find Heqaib."

"Begging your pardon, my lady, if you are veiled and I am not, might it not arouse suspicion?"

"Good point," Asenath said, reaching to unclasp her veil.

"Surely you do not mean to exit your chambers with an unveiled face, my lady?" Semat asked, her eyes wide with alarm.

"Have you a better idea, Semat?"

"Perhaps I might also don one of my lady's black veils, with your permission."

"An astute plan. Retrieve one forthwith."

Semat hastily did as she was told.

Asenath surveyed her handmaiden's partially hidden face with

117

approval. "Excellent. Now, let us make haste."

Semat exited and after a last glance at the docile Tsillah, Asenath followed. They hurried through the hallways silently. Just as they turned into the south wing, they collided with Wadjenes, who dropped a scroll and cursed.

"What gives? Do you walk asleep?" Wadjenes inquired.

"We could ask you the same!" Asenath retorted.

"What say you? Speak up, virgin; I do not bite!"

Semat hurriedly responded, "We . . . we are morbid with shame! We beg a thousand pardons. My lady asks that we bring a message to HEQAIB, IF HE IS HERE!"

"The curses of Ra! Must you bellow? I am not deaf! Or at least, I was not," Wadjenes grumbled, massaging his assaulted ear as he bent over to retrieve the fallen scroll. Asenath was glad to see Semat's increased volume achieved the intended result. Heqaib emerged from a nearby chamber.

"There you are, Heqaib. These virgins bring you a message from their queen."

Heqaib approached them. "What is it? Is my lady all right?"

"The question of the hour!" Wadjenes interrupted. "Tell me, is she returned to normal activity?"

Asenath kept her tongue still and her eyes lowered, letting Semat answer. "Not yet, my lord."

"Then I may as well save myself a trip to the north wing."

"My lord?" Semat inquired, confused.

Raising the scroll, he said, "His Eminence asked that this be hand-delivered to her, and seen by no other eyes."

Asenath jabbed Semat in the ribs.

"I will deliver it," Semat said, reaching out her hand.

"I think not," Wadjenes scoffed, whisking the scroll well out of reach.

"My lady gave express orders she would see and speak to no one but her handmaidens until further notice."

"Then I shall wait."

Asenath spoke, making her voice as high-pitched and nasal as possible. "Suppose the contents of the scroll require urgent attention? Surely you would not want my lady to miss a message from His Eminence, especially given the present circumstances."

Stealing a glance at the men, she noticed Heqaib eyeing her curiously, even as Wadjenes's eyes shifted doubtfully. "Well . . . no . . . but my orders—"

"She has a point, Wadjenes," Heqaib chimed in. "My lady trusts Semat with her life. If I were in your sandals, I would hand Semat the scroll and consider it *hand-delivered*."

After a moment's hesitation, Wadjenes conceded. "See that she gets it without delay. If things turn awry, I shall deny this conversation. Now, if you will excuse me, there is a goblet of wine with my name on it. But you virgins are welcome to join me," he hinted, strolling casually toward his chamber.

Heqaib stared at Asenath suspiciously but addressed Semat. "Why do I feel as though you are hiding something, Semat? Tell me the truth; is my lady well?"

"Yes, my lord. She asks that you take Tsillah to His Reverence's villa, urgently, to deliver a private message to Na'eemah."

"Tsillah? I have never known my lady to trust anyone but you with a *private* message."

"She needs me to remain at her side, being that she is unwell."

"Unwell? You just said she was well." Heqaib started to head for the women's quarters. "I want to hear the instruction directly from her."

"Wait, she asked not to be disturbed," Asenath said in her false voice.

He glared at Asenath, disguised as Tsillah. "Then tell me the message. Na'eemah is my mother, is she not?"

Asenath, keeping her eyes lowered, showed her unwillingness to comply by briskly shaking her head from side to side.

Heqaib stood directly in front of her, arms crossed. "Either you tell me the message, or take me to my lady," he said firmly. "I will not set one foot outside this house until one or the other happens."

Not wanting them to remain within earshot of Wadjenes, Asenath raised her head and looked him directly in the eyes.

Heqaib sucked in a breath. There was no mistaking those amber eyes. She lifted a finger to her veiled mouth, signaling silence, and then pointed toward the corridor. Maintaining her nasal, high pitch, she said, "Very well. I will tell you the message, but only in private."

The three of them headed down the hallway leading to the exit closest to the stables. As soon as they were outside, Heqaib turned to Asenath. "By the life of Pharaoh, *what* are you doing?"

Asenath turned to Semat. "Return to Tsillah. Remember my instructions. By the favor of Ra, you will see me again soon."

"Yes, my lady." Holding out the scroll, she said, "Your missive."

I could not care less what it says. Scowling, she took the scroll and sequestered it beneath her riding cloak.

Trembling like she might suffer a stroke at any moment, Semat bowed and went back inside.

Asenath turned to Heqaib. "Take me to Na'eemah."

"Surely you jest," he said, shocked.

"I have never been more serious."

"My lady, you know I would die for you; but if I am to remove you secretly from your *matrimonial home*, I need to have an impervious reason to give your father."

"Then I give you the assurance of my *unhappiness*. He is . . . I cannot . . . I cannot do this," she said, brushing an arm over her sore forehead.

Noting her bruise, Heqaib's hands curled into fists at his side. "Did he . . ." He swallowed. "Did he hurt you?"

He may have left a sour taste in her mouth, but Asenath could not bring herself to slander the vizier. "No, Heqaib. I fainted and apparently fell into the river. I thought everyone knew. Notwithstanding, this is neither the time nor the place. For now, know that he asks more than I am willing to give." Asenath's voice broke. "I have never missed my mother more than I do at this moment, but I am grateful yours still lives. She is the only one I can trust with the burden I now bear. Will you please take me to her?"

"Without further question."

"And our fastest means?"

"Your father's barge; but it will draw attention. A hard horse ride would be best. *If* you can stand the heat," Heqaib said.

"If I could not stand the heat, I would not be starting a fire," Asenath quipped.

Heqaib stifled a smile. "Duly noted. If we are to leave without being questioned, I must inform Wadjenes I am . . ."

"Escorting my maiden to deliver my private message."

"Indeed. Since we cannot risk him seeing through your disguise, I suggest you wait here. Better still, head for the stables and I will meet you there."

Asenath nodded. She secured her cloak about herself and kept her eyes lowered as she walked. Once within the stables, she happened upon a ruddy stable boy.

"Blessings of the dawn, lad."

"Blessings of the dawn."

"I would hazard a guess that a smart fellow like you knows which of these are the fastest steeds."

Blushing, the boy pointed out two.

"I knew I could count on you," Asenath said, winking at him. "Now never mind me, I am just waiting for my lord."

Heqaib entered the barn moments later.

"Is all well, my lord?" she asked.

He nodded.

"I hear those two run like the wind," she said, pointing out the horses the boy had indicated.

"Excellent," Heqaib replied. "I will return momentarily." He went off to find the keeper of the horses. A few moments later, he came back with a burly man who was the spitting, albeit older, image of the stable boy. The man untethered the requested steeds and handed them over. "See that you bring them back in the same condition."

"Naturally. Thank you," Heqaib said.

"Ready my—Tsillah?" he asked Asenath.

"Yes, my lord!" Asenath answered, thankful her veil hid her smile.

He gave her a leg up onto the first horse and mounted the second. They made their way out of the stables and out of the villa. But it was only thanks to Heqaib's military background they made their way out of the north gate of the palace with no obstructions.

Once outside the bustling city, Heqaib explained they had a straight path over wide open fields.

Time to pick up the pace, Asenath thought. She took a drink from her water container. Then she looked at him. "Heqaib . . ."

"Yes?"

"Do try to keep up, will you?" Kicking her horse with both heels, Asenath took off. She rode like she was being pursued by all the spirits of the underworld. She was pleased that Heqaib matched her pace with equal fury. Hours later, he led them off the path into a beautiful little oasis of oak trees that lay next to a stream. He stopped and gestured toward it. Asenath led her mare to the stream and dismounted, letting it dunk its entire head into the water. She wished she could do the same. Drenched in perspiration, she was determined not to give in to weariness just yet. She noticed Heqaib had dismounted and was walking toward her. She raised her hand, palm forward. He stopped.

"May I have a moment?" she asked.

"Certainly." He turned his back to her.

She unveiled herself, took off her riding cloak, and dipped her entire head into the water alongside her horse. It was refreshing. She would dip her whole body in if she dared. The water trickling down her curly tresses brought a welcome coolness. She savored it for a few moments and then squeezed her hair as dry as she could. She put her riding cape back on and was about to refasten her veil when a thought stopped her.

What have I got to lose? If ever there was a moment to dare this, it is now. Leaving her wet face unveiled, she walked up to Heqaib quietly and placed a hand on his shoulder.

He started speaking before he turned. "I thought you would ride us into the—" He stopped, mouth agape, when he saw her. For a second, it seemed like time had stopped. He stood transfixed, his eyes perusing her face. Then, as if catching himself in the act, he turned away. "What have you . . . what have I done?"

Asenath spoke softly. "Heqaib, look at me. Please."

Heqaib turned around slowly. He looked as though he gazed at something supernatural.

"You are a man, and I need the truth—from a man. If you knew nothing about me, but saw me as you do now, would I please you?"

"Please me?" His brow furrowed slightly as he inclined his head.

Asenath felt heat rise to her face. "I mean . . . would you find my form . . . my face . . . comely?"

He raised both eyebrows. "How can that even be a question?"

Asenath looked away. "I do not know. I thought . . . but the vizier . . . he . . . I do not think . . ." Sighing, she looked at him. "He does not want me."

Heqaib looked at her as though she had suddenly sprouted a second head. "Then he is a fool. A blind one at best, a mad one at worst, but a fool either way."

Asenath gave a weak smile. "He interpreted dreams that confounded the wisest in the land; he is no fool, Heqaib. But tell me sincerely. How would you describe me to someone else?"

This time, it was Heqaib who blushed. "I do not possess a vocabulary rich enough to give a worthy description of what my eyes presently behold. You rightly said I am a man. And speaking as one, let this suffice; there is not a man alive who would not consider it a blessing from the gods to have the pleasure of gazing upon your face even for a moment, let alone a lifetime. Yours is a face beyond compare. Its lovely image is now engraved in my mind, and will remain so until the day I die."

Asenath's eyes watered. His words were a salve to her wounded heart.

Heqaib reached his hand toward her face. "Asenath . . ." Pausing just shy of touching it, he dropped his hand and curled it into a fist. "I do not know what that man has done, or not done, to make you doubt yourself. However, it is not your beauty you should question, it is his sanity."

"Thank you, Heqaib. Your words mean more than you know."

His eyes perused her face for a moment, his gaze lingering on her full, moist lips. Then he shut his eyes, turned around, and released a slow breath. "We should ride, my lady; but I need a moment." He headed for the stream.

"Take all the time you need." Asenath hid her face once more, but she could not hide her smile. She had just broken a rule she had spent a third of her life upholding. Hopefully, this indiscretion would not earn her a punishment from Ra, but in this moment, her defiance felt well worth whatever consequences may lie ahead. She felt seen. And desired. She could not remember ever feeling this way. The look in Heqaib's eyes said what his lips dared not. She traveled the rest of the hard road, feeling as though she was riding on the clouds.

Part II:

Unveiled

13

Soft may be its fur
Yet the tamest mongrel
Cornered, bares its fangs

***

Apprehensive.

The sense of freedom that escaping her proposed matrimonial home brought vanished the instant she set foot in her father's villa. Mercifully, the cover of night had made it easy for her and Heqaib to do so surreptitiously using the servant's entrance. They both knew where Na'eemah would be; she was a creature of habit. Deliberately lagging, Asenath let Heqaib enter the courtyard first. From her position behind a curtain, she could both hear and see the ensuing exchange.

"Blessings of the evening, Mother."

"Heqaib?!"

"I hope you have not lost your appetite for surprises," he added, embracing his visibly stunned mother, and kissing her on both cheeks.

"What in the name of all the gods are you doing *here*?"

"I am not sure I should answer that. And before the scolding begins, let me just say this was not my idea."

"Not your idea? What are you—" Na'eemah's jaw dropped as Asenath stepped into the courtyard. Asenath saw the shocked woman take her in from scalp to soles. No doubt her servant's garb and disheveled appearance were part of the reason Na'eemah's eyes had just doubled in size. She drew her gaze from Asenath to Heqaib, and her eyes narrowed. "What have you done?"

Heqaib threw his hands up in the air. "What I did, I did at her command. And now, I believe I would be safest elsewhere." Without waiting for a retort, he hastily exited.

Asenath was now the object of Na'eemah's stern look. "By the life of Pharaoh, tell me what you have done."

"Nothing, Mother. I merely escaped the house of a madman to seek solace with you."

"A madman? Asenath, daughter of Potiphera, explain yourself! And spare me the theatrics—I want facts."

"Very well. May I at least have a bath and some refreshments first?" Brushing her fingers lightly against her bruise, she added, "I am weary; it has not been long since I fainted after falling into the Nile—"

"By the mercy of Hapi!" Na'eemah gasped, reaching a hand over her heart. "Fainted? In the Nile? . . . This child will be the death of me!" Rushing over, she placed an arm around Asenath and guided her onto a stone stool. "Sit here while I order a healing bath to be drawn." With that, she strode into the hallway, yelling for a servant.

Asenath dropped her bruised head into her hands and sighed. *Bathe, eat, and sleep. That is all you need to dwell on presently.*

***

The warm water felt like a deep, soothing caress to her aching limbs. She kept her eyes closed, and deeply inhaled the wafts of steam, letting the essences of lemongrass and mint leaves soothe her. Her face tingled under the thick mixture of honey and spices lathered on it. Her eyelids bore the light weight of fresh cucumber slices. Asenath could feel her completely immersed body slowly relaxing. Getting her mind to follow suit was a lost cause, for it was rapidly reviewing the unusual events of the last two days.

Na'eemah wanted facts. *How best do I present them?* She was still contemplating that when the weariness in her body overcame the busyness of her mind. When she felt someone rousing her, she was unsure of how much time had passed. She let strong arms pull her out of the bath and wrap her in drying cloths. She felt herself being led, but remembered nothing else until she awakened to the smell of a familiar fragrance. Lilies and spices. *Na'eemah.* Even with her eyes closed, she knew the woman sat patiently beside her. All Asenath wanted to do was lie here, in the comfort of her childhood chamber, next to the only person who truly loved her.

"I know you are awake. Your breathing lightened."

Sighing, Asenath opened her weary eyes and gazed into Na'eemah's concerned ones.

"Blessings of the morn, my sunshine."

Morn? "I slept all night?" Asenath asked, sitting up.

"You were weary indeed. Despite my immense curiosity, I had not the heart to wake you." Asenath felt Na'eemah's soft, plump hand cup her face. "Tell me, how do you feel?"

The motherly woman's warmth unlocked the well of emotions within her. She could not stop herself from dissolving into tears.

"O my child! What troubles you so?" As Na'eemah's arms encircled her and gently stroked her back, she wrapped her own arms around the woman's broad waist and wept. "Come now, my sunshine, whatever it is, we will find a resolution together."

She let Na'eemah rock her and stroke her hair, and Na'eemah let her give rein to her troubled emotions. After Asenath's sobs had reduced to sporadic sniffs, her concerned caregiver released her. "Here, have some tea," Na'eemah said, pouring steaming liquid into a cup. "'Tis lemon and honey."

"Thank you," Asenath said softly, taking the cup. She sipped the tea briefly and then, setting it aside, she spilled her heart. Na'eemah let her talk, giving her undivided attention. Asenath left out no details. Concluding her tirade, she said, "There you have it. Now you see why I cannot go back!"

Na'eemah paused for a moment, then spoke softly. "I fear what I see is that you *must* go back."

Go back? Asenath looked at Na'eemah as if the woman had succumbed to a sudden stroke of insanity. "You jest, surely!"

"This is no time for jesting, Asenath. I am truly sorry to know that things have not gone as anticipated. But entering a marriage is not akin to taking up a sport of leisure. You cannot simply drop it if it no longer fascinates."

"When has marriage ever fascinated, Na'eemah?"

"I know, I know. It is more an obligation than a fascination; but we are talking about your future. As decided by Pharaoh, Lord of Egypt—long may he live—and sanctioned by your father. Appealing or not, unless your husband himself sends you back to your father's house, Ra forbid, there is no escaping your matrimonial home. You simply must return."

"And forsake *everything* I believe in? My father is *high priest of Ra,* for the entirety of Heliopolis! How can his only daughter worship a foreign deity?"

"If her husband, who is appointed by the lord of Egypt, commands it, she can and she should."

"Am I to have no say in the matter, even though it is *my* life?"

"You toy with the fate of the house of Potiphera, and have the audacity to demand a say?" a deep voice asked.

"Father!" Asenath said, leaping to her feet.

"You cannot be nearly as shocked to see me in my home as I am to see *you* in it!" Potiphera declared.

"Blessings of the day, Your Reverence," Na'eemah said, rising and bowing.

"Leave us!" Potiphera ordered. Na'eemah hastily complied.

Asenath swallowed. "How did you . . . I thought you . . ."

"You thought you could flee your matrimonial home and keep it from me? Ra be praised that Heqaib is not as foolish as you."

Heqaib! How could he?

"Fortunate for you he has explained your recent plunge into your worst fear may have clouded your judgment, for I would otherwise have failed to understand your senseless actions."

Asenath kept her eyes lowered as her mind raced.

"You were speaking so freely moments before. Why the silence now?" Potiphera said, seating himself on her couch. "Be seated, and explain why I have had to suffer yet another rude interruption to my month of priestly duties."

Asenath bowed and slowly perched herself on the edge of her bed.

"Forgive me, Father, but not only has Zaphnath-Paaneah stipulated a heretic condition for this marriage, I have had reason to fear for my life."

Potiphera's broad brows arched. "Are you implying your dip in the Nile was no accident?"

128

"I am sure the vizier would term it as such, but I cannot, for it was shown to me in a dream, Father, the very morning of your palatial summons."

"Neither of us had the faintest idea of who he was then; yet you saw him in a vision of the night?"

"I saw a strange and powerful oarsman leading us to an unknown destination. He was clearly a sorcerer, for he controlled the elements against us. And when I pleaded for the mercy of Ra, he tried to end my life, first by suffocation and then by drowning me in the Nile," Asenath said, leaving unsaid what she feared was about to happen: *And you were powerless to stop him!*

"And because you fell in the Nile, you believe Zaphnath-Paaneah to be this . . . mysterious oarsman?" Potiphera asked, his brow raised.

"He is clearly a powerful diviner, Father, and a man with bewitching power over people, or he could not have got the lord of Egypt to sanction his unreasonable condition."

"You mean the one I caught as I approached? That you worship a foreign deity?"

"Yes, Father."

"I hardly call that unreasonable. He is a foreigner. We already expected he would have some nontraditional customs."

"It is one thing to worship only one deity, but an invisible God with no name, Father?"

Potiphera's burst of laughter was completely unexpected.

"How can you laugh?"

"In all my years of priesthood, I have heard nothing more ridiculous. I am trying to imagine how one appeases a god one can neither see nor name."

"He not only expects me to do so, he further demands that I forsake allegiance to all other gods. Do you find *that* amusing?"

Her father sobered. "No. Arrogantly absurd, but not amusing."

"I thought the same."

"Then I do not fault your thought, but your subsequent deed. A missive would have sufficed. You need not have fled, and you shall certainly return."

"I do not understand, Father. Returning implies accepting his conditions."

"There was more than one?"

"The other is inconsequential by comparison. He merely stated that only *after* a public wedding ceremony would he . . . consummate the marriage."

"Am I to understand you fled your matrimonial home still a VIRGIN?!" Potiphera bellowed.

"It was not for lack of trying, Father."

"I ought to demand a full refund from Mayet. She clearly taught you NOTHING!"

"He is not an ordinary man—"

"He is a man of flesh and blood. Any man would ravish any maiden with half your beauty in a moment! I have heard enough of this foolishness. Clearly, you are still too childish to make sound decisions, so I shall make them for you. You will return; you will beg his forgiveness; you will accept his conditions—"

"But if I do, I will incur the wrath of Ra—"

"I am not finished. You will accept his conditions, and humor his invisible deity, like a dutiful wife. Simply maintain proper worship privately, and might I add, fervently. You need the mercy of Ra now, more than ever!"

"You are asking me to lie to my husband, Father?"

"I am advising you to do what wives have done since the beginning of time: keep a secret from your husband."

"He is a diviner, Father. What if he finds out?"

Potiphera scoffed. "You give him too much credit. Granted, he exhibits more powers than most men, but he is not more powerful than the gods we serve."

He is not, but what if his God is? Asenath kept the troubling thought to herself, while her father continued confidently.

"About your vision of the night; tell me, did you die?"

"No."

"How exactly did you escape a watery grave?"

"A yellow light from the heavens streamed down and saved me."

Potiphera spread his arms out and smiled. "If that was not the supernatural sunlight of Ra himself, I am unworthy of the high priesthood. Even your own dream tells you, Ra will protect you as long as you appease him."

Appease him I will, along with all our other gods. No matter how powerful, his invisible God is still but one god, and no match against a host of deities. Offering her father a weak smile, Asenath said, "You are right, Father."

"Indubitably! You have nothing to fear. I shall furnish you with a new set of amulets for your protection and some charms to secret in strategic places around your new home."

"Thank you, Father."

"Good. Lest I forget, in the event your husband presents any further surprises, and you find yourself with another urge to flee, seek out His Radiance, Akhom. He generously assured me he would look out for your best interests at all times. Is that understood?"

"Perfectly, Father."

"Excellent. As for your return, since Heqaib was thoughtless enough to leave my barge behind, I shall have another ferry you both to Avaris at first light tomorrow."

Tomorrow? So soon. "That is most gracious, Father," Asenath said, bowing deeply.

"Think nothing of it, gift of Ra," he said, rising. "If you will excuse me, I must return to my duties. May the blessings of Ra remain ever upon you." Asenath watched him head toward her door, and then pause. Turning a piercing gaze on her, he said, "Now that we know your husband mandates a wedding feast, I look forward to it. And make no mistake, should I fail to receive your invitation to it within the week, it is not the wrath of the vizier you will have cause to fear."

What have I done? Asenath waited until her father's exit before sinking her trembling form to the floor.

Scarcely had her father left, than Na'eemah returned, rushing to her side. Sitting on the bed, she placed a hand on Asenath's head, "I am sorry, my sunshine, I heard it all."

Asenath looked up at her. "What have you to apologize for? It is Heqaib who betrayed me."

"No, my child, it is I. I sent him to your father at first light."

"You?" Asenath asked, leaping to her feet. "Why would you do that?! I came to you for comfort and advice!" *Not a knife in my back!*

"I have tried to provide the former, but the latter . . . this was beyond my expertise, Asenath."

"No, it was not!" Asenath said, turning away. "You did not even hear me out before reporting my presence to him."

"You were already a night here. If he found out on his own, it is Heqaib who would have borne his wrath."

"Instead, I did," she said, facing Na'eemah with eyes blazing.

"He is your father. No matter how angered, he will temper mercy in dealing with you."

But he would not do so in dealing with Heqaib. And that would have been my fault.

Asenath lowered her head. "You are right. I put his employment, and yours, in danger. It was thoughtless . . . selfish of me." Sitting next to her mother figure, she asked meekly, "Forgive me?"

"As long as you forgive me," Na'eemah said, kissing Asenath's curly head.

Asenath leaned over, adjusting herself so her head lay in Na'eemah's broad lap. The compassionate woman stroked her curls. "I love you like my own child, Asenath. It breaks my heart that you are unhappy in your new home. I wish there was another way to resolve this challenge, and as much as I know you hate to hear it, your father's advice stands to reason."

The sigh that escaped the runaway bride's lips came from a weary, troubled soul. Na'eemah loved her; that was not in question. Regardless of whether she agreed with what her mother figure said, she could always trust her love. She had a mother's heart—pure and loyal. If anyone would want to see Asenath happy, it was Na'eemah. But that truth did not prevent Asenath from feeling like an entire pyramid lay upon her, crushing her into nothingness. Liberty had yet again eluded her grasp. She felt familiar walls close in around her. For what felt like the thousandth time in her life, she faced an irrefutable, irreconcilable fact: *I, Asenath, am nothing but a prisoner of fate.*

A weighty silence hung in her chamber for what seemed an eternity, but through it all, she felt Na'eemah's warm hand gently resting upon her shoulder. Eventually, the silence was broken by the entrance of a maidservant.

"What is it?" Na'eemah asked.

"Pardon me. I retrieved this while cleaning my lady's travel cloak," she said, holding out a scroll. Na'eemah held out her hand, and the servant placed the parchment in it.

The vizier's missive! Asenath recalled sitting up.

"Thank you. You may go," Na'eemah dismissed her, before turning to Asenath. "What is this?"

"A missive the vizier left for me. It was delivered just before we left his villa. I have not had a chance to read it."

"Do you not think you should?"

"No, thank you. I could do without any more morbid surprises."

"Nonsense. It might be a love poem for all you know," Na'eemah teased, gently shoving Asenath's shoulder with hers.

"Really? And you say I am the one with the wild imagination?"

"Here." She handed the scroll to Asenath. "Go on, read it."

Asenath massaged her temples. "My kingdom for a moment's peace!"

"Let us secure you a kingdom first, shall we? Read!"

Reluctantly taking the roll of papyrus, Asenath unrolled it.

Na'eemah rose. "I shall return momentarily, then you can tell me what he says."

The weary young lady focused on the impressive penmanship before her.

Asenath, daughter of Potiphera, high priest of Heliopolis

My lady,

> *I am deeply disturbed that the terms of our proposed union distressed you. In retrospect, I should have been more sensitive in my disclosure; please, forgive me. It grieves me even more, having learned of your understandable aversion for the Nile. I am truly sorry to have caused you to relive a memory so painful. Since you are reading this, I hope you are in much better health than you were when I last saw you. (I left strict instructions that this was not to be delivered until your strength was restored.)*

> *I am further displeased because I am not present to see to your recovery myself, as I would have preferred. As I pen this, I have just learned that my presence is urgently required on*

matters of security in Memphis.

Memphis?! He is just south of Heliopolis!

I hastily write this to inform you, since I may not return for several days. Although, I am hoping this journey turns out shorter, rather than longer. We have only spent a fraction of the time I had planned that we would spend together. Even then, I must say, it has been a pleasure getting to know you so far.

A pleasure? I wish I could say the same!

I confess our evenings together have been the highlight of my days, and I hope we can resume them upon my return. I am also aware I have said very little to answer the myriad of questions you must have about me, and how I, a foreigner, came to be in Egypt. Rest assured, I shall answer those and anything else you desire to know when I return.

In the meantime, please consider my villa, yours. Wadjenes, and all of my staff, are entirely at your disposal. Do not hesitate to summon them day or night should you require anything to make you feel more at home.

I look forward to seeing you soon.

His Eminence, Zaphnath-Paaneah, vizier of Egypt

Asenath laid the scroll on her bed, processing the thoughts it inspired. *I need not have left, after all! This voyage only incited Father's anger . . . Mercifully, I shall not have to face the vizier tomorrow; hopefully for several more days . . . He need never know I left if Semat and Tsillah have maintained the ruse successfu—*

"You look brighter! Do not tell me I was right about the missive?" Na'eemah asked, interrupting Asenath's racing thoughts.

She looked up to see the soft-hearted woman approach, bearing a heavily laden tray of foods. She grinned. "No, it was not a romantic verse; but I am far happier for reading it."

"Victory for the wisdom of the aged!" Na'eemah thundered, setting the tray beside a smiling Asenath. "I want details! But first, behold: your favorites."

Asenath took in the dried dates, raw almonds, pomegranates, fresh bread rolls, lightly roasted fish, and steaming goat's milk in one glance. Placing a hand on her heart, she sighed. "A slice of paradise."

"One who has trod through Hades deserves no less."

"Thank you," the grateful young woman said, rising. Throwing her arms around Na'eemah, she added, "Thank you for this, for everything." *I wish I could take you back with me.*

"For nothing. Fate may not permit me to return with you in person, but it cannot prevent me from doing so in heart. May the favor of Ra go with you, my sunshine," she whispered.

Asenath felt the gentle circles Na'eemah's soft, plump hand was making on her back, and she knew with all certainty: her voyage may have been unnecessary, but it had not been in vain. She would have journeyed a thousand times farther, to feel the warmth within which she was presently embraced. The thought of returning to live a life devoid of such love was utterly unbearable.

Drawing strength from Na'eemah's affection, Asenath reached a new resolution. Undoubtedly, she had to go back. But she did *not* have to let any man lead her into a loveless life, like a lamb to the slaughter. Ironically, it was her father who had made the singular comment that now fueled her newfound resolve.

The vizier is indeed a man of flesh and blood. And every man has a weakness. Asenath would return as a woman with a renewed mission: find his frailty and exploit it to secure her freedom.

14

Beneath the mask
Of the mighty man
Hides a little lad
Starving, for want of love

***

*I*mpressive.

Such was Asenath's one-word thought, as she stood in the vizier's library, unable to hold back a smile. Her chief handmaiden had not exaggerated—this was indeed a grand chamber of knowledge. Seeing Asenath return safe and sound, Semat, who had been severely sleep-deprived and nearly feverish with fright, had slept for nearly an entire day. As for Tsillah, weary of idling in bed consuming copious quantities of tea, she had begged to not so much as see an amphora of tea anytime in the near future. Immensely grateful to have her absence undiscovered, Asenath had indulged them both.

That was two days ago, and mercifully, the vizier was still away. Asenath was not sure how much time she had before his return, but she was focusing every minute on her newfound mission. A man this mysterious surely had secrets. It stood to reason that if the people within his home did not hold those secrets, perhaps the parchments would. Despite surreptitiously and thoroughly searching his chamber last night, she was yet to find anything useful. Hence her present location.

What mysteries lie within these walls? Asenath glanced around. The writing table in the heart of the vast library seemed a good enough place to begin her search. She discovered it was meticulously crafted, complete with several storage compartments. Atop the desk lay a reed pen next to an ink canister, beside which rested a parchment. It held a rectangular drawing of sorts.

What might you be? Upon inspection, she discovered it was an outline of the palace, divided into sections by occupancy. Curious, she studied it. There was an outer court, an inner court, and Pharaoh's sanctuary, represented by three squares. The smallest square was Pharaoh's chambers. It lay in the center of a second square, the inner court. Moving circularly from northeast to southeast, the sections of the inner court were marked as follows: *Royal wives and children. Pharaoh's private temple. Vizier and chief advisors. Royal guest halls.* They were all surrounded by a large square that no doubt represented the extremely high, impregnable palace walls, upon which several chariots could easily race side by side.

The largest square was the outer court. It was enclosed by a perimeter wall that was far less intimidating. And the south walls were split by the Nile. The entire northern half of the outer court was marked *Nobles*, with the north gate indicated centrally. The southeast quadrant was titled *Temple of Seth*, while the southwest quadrant read *Military Elite*. There was also an asterisk in a corner of that quadrant with the word *Home* next to it.

That is where we are! Noticing the military encampments were asterisked, she numbered five of them at various points in the outer courtyard. Two of them were at the south gate—one on each side of the river. And that gate was a stone's throw downhill from their residence, and accessible by foot, horseback, or boat ride.

He told no lie when he said this location afforded heightened security, she grudgingly admitted. *But a map of the palace is not what I seek.*

She rifled through the compartments of the table, but found nothing of interest. Slowly walking away, her eye caught some wooden shelves upon which sat several small cedar chests. Each had an inscription engraved on its lower right corner.

Palace protocol. Territories of Egypt. Royal projects.

She moved to a different section of chests. *Deities. Maxims. Gardening.*

Gardening? What is it with him and gardens? The chest beside that one was marked *Tales & Fables.*

Asenath smiled. A good story might just be the perfect escape from her unpleasant reality. She reached for the chest of tales and tried to withdraw it, inadvertently shifting the gardening chest out of place. Letting go of the former, she tried to push the latter back in its proper position. She noticed it did not go as far back as the chest beside it. She pulled it out completely to see if there was an obstruction of any kind.

What have we here?

A worn leather pouch protruded from an opening in the shelf. Asenath laid the chest aside and pulled out the pouch. Scratched into the brown leather was one word: *Dreamer.* She unrolled the leather straps and peered into the pouch. It housed a collection of parchments, in a familiarly flawless hieratic script.

She pulled out the collection and read the inscription on the first papyrus:

> *The journal of Joseph, ben Jacob, ben Isaac, ben Abraham*
> *—friend of the invisible God*

His personal journals? Asenath smiled. *Our seaside dinner was not a total misfortune, after all.* Without that, she would not have discovered the vizier's Hebrew name. Nor would she have now recognized that she had stumbled upon what was no doubt a treasure chest of secrets.

Well, Joseph, let us see exactly what manner of man you are. Ensconcing herself on the nearest cushion, Asenath laid the pile of parchments on the floor before her. She examined the scroll following the premier one. It held a drawing that resembled a tree, but instead of leaves, the branches sprouted names. She recognized the names at the root of the tree: Abraham and Sarah.

This must be his genealogy, all the way back to the fourth generation. She also recognized the names Jacob, Rachel, and Joseph, and noted by their positions in the diagram that he had listed his brothers' names in order from oldest to youngest, which meant his eldest brother was named Reuben, and his youngest, Benjamin.

A large family indeed.

Setting the second papyrus aside and rifling through the remaining parchments, Asenath discovered they were dated and appeared to be placed in order from oldest to newest. She picked up one at random and began to read.

The happiest of my days began like any other. Abba had sent me out early, laden with meats and cheeses, to see how my brothers were doing in the fields. Alas, I did not have good news to report. They had been gambling again, and had to pay their losses with some of our sheep. As I lifted the tent flap and entered to greet Abba with a kiss, my eye caught an unusual, brightly colored fabric lying beside him. Abba was not pleased to hear the report on my brothers, but he praised me for being his eyes in the fields.

With a broad smile, he picked up the cloth beside him and handed it to me. Only when he said to put it on did I realize it was a tunic. It was like none I had ever seen. The fabric felt as smooth as fresh butter as I draped it over my shoulders and put my hands through its long, spacious sleeves. I must have turned around with the most astonished look in my eyes, because Abba laughed out loud.

How I miss the rich sound of his laughter.

When I asked him why he was gifting me a garment so magnificent, he rose, placed his hand on my head, and said words I repeated to myself so many times thereafter, I can never forget them:

"Joseph, my son, firstborn of my one true love, I clothe you in this tunic today because you are my delight. Wear it with my blessing, and these truths in your heart:

It is colorful and bright—for you bring radiance everywhere you go.

It is a raiment fit for royalty—for you are a son of the Most High God.

It covers you from shoulders to soles—let that be a reminder that you are covered by the invisible God, who sees all and knows all.

Many are the colors on the outside, but few on the inside—never judge by the outward appearance alone. There is more to every person than meets the eye. You cannot be friend to all, but you must be fair to all. Now may the Lord our God bless you and make his face shine upon you from this day forward, and forevermore."

I was but a lad of seventeen then, yet even now, my heart stirs at the memory of that moment. I have never felt more loved, or more special, than I did then. Of twelve sons, he chose me to receive that rare robe. I wore it with pride everywhere I went. Now that day feels like a dream. A long-lost dream in someone else's life.

Had I been told that precious tunic of many colors would be ripped from my shoulders, by my own flesh and blood, and discarded like a beggar's rags, I would have laughed in disbelief. Alas, a beggar's rags I would much rather wear now than the prosaic shendyt that surrounds my loins. Far better that my raiment proclaims me as indigent than as a criminal.

O Lord God, let it not be that I have already lived the happiest day of my life.

So he was his father's favorite son! Asenath thought. His tale was no fable, then. Jacob must have indeed loved Rachel deeply to have so cherished the son that opened her womb. But was it wise to make it obvious that he favored one son above the others? . . . And why am I asking myself questions when a pouch full of answers lies before me? Ignoring the hunger pangs beginning to gnawing at her belly, Asenath reached for another parchment.

My brothers called me 'Dreamer.' It was not in endearment but in derision. I dreamed often as a boy, even though nothing seemed to come of my dreams. I have forgotten most of them, with the exception of two. These I cannot forget for the angst they aroused in my family.

It was harvest time in the first dream. All twelve of us brothers were out in a massive wheat field. We gathered the wheat into sheaves, each of us making a bundle. To our greatest amazement, the bundles began to move on their own accord. All but mine, that is. The other eleven bundles were marching to some sort of imperceptible rhythm until they

141

formed a circle around my bundle. And then they bowed down and made obeisance to mine.

My older brothers were enraged when I shared it. Ten against one—no surprise there. What was surprising was Abba's visible displeasure at my second vision of the night. It is one of the few times I saw his anger directed at me. I still do not understand their fury. I did not cause myself to dream; I merely recounted what I saw. Even now, I close my eyes and my second dream is as vivid as the night I first dreamed it.

There I stood at the top of a mountain so high it felt like I was standing in the clouds. It was too dark to be called day, and too bright to be called night. Even more confusing, I could see both a brilliant sun and a glowing moon in the sky at the same time. But rather than a host of stars, there were exactly eleven stars encircling the moon, arranged in order from the biggest to the smallest. Before I could comprehend that incredible sight, something extraordinary happened: The sun leaned slowly, as though it was folding in half, or nodding in my direction. It was such a graceful movement. As the sun raised itself up again, the moon then made the same motion. Then the largest star, the second largest one, on and on until the smallest star had done the same. And that was when I understood: all these celestial elements were bowing to ME!

I am still as confused now as I was when I awakened from that dream. I still wonder at its meaning.

A sentiment all too familiar, Asenath admitted. It appears even the revered revealer of secrets is himself, sometimes mystified by visions of the night. Perhaps Father was right. I attribute too much power to him. She continued the journal entry with rapt attention.

This time, I was subjected to my entire family's wrath. Abba asked if I implied that he, Ima Leah, and my brothers would all come bowing to me! Judah was furious that I would dare imagine myself to be ruler over them. I think were it not for Abba's presence, he would surely have struck me then and there.

What a fool I was to have shared those night visions so unrestrainedly. They were naught but the idle imaginations of a favored son. For what cause would my family ever bow to me, the eleventh of twelve sons? I, Joseph, leader of the Bar-Jacob clan? Ludicrous.

If my brothers could see me now, they would not fume, they would laugh. And congratulate each other for successfully putting an end to my foolish fantasies.

His brothers put an end to his dreams? How—

"Forgive the intrusion, my lady."

Startled, Asenath dropped the parchment in her hand. "The mercy of Ra! You gave me a fright."

"My apologies, my lady," Semat said, dipping her head.

"What is it?"

"I just wanted to make sure all is well."

Asenath had not shared details of her intentions for visiting the library, and she was not inclined to do so just yet. "All is well, Semat," she said with a reassuring smile.

"Shall I send for a meal, my lady?"

The sudden rumble of her belly answered before she could. Semat tried to mask a smile.

Placing a hand on her noisy abdomen, Asenath said, "Yes, thank you. Serve it in my chambers. I shall be along momentarily."

"Yes, my lady."

Asenath watched Semat leave, a war of two hungers raging within her. It was a brief battle, and her mind won over her belly. *Just one more entry, and then I shall eat.*

She flew through another parchment, which detailed how the keeper of the king's prisoners placed Joseph in charge of the prisoners' welfare, and supplied him with scrolls upon which to make weekly reports about the prisoners. The warden gave Joseph permission to use any extra scrolls as he saw fit.

That explains how he got writing materials in prison! She thought as she dove into the next journal entry. This one revealed that several months before his writing it, Joseph had interpreted the dreams of two prisoners he had been assigned to serve: Pharaoh's chief baker, Wehemmesu, and his chief butler,

Pehernefer. True to his prophetic interpretations, the baker had faced execution three days after his dream and the butler had been restored. Therefore, for the first time, Joseph had been hopeful that he might be liberated, because he had asked that Pehernefer speak kindly of him once back in service to Pharaoh. Alas, months had passed, and he still pined in prison. Asenath noted the date on the entry.

He penned this almost two years ago. He must have spent several years in prison. But for what exactly was he sent there in the first place? That question begged to be answered. Deafening her ears to the grumbles of her empty stomach, she reached for another scroll.

I had never before seen anyone as striking as she. Her skin was as fair as milk, yet her hair, as dark as ink. Like a curtain, it hung down to her slender waist. Her face was so perfectly painted, she looked like a mural come to life, and it was impossible to guess her age. Her voice was arrestingly shrill, but her steps, utterly silent. She did not walk, she sauntered, as one dancing for an invisible audience. She had dark, almost lifeless eyes, but what is forever engraved in my mind is her gaze. Not before or since has anyone looked at me in such a manner.

Clearly, Joseph is NOT blind to beauty, Asenath mused, as she continued reading.

I remember the first time I stood before her. Her eyes perused me from my tousled locks to my bare feet. She circled around me slowly. I felt the hairs on the back of my neck rise, and I could not quite shake off the foreboding feeling that filled me.

She asked my name, and I gave it. She inquired as to its meaning, and when I shared that, she said, "Savior? Well, you are welcome to save me anytime," and cackled a strange laughter that did nothing to warm her cold eyes.

Yes, hers was a gaze that left me discomfited.

No, hers is not a face I could ever forget. It is the flawlessly frightening face I still see in my nightmares. Cursed be the day I laid my eyes on that face.

Cursed be the day? Asenath did not yet know who the woman was, but she could feel Joseph's hatred of her leaping off the scroll. The man who penned these words sounded nothing like the man that had regaled her with tales of love during a seaside dinner. *Which man is the real Joseph?* The hairs on the back of her neck rose. Ready or not, Asenath knew she was about to uncover a significant secret.

15

Secrets
Should they reveal
An enemy's old wounds
Mirror your scars, call such not foe
But friend

***

Insatiable.

Riddled with curiosity, Asenath adjusted herself on the plump cushion, and let her eyes race through the rest of the intriguing entry.

Cursed be the day I laid my eyes on that face.

It adorned the coldest heart I have ever had the misfortune of meeting. Yet, it was adored by the kindest soul I ever served. The captain of the king's guard deserved better than a serpent for a spouse. What was I but a starving slave when he bought me?

A slave? How did a favored son become a slave? The question flashed in her mind, but only for a moment, as she hastily read on.

Why he chose me from the many at the slave market, I still do not know. I must have resembled a lad at death's door after that harrowing journey from the land of Canaan. Surely, it was the hand of the Lord that compelled him. One more night there and I might not have lived to tell the tale. He was, in that moment, my savior. I think out of sheer gratitude, I could have served as his slave the rest of my days, how much more when he appointed me steward of his entire household. Alas, it was not to be so. How could I forget the day he looked upon me and it was not approval but disgust that filled his eyes?

My heart bleeds still. And her face haunts me. As does the sound of her voice, pleading again and again that I lie with her, as if I would ever commit such a sin against God! I wish I had left for an afternoon respite, like all the other servants had done. Then I would not have been there, alone, when the serpent struck.

Her pungent perfume assaulted my nostrils long before her hand touched my back. She accused me of hiding from her again; she said it was futile since she would find me anywhere. Stepping out of her reach, I asked if there was anything I could do for her. She claimed her most expensive usekh was missing, and she wanted me to search her chamber for it. Not wanting to enter her chamber unaccompanied, I pointed out her handmaidens would be better suited, but she insisted they had already searched obvious places to no avail, and a man's strength was needed to lift her bed and search beneath it.

Like a lamb to the slaughter, I followed my mistress to her chamber. No sooner had I leaned to raise the wooden frame that supported the bed cushions than I felt her arms wrap around me from behind. She pressed her body against mine, grabbed my tunic and once again voiced her adulterous plea:

"Lie with me, Joseph, just this once! For how long must I beg you?"

I rose quickly, trying to extricate myself from her viselike grasp, as well as reason with her. I told her she was the only thing my master had not put in my charge, and I could not commit so great a sin against God. Undeterred, she said she was not betrothed to any god, and though her beauty rivaled that of a goddess, she was a woman in every way. Pressing the curves of her chest against me, she tried to disrobe me. Trying to escape without causing her harm, I tore myself from my tunic and fled, bare-chested, from her chambers. I kept on running until I was outside the house. I could hear distant screams coming from within, yet I could not bring myself to stop running. She was screaming as though she was being attacked. Little did I know she was preparing a performance that would put a seasoned actor to shame.

She must have played the innocent with unrivaled excellence, for when I returned that same evening, it was to face my master's wrath. I had seen him displeased once, at another servant for stealing, but it was nothing like this. His wife was standing by his side, sobbing. He held my rent garment in one hand.

I immediately threw myself at his feet, but he did not let me speak. His eyes held a look that torments me to this day: a mixture of disgust, rage, and hate. His simple question still wounds my soul. "How could you?"

There was nothing I could say, and there was no chance to say anything. He had passed his judgment, and his sentence followed swiftly, as a three-word command that still echoes in my nightmares: "Take. Him. Away!"

As the guards dragged me out, I was convinced I was en route to his executioner. In some ways I would have welcomed death, for what I received in its place was a fate worse: a life indefinitely confined to the dungeons, sharing chambers with criminals.

What did I ever do to deserve twain piercings from the ruthless sword of treachery? A betrayal led me into the house of Potiphar as a slave and another one took me out of it as a prisoner.

O Lord God, you who see all and know all, when will you vindicate me?

Asenath closed her eyes for a second. Her belly was roiling with hunger, but her head was bursting with insights. *Joseph was sentenced on the false accusation of a woman scorned! He was not guilty of rape; he was nearly a victim of it! And he was never given a chance to tell his story, not that anyone would have believed a slave over his mistress. Small wonder he did not take too kindly to my forwardness the night we met; I must have seemed the very resurrection of the shameless woman's phantom!*

149

In hindsight, Asenath almost laughed at how ill-advised her 'enter and conquer' strategy had been. It had been guaranteed to fail. This experience she had just read about alone would have foiled her plan, even without taking his beliefs into consideration. There was one small comfort she could derive from all of this: she was not the only woman from whom he had fled in a chamber. Granted, the circumstances were vastly different. That woman had been his master's wife, making adulterous advances, not his virgin bride attempting to arouse his passions. *He is certainly a man of admirable character regarding women; a pity he does not seem to have had much fortune with my sex.*

Asenath caught herself feeling sympathetic toward him. *A perspective that clearly sees all sides is indeed an indispensable gift.* The more she got to know this mysterious Joseph, the harder it was to harbor ill feelings toward him. It was unimaginable, spending years in prison for a crime one did not commit.

What a bitter betrayal. Wait, he mentioned twain betrayals. Asenath looked at the groups of parchments before her. The pile yet unread seemed smaller than that read, but it definitely included a few more scrolls. The sharp pang that pierced her lower abdomen told her she was treading dangerously close to starvation, and there would be consequences if she did not alter her course. *Necessity mandates novelty,* Na'eemah often said. If ever there was a time to implement that, it was now. She would never dine in a chamber of knowledge, but that did not mean she could not glean knowledge where, and while she dined. More so, when the food awaited in the privacy of her chamber.

Carefully but swiftly, Asenath sequestered the scrolls back into their worn leather home. Then she hastily returned the chests back to their previous locations on the shelf. Taking one last look around, she was satisfied the room was as she had met it. There was only one thing left to do: take the journals with her in such a surreptitious manner that anyone she ran into would be none the wiser. There was no room in her formfitting *kalasiris* to hide a pouch of this size. *Dare I simply walk out, pouch in hand, and hope for the best?* Asenath headed for the door, but stopped when she reached it. The grand curtains that hung from the ceiling were each tied with a wide cloth to keep them open in the day. She unfastened the cloth and spread it about her shoulders like a cloak. Then she sequestered Joseph's pouch of journals underneath her arm and strode confidently to her chamber.

Semat's curious gaze accosted her as soon as she entered the chamber. Giving her handmaiden no chance to begin an inquiry about either her tardiness or her strange attire, she said, "I know, I know. I shall eat the meal, cold as it is. Thank you."

"Very well, my lady," Semat said.

"And I shall serve myself. Please ensure I am undisturbed for the rest of the day."

"Am I still to schedule your evening audience with Wadjenes?"

I forgot about that! Should her search of the library have proven unfruitful, Asenath had intended to tell Semat her plans, and have her search Wadjenes' chamber, while she herself was meeting with him.

"No, it is no longer necessary. Thank you."

Semat bowed and turned to leave.

"Semat?"

Her handmaiden turned back and looked at her, unable to mask her concerned curiosity.

"Be at ease. All is well. In fact, I might have a gripping tale to tell you later."

Semat's doe eyes brightened as she smiled. "I look forward to it, my lady."

No sooner was her handmaiden out of sight than Asenath rid herself of her makeshift cloak and hid the pouch under her pillow. After hastily swallowing a reasonable amount of her cold meal, she rifled through the remaining unread texts, skimming the first few lines of each until she found one with an opening line that was so arrestingly familiar, if she had not known better she might have said she wrote it:

> *I curse that black day.*
> *Were I to live a thousand lifetimes, I could not forget it.*
> *Would that I had died before I met its darkness.*

He too had a black day! For the first time since beginning to read, Asenath felt uncomfortable. She was possibly peering into someone's greatest sorrow uninvited. But it was too late to stop now. She had to know what transpired on his black day.

How beautiful the Valley of Hebron was that day. So still, so serene. When I kissed Abba as I left home, I did not know it would be for the last time. Had I known, I would have lingered to drink in his face and his scent. Tarried to listen to his voice just a little longer. I promised Benjamin I would teach him how to fight with his shepherd's staff when I got back. It was a promise I would never fulfill.

I left home blissfully ignorant. En route, once again, to see to my brothers' welfare. I made my way out of the valley across the plains and ended up wandering all morning. Each passing hour brought me more confusion until I ran into a man at Shechem. Upon describing my brothers and our flocks in detail, he was sure they had left Shechem for Dothan. Delighted, I headed on to Dothan, like a lamb to the slaughter. Would that I had remained lost, for then I might have found a better fate.

Making my way up the hills of Dothan, I saw my brothers in the distance. I waved at them. They did not wave back. That should have been the first sign of things to come. The angry voices I heard as I approached them should have been another. Blissfully ignorant, I missed both signs and greeted them cheerfully.

Levi returned my greeting as usual: "All hail the king of dreams!" Before I could comment, Judah accused me of coming to spy on them again, and said this time I would not have the chance to tell Abba any tales. Not one word of defense had escaped my lips before they collectively attacked me. I felt their rough hands rip off my precious tunic. Their blows and kicks inundated me as they dragged me downhill.

But the blows were not comparable to Simeon's unforgettable words: "Let us kill him and end this once and for all!"

Kill him? Their own brother? Shocked, Asenath could feel her heart racing as she sped through the rest of the entry.

Images of a bloody death flooded my soul as many of my brothers agreed with him. It must have been the mercy of the Lord that stirred Reuben to contradict them. He asked why they should bear the stain of my blood on their hands. Then he reminded them of a nearby well and suggested they throw me in it while they decide my fate.

Moments later, I felt myself being hoisted into the air and I landed in a dark, deep well. Their laughter rang in my ears. I can still hear it. It terrifies me now, as much as it did then. I screamed, asking what my crime was and begging them to let me out. I screamed until I lost my voice. Alas, no one responded.

Mercifully, the well was devoid of water, but it was both damp and cold. I tried in vain to climb the moist walls, sullying my body in mud and my fingers in my blood. Exhausted, I wept and then I prayed. I begged the invisible God not to let them leave me there to die. What had I done to deserve death, and such a slow one as dying of starvation?

It seemed like an eternity had elapsed when I heard Simeon yell for me to take hold of a descending rope. Relief washed over me. They had not abandoned me to die. My relief was short-lived.

Awaiting me upon land were not only my brothers, but also a group of Midianite and Ishmaelite merchants upon camels. Judah was talking to them. Simeon bound my hands with the cords they used to pull me out of the well, while my other brothers stood guard. Shocked, confused, and afraid, I struggled. I asked why they were attacking me so. Simeon's response astounds me to this day. "You have flaunted Abba's favor in our faces long enough! No more!"

Suddenly, Judah walked up to us, smiling and shaking a small pouch. I heard the coins within it. "Twenty pieces of silver!" he declared. "Not bad for an afternoon's labors. Who knew the dreamer was not worthless, after all? Hand him over to his new masters!"

As they shoved me forward, I fell to the ground. I looked up at Judah, pleading with every ounce of strength I had left. I begged him to have mercy upon me, but my pleas fell on deaf ears. *I will never forget his last words to me: "Let us see what becomes of your dreams now!" Nor will I ever forget the look in his eyes as he said them. That look silenced my pleas. It haunts me still. It was unadulterated, unbridled hatred.*

As the merchants dragged me away, I wept. It was not my physical pain that caused my cries; it was the harsh realization that my own brothers hated me. So much that they sought to end my life before I had even lived it. I was but a lad of seventeen, and my flesh and blood had stripped me of the very will to live.

My heart was broken into a thousand pieces, each bleeding into my soul. One singular, sinister act of betrayal broke my faith in the bonds of brotherhood. In one moment, I was transformed from a favored son into a frightened slave. Worse, a slave en route to a foreign land. I had nothing left. Neither father nor family, neither home nor hope; nothing but one question etched in my mind that fearful day. It is a question that plagues me even now:

Why me?

Asenath laid the parchment aside and placed her head in her hands, trying to make sense of that which her misty eyes had just read. *This cannot be! If I thought the other betrayal bitter, this one is brutal.* She had heard Satiah share tales of the rivalry among siblings, but none was comparable to this. This was cruel, calculated, and cold-hearted. A man would have to be devoid of a conscience to sell his own flesh and blood into slavery. *What reason could they possibly have had to execute such treachery? Jealousy? Surely jealousy alone cannot inspire this much hatred. Or can it? . . . To think that as a child I had thought myself unfortunate for not having brothers! Ra be praised for making me an only child!*

Her heart ached for the sad boy hiding within the cheerful man she met. He had been the same age then as she was now. She did not know what she would do if she were suddenly torn from her family and her homeland and enslaved in a foreign country. But to have that done to her by her own flesh and blood, after they voiced their desire to kill her; it was unimaginable! Even now, she felt like raining down the curses of all the gods upon his hateful brothers. *They deserve to be locked in the darkest part of the dungeons! Were I the jailer, I would leave the keys to their prison chambers rotting at the bottom of the Nile!*

What horrors must Joseph have endured as a slave? How was it he could even speak of love and family with such hopefulness? Had she not read his journals, she would never have imagined he had endured such evil at the hands of family.

Asenath rose and traversed back and forth across the length of her chamber. Yet another plan of hers had gone up in flames. She had found secrets, and what secrets! Unfortunately, they were not the kind she could use against the vizier. If anything, she was now riddled with guilt at the thought of ever wanting to manipulate him into setting her free. The man had been twice betrayed by the people closest to him, including his own flesh and blood. The deception her father had demanded she perpetrate would be a third betrayal. *I cannot do it; not knowing what I know now.*

A sense of kinship with Joseph suddenly overwhelmed her. Incredibly, they had far more in common than she could ever have imagined. Were it not for their opposing faiths, they might have made a good match. Alas, her feelings may have changed, but the truth was still too bitter a cure to swallow. She could not live honestly with Joseph if she accepted his marital condition, and she could not live with herself if she accepted her father's deceptive proposition.

What am I to do now?

16

The eye that beholds
End from beginning
Peers from the face of one
Whose hand cradles fate

***

Ambivalent.

Asenath found herself completely at a loss. She did not know what she was going to do. But she knew she would not cause any further anguish to one who was clearly a fellow prisoner of fate. Particularly when the darkness of her black day now paled compared to his. She was still musing and pacing when an immediate course of action came to mind.

I need to return his journal. With that thought, she ceased her aimless walking and began arranging the parchments in order from oldest to newest. She noticed the date on the final entry was rather recent, and it seemed vaguely familiar, though the reason eluded her. The papyrus looked comparatively less worn than the others, yet the ink had bled in quite a few places, as though the parchment had suffered water damage.

I do not remember seeing this one. Asenath noted this entry was brief, and written as a verse:

A fool I have been to trust in man
Vain is the help of the arm of flesh
The days have grown into months
The months have stretched into years
I remember no more that sound

That melody they call hope

What have I done that each one
Repays my good with evil?
Why do those who should love me
At best, forget me; at worst, hate me?
Alas, those who should preserve my life
Are the very ones eager to end it

Where be the spice to wash away
The lingering taste of bitterness?
Where be the cloth to scrub away
The memories of my sorrows?
Where be the hand to reverse time
And undo the wrongs done to me?

I am but a memory, forgotten by all
A man, beloved by none
I am but a dreamer, with no vision
A prisoner, with no future
I am as an orphan, with no family
As one living, with no life

O Lord, God of my fathers
Have mercy upon my weary soul
I have not the strength to bear
The crushing weight of my burdens
Deliver me with your mighty hand
For no savior compares to you

Creator of heaven and earth
You know the number of my days
Should it be my eyes never again
See a dawn beyond this dungeon
Your praise shall stay upon my lips
So long as you grant me breath

O Lord, the omnipotent God

Who sees all and knows all
Though all the annals of time
Hold no record of my name
May 'Joseph' be inscribed upon
The palm of your eternal hand

Tears fell unbidden from Asenath's eyes. She tried to wipe a teardrop that had fallen in the middle of the papyrus, but it made the ink bleed. And in that moment, she realized what the strange, circular marks scattered on the parchment were. *Joseph had been crying while he scripted this heart-wrenching poem! If it was this painful to read, what agony must he have been in to write it?* Laying the parchment aside, Asenath wiped her tears and dried her hands carefully. Then she picked it up and read the verse a second time. She sat in silence, staring at the moving words, when her eyes caught the date on the parchment again.

Why is this date familiar? Suddenly, the answer rang in her mind as loudly as the sound of a temple gong.

"No. It cannot be . . ." she whispered, as the breath caught in her chest. But it was. Without a shadow of doubt, the parchment in her hand was dated the exact day of the festival of Ra. The infamous one during which her father had received the palatial summons. Like a freshly lit torch lighting up a previously dark chamber, the significance of this illuminated her mind, leaving her utterly amazed: While Joseph was in the depths of despair, pouring out his heart on a prisoner's parchment, surrendering to the will of the invisible God, his God had already inspired Pharaoh to have the mysterious duo of dreams. He had then withheld their interpretations from every wise man in Egypt, thereby orchestrating the events that led not only to Joseph's liberation, but to his unprecedented promotion from prisoner to vizier! *Before Joseph penned his poetic plea, while it was yet an unformed cry in his heart, his God had known it, and answered it. Not only that, the answer he gave went exceedingly beyond every imaginable outcome of the prayer.*

She felt the hairs on her arms rise. *What manner of God is this?* She may have lost reason to fear Joseph's powers, but she had just gained ample reason to fear the power of his God. Asenath fell to her knees and raised her hands skyward, as she had seen Joseph do in the garden. "Great invisible God, I do not know if you will hear the voice of such as me. I am a woman, an Egyptian, and a worshiper of many gods. If truly you see all things and know all things, I beg you to forgive me, for I have been wrong about your servant. My thoughts toward him before now were not gracious. Everything I hitherto believed as to why fate crossed our paths, I now question. I no longer see his as the hand that seeks to drown me in a watery grave. Yet, I am uncertain which path to take. Furthermore, I fear what divine consequences may await at the end of whichever road I choose. If I take his hand, I offend the gods I have served all my life. If I spurn it, do I not then invite the wrath of a God as powerful as you appear to be? Forgive my boldness, O great invisible God. But if it is true that you befriend mere mortals, and you would deign to care for one such as me, please show me a sign."

Asenath lowered her trembling hands. She thought her heart would beat its way out of her chest. A fresh anxiety saturated her mind. *Perhaps I should ask for a specific sign. Otherwise, how am I to know if he answers my prayer? What if the invisible God will not accept my prayer from here? Maybe I have to offer it from the stones in the garden, with a fire, just like Joseph did.* Her last thought hastened her to her feet. If she must do it from the garden, she preferred to offer her prayer under the blanket of nightfall. But first, she must return the journals to their rightful place.

***

The moon hung high in the sky on this windy night. Cloaked in black and carrying a torch, Asenath made her way through the maze. Standing before the stony mound, she scanned the perimeter. Assured of her solitude, she set the torch to the sticks upon the altar. Once the fire gained intensity, she gingerly brought herself to her knees. Lifting her hands to the heavens, she repeated her prayer, but this time, she extended it.

"O God of Joseph, son of Jacob, if truly you spared his life, delivered him from the pit and freed him from the prison, if it was indeed by your might that he received such unprecedented favor before the lord of Egypt, then I humbly ask for a small sign, that by it I may know you see me. The sign I request is thus: let my eyes see my favorite bloom. Your servant does not know it, but if truly you are omniscient, then you do. Surely to grow a flower out of its season is no hard thing for a God who caused a barren woman to conceive at ninety. Forgive my boldness in making a request of you, when I have offered you nothing. I know not yet how to appease you. But should you grant me this sign, then I shall know not only that you are the one true God, but that you would deign to accept me as your humble servant."

Asenath was not sure what else to do or say. *Is there a chant, or a hymn perhaps? How does one end a prayer to the invisible God?*

"What are you doing?" a familiar male voice asked, startling her.

"Nothing!" Asenath said, leaping off her knees and straightening her garments. "I was just . . . getting some fresh air."

"On your knees?"

"Retrieving a fallen earring," she lied.

"And the fire?"

"I . . . I thought it might keep me warm."

Heqaib arched an eyebrow. "I see."

Asenath felt the fool. Clearly, it was not a chilly night. She should have given a more plausible answer.

He stepped closer to her. "Feeling well tonight, my lady?"

"Well enough. What are you doing here?"

"Circling the grounds to kill time. I find myself with more of it on my hands than I am accustomed to. The fire caught my attention."

"I see. I am sorry my unsettled matrimony is keeping you away from your true duties for so long."

"Think nothing of it. Truthfully, I am pleased to be able to see you. I worry about your happiness and I am glad your father assigned me to ensure it. Especially since our recent adventure." Heqaib took a step closer and looked directly into her eyes.

Asenath averted her gaze. "You need not worry, Heqaib. I am . . . all will be well."

"I am delighted to hear you sound so hopeful. Especially with your . . . husband, expected back at any moment. Have you had any word from him recently?"

"No. Why?"

"I heard rumors about bandits raiding the royal construction site in Memphis. Since he went to Memphis, I can only assume it was to ensure the security of Pharaoh's assets."

Bandits? "Are you saying he is in danger?" Asenath asked, genuinely concerned.

"No, no. I am certain as vizier he is well-guarded. Please dismiss my thoughtless comments. I did not intend to alarm you."

True, he would indeed be well-guarded. "You are right. I have no cause for concern. Other than the obvious."

"Indeed. Well, are you ready to face him again?"

Asenath let out a breath. "More so than I was a night ago," she answered truthfully.

"You seem more at peace tonight."

"I am," she said, standing taller. "Thanks to a fresh perspective."

"Does the lady care to share this new perspective?"

Asenath smiled. "Not just yet."

"Very well. If I may be permitted to inquire, does your new viewpoint imply you no longer think he asks too much of you?"

"No. But it affords me an understanding of why he asks it."

Heqaib nodded. "Ultimately, do you think you can give it?"

"I am uncertain. Truthfully, I am waiting for a sign."

"A sign?"

"Yes, a divine one. And do not ask, because I cannot explain it to you. I am still trying to understand it all myself."

"In that case, I pray you get what you are expecting soon. For neither your father, nor my mother, will rest until they receive the full assurance of your happiness."

Asenath silently seconded his prayer. *From your mouth to the ears of the invisible God.*

The sound of a twig snapping underfoot caught her attention.

"Who goes there?" Heqaib asked, stepping protectively in front of Asenath.

"It is I," Semat answered, walking into the light. "Blessings of the evening, my lady, Captain Heqaib."

"And to you, Semat," Heqaib answered.

"Forgive the intrusion, my lady," Semat added, dipping her head.

"I hazard a guess that you are coming from my chamber?"

"Yes, my lady."

"Alas, Heqaib, though I make my bed in Hades, I cannot escape Semat's watchful eye!"

As Heqaib laughed, Asenath noticed her handmaiden's cheeks redden. *Do my eyes deceive, or does she blush?*

"I only tease, Semat. You well know I would be lost without you."

Semat smiled shyly. "Would my lady care for a meal?"

"The hour is late. Some tea perhaps."

"Very well." Looking up at Heqaib, Semat added, "Tea for you too, Captain Heqaib? Perhaps with some honey cakes?"

His favorite treat. Asenath thought, watching the exchange curiously.

"An offer I cannot refuse. Thank you, Semat," Heqaib said, casually.

Semat dipped her head and bounded away, but not before Asenath caught her broad smile. She looked at Heqaib. His expression was nothing out of the ordinary. *He has not the faintest idea.*

She had promised Semat a story; perhaps it was Semat who needed to tell her one. Either way, she did not need powers of divination to foretell an interesting conversation loomed ahead.

"What are you smiling about?" Heqaib asked.

"Was I? Perhaps your eyes deceive you, Heqaib."

Heqaib grunted. "My eyes see perfectly."

"If you say so," Asenath said, trying to hide her amusement. "Come, we had better return or she will—with a posse. One way or another, that tea will be consumed while it yet steams!"

***

The night proved unrestful for Asenath, and dawn brought a disconcerting feeling with it. She sought solace in the gardens, keeping a watchful eye out for her divine sign. Her favorite flower was nowhere in sight. Before returning to begin her morning routine, she kneeled at the altar and offered last night's prayer again. Remembering Heqaib's swiftly masked concern, she added a petition for Joseph's safety.

The rest of the morning, she could not stop thinking about him. As much as her disposition toward him had changed, she still did not know what she would do if her sign did not appear before he returned.

She had just finished a soak in the fragrances of jasmine, frankincense, and lilacs when Semat's voice drew her out of her anxious musings.

"Is all well, my lady?"

"What do you mean, Semat?"

"Only that you have been rather reserved this morning. In fact, I believe you have sighed half a dozen times."

"Have I?" *I know of only one other who keeps count of my sighs. He and she are cut from the same cloth.*

"Is there anything I can do to ease whatever troubles you, my lady?"

Perhaps the time had come to tell her confidante everything. Yet she hesitated. It occurred to her she should get Semat's unbiased opinion on Joseph before she shared her own reservations.

"You are doing it now, Semat. I know I have kept the things on my mind to myself lately, but it is because my thoughts are yet unclear to me. They mostly concern my mysterious husband-to-be, as you must have surmised."

"Do you still wish me to inquire if any of the servants might know something about him?"

"No, that will not be necessary. I would not want them to become wary of you. They have been treating you and my other handmaidens well, I hope?"

"Yes, my lady."

"No conflicts or difficulties among yourselves?"

"Nothing noteworthy."

"Anything at all?"

"Wadjenes is no worse than you saw yourself the day you departed, but his coarse jesting is only verbal."

"If it ever becomes anything else, you must let me know at once. My handmaidens are all very important to me, and so is your safety."

"Yes, my lady. Thank you."

"Tell me, what do the staff say about the lord of the villa?"

"Only good things, my lady. They tell us tales of his kindness and generosity."

Interesting. "And you? I know we have not had many days with him, but what do you make of him? You may speak freely."

"He seems very kind, my lady, in his manner. I was most moved by the way he showed great concern for you the night you fainted in the Nile. Even with an entire household to care for you, he would hardly leave your side. And . . ."

"And what? Hold nothing back, Semat."

Her handmaiden's face colored. "I have never seen a man more handsome."

Asenath smiled. *Neither have I, Semat, neither have I.*

"His handsomeness is only rivaled by your beauty, my lady. All the maidens blush in his presence."

"It would seem some blush even in his absence," Asenath said, grinning at Semat's now crimson face.

"I would not dream of it, my lady. It is not my place."

"But you would dream of a man's love?"

"What maiden does not?"

"And when you dream, the man would not happen to have auburn brows, would he?"

Semat gasped, her eyes doubled in size.

"I see I am not the only one keeping things to myself, am I?"

"How could you know, my lady? I have said nothing. To anyone!"

"Would you like me to put in a favorable word on your account?"

"No! I would be mortified, my lady. Promise me you will say nothing to him."

"Very well, I will say nothing." *That does not stop me from writing something.*

"Thank you, my lady. It is merely a dream. I know my place, and the life to which I am called."

"For what it is worth, I would be delighted if it came true. To love and be loved is the best life imaginable."

"It will be your life, my lady, soon."

"I am afraid I do not share your confidence, Semat."

"No? But why not?"

"Where do I begin? It turns out—"

"Forgive the intrusion, my lady."

"What is it, Merit?"

"Wadjenes demands I inform my lady, as follows: 'Pharaoh, lord of Egypt—long may he live—requests the presence of the daughter of Potiphera, high priest of Heliopolis. The captain of the palace guards awaits to convey her immediately.'"

What? A royal summons? Her heart skipped a beat. *Why would Pharaoh send for me?* A nagging premonition arose within her.

"Tell Wadjenes my lady will arrive momentarily," Semat said, giving the answer that Asenath's shocked tongue had failed to.

"Yes, Merit, go." Asenath confirmed, regaining her composure and rising to her feet. "And send Tsillah and the other handmaidens back to assist with dressing me," she yelled at Merit's hurriedly departing form. She turned to find Semat already standing before her mistresses' neatly arranged collection of raiment.

"Can you believe this, Semat? What in the name of Ra, does one wear for an impromptu audience with her sovereign?"

"The attire of a queen, my lady. What else?"

Her handmaiden was right. She had not the faintest idea of how this royal audience would unfold, but she would be sure to arrive adorned like royalty.

17

A lonely road forks
Two paths. Great mountains beyond
One step. Fate is sealed

***

Effulgent.

Despite having to make short work of dressing, Asenath was radiant. She was arrayed in a sleeveless, royal blue *kalasiris* that matched her deep eyeshadow. The *usekh* that graced her neck was that gifted to her by the one who now summoned her. Atop her ceremonial wig sat a tall, multicolored headdress, shaped like an upside-down pyramid. The exquisite, bejeweled veil on her face was the finishing touch to her dazzling attire.

Heads turned as she strode elegantly down the massive palace halls. The statuesque guards that escorted her ushered her into an elaborately furnished chamber. There, a well-built, superbly dressed man with a slightly effeminate gait approached her.

"I am Metjen," he said, in a surprisingly high-pitched voice. "Overseer of the women fortunate enough to receive the favor of Akhenaten, Pharaoh of Egypt. It is indeed a pleasure to receive the resplendent daughter of Potiphera, high priest of Heliopolis." He gave a slight bow.

"Thank you, Metjen. I am pleased to be so graciously received." Asenath returned the gesture with a graceful dip of her head.

"Pharaoh, lord of Egypt—long may he live—has requested your presence. He will grant you an audience momentarily. Please be seated. I shall return to usher you in."

Asenath took the seat he offered, drying her sweating palms on her bare shoulders. She mentally attempted to review her lessons on the protocol for an audience with Pharaoh, but her thoughts kept going back to Joseph. *What delays his return? And why am I to have an audience with Pharaoh in his absence?* Answers eluded her. Nonetheless, she had a feeling whatever was about to happen could determine the course of the rest of her life.

Moments later, Metjen returned for her, and escorted her into a grandiose hall. It was occupied with several servants and a few nobles, each there to perform a duty. Metjen walked ahead of her as the palatial announcer made her presence known.

"The gift of Ra: Asenath, daughter of His Reverence Potiphera, high priest of Heliopolis!"

A hush fell upon the hall. She could feel dozens of eyes boring down on the mysterious curiosity all had heard about but no one had seen. She could not remember being more grateful for the veil that partially hid her face. Holding her head high, she kept her eyes on the back of Metjen's gleaming, bald head. He reached the bottom of the stairs leading up to Pharaoh's raised dais and bowed. Asenath, two paces behind him, did the same.

"The gift of Ra. Approach!" Pharaoh ordered, beckoning her with a wave of his ring-laden fingers.

Asenath began ascending the short flight of stairs, sure that everyone could hear her pounding heart. If the eyes of the nobles present had felt intimidating, the heavily lined, dark pair she approached were even more so. They were bordered by dark, angular eyebrows and set in the aquiline face of the man who ruled all of Egypt.

To his subjects, Pharaoh was more than a man, he was divinely appointed and himself revered as a god—hence his wielding a scepter. Thus, walking up to the large, gold throne, upon which he sat, was indeed intimidating. She took in the majestic, gold-rimmed *nemes* that crowned his bald head, and the long, midnight black false beard that fell from his chin. Earrings sparkled from both of his ears, as did hieroglyph-bearing armbands on his lower arms and gold rings from almost every finger. Gracing his square shoulders was a broad collar bedecked with glistening *chesbet* stones.

Stopping two steps shy of the throne, she bowed again.

"Come closer. Pharaoh does not bite."

As if on cue, the advisors seated on his left and right laughed politely. Asenath ascended the last two steps and bowed to the ground. "Life, prosperity, and health, Your Divine Magnificence," she said, keeping her face lowered. Pharaoh rose from his throne, leaned over, cupped her chin with his hand, and lifted her face, forcing her to rise. She stood directly before him. He slowly circled her, meticulously taking in her appearance.

"A rare prize indeed."

"Such unusual eyes," said the man on Pharaoh's right.

When she followed the voice, she saw the man vaguely resembled the lord of Egypt, except his eyes resembled a hawk's, and a lifeless one at that.

"Unusual indeed, Akhom."

So that is His Radiance! Asenath thought, taking in Akhom's hardened features more attentively.

Seating himself on his throne again, Pharaoh asked, "Tell us, daughter of Potiphera, is it true that the flower of your youth remains untainted?"

Asenath gasped at his bluntness. Quickly recovering her composure, she answered, "Yes, Your Divine Magnificence."

Whispers of disbelief rippled across the hall.

"Incredible! If Pharaoh had not witnessed his wisdom firsthand, Pharaoh would have concluded Zaphnath-Paaneah a fool." Looking around at his nobles, he asked, "Is there a single one of you who would not give his right arm to ravish a prize like she which stands before us now?"

There were murmurs and shaking heads.

"I thought it a jest when he admitted not having much experience with women. But if he has left such a beauty untouched, perhaps his desires lie elsewhere." Akhom's insinuation drew a few sniggers from the nobles, but only intensified Asenath's discomfort. Mercifully, the lord of Egypt contradicted him.

"Pharaoh did not gather that from our conversation. He seemed eager for a wife, but he made it clear he will not take an unwilling bride. In any case, the number of noble women that grace the palace whenever he sits in court is a testament to his charm."

Which means he has his pick of eager royal women.

Pharaoh continued, "The question then falls to you, gift of Ra. Do you not find him pleasing?"

"No, Your Divine Magnifi—"

"No?" he interrupted, clearly surprised.

"I mean, yes. He is most pleasing to behold, Your Divine Magnificence."

"Then to what does Zaphnath-Paaneah allude when he pronounces you *unwilling*?"

He has told Pharaoh I am unwilling! she thought, panicking. "Well, I . . . It must regard the marital condition he stipulated," she said, beads of sweat breaking out on her smooth brow.

"Condition?"

"That his wife must worship his God and none other, Your Divine Magnificence."

"Yes . . . Pharaoh seems to recall him mentioning that," he said, stroking his lengthy, false beard. "Nonetheless, Zaphnath-Paaneah is unlike any other man. He has earned the favor and admiration of Pharaoh. He is fiercely loyal to his God, and who can find fault in him in this regard? His God has made him wiser than all the seers in Egypt! Be that as it may, Pharaoh can see how that condition might not be acceptable to the daughter of Potiphera. Make no mistake, Pharaoh has given his word. Zaphnath-Paaneah shall worship as he sees fit, he and his household."

And where does that leave me? Asenath wondered, lowering her eyes.

The lord of Egypt carried on. "Pharaoh sent word that my vizier journey on from Memphis, and carry out his planned tour of all the provinces. Imagine Pharaoh's surprise when he sent back a missive requesting that the matter of his bride be settled first! It is a matter Pharaoh thought long ago settled. Incredibly, he has requested that you, gift of Ra, be given liberty to choose. Per our agreement—and since defying all human understanding, you yet remain chaste—let it be known that you must make your choice before the sun sets this day."

"Your Divine Magnificence, if I may suggest, I think the matter of her groom should be settled at once if she does not wish to accept his condition, and understandably so. She is clearly a rare prize, and worthy of a royal husband," Akhom said, leering at her.

Who does he have in mind?

"You have spoken wisely," Pharaoh nodded. Turning to his scribe, he ordered, "Send a missive to inform my vizier to return for a marriage feast. The maiden's choice will determine if he attends as groom or guest."

My choice? Between Joseph and who?

"Gift of Ra," Pharaoh said, his intimidating, dark eyes piercing her, "if you are unwilling to be wife to Zaphnath-Paaneah, it pleases the lord of Egypt to welcome you forthwith into the illustrious company of Pharaoh's wives, with all the privileges thereof. A more enviable choice no maiden before you has been given the luxury of making."

No! Join Pharaoh's bevy of wives? Oblivious to both her widened eyes, and the shocked expression on Akhom's face, the lord of Egypt leaned in to within a handbreadth of Asenath, and dropped his voice to a whisper.

"Should Pharaoh have the delight of your pleasure in his bed, rest assured, you will leave it laden with gifts, but your virginity will not be one of them."

Asenath felt her face grow warm. Too stunned to speak, she lowered her eyes.

Rising, Pharaoh commanded, "Metjen, escort the gift of Ra. See that she is comfortable and honor her choice with the appropriate gifts."

Asenath bowed low before Pharaoh once more, trying to maintain a calm exterior while her heart was furiously pounding itself against her chest. The lord of Egypt had all but welcomed her into his harem with open arms. It appeared her greatest childhood fear may yet catch up with her. She gracefully descended the stairs to meet Metjen, who led her out of the grand hall through a side door.

"I shall escort you to private chambers reserved for Pharaoh's special guests, my lady. Please follow me," the steward of the royal wives said.

As they meandered eastward through private hallways, Asenath remembered the map of the palace. Unless she was mistaken, they were heading towards the wing that housed Pharaoh's bevy of women. Asenath felt a foreboding chill crawl up her spine.

Moments later, Metjen ushered her into a luxuriously furnished chamber that was more like a miniature villa than private quarters. It had a receiving chamber, writing desk, dining section, and a sleeping chamber all enclosed within its extensive space.

"Please make yourself comfortable, my lady. I shall return shortly."

"Thank you," Asenath said.

She sank into an inviting couch in the receiving area. Laying her elaborate headdress down at her side, she let her now aching head fall into her open palms. Thoughts sped through her mind faster than she could process them.

Did the lord of Egypt just offer me, Asenath, a place in his harem? . . . If Joseph has told Pharaoh I am unwilling, then perhaps he does not want me after all. The thought stung, though she could hardly fault him. She was unwilling by his standards, and he had a palace full of all too eager alternatives from which to choose. She, on the other hand, had a singular, shocking alternative: her sovereign. This morning she awakened, thinking herself to be in a conundrum regarding what she would do when Joseph returned. Now, she was the very apex of a terrifying marital triangle that included the two most powerful men in all of Egypt. By choosing one, she would inevitably slight the other, and a powerful man with a bruised ego would make a formidable adversary. *Pharaoh did mention it was Joseph who insisted I be given freedom of choice. Even the lord of Egypt admits no royal bride has ever had such a liberty.* That Joseph would grant her such a choice—something neither her father nor her Pharaoh previously did—spoke volumes about the kind of man he was. One that once chose to face the wrath of a mistress scorned, rather than accept her adulterous offer. He was obviously the better man between her choices, but with whom would she be the better woman? *I would not have to recant my beliefs as a wife of Pharaoh. Our marriage would not be based on deceit.* Even as she thought about it, she knew that being one of a plethora of royal wives fighting for their husband's attention would be the realization of her childhood nightmare. There was no doubt the lord of Egypt wanted her. His eyes had made her feel like she was a cornered fawn and he a ravenous lion. But with sixty-six wives to choose from, not counting concubines, she would soon be abandoned to a lavish, but loveless life.

She recalled her mother's admonishment. *Better a small wedding to be the only wife than a royal wedding to be one of many wives.*

What would you do, Mother? She was not certain what her mother would do if put in this position, but she knew exactly what her father would say—he had made his aspirations clear since the black day. There was no surer way for Potiphera to gain the 'eternal favor of Pharaoh' than to become his father by marriage. But her father was not here. She wondered what Na'eemah would advise and what Heqaib would think. She even wondered what Semat might suggest.

But none of that mattered. At this moment, there was no one to tell her what to do.

You are a woman now, Asenath. You must decide for yourself.

She felt acutely alone.

Alone, afraid, uncertain, and unloved.

From deep in the recesses of her anxious mind, Joseph's words filtered to the surface. *Gazing upon your face would be a rare privilege. One that should be earned by love, not granted by law.*

Were she to live a thousand lives, she could never forget those words. Nor would his definition of love ever fade from her memory.

Jacob loved her all of her life, and he never loved another woman like he did her . . . That level of sacrifice . . . devotion . . . affection . . . Staying true . . . in life, in death, and beyond; that is what love is to me.

What would it be like to love, and be loved by a man of such character? It would be a dream come true, no doubt. After a past as harrowing as his, Asenath knew this much: Joseph deserved to have that dream come true. He deserved a wife that would embrace all of him and offer all of her. If she could not be such a woman, she would not stand in the way of his finding that woman.

Better I live without love than live a lie. Asenath heard a distinct throat clear and looked up to see Metjen.

He gave a slight bow. "Forgive the intrusion. Apparently when His Eminence, Zaphnath-Paaneah dispatched an urgent missive for

His Divine Magnificence yesterday, he also sent this, for you." He handed her a small leather pouch.

Joseph sent word? Asenath's pulse quickened involuntarily.

"The rider must be new. He inadvertently left here it at the palace. I have only just discovered it; my apologies."

Asenath took it, her curiosity peaked. "Thank you, Metjen."

"A pleasure, my lady. I do hope you have come to your decision. Pray tell me, what should the invitation to His Eminence state?"

"Forgive me Metjen. . . may I examine the contents before I give my answer?"

"Certainly, my lady."

Asenath opened the pouch and saw a scroll. Her hands trembled slightly as she pulled it out and unrolled it.

Asenath, daughter of Potiphera, high priest of Heliopolis

I hope this finds you in good health. I am sorry for my prolonged absence. Matters of state have kept me here longer than I would prefer, and will further extend my time away from Avaris. Hence, I was obligated to pen a letter informing Pharaoh, lord of Egypt—long may he live, that the matter of our marriage is yet unsettled, for which I take full responsibility. I imagine he may ask to hear your wishes to that end. And I have asked that they be fully honored.

I do not think it fair that you be forced to remain in my home indefinitely, without my presence, while I tour the land, especially since you do not find my proposal favorable. Please know that should you choose to leave, I shall hold no hard feelings toward you. My feelings are quite the contrary, Asenath. You have consumed my thoughts and prayers since the night I first saw you. It may be foolish of me to admit this, but then again, this may be the only opportunity I ever have to do so.

There is not much to see here, at a construction site. But yesterday, I saw something out of the ordinary. Sprouting from the desert sands was a lone bloom. It was a surprise to encounter, but impossible to forget, for it stood out from everything around it. Exquisitely lovely with a fragrance sweeter than perfume, it drew me in effortlessly. I could not take my eyes off it. Wondering what strength it must have to blossom against the odds, I was compelled to pick it up. It has been in my travel cloak since. Though it is worse for wear, and merely a sentimental gift, I could not resist enclosing it here, for the one that embodies everything it called to mind, and so much more.

Should our paths become uncrossed, please know that if ever there is anything I can do for you in the future, it would be my pleasure.

With sincerity of heart,

Joseph

Asenath could hardly breathe. She felt like time had stopped. Now completely oblivious to Metjen's presence, she raised the flap of the pouch once more, silently praying, *Please let it be, please . . .* When her eyes fell on the crumpled flower lying at the bottom of the pouch, she could not stop the gasp that escaped her lips. It was her favorite flower: a purple iris.

The invisible God sees me!

Overcome with emotion, Asenath fell to her knees. She could not stifle the sobs of relief and joy that broke forth from her belly.

"My lady, are you all right?" Metjen asked, alarmed, as he reached toward her.

"Yes," she said, through the tears of joy and relief.

The God of Joseph heard my prayer! He welcomes my worship! Asenath could not stop the laughter that bubbled up from her newly unburdened heart.

"Yes, Metjen," she said, rising. "I am well; all is well. Please have His Eminence, Zaphnath-Paaneah's invitation to the wedding feast state thus: '*Asenath, daughter of Potiphera, will be honored to have you as groom.*'"

Metjen's brows shot upward. "Very well, my lady," he said with a slight dip of his head. "Nonetheless, His Divine Magnificence has extended you an invitation to remain at the palace until your wedding feast. I shall send for your maidens. If there is anything you need to ensure your utmost comfort, please do not hesitate to send for me."

"I am most grateful, Metjen," Asenath said, wishing she could share just how thankful she was. He had scarcely reached the door when Asenath pulled out the single stem whose arrival had just changed the course of her life. It was falling apart, yet she did not think anything more beautiful. It was dying, but nothing could have given her more life.

Affection. Like a tiny spark that lights a forest on fire. That was what she felt kindling in the depth of her heart and spreading through her being. She did not bother to stop the tears effortlessly trickling down her cheeks. Why should she? She was not alone, unseen, or unloved. *He sees me; he loves me; he wants me!* It was utterly beyond comprehension, but the God of Joseph, Jacob, Isaac, and Abraham cared about a woman that he should consider naught but an insignificant pagan. And he cared enough to show her he did.

Asenath read the missive once more. He may not have explicitly stated that he loved her, but he wrote enough to give her hope. For one thing, he signed this letter with his true name.

"Joseph . . . I am to be the wife of Joseph." Asenath pressed the parchment to her breast and let herself enjoy the wonder of the strange, warm feelings flooding her heart.

18

Girl. Gone
The whims of men
My will no more control
Behold I choose my path. I am
Woman

***

ounting.

Metjen had said the royal feast celebrating Asenath's marriage would commence in five days. By order of Pharaoh, the three-day festivity was to be held in the palace, and the bride-to-be was welcome to remain therein. Having chosen to wed Egypt's vizier and not her Pharaoh, Asenath had requested, and been allowed, to return to the seaside villa she now considered home. Her first order of business upon returning was to swiftly dispatch what her father had demanded: an invitation to her wedding feast. She could imagine his surprised delight at discovering it was to be held at the palace. She could hardly believe it herself.

Three days had since elapsed. Besides being daily steeped in preparations for her nuptials, she had acquired two new habits: she went on her knees and praised the invisible God every morning, and she read Joseph's timely letter to her every night. Her morning habit filled her with an almost indescribable sense of peace, and her nightly one fanned the flame of her hopeful anticipation.

Joseph returns today! Our wedding is tomorrow! And a royal ceremony, no less! Those three happy thoughts were Asenath's awakening musings this morning. They had filled her with a sense of excitement. That third thought had inspired a series of daydreams about various aspects of her impending wedding ceremony. It was somewhere in those exciting imaginations that a concern crossed her mind. *A palatial ceremony would only have Egyptian customs, but I am marrying Joseph. Should he not have some part of his culture at his wedding? That would be ideal . . . Alas I do not know any Hebrew wedding customs, other than the brides being veiled, which I already am . . .* Asenath wondered if there were any others she might imbibe. The more she mused, the more the desire grew. *Where can I find a mature, experienced, Hebrew woman to enlighten me this very day?* Fortunately, Merit's timely entrance to her chamber at that moment provided her answer. The mother of her most reserved handmaiden was such a woman, and she happened to reside in Avaris. Asenath lost no time in giving her first instruction of the day—dispatching Merit to fetch her mother.

By early afternoon, Asenath was standing before her *kalasiris*-ridden bed, trying to make yet another decision about her life-changing day: what to wear.

"Should Merit not have returned by now?" Asenath asked Semat, who was holding up two of her mistress's garments.

"Perhaps they are securing some items for you, my lady."

"Perhaps."

"I am certain she will come straight here upon her return. What about one of these?" Semat asked, waving her arms.

"Possibly. It should be stunning, but less grand than the *kalasiris* for the marriage ceremony," Asenath replied.

"Do you have a preferred shade in mind, my lady?"

"Something light would contrast the night well."

"It is fortunate I brought the gift I did then," a third voice said from the door to Asenath's chamber.

The bride-to-be turned and let out a cry of delight. "You are here! And early!" She said, rushing to embrace the plump, beaming Na'eemah. Trailing behind her, with a small chest, was Tsillah.

"You can thank your father for that, my sunshine," Na'eemah said, returning the embrace warmly.

"Where is he? I have missed you terribly! I have so much to tell you!"

"And I can hardly wait to hear it all! But your father will talk my ear off if I do not send you out directly. He has an audience at the palace, but wants to see you first."

"I take it he is in the guest chambers."

"You know your father. *Protocol must be upheld at all times —*"

"*And in all circumstances!*" Asenath finished, holding up her right index finger, and deepening her voice to give her best imitation of Potiphera.

The two women laughed.

"Now, go. You can try that on for size when you return. I am curious to see what you make of it," Na'eemah said, indicating the chest Tsillah had deposited on a nearby table.

"I am beside myself with anticipation!" Asenath said, clapping her hands together like an overexcited child. With that, she raced out of her chamber.

Potiphera rose to greet the lady of the villa as soon as she entered the guest chamber.

"Blessings of the day, gift of Ra," he said with a smile.

"Blessings of the day, Father," Asenath answered, bowing deeply. "And what a delightful surprise!" She added, rising with a genuine, broad smile.

"Indeed! It is a joy to see you positively glowing! As well you should be, a royal bride days away from her *palatial* wedding feast!" Potiphera said, kissing both her cheeks.

"Thank you, Father."

"I am pleased you have embraced your destiny. I could not be more proud! This is indeed a time for celebration! Where is a goblet when you need one?"

Asenath signaled a servant standing by, who poured out two goblets of wine, and handed one each to her father and herself.

"Life, prosperity, and health, to the royal bride!" Potiphera said, raising his goblet.

"And to her groom," Asenath added, raising hers too.

"Her most *fortunate* groom, to be marrying such a rare prize."

Asenath smiled, "Thank you, Father. I am looking forward to wedding Joseph."

"Joseph?" Potiphera asked, a puzzled expression on his round face.

"Zaphnath-Paaneah, Father. Your future son by marriage. Joseph is his name, as given by his father. It means savior."

"Interesting. A revealer of divine secrets would naturally be a savior of sorts."

"Yes, Father." *He is certainly saving me from a loveless future in the royal harem.*

"Admirable qualities to have in a leader, whether as vizier or as husband. Do you not agree?"

"Absolutely, Father. He has many admirable traits."

"I am immensely pleased to hear you speak thus, especially after our last conversation. I may not have made it apparent, but I want you to have a marriage filled with love and the fruits of love. In fact, I have brought you something to ensure that is the case!" Potiphera said, reaching into a leather pouch on the couch beside him. He pulled out a small, beautifully carved ebony chest.

"What is it, Father?"

"See for yourself, daughter," Potiphera said, smiling.

Asenath accepted the chest and opened it. It contained a gold jewelry set: an anklet and a matching waist chain. Her heart skipped a beat. It was no ordinary jewelry; it was a talisman. Each piece was fully engraved with symbols of the goddess of fertility and childbirth.

How do I tell him I can no longer wear these? Asenath kept her eyes on the chest. "These are beautiful, Father."

"Only the finest for the gift of Ra. Satiah has worn a similar set since her wedding night, and she has just delivered her third child! You keep them on and they will ignite in your husband undying flames of love for you."

Asenath swallowed, then said softly, "I am indeed delighted to hear my beloved Satiah is now a mother three times over. And I do hope I know that pleasure someday. But . . ."

"But?" Potiphera said, raising a bushy eyebrow.

Asenath cleared her throat. "I cannot accept these, Father."

Potiphera's eyes darkened slightly. "You *cannot* accept them?"

"I mean . . . I cannot wear them, Father."

"Why, in the name of Isis, not?"

"Because talismans, and any other objects bearing symbols of the gods, are unwelcome in this house. To wear them would be to violate the laws of the invisible God."

"Of course. . ." he said, both brows rising in realization. "You refer to the marital condition. I thought I made it clear you were to accept it in word but not in deed, so the marriage goes on as planned?"

"Yes Father, but in doing so, I would be betraying my husband," she said, looking him directly in the eye.

"Asenath, *you* know the meaning of the engravings, but *he* need not. In his eyes, these would just be exquisite jewelry. A wedding gift from your father."

"Even if he does not know, the invisible God sees all and knows all, and he is a jealous God."

"I take it you speak of *his* God?"

Gaze unflinching, she responded, "And mine, Father. I had heard stories of his power, but now I have experienced it for myself. So I too will worship him, in public and in private, forsaking all others."

Potiphera's face went ashen. "Surely you jest."

Asenath squared her shoulders. "No, Father. I do not."

"Have you lost your mind entirely? You intend to forsake ALL our gods?"

"I already have."

"No! If I drove you to this madness, I will never forgive myself!"

"I have never been more mentally sound, or at peace, Father."

"Are you so foolish as to think there will not be consequences for forsaking Ra?"

Asenath was silent, contemplating her father's troubling comment.

"Surely you do not believe Zaphnath-Paaneah is powerful enough to save you from the wrath of Ra?" Potiphera said derisively.

His tone stung, and Asenath raised her chin. "My faith is not in his power, but that of his—*our* God. I have made my decision, Father," she concluded, holding the wooden chest out to him.

Potiphera blinked. He took the rejected gift and looked away, speaking as though to himself, "Have I lost my only child?"

Asenath felt a lump rise in her throat. This was the kind of sentiment she had longed to see from her father her entire childhood. It was bittersweet; medicine after death. She felt sorry for him. But there was nothing to be done, except offer him the truth.

"Father, you have lost a child, for I am now a woman; but you will never lose your daughter." She took his robust hand in hers and said, "I will always love you." Raising it to her lips, she kissed it gently. Looking up at his face, she was glad to see its paleness gaining color. "Notwithstanding, Father, have no doubt about this: while I embrace the rich heritage of my father, and his fathers before him, I will teach my children to embrace the robust faith of their father, and his fathers before him."

A strange expression formed on her father's round face. If Asenath was not mistaken, it was anger combined with, dare she say, admiration.

She had just declared independence from her father and his faith. Her heart picked up pace in anticipation of the fury that might immediately be unleashed upon her.

Potiphera held her gaze, neither flinching. Finally, he bowed his head and sighed. Speaking softly, he said, "I see . . . I have indeed lost my child." Raising his eyes to hers, he added, "This strong, decisive daughter standing before me is a woman."

Asenath's eyes misted. "Thank you, Father."

Abruptly shaking his head, Potiphera added, "Wise or not, you have made your choice. Let us not dampen this festive season with differences. You, gift of Ra, are on the verge of fulfilling your destiny. And your father merely came to wish you every happiness. All the same, if you change your mind, you know where to get this," he said, waving the small chest.

I will not change my mind, Father. Asenath left her sentiment unvoiced. She had made herself abundantly clear. Whether or not he believed her, it was best to keep the peace and focus on the joyous occasion that brought him here. She was wondering how to break the uncomfortable silence when Semat's appearance saved the moment.

"Forgive the intrusion, my lady," her handmaiden said cautiously from the doorway. Asenath bid her come in. Semat entered, bowing deeply.

"Blessings of the day, Your Reverence. We are most honored to have you here."

"Blessings of the day," Potiphera replied.

Semat lifted her head and looked at her mistress. "I thought you would want to know: Merit has returned."

"With her mother?"

"Yes, my lady."

Yes! "Thank you. I shall be with them momentarily."

As Semat walked away, Wadjenes walked in with a manservant in tow, carrying a colorful, fragrant floral arrangement.

"Blessings of the day, Your Reverence, my lady. These flowers just arrived along with this," he said, indicating a scroll in his hand.

Asenath held out her hand. "Thank you, Wadjenes." As he gave her the parchment, she said, "Permit me to introduce my father, His Reverence Potiphera, high priest of Heliopolis. Father, Wadjenes, illustrious steward of my new home."

Wadjenes bowed deeply. "It is an honor, Your Reverence."

Asenath read the missive while her father exchanged a few words with Wadjenes.

Asenath,

I have never been more pleasantly surprised than when I received a royal invitation to my wedding! Words fail me in expressing my delight at knowing you willingly become my wife. I am back in Avaris and eager to hear what inspired your change of heart, especially when there is still so much about myself I have not yet shared. Alas, palatial matters may keep us apart for one more night. I have a host of meetings to resolve pressing issues due to my absences, both past and impending. By the favor of God, Pharaoh has granted me five additional days off from royal obligations, after our marriage feasts, to spend with my bride. I leave it up to you where, and how, we spend our first days as man and wife. As for me, I can hardly wait!

~ Joseph

"Good tidings, I presume?" asked her father, draining the contents of his large goblet.

Better than good! "You presume correctly, Father."

"Then I leave you on that positive note," Potiphera said, rising.

"Already? Will you not at least have something to eat?" Asenath asked, also standing to her feet.

"Do not trouble yourself. Clearly you have matters to attend to, and so do I."

"When should we expect your return?"

"When does our illustrious vizier arrive?"

"He is already in Avaris, but it appears he may be occupied at the palace right up to the feast!"

"In that case, I shall return when I return. Rest assured, if we do not see again before your feast, we shall see there."

"Very well. I am truly pleased you will be there."

"With the largest goblet and the loudest cheer!" he said dramatically.

Asenath laughed. Her family were guests in her home. She was but hours from her royal wedding, and best of all, the groom of her choosing was excited to marry her. She felt a lightness of heart that was unfamiliar, but warmly welcome.

19

***

Incandescent.

From scalp to soles, the radiant royal bride was adorned in golden shades. Her figure-flattering *kalasiris* was made of a rare, light fabric that shimmered like liquid gold. Cinched at the waist by a slender belt, the dress left her broad, sun-kissed shoulders bare. The green shadows around her kohl-lined, amber eyes only added to their magnetism. Beneath her arresting eyes rested a specially crafted, bejeweled veil, made from a sheer, pale yellow fabric. The plethora of minute, precious stones on the edges of the veil flowed like a jeweled stream from the bridge of her nose across her cheeks, disappearing behind each earring-filled ear. Just below her veil, hanging from her elegant neck, was her mother's *usekh*, its lapis lazuli stone resting squarely in the center of her bust.

Her mesmerizing bridal look featured two unique finishing pieces:

A thin, long cloak, fashioned from the same sheer fabric as her veil, that fell from her bare shoulders all the way down past her dainty feet, extending into a short train.

And a jewel-encrusted, dome-shaped, gold headdress, that spanned from her forehead almost to the base of her head, elegantly crowning her intricately styled, waist-length ceremonial wig.

Standing before the grand, ebony doors to the royal feasting hall, surrounded by her septet of maidens, Asenath had never felt more beautiful, or more nervously excited, in all her life. Everyone who was anyone in the palace, was awaiting within the grandiose chamber to see her. But of all of them, she was eager to lay her eyes on just one person. By one twist of fate after another, she had not seen him since the night of her unexpected plunge into the Nile. True to his predictions, he had been in an endless series of meetings at the palace right until this morning. Asenath's deliciously impatient sentiment was soured by the absence of the woman who had been dreaming with her, the very first time her blissful, childish heart had imagined this day.

Clutching the jewel on her *usekh,* Asenath closed her eyes for a moment.

It is happening, Mother. I am wearing a beautiful kalasiris and on the verge of my grand wedding feast at the palace. And I did not have to marry Pharaoh to get here. If only you could see me now.

"If only your mother could see you now."

Asenath opened her eyes and looked into Na'eemah's. They were moist and held pride, admiration, affection, and sadness, all combined into one heart-warming, gut-wrenching gaze.

"There you go, reading my mind again!" Asenath said, rapidly blinking back the tears that threatened to mar her flawless makeup.

Not bothering to stop her own tears, Na'eemah walked up and gently embraced her. "My pride in you today is only superseded by my happiness for you, my sunshine. May your union be filled with love, and the fruits of love, always."

"So let it be, *Mother.*" She let Na'eemah lightly kiss her veiled cheeks right as the thunderous sound of the gong reverberated all around them.

It is time!

Na'eemah hurriedly stepped back as the intimidating doors were swung open by menacing, muscular guards. Simultaneously, her septet of maidens collectively ululated as though with one voice.

Their long, shrill wail echoed from the furthest enclave of the hallway to the smallest corner of the chamber.

A hush fell upon the royal feasting hall. Every eye turned toward the entrance, eager to see the bridal procession. And what a procession it was.

Like a golden goddess rising from a sea of white, Asenath stood amidst her barefooted maidens. All seven of them wore narrow, strapless white sashes across their busts that left their bellies bare. Beneath their revealing upper garments flowed long white skirts that hung low on their hips and fell down to a handbreadth above their bejeweled ankles. Each maiden's wig was skillfully woven, with white seashells intermittently twisted into the long, raven braids. Broad, layered *usekhs* on their shoulders boasted the popular blue-green faience stones, as did the wide bracelets on their henna-painted hands. Other than sharing the same blue shadows around their heavily lined eyes, each of their faces was different, yet every one bore a brilliant smile.

The deep, throbbing sound of large drums felt like gigantic hearts beating within Asenath's chest. That was the signal that her resplendent bridal party should begin making their way down the aisle. As musicians began a wedding chant, Semat, who led the party of maidens, gracefully threw fistfuls of white lily petals into the air. She danced forward after each toss as the petals floated down to the gleaming marble floors, forming a fragrant carpet beneath the bride's sandaled feet.

Led by Tsillah and Merit, both trios of maidens on Asenath's right and left did the most vigorous dancing of all. They started out facing the audience with their backs to their mistress, side-stepping as they slowly progressed. Then they spun around and reversed positions, dancing first toward, and then away from the bride. Repeating their fascinating, synchronized steps and smiling from ear to ear, they inched forward.

From their midst, the beautiful bride took short, soft strides. With each one, her henna-painted, perfectly pointed feet peeped out from under her golden hems, while she simultaneously made gentle, graceful gestures with her dainty, decorated hands.

As she danced, her eyes took in the surrounding opulence. The festively decorated, brightly lit hall was packed. Groups of glamorously attired guests reclined around lengthy ebony tables. Beside each stood servants dressed in celebratory raiment, ready to dish out every Egyptian delicacy and others imported from nearby lands. Diverse parties of artisans awaited, from belly dancers to fire eaters, eager to display their crafts.

As the virginal octet progressed closer to the dais, Asenath's darting eyes settled on the piercing pair she had been most excited to see.

Joseph. Her heart fluttered at his mesmerizing gaze. For a moment, she forgot there was anyone else in the room.

He could not look more royal. Standing tall at the foot of the steps leading up to the dais, he was dressed in the purest white tunic, and adorned with gold accessories, including forearm bands, wristbands, a broad collar, and a thin, circular headdress atop his short, dark wig. When their eyes met, they remained locked as Asenath danced all the way to his side.

Potiphera, who had been standing at a table a short distance to Joseph's right, approached and stood beside his daughter and her groom. All three of them turned to face Pharaoh's elevated dais and bowed low.

At the sound of the gong, every guest seated stood to their feet.

Finally, the lord of Egypt arose majestically from his golden seat. Brandishing his scepter, he proclaimed: "Let it be known this day that Akhenaten, lord of Egypt, being so pleased and so inclined, bestows upon Zaphnath-Paaneah, vizier of Egypt, the distinct favor of receiving the gift of Ra—Asenath, daughter of Potiphera, high priest of Heliopolis—as his bride."

Upon this royal declaration, the bride and groom faced each other. Their gazes unflinching, Asenath returned Joseph's dazzling smile with one of her own, as Potiphera took his daughter's hand and placed it in her groom's. A servant swiftly appeared and handed the high priest a thick, white cord, which he used to bind their right hands together. Once bound, Potiphera lifted their hands up as high as he could, and held them in the air.

Raising his scepter-bearing right hand high, the lord of Egypt continued his pronouncement: "They are henceforth man and wife, with all the rights and privileges afforded the highest-ranking nobles. Hear Pharaoh well, anyone foolish enough to come between them shall enjoy the unbridled wrath of Akhenaten, lord of Egypt." With that, Pharaoh struck his scepter on the polished floor once. The resulting unique, piercing sound echoed throughout the chamber, while Egypt's sovereign regally reseated himself on his throne.

As Potiphera lowered and unbound the new couple's hands, Pharaoh stretched his left hand sideways, his fingers slightly curved as though holding an invisible cup. Pehernefer, his chief butler, appeared as if from thin air and handed Pharaoh his golden goblet. Raising it, he offered the marital toast: "May their marriage be filled with love, and the fruits of love. So let it be!"

Every guest raised a goblet and echoed the sentiment, "So let it be!"

As the gong clanged once more, Asenath, her husband, and her father, bowed low before Pharaoh, who thundered, "Life, prosperity, and health! Let the feasting begin!"

As the sound of festive music filled the hall, the bowed trio lifted their faces and looked at each other. Potiphera kissed his daughter on her veiled cheeks and made his way back to his table to join the merrymaking.

Asenath felt Joseph's warm hand envelop hers as he leaned in, his lips nearly grazing her ear. "I can hardly wait to unveil you," he whispered, sending warmth spreading through her body.

Her glowing eyes lowered shyly as she smiled.

The music changed, and Asenath raised her eyes to her husband's. "Turn around," she said.

"Why?" her husband asked, a puzzled expression on his handsome face.

Just then, her seven maidens formed a circle around the newlyweds and began a triumphantly animated dance about them.

"Turn around, lean on me, and clap!" Asenath yelled, trying to make sure he heard her above the festive din. She felt his back rest lightly against her shoulders. They both clapped as the dance continued, and then her six secondary maidens spread out to dance in a much wider circle.

At Semat's approach, Asenath gently nudged Joseph away and turned to face him. She watched his eyes widen as her handmaiden swept off her cloak in one fluid motion.

Smiling, she said, "Just stand there and keep clapping!" With a grace born out of a newfound joy, Asenath slid away from her husband, picked up the skirt of her shimmering *kalasiris*, and began a graceful circular dance around him. The entire crowd joined in the clapping and the music heightened. Her heart beating wildly, Asenath moved faster and faster around him. Finally, she twirled on the tips of her toes and spun out into an elegant pose right in front of him, as her maidens fell to the ground, bringing the lively dance to a dramatic finish.

The guests cheered, thumping their goblets on the tables in excitement. The familiar sound of the gong rang again. Deep drum beats filled the hall as six bearers in white *shendyts*, who looked more like chiseled bronze statues than men, came in chanting. They swiftly approached the newlyweds and bowed, laying an ostentatious carriage at their feet.

Asenath turned to her husband. Inclining her head toward her father's table, she said, "Now, you feast!" Potiphera stood with one arm outstretched, ready to welcome his son by marriage.

"And you?" Joseph asked.

"I go to our home to prepare for my unveiling."

Kissing her veiled cheeks, Joseph said, "Go then, my wife."

His addressing her possessively was akin to being wrapped in a soft, thick cloak on a winter night. Smiling from ear to ear, Asenath seated herself majestically on the carriage and the bearers hoisted her into the air. With Semat leading, and a maiden beside each bearer, the girls chanted their way out of the palatial hall.

***

The blushing bride felt thoroughly refreshed after a cool, scented bath. In significant contrast to her first night in Joseph's chamber, she had chosen to wear the purest of whites and present herself in her most natural state, for her true wedding night. Her look for tonight was inspired by the wisdom of Merit's mother, but made possible by Na'eemah's timely gift.

Standing before her bronze-framed mirror, she let her eyes take in the familiar, exquisite, one-shouldered *kalasiris* that framed her sun-kissed slender form as elegantly as it had her mother's. She had thought her heart would burst when she opened the chest Na'eemah gifted her and discovered its long-forgotten, dearly beloved content. Na'eemah had told her she hid the garment on the night of Asenath's black day, after her sorrow-filled childish heart, mourning her crushed dreams, had declared it unwanted. The motherly woman had only recently unearthed it, from the dark depths of her old, worn chest of raiments. Asenath's bittersweet tears had come unbidden then, and a lone one streaked down her bare cheek even now.

I am finally grown up enough to wear it. She could not think of a better occasion to wear it than her own bridal unveiling.

"What dampens your spirit on such a joyous day, my lady?" Semat asked.

"Nothing," Asenath said, wiping her cheek. "Absolutely nothing, Semat. I was merely feeling nostalgic, but I could not be happier."

"I, too, am most happy for you, my lady. Now, with what jewels would you like to be adorned?"

"None."

"None?"

"Not a one. Tonight, I want the only things that shine to be the twain amber windows to my soul."

She laughed at the reflection of Semat's stunned face. Looking from Semat's lined eyes to her unlined ones, she realized that without the usual dark liners and bright shadows that magnified her eyes, they appeared softer, and she looked more youthful.

Bending over, she shook out her long, thick hair. When she flipped herself back up, a mass of chestnut curls beautifully framed her unenhanced, flawless face.

This is me, for better or worse. I hope he is not disappointed.

There was only one thing missing. "Veil me," she ordered. As Semat retrieved and secured a sheer, white veil upon Asenath's face, Tsillah arranged the shiny, curly mane that stretched from her head to her waist. Both maidens stepped back when their finishing touches were complete.

Simultaneously nervous and excited, the bride turned from her mirror and faced her maidens. It was almost time for her bridal party to make its way from her chamber to her husband's.

It occurred to Asenath that a hush had overtaken the room. She took in the look of wonder on Semat's face, and the similarly awed expressions on the other six faces in the room.

"What is it? . . . Semat?"

"Forgive me, my lady. I just . . . I never imagined you could look so lovely in such simplicity."

"You are breathtaking, my lady," the typically quiet Merit added, dipping her head. The other maidens nodded and murmured their agreement.

"Thank you," Asenath said, looking each of them in the eye. "I am profoundly grateful to all of you. You are all beautiful, from within to without. You have served me selflessly, and I pray you experience the joy and love that I am starting to realize exists in this life. I will miss you deeply." Stepping closer to Semat, she placed an arm around her. "Except for you, my ever-faithful one."

Aglow from her mistresses' praise, Semat looked around at her fellow handmaidens and said, "I will miss you all too, sisters."

Asenath scanned the misty-eyed group and fanned her face with her fingers. "No, no tears allowed tonight. Only celebration. Where's a harpist when you need—" Snapping her fingers as though recollecting something, she focused on Merit. "Did you remember the musician?"

"Yes, my lady. I shall give the signal as you enter the chamber."

"Superb. I—"

A sudden disturbance interrupted Asenath. It sounded like drums, musicians, and clapping. Eight pairs of eyes turned toward the entrance to her chamber. Semat swiftly exited to see what the clamor was about. Within moments, the handmaid hurried back, with a surprised look on her face. "His Eminence approaches, my lady."

Joseph? Asenath's eyes widened.

Just then, she heard Wadjenes' voice announce, "His Eminence Zaphnath-Paaneah, vizier of Egypt, has come for his bride."

He has come for me? With a dropped jaw, Asenath looked from Semat to the entrance of her chamber and back. The maidens whispered to each other, shocked and confused. Asenath raised her hand to silence them.

"Order. My husband is here." As her secondary maidens instantly fell into their usual formation around her, she nodded at Semat.

Signal understood, her chief handmaiden went to the entrance of her chamber and announced: "Her Eminence Asenath, wife of His Eminence Zaphnath-Paaneah, vizier of Egypt."

Asenath tingled with pleasure at hearing herself announced this way for the first time. She lifted her head, squared her shoulders, and strode elegantly out of the chamber. As she stepped into the hallway, she paused. The entourage there bowed. Her husband, beaming like one who had just discovered a lost treasure, stared at her with dark, dancing eyes.

In a low voice, he said, "You are the perfect picture of a virgin bride. And I am not waiting another moment to unveil you." Before she realized what was happening, he swooped down and swept her off her feet effortlessly.

Asenath gasped in shock, throwing her arms about his strong shoulders. Joseph spun around and headed directly for his chambers. His passel of supporters cheered and clapped as the drummers and musicians resumed playing. Their formation forgotten in the excitement, her maidens hurriedly tried to keep up with Joseph's long strides. Once they arrived at his chambers, two guards swung open the doors. The eager groom stepped in without a backward glance, his bride still cradled in his arms. She felt herself gently lowered until her sandaled feet touched his polished floor.

"My wife . . ." he said, staring at her adoringly. Reaching toward her face, he fingered one of her thick curls. "Is this your real hair?"

"In its most natural state. Does it please?"

"Immensely. It adorns you like a crown of chestnut curls—" The sudden sound of a lyre's melody interrupted Joseph. Asenath saw his eyes widen as he recognized the traditional Hebrew wedding tune.

That is my signal. She gazed into his magnetic eyes and spoke in well-rehearsed Hebrew. "After so many years in a foreign land, enduring strange customs, should a groom not enjoy something familiar on his wedding day?"

His eyes watered as he took her hand and gently kissed it. "Truly, you are a gift; an absolutely divine one." Holding her hand between both of his, he closed his eyes. Like it was the most natural thing in the world to do, he prayed, "Blessed be the Lord Most High, creator of earth and sky, man and beast. The giver of all good gifts who has this day, blessed groom with bride." Then he looked at her. "Blessed are you among women and blessed be the fruit of your womb, my wife." He placed her hand on his chest, pulling her close.

Asenath felt the rapid beating of his heart beneath her palm, followed by the tender moistness of his lips upon her forehead. When he gently lifted her face to his, and reached toward her veil, he asked, "May I?"

He asks, even now? Asenath could not believe that when she rightfully belonged to him, he would still ask permission. She nodded, still staring into his eyes. She wanted to see his face when he saw hers.

"Wait. First, this goes," he said, ripping off his ceremonial wig and flinging it toward a nearby couch, without breaking their locked gazes. She smiled as he continued, his freshly exposed bald head gleaming.

"Now, this," he whispered, slowly unclasping her veil. She saw his eyes widen slightly, as they roamed all over her naked face. "From the first moment I saw you glide into this very chamber, I imagined what lay beneath the veil . . ."

Her pulse quickened as he ran his fingers gently across her right brow, down her right cheek, and across her lips. When he cupped her face with one hand, a shiver ran up and down her spine.

"Lovelier. More so than anything I imagined. The gift of the sun outshines her giver." As Joseph leaned his face toward hers, Asenath swallowed involuntarily. When his lips met hers, they were soft. Soft in feel and in kiss, but they lingered. Joseph pulled back for a moment and picked her up. Then he made his way to his luxurious white bed and tenderly placed her on it. Asenath watched him untie his belt, lay it aside, and then remove his tunic. Her eyes took in his chiseled, masculine torso as he unfastened and shed his jewelry, her body steadily growing warmer. Muscles rippling under

194

flawless skin, he kneeled at her feet and unfastened each of her sandals, placing a kiss on each dainty foot.

Asenath's breathing intensified. She felt his fingers softly and slowly trace their way from her right foot all the way to her right shoulder, where he unfastened the singular clasp holding up her *kalasiris*. As the soft white fabric fell from her shoulder, Joseph paused. She watched his gaze drift over her feminine figure slowly, then rise to her eyes. When he whispered, "Asenath . . ." she thought she would melt at the depth of the desire in his eyes. Their lips met again, and this time, the kiss was strong. It only grew in its sweet intensity, and soon, all else was forgotten in the unreserved uniting of their beautiful bodies.

20

A man
Finding a wife
Discovers a treasure
Richly blessed is he with favor
Divine

***

T ranquil.

Asenath awakened, feeling entirely relaxed. She made a half-turn in the tremendously comfortable bed, expecting to see her husband. Only wrinkled, empty sheets lay where he had.

Where is he? A glance at the high, latticed windows told her it was still dark. She shifted her gaze around the large chamber, and caught a low light seeping in from beneath the door to Joseph's adjoining, private receiving room. Curious, Asenath slid off the bed, wrapped a linen around her unclad, slender form, and stealthily approached the light. Gently pushing the door open a little, she peeped into the room. Her completely preoccupied husband sat at a table. A lamp before him, an ink cake beside him, and a reed pen in his hand, he scribbled on a papyrus scroll.

He is working; on our wedding night? Her thought stung. Quietly pulling the door closed, she made her way back to bed. After the explosive tenderness of their marital consummation, she felt like she could have laid in his arms forever. It was alarming thinking he may not have shared her sentiment. *If I cannot hold his attention on our first night together, what hope do I have of keeping it in the nights ahead?* Doubts crept around her mind, keeping her awake for a while, but exhaustion eventually overtook her misgivings.

She reawakened to full daylight. The sun shone like it had been in the sky for hours. Realizing she was still the sole occupant of Joseph's chamber, disappointment made itself at home in her heart. As she sat up, her eyes were drawn to a crumpled purple iris. It sat in the center of a papyrus, positioned where her husband had laid the night before. Her heart fluttered as she reached for the papyrus. She recognized Joseph's elegant penmanship, instantly. Lifting the fading flower gently, she read:

Her beauty, beyond compare
Her lips, sweeter than honey
Her skin, smoother than butter
Her hair, softer than wool

How the glow in her eyes
Kindles a spark in my heart
And the light of her smile
Ignites an ember in my soul

How the melody of her voice
Inspires a song in my spirit
And the music in her laughter
Sparks a dance in my loins

How the passion of her spirit
Arouses a fire in my being
And the warmth of her soul
Melts down all my defenses

I lay naked, unashamed
Before love's eternal flame
Its brilliance in her gaze
Its fervor in her touch

I stand strong, unafraid
Before life's great mystery
Its answer in our honesty

Its meaning in our unity

O the beauty of her face
O the glory of her kiss
Leave me lost in her embrace
For therein I find my bliss

My beloved is mine and I, hers
My heart sings a song like no other
Unending be my song of songs
Unfading be my purple iris

He calls me his purple iris! Heart bursting with emotion, Asenath leaped out of bed with renewed vigor. Not only had his verse taken her breath away, it had dispelled every lingering trace of doubt from last night. She yelled in the direction of the entrance to his bedchamber.

"Semat! . . . Semat, are you there? I need a *kalasiris*, something stunning . . ."

The curtains parted. "May I suggest one?" She tingled at the unmistakable baritone voice. Her husband stood there, casually leaning against the doorframe, a disarming smile on his striking face.

"You are familiar with my array of raiment?" Asenath asked skeptically.

Without breaking his gaze, he casually strode toward her. "One in particular is quite memorable." He had a mischievous look in his eye. "Flaming. Immensely flattering. And, I believe, very well suited for dancing."

"You believe, do you?" she replied, catching his teasing drift.

Joseph reached her in three strides, and his bare arms encircled her slender waist. "I would give my right arm to see it again."

"There's no need for dismemberment, as long as you promise neither to run away, nor interrupt my . . . movements."

Joseph raised his right hand. "I solemnly promise the former, but the latter . . ." he said, giving her a knowing look, "I am a man, not a god." Kissing each of her plump, pink lips individually, he added, "A man in love." He released her, casually strode to his bed, and reclined himself on its lengthier edge.

You may not be a god, but you certainly look divine. Asenath thought, staring at his bare-chested body.

"Your audience awaits with bated breath, my eminent lady."

"Not for long, my eminent lord," she responded, heading for the doors to dispatch orders to her recently surfaced handmaiden.

"Blessings of the morn, my lady."

"And to you, Semat. Quickly, retrieve the *kalasiris* Mayet gifted me, and return forthwith."

"Is that all you want, my lady?"

"For now. But lest I forget upon your return, see that you find Heqaib and convey these exact words to him from me: 'Assurance of happiness acquired.'"

"Assurance of happiness acquired?"

"Precisely. And Semat, no need to hasten away from him. I shall not need anything else for quite some time." Asenath smiled at the growing color that filled her handmaiden's cheeks.

Moments later, when she once again donned her fiery garment, Joseph let her begin the infamous *Raqs Baladi* routine. This time, he did not blush; his gaze was so intense he barely blinked. Once again, the dance did not end as choreographed. But this time, it was because he could not contain his passion, and she did not restrain hers.

***

Man and wife lay basking in the afterglow of their love. Their long limbs intertwined, the darker shade of her skin beautifully contrasting the lighter hue of his. The day-old husband was drinking in the sweetly enigmatic scent of his wife. Her head lay on his strong chest, and his on her soft curls, the silence undisturbed save for their contented breathing. He had been dreaming of moments like this one since their infamous first meeting. He smiled at the memory of his near failure to resist temptation.

I should tell her. "I have a confession, my purple iris."

Her amber eyes danced as she lifted her face to his. "Pray tell."

"I almost came back in here that first night, after my hurried exit. I stopped outside the chamber to calm my pounding heart. But the thought of you in here, naked . . . only the strength of God kept me from running back in to take you in my arms."

He registered her surprise. "You wanted me then?"

"I wanted you from the moment I laid eyes on you."

Smiling, she lowered her eyes and bit her lower lip for the briefest of moments.

How adorable—her embarrassment manifests as a lip bite, while those of us with sun-shy skin turn crimson. "Nothing to say to your husband?"

"You hid your desire well."

He laughed. "Only by the grace of the Lord."

Her answering smile soothed like the first rain after a drought. Sobering, he added, "But when I knew I loved you, I also knew I would not be able to hide it any longer."

"When did you know?" she inquired, her melodious voice barely above a whisper.

"When I held your fainted, wet form in my arms and feared you may never be mine."

When she placed her hand on his heart and said, "You need never fear that now," the warmth of her dainty hand reached his soul.

"I know," he said, taking her hand and kissing her palm. "What I do not know is what inspired your change of heart. You knew hardly anything about me before I saddled you with my conditional proposal and left you recuperating from a frightful plunge. How I prayed for you that night. I had not known you but three days, yet my heart ached at the thought of leaving you."

"Truly?" she asked, her expression wondrous.

"Truly. I could not stop thinking about you, or what you must have thought of my brashness. Even as I left Avaris, I prayed earnestly that God would show you my heart."

"He did."

He did? "How?"

"Alas, 'tis my turn to confess," she said, lowering her eyes and pulling away from him. "I searched your texts. At the time, I was hoping to find something I might use to get myself out of our proposed marriage. But then I found your journal."

She read my journal?

He noticed her swallow nervously before she went on. "It was raw, real, and brutally bare. And in it, I saw you: painfully beautiful. I realized we were both prisoners of fate. Except, you seemed so . . . free."

"I am . . . stunned."

Her eyes were misty when they met his. "I am sorry I read them without your permission, but I am not sorry that I saw you."

Thank you, Lord. "Neither am I. I may not have had the confidence to share them with you right away, but I wanted you to see me. What stuns me is how the Lord saw fit to answer my prayer. I am amazed by his loving-kindness."

"As am I. His answer to my prayer is what solidified my change of heart."

"You prayed? To the *invisible* God?"

She grinned and nodded enthusiastically.

This I have to hear! "What did you request?" he asked, sitting up.

"A sighting of my favorite bloom, which was out of season. I feared I had prayed in vain when Pharaoh issued me an ultimatum in your absence. I was moments from naming Pharaoh my choice of groom, so I would not deprive you of a willing, wholehearted wife when I opened your missive and saw the answer to my prayer."

The purple iris! "The Lord uses foolish things to confound the wise. I was inexplicably drawn to that flower. When I looked at it, I felt like I saw you."

"And when I looked at it, I saw a profound truth: your God saw *me*, and he cared enough to let me know so. If this was the God you wanted me to worship wholeheartedly, then your request was not so much a burdensome condition, but a delightful invitation. One I had the privilege and liberty of accepting or rejecting. It was to be *my* choice."

How beautifully apt. "Indeed. He gives that choice to all, male or female."

"Is that why you gave it to me?"

"Absolutely. How could I possibly demand something God sees fit only to request?"

As she smiled, he noticed she dipped her head in the most charming manner.

"After your journal, that is what most endeared you to me."

"Letting you choose my faith?"

"No. Letting me choose my husband. But for you, neither Father nor Pharaoh would have granted me the power of choice in that regard. As a child, I grew up dreading a loveless marriage that my father told me was my divine destiny. I accepted that as my only option until you showed me another, and let *me* choose."

"Do not applaud me; but for the grace of God, I would not have had the courage to do so. I thought surely my condition would drive you into Pharaoh's bedchamber."

Her ensuing laugh sounded like a joyful melody. "Indeed, it drove me, but not into Pharaoh's bedchamber. Just out of your house."

What? "I do not understand."

"You will after I make my final confessions."

Confessions? "You have my ears." Joseph said, reclining with his arms crossed beneath his head.

She adjusted herself so she sat cross-legged, facing him. The sight of her hair cascading across her otherwise bare chest was akin to twain waterfalls covering magnificent mountains.

Focus, Joseph. Your wife is confessing.

"I fled this house. The day you left for Memphis."

"You jest!"

"I do not. At the time, I did not know you had left. I made Heqaib take me back to Na'eemah in order to tell her I could not be yours. But she said I had to return; and my father literally shipped me back."

"Remind me to send them both generous gifts!"

She giggled, then sobered before proceeding. "I really thought then that you did not want me; that perhaps I was not as comely as my loved ones had led me to believe. While en route to my father's house with Heqaib, I . . ." Her gaze flinched.

What?

"I asked him what he thought of me, and I did it with an unveiled face. . . Forgive me for letting another man see my face before you."

203

This goddess of a woman did not think herself lovely? It was my fault. He sat up and faced her, imitating her cross-legged posture. Cradling her chin, he gently lifted it, until her misty eyes met his.

"It is I who should ask forgiveness for distressing you so much you felt it necessary to do so. I am sorry, my purple iris."

"So am I."

O Lord, she is so beautiful! Slowly tracing a finger across her flawless facial features, he said, "Heqaib glimpsed your face for a moment, but I get to gaze upon it . . . caress it . . . cherish it . . . and kiss it, for a lifetime." As he kissed her sensationally soft, moist lips, he felt her arms encircle his back and stroked hers in return. When they broke for breath, he said, "But let this console you: Heqaib did not see your face before me."

Her smooth brow instantly furrowed. "Explain."

"Fearing for your safety after I hastily rescued you from the Nile, I pulled your veil down to let you breathe. Granted, your eyes were closed and your forehead was bleeding. And while I was racing back into the house cradling you in my arms, uppermost in my mind was securing you help, and quickly. Still, I cast my eyes upon your wet, bruised visage, and I carried its beautifully haunting image with me throughout my travels. I confess, I chided myself for seeing your face before I had earned the privilege of doing so."

Her eyes held both amazement and relief. "You saved my life that fateful night. I say, that privilege was duly earned."

How sweet. He placed a tender kiss on her forehead.

Lifting her eyes to his, she grinned. "I must say, if any man had told me a husband of my choice would come from me falling in the Nile, I would have dismissed him as a liar and lunatic."

Joseph chuckled. "I have no doubt! So tell me, are you happy with your choice?"

With one brow arched, she quipped, "You are the diviner; you tell me."

Throwing his head back, he roared. "The last time I heard those words, I knew my wisdom alone would be unequal to the task of making even a small crack in the walls that surrounded your heart."

"Not walls, husband. A fortress."

"My mistake, wife. Did you let your husband into this fortress, or did you let yourself out?"

"You have a lifetime to divine the answer to that," she said, fluttering her long lashes.

Indeed, I do. "My beloved is mine, and I, hers."

"One of my favorite lines from your breathtaking verse."

"Was it?"

"Yes. You have written me the loveliest lines I have ever read. Yet I have penned you none."

"I demand none. I am content that you take pleasure in mine."

"But I am not!" she said, suddenly scrambling out of his bed. He watched in confusion as she snatched the lightest of the bed linens and began wrapping it around her beautiful body.

"What are you doing?"

"In lieu of a written verse, will my husband accept a spoken one?"

A recitation! "Actually, I would prefer it—coming straight from your lovely lips."

She bit her bottom lip again. "Thank you." Glancing around, she picked up a discarded cloak from the floor and wrapped it around her head in a surprisingly well-shaped makeshift headdress. "Now, I warn you, I am no poet, at least not one of your caliber. And this is impromptu, so give me a moment to collect my thoughts."

"Take all the time you need."

He watched as she closed her eyes and took a deep breath. She was statuesque for several moments before a small smile parted her lips. When she opened her eyes, his heart skipped a beat. They glowed like twain suns.

"To the eleventh son of Jacob, the son of Isaac, the son of Abraham," she said with an exaggerated bow. Rising, she cleared her throat, then giggled.

She is enchanting.

Her expression grew sober before she proceeded. "Joseph, you are the dream I never knew I had until it came true. I am still amazed at the magnificence of my fortune. To be offered not only your love, but the love of divinity is . . . an imagination too wild for my minute mind.

"Standing before Pharaoh, I chose you. Standing before the invisible God, I choose you. And for all of my days, I will choose you.

"Where you lay, I will lay. Where you live, I will live. Where you die, I will die, and be buried at your side.

"Your God is my God. Our children and their children will know no other god beside the unseen one who sees all, and knows all."

His heart melted as listened to her speak. *What wonder have you wrought, Lord, that stands before me thus?*

"Since our God has blessed you with such unprecedented favor, I know the annals of time will hold your name esteemed as Zaphnath-Paaneah, the Hebrew prisoner turned vizier of Egypt. But I," she said, placing a hand on her chest, "I am content simply to be Asenath, devoted wife of Joseph, servant of the Most High God."

"My purple iris . . ." He whispered, blinking furiously in an attempt to hold back the tears swiftly gathering in his eyes. As Asenath made her way back toward him, he shuffled forward until they met at the edge of the bed. When she sat beside him, he felt her soft hands envelop his rough ones. He tried to speak, but all he could say were three words, uttered in a breaking voice: "Words fail me . . ."

"Then it is a mercy that I have yet a little more to say, my beloved dreamer. I do not know that for which you now dream, but my dream for you is family. Though the family of your birth embraces you no more, the family of your choice will never forsake you. I am your family now, and you are mine."

I, Joseph, beloved by family? Never again to be forsaken? Do I dream? He wondered, swiftly losing the battle to contain his emotions.

As his wife gently brushed away the lone tear that rolled down his cheek, the tenderness of her gesture proved mightier than the strength of his will. The walls he had not even realized surrounded his heart, crumbled.

Like an orphaned child seeking comfort, he laid his head on her bosom and wept.

PART III:

THE CURSE OF CAPTIVITY

21

A hive's golden milk
In the face of love's wine
Cannot boast of sweetness

***

TWO YEARS LATER (THE SECOND YEAR OF PLENTY)

Cool.

The sea breeze was a welcome contrast to the morning's already strong sunshine. Asenath savored the feel of the air on her unveiled face. Freedom from the veil was just one of the blessings for which she was grateful since marrying Joseph. In their two years of matrimony, he had superseded even her wildest dreams about what a good husband might be like. Palatial duties kept them both busy, but he always found ways to carve out time for just the two of them in the busyness. A classic instance being this morning's imminent sea adventure—a boat ride to the palace—for which he insisted on taking the oars himself.

As memories surfaced, Asenath smiled at how much she had changed in the past two years. She had once thought Joseph the nefarious oarsman of her nightmares. And after her infamous plunge into the Nile, she would sooner have been stung by a thousand scorpions than let him row her anywhere again. Now, she could hardly wait for their imminent, albeit brief, sea adventure.

The small sea vessel rocked as a manservant untethered it. Her husband stepped toward it and turned to her, his hand extended with palm facing up. "Your Eminence."

She took his hand with a playful smile. "His Eminence is too kind."

"'Tis but one of my many flaws," Joseph teased, as he helped her into the boat. Their carefree laughs echoed over the waves as they ensconced themselves on plump cushions.

Once they were seated, Joseph accepted his leather pouch from his awaiting steward. "Thank you, Wadjenes. That will be all for now."

"Yes, Your Eminence," Wadjenes answered, dipping his head.

Just then, the breeze intensified, tousling Asenath's curls slightly.

Feels colder than I thought. I should have brought a—

"Your Eminence, I thought you could use this," a feminine voice said.

Asenath looked at her handmaiden, who held out a thick cloak. Merit might be more reserved than Semat, but the wiry woman anticipated her needs with a consistency and precision that was both refreshing and astounding. "You thought wisely, as always. Thank you, Merit," she said, accepting the cloak and draping it around her shoulders. "You may go."

Merit gave the faintest hint of a smile as she bowed.

As their servants walked back towards the house, Asenath turned to find her husband's dark eyes fixed on her.

"What is it?"

"Can a husband not admire his wife's beauty?"

She grinned. "He can, as long as he remembers, duty calls. Start rowing, oarsman."

"At once, Your Eminence," he said, feigning an apologetic bow.

Asenath laughed. Admiring the powerful muscles rippling on his arms as he began paddling the oars, she asked herself. *How did I get so fortunate?*

They rowed in contented silence until the grassy shore of their villa's north end began to fade. Then Joseph spoke.

"Merit seems to be growing on you."

"Indeed. I am increasingly thankful she chose to stay. I dare say you and she might be woven from the same threads. Tell me, is there something in the milk of Hebrew mothers that gives their children powers of divination?"

His long, hearty laugh still enveloped her like a warm wrap on an icy night.

"You laugh, but you cannot convince me she was not a diviner in a past life."

"I am glad she is so efficient. I know you miss Semat."

I do. But she is happy, and that makes me happy.

"It was a good thing you did, letting her go."

"I could not deny her a chance at the happiness we have. And now, she has found it."

"Thanks to your matchmaking prowess—Merit and I are not the only diviners in the family. How did you know to pair those two?"

"A woman in love can always recognize another. Even though Semat swore me to silence, I tried to find reasons to ensure their paths crossed. And I noticed how moody she became after he left. I had to give her the same choice the others had been given—stay in my employ or return to their families. Yet I knew, even after returning to her family home in Heliopolis, their paths might not have crossed as he was too blind to see, and she too proper to say anything. Hence my writing him an enlightening missive; the rest was up to him."

"He is a good man, Heqaib."

"Indeed. And almost a father by now. Semat's time draws nigh."

It had been several months since she received Heqaib's last missive excitedly announcing his wife's pregnancy. The news had been bittersweet. Asenath was thrilled for both of them, yet it had reminded her of the dark cloud that hung over her marriage. Semat had not yet been married a year and was already with child. She, on the other hand, had not been able to give Joseph the one thing she had promised him: a family of his own. And it was not for lack of trying. The flames of their love still burned brightly, almost nightly.

When will my time come? Asenath wondered for the thousandth time. She still could not voice what she feared: her failure to conceive was a consequence of her forsaking the gods of her father. Every time the frightening thought crossed her mind, she asked herself the same question: *Is the God who transformed a Hebrew prisoner into Egypt's vizier in a day not powerful enough to deliver me from the lawful captivity of Ra?*

As though privy to her thoughts, Joseph said softly, "Your time will come, my purple iris."

Asenath tried to put on a brave face for him. "From your mouth to the ears of our God."

They fell silent for a few moments, but it was not a comfortable one, and thankfully, Joseph broke it.

"So, what is on the agenda of the illustrious instructor of the royal wives today?"

"It appears I have a fresh addition to my students. I am yet to meet her, but Metjen mentioned she is a Nubian princess."

"That must be Her Radiance, Neferubity. Take care with that one—she is quite . . . spirited," he said, with a mysterious smile and a gleam in his eye.

Something about the way he said it aroused her curiosity.

"Spirited?"

"I was present when she was first presented to His Divine Magnificence, and so was His Radiance. Suffice it to say, she did not take too kindly to Akhom's lack of discretion."

If her husband was sharing a rare piece of palatial gossip, she was all ears. "Pray, tell."

"I gather she is a highly skilled warrior. When the Lord of Egypt said her father was most gracious to present him with a prize like her, she responded by saying her father gave gifts when he should draw swords."

"Bold!"

"If you only knew. When he then asked what she knew about drawing swords, His Radiance chimed in, saying a woman with her assets was best suited for gracing a royal bed."

Asenath gasped. "Such insolence! Someone ought to tell him a thing or two."

"Her Radiance wasted no words."

"What did she say?"

"She said, and I quote: *'Five minutes in your bed and my sword will render you powerless to ever ravish another woman in it!'*"

Joseph's laughter drew hers out effortlessly.

"I like her already," Asenath said.

"You are not the only one."

"No?" Asenath was surprised he would admit a fondness for another woman.

"His Divine Magnificence was completely charmed. It is safe to say the hunter in him cannot wait to tame the wild creature in her."

"She must be quite beautiful," Asenath asked, trying to judge his feelings.

"There is none whose beauty could ever compare to yours."

"Says the wisest man in all of Egypt," Asenath responded, amused by his diplomacy. He did not say whether the princess was comely. She knew he was not blind to the beauty of the women at the palace, especially when they found reasons to "accidentally" flaunt it in his face. After all, he was the most attractive noble in the palace, and that was not just her biased opinion. She chided herself for being even a little jealous—he had never given her the faintest reason to be.

The south entrance to the palace was in sight. Their one-on-one time was almost over.

"What about you? What begs for the attention of Egypt's vizier today?"

"If I am not too distracted by thoughts about my lovely wife, I might attend to those," he said, tilting his head toward the pouch that lay beside him. No doubt "those" would be the most pressing matters on his seemingly endless list of vizier duties. In addition to reviewing reports from a host of palace officials, the vizier oversaw everything from sampling a city's water supply to sitting in high court, from supervising a construction project to recording trade. Since he was also responsible for the security of Egypt's sovereign, he oversaw incoming and outgoing visitors to the palace. Whatever "those" were, she did not think he was inclined to share details about them.

"It appears you will have your hands full today."

"As always."

Guards were already waiting on the raised dock to receive them. So were two quartets of bearers manning two carriages. As they transitioned from boat to dock, she knew his attention would be shifting into work in seconds, so she said, "Beloved . . ."

He turned immediately, his brows arched.

"May the blessings of our Lord grace your day."

"And yours," he replied, as he took her hand and lifted it to his lips in a gentle kiss.

***

Lord, grant me patience, Asenath prayed silently. The forty-fifth wife of Pharaoh may still be able to turn heads, but underneath her fiery tresses lay a barren head. Asenath had lost count of how many times she had repeated her instruction to the woman. Unable to replicate the hieroglyphs adequately, the royal's frustration was mounting quickly.

"Perhaps Her Magnificence would like to take a brief break," Asenath hinted.

"More like a permanent one," Aneski replied, laying down her reed pen. "I do not know why I bother. There are scribes aplenty, ready to take down letters anytime."

"Indeed, but if Her Magnificence can pen them herself, she should stand out in a sea of beautiful women."

Aneski's smooth brow furrowed. Slowly, she picked up her pen, dipped it in ink and tried again.

Asenath smiled. Nothing motivated the wives of Pharaoh like the possibility of outshining each other. She was profoundly grateful to be teaching some of them, rather than being one of them. Noticing movement at the door to their learning chamber, she walked toward it.

"Are you going to announce me, or shall I do it myself?" asked an authoritative voice with a faint accent.

"I beg your pardon, but Her Eminence says all who wish to may enter freely," a nervous guard responded.

Asenath took in the unfamiliar female at the entrance with one glance. She had skin the shade of a moonless night, yet it shone. Her dark, thick mane seemed to defy gravity, and was being temporarily tamed by two circular gold headbands, spaced out one on top of the other. The overall updo was reminiscent of two balls of hair sitting atop her lovely head, with the lower ball boasting two thin, intricately fashioned ebony sticks criss-crossed through it. The lower gold band had a pyramid-shaped green jewel sitting front and center that sparkled every time she moved. Her arms bore gold bracelets with similar stones. The striking stranger's attire was made of two pieces of white fabric covering her upper torso and hips respectively, leaving little to the imagination.

"What seems to be the trouble?" Asenath asked, looking at the unknown face.

"It appears some of the royal staff lack proper training. I merely asked to be announced, as protocol demands."

Definitely a royal! No informalities for this one. "Excuse him, the fault is mine. Whom do I have the pleasure of receiving?"

Hoisting her head high, the dark beauty glared at the guard, who quickly cleared his throat and announced: "Her Radiance Neferubity, daughter of Panehesy, King of Nubia."

The warrior! Beloved was right. "And I am Asenath, wife of His Eminence, Zaphnath-Paaneah."

"The vizier's wife."

"Delighted to be."

She noticed Neferubity take her in from scalp to soles. "I am not sure I have met a more striking couple. Your Eminences must collectively have more enemies than a stray hound has fleas."

Asenath laughed. "I certainly hope not. But Her Radiance is most gracious, and most welcome." Gesturing towards the chamber, Asenath stepped aside. Neferubity walked in.

Switching to the Nubian dialect, Asenath asked, "Is it reading or writing that interests Your Radiance?"

Neferubity's large brown eyes registered surprise. "Your Eminence's command of my language is impressive."

Asenath smiled and gave the slightest dip of her head.

The radiant royal continued. "To answer the question, neither reading nor writing. I already do both, excellently. But, since my father has seen fit to trade me for peace between our nations, I thought this might be a way to pass the time. I find I suddenly have so much of it."

"I am sorry to learn Her Radiance did not come to Egypt voluntarily. If I may be so bold, what formerly occupied your time?"

Reaching below her right hip, Neferubity whisked out a small knife.

Asenath was surprised such sparse attire still provided enough room to secret a weapon.

Tracing her finger from its bejeweled handle across its slightly curved blade, Neferubity answered. "Sparring. Training. Strategizing. Duties of the fiercest warriors in all of Nubia, even if my brother and father would rather deny that fact. They know not the privileges they enjoy by the virtue of their gender. They fight for Nubia because they have to, but I did, because I chose to. Even if I had to trade my sword for a skirt."

She is here for the love of country and family. Asenath felt a newfound respect for the young warrior. An idea crossed her mind.

"Perhaps Her Radiance would not mind imparting some of her skills to an eager, welcoming audience."

"I hardly think Her Eminence's students would see me as anything other than a rival."

"I speak not of the royal wives, but of the royal children."

Neferubity inclined her head slightly and then smiled. "I am not opposed to the idea. But forgive me if I fail to see how you could arrange it."

"Her Radiance wages wars with swords, but I do so with words."

Neferubity smiled, a brilliant white, genuine smile that lit up her entire face.

"Please, call me Neferubity."

"In that case, call me Ase—"

"Forgive the intrusion, Your Eminence," said a suddenly appearing Merit, as she briskly approached Asenath. "An urgent missive came."

"Please excuse me, Your Radia—Neferubity." Turning towards Merit, she took the scroll.

Father's seal. She thought, breaking it. She read the letter silently, but quickly, and felt like someone had punched her in the gut.

"Is all well?" Neferubity inquired.

"I fear we must resume this conversation at a later time. Urgent family matter."

"By all means, Asenath. I look forward to speaking again."

Asenath made short work of explaining her hasty departure to the other ladies present, as Merit gathered her belongings. Then the two of them headed out the door. Once they reached the courtyard, Asenath dispatched an order. "Merit, return home and pack for an urgent but indefinite journey. I shall be along shortly."

"Yes, Your Eminence."

Turning to the bearers, she said, "Take me to His Eminence's quarters."

Lost in a sea of anxiety, she missed their arrival at the vizier's official chambers until the bearers called on her. Without waiting to be announced, she strode into her husband's receiving chamber. Mercifully, he was alone.

She registered his surprise, undoubtedly as easily as he registered her worry. When his wide-eyed gaze met hers, he only said two words: "What happened?"

"Father is ill. He sent his barge. I must leave for Heliopolis at dawn."

His eyebrows shot skyward, then descended forming a faint frown. Asenath was willing to wager the expression on his face now matched hers.

***

The journey to Heliopolis was smooth, swift, and serene. Asenath, on the other hand, was anything but calm. Joseph had been both gracious and supportive; they had spent time together in the garden praying the evening before. But emotions seemed to be getting the better of her today. She was feeling alone, even though Merit journeyed with her. It was the first time she had been apart from her husband since they wed. She had not realized how much comfort and joy his presence brought until she found herself suddenly without it. But anxiety overshadowed her loneliness. The missive had not detailed her father's illness, only that he was unwell and her presence was needed *urgently*. She had more questions than answers, but not for long.

Na'eemah was standing outside the main entrance to her childhood home.

O Lord God, please give me strength to face whatever awaits me.

Asenath ascended the short flight of stairs quickly; Merit trailing behind her.

"I am truly glad to see you," Na'eemah said, arms spread out, inviting an embrace.

"Likewise, though I wish we were seeing each other under different circumstances," Asenath said, briefly wrapping her arms around Na'eemah. Dispensing with any pleasantries, she asked, "Where is he?"

"In his chamber."

Asenath turned and began heading towards her father's wing briskly.

"Wait, I need to talk to you before—"

"Afterward, Na'eemah," Asenath called back over her shoulder. She needed to see her father first; everything else would have to wait.

Potiphera was reclined on his couch, a bowl of partially eaten pomegranates next to a half-full goblet of wine on a table beside him.

"Life, peace, and prosperity to you, Father," Asenath said soberly, entering unannounced.

His countenance brightened. "Gift of Ra, you are here!" he said in a lively voice.

Kneeling beside her father, she took his hand, kissed it, and held it in both of hers. "Undoubtedly, Father; I came as quickly as possible. Tell me, what ails you?" she asked, her eyes searching his fleshy frame for any signs of weakness or discomfort.

"It is a malady of the heart, daughter."

"Heart?! What kind of malady, Father? Does it flutter or race? Or does it hurt? What do the physicians say?" Asenath said, bombarding him with questions.

"I did not see a physician."

Has Father run mad? "How could you not see one, Father? I do not understand."

"Because the cure does not lie in the hands of a physician."

"In whose hands, then?"

"Yours."

"Mine?!" Asenath exclaimed, looking at her hands as though they held some mystery she was yet to uncover.

"Yes, yours."

"Father, surely if I knew the cure I would not hesitate to administer it, but I am yet to even understand the ailment."

"Then let me enlighten you," he said, sitting up. He pulled a small, engraved ebony chest out from under the cushion he had been resting on. It looked disturbingly familiar. "My heart aches at the thought of you sending me to the afterlife without grandsons."

A slap would have stung less than what Asenath's ears had just heard. She felt like a sword had pierced her heart. It physically hurt. Now the ebony chest registered—the only wedding present she rejected. *He brought me here for this?* Pushing herself away from his couch, she rose slowly, her hands trembling with a fury she had never felt before.

22

The knife of a foe
Spills not as much blood
As the needle of a friend

***

Infuriated.

Anger had simultaneously replaced Asenath's anxiety and sharpened her tongue. Leveling a quelling gaze at her father, she turned her last thought into a question.

"You brought me here for *this*?" she said, pointing a shaking finger at the chest.

"Is it not reason enough?" he asked, seemingly unphased.

"I left husband, home, and responsibilities, just so you could throw my empty womb IN MY FACE?"

"YOU DARE RAISE YOUR VOICE TO YOUR FATHER?" Potiphera thundered.

Her voice laced with an icy coolness, Asenath responded, "A father would not do what you did." She looked at her father, completely devoid of any fear of him. As her head shook from side to side, a bitter laugh escaped her lips. "The irony. I was nearly sick at the thought of harm coming to you, yet you wound me without a second thought. I have looked back at my life many times since becoming a wife, and somewhere deep within me I believed you loved me, but perhaps did not know how to show it. I was mistaken. It is an error I will never repeat." Turning her back on him, she began walking away.

"Asenath! Think about this: no woman in the lineage of your father has ever been childless. For none was foolish enough to forsake the favor of our gods!"

Except me. I am the fool. Heart pounding, she strode hastily out of his chamber and headed straight for the women's quarters. But she never made it there. Standing in their luxurious guest chamber was a sight that only rubbed salt in her fresh wounds: Na'eemah, Heqaib, and a heavily pregnant Semat, wearing a fertility amulet.

"You were all privy to this." It was a statement; the question, unnecessary. The guilty expressions on their faces were answer enough. Anger, hurt, and frustration battled for the first place in the fierce race of emotions within her soul.

Na'eemah responded first. "I tried to warn you before you—"

"You should have warned me before I ever left my home!"

Heqaib chimed in softly. "You know you would not have come —"

"Stay out of this, Heqaib! You are a *man*; you will NEVER understand!" Fixing her eyes on Semat, Asenath asked softly. "How could you?"

"I am sorry, my la—Your Eminence. I did not want anyone to deceive you, but how could I stop them when we saw no other way to help you?"

"I never thought I would see the day when you would betray me, Semat. Them, maybe, but not you."

Semat's eyes lowered. "Forgive me, Your Eminence, please. I only want—"

"What is best for me? Well, that is not for you to decide." Asenath turned and began storming away. She wanted to get away from all of them—to be alone and clear her head.

A deep, agonizing groan from Semat stopped her in her tracks. The sound raised every hair on the back of her neck.

"What is it, my love?" she heard Heqaib ask his wife. As she turned around, two things registered:

One, Semat was grabbing her enormous belly with both hands.

Two, the marble floor underneath Semat was freshly wet.

"The baby comes!" Na'eemah said, alarm heightening her pitch.

"Now?" Heqaib asked, panicking. "No. I must take her home."

"There is no time; she has to have it here." Not until three pairs of eyes fixed on Asenath, did she realize she had voiced her thought. Shifting her gaze to her ever-present handmaiden, she said, "Do not just stand there, Merit. Go and prepare my chamber—it has the most light." As Merit hurried away, she turned to face the father-to-be. "Now would be a good time to get the midwife, just in case." Semat groaned again, and Heqaib looked torn.

"We will take care of her, son. Just hurry," Na'eemah said, trying to hold Semat's full weight.

Asenath took Semat's hand from Heqaib and placed her former handmaiden's arm around her own shoulder, her fury suddenly forgotten.

***

Twins. Asenath stood in the chamber she had practically grown up in, watching the new mother and father each hold a son. Heqaib and Semat were speechless with a joy and wonder that Asenath knew she could not describe, and feared she may never experience. She did not know whether to laugh or cry. This day had unleashed a whirlwind of emotions.

"Your Eminence," Semat said, extending a hand out in invitation.

Asenath walked to her side and took her hand.

"Would you like to hold him?"

Asenath nodded and took the baby gingerly in her arms. *He is perfect.*

"Thank you," Semat said, her eyes misty. "Were it not for Your Eminence, I would never have known this joy."

Asenath nodded, too emotional to speak. She fully grasped the gravity of Semat's gratitude. Before Heqaib had returned with the midwife, she and Na'eemah had already seen both boys safely ushered into this world. But beyond that, it was her bold missive that had inspired Heqaib's reciprocity of Semat's love. By his own admission, her words had helped him see what a prize the doe-eyed, kindhearted girl was.

After a brief silence, Semat added, "Forgive me, and know that all I want is for Your Eminence to know the same joy. Please, let us help."

"I forgive you, Semat. And I too, apologize. But let us not speak of sorrows in so joyous a moment. You are a mother; of twin sons, no less! What shall you call them?" she asked, handing the baby back to his mother.

"Meriiti," Heqaib answered, looking at the baby in his arms.

'Beloved of the father,' Asenath thought, smiling.

"And? . . ." The new father asked, raising his eyes towards his wife.

Looking from the baby in her arms to her husband, and back, she said, "You are the mirror image of your father. I call you, 'Inyotef.'"

'Whom his father brought.' How apt.

"Befitting names for my grandsons," Na'eemah said, gushing.

"Long live Meriiti and Inyotef," Asenath said. "May they have the strength of their father, and the sweetness of their mother."

"May they also have their grandmother's wisdom," Na'eemah added.

"And their father's irresistible charm."

Asenath rolled her eyes. "In that case, Semat, good luck handling not two, but four inflated heads!"

The room rang with laughter. It was enough for the moment, but it did not stop seeds of doubt from taking root in Asenath's soul.

***

Joseph's wife had returned from Heliopolis three days ago, and filled him in on her surprise-laden visit, but she had yet to sleep in his chamber. He had every intention that they would spend tonight together. If she would not invite herself to his chamber, he had no qualms about doing the reverse. To that end, he had returned home slightly earlier than usual, with a head full of romantic ideas. One in particular now propelled him into her chamber, unannounced.

"I take it my wife is yet to return?"

"Your Eminence!" said the startled handmaiden, jumping to her feet.

"I apologize for alarming you, Merit."

She dipped her head, "Forgive me, Your Eminence. No, she has not returned. Blessings of the evening."

"And to you. Now, here is what I want you to do . . . "

Having given detailed instructions, Joseph positioned himself somewhere where his wife would least expect him to be this night. Imagining her reaction to his presence made his indefinite time of waiting pass quicker. He was just contemplating a change of position when he heard footsteps.

She is here!

The sight of his wife casually strolling into her private bathhouse made his pulse pick up pace. Oblivious to his presence, she slipped out of her loose linen *kalasiris* and slowly began stretching her slender, unclad frame. Joseph temporarily held his breath, mesmerized by her lithe, deliberate movements. *And I thought I was the one that would be handing out the pleasant surprise tonight.* He let out a slow, silent breath, sure that the sound of his now wildly beating heart would give him away at any moment.

Unfurling herself from her final position, Asenath slowly eased into the steaming bath waters. From the aroma of the mist, she was immersed in goat's milk and lemon grass, among other things.

Her show is over, Joseph. Your turn. He gave a single, gentle clearing of his throat.

Not bothering to open her eyes, Asenath said, "Enter Merit, and I hope you brought a strong cloth because I need it tonight."

"Will some strong arms do?" Joseph asked, smiling.

Asenath sat up and spun around instantly. "Beloved!"

Her eyes could not have been any wider as they took him in from scalp to soles at one glance. Clearly, the fact that he was casually leaning back against a wall in her bathhouse, wearing nothing but a tiny white *shendyt,* had the desired effect.

"What are you—How long have you been standing there?"

"Long enough to appreciate the divine creator's exquisite handiwork."

She bit her lip and lowered her eyes, which only broadened his already wide smile.

"I instructed Merit to draw you a bath," Joseph said, easing himself off the wall, and slowly walking toward her.

"*You* did!"

"I thought you might need one. Was I wrong?"

She briskly shook her head from side to side, her dancing curls dolling out droplets of water.

He paused and gave an exaggerated bow. "I hope Her Eminence is willing to make do with my assistance tonight; Merit will not be back anytime soon."

He had not thought it possible for her eyes to get any bigger, but they did. "She told me she was retrieving a washcloth."

"I know," he said, pulling out a washcloth tucked into the low waistline of his *shendyt* and twirling it.

She visibly swallowed.

He reached her in two more strides and kneeled beside the bath. After dipping the cloth in the warm water, he held it close enough to her skin so the drops of water began falling on her shoulder without him touching her yet. "May I?"

She tilted her head and gave the briefest flutter of her long, wet lashes, before nodding.

Joseph needed no further invitation. Placing one hand on her back, he used the cloth in the other to rub her flawless skin. His touch was gentle at first. Then, with increasing pressure, he moved the cloth in circular motions on her back.

She uttered a wordless sound of pleasure that intensified his breathing. He moved to her shoulders next. Then, making his way around, he bathed her chest. Her breathing was fast, catching up to the intensity of his.

Leaning in till his lips were almost touching her ear, he whispered, "I could do this a lot better if I was in there with you."

"No!" Asenath said, pulling away from him with a speed that simultaneously stunned and stung.

"No?" Joseph asked, puzzled.

She avoided his eyes. "I mean, no need to get yourself entirely wet, when you are already doing a better job than Merit."

Something is amiss. Joseph dropped the cloth and sat on the wet floor. "What is wrong?"

"Nothing," Asenath said, averting her eyes from his.

He cupped her wet face in his hand. "Look at me, my purple iris."

When her eyes met his, the pain in them twisted his heart into a knot. "You have never lied to me before. Please do not begin now. You have been back three nights, and we have spent them apart, for one reason or another. Now you refuse to let me in there with you. Either I have inadvertently done something to hurt you or something else happened in Heliopolis that you are keeping from me. Which is it?"

"I am sorry, Beloved." Her voice was barely above a whisper.

"For what exactly are you sorry?"

"Promise me you will not be angry."

"I cannot make an uninformed promise. But I do promise to listen."

"Twins. Semat had twins, Beloved, in under a year of marriage. She gave me what she used because she loves me, and I took them because I could not argue with the evidence."

"Took what?"

"An ointment. To rub on my belly for ten days, before spending the night with you."

Ten days? "That is why you have been avoiding me."

"Yes."

"Why did you not tell me?"

"Because I was afraid."

"Of what?"

"Of what you would do when you saw this." Asenath lifted her right leg out of the bath.

No! Joseph sucked in his breath. There, glistening on her ankle, was a fertility amulet.

"What have you done, Asenath? You told me you did not take your father's gift."

"I did not," she said, dropping her leg swiftly. "This was Semat's. She begged me to try it for a few months. What harm could it do, Beloved?" she asked, her eyes pleading.

Joseph fell to his knees and bowed his face to the ground. *O Lord, have mercy, she knows not what she does.* Raising his face to hers, he said simply, "You have to destroy it. I have never hidden the fact that I will permit no graven images or idol worship in my home."

Asenath raised herself to a kneeling position. "I am not worshiping any idols, I promise! I just need the favor of Isis to bear you a child, and that is all."

"No, you do not! You need the blessing of the invisible God and He will NOT bless unfaithfulness."

"What if He does not bless me? Or, worse, is not strong enough to undo what Ra has done?"

"What has Ra done?"

"Father said no other woman in our lineage has ever been barren, as none was foolish enough to forsake the favor of the gods. Except me. And now I am the fool whose womb Ra has closed. Do you not see? I have to appease him," Asenath said, her eyes brimming with tears.

Lord God, have mercy. Joseph rose and paced silently. *I cannot believe she would do this. Clearly, I have failed to provide the right guidance. Help me now, to look past my frustration and speak with wisdom and grace.* He was still pacing when she made her next appeal.

"Please, Beloved. You do not know what it feels like to watch the women I love become mothers while I remain childless."

He stopped and looked at her. "You are still young. There is plenty of time for you to bear children."

She threw her hands up and shook her head. "I cannot! I am barren."

Joseph's heart stopped. *Barren?* "What are you not telling me?"

Tears streaming down her face, she answered in a shaky voice. "I saw a physician while I was there. An expert on women's matters. He said my womb is blocked. He also said he has been seeing cases for three decades, and mine is beyond human solutions. Do you not see? I need divine intervention or I will NEVER be a mother."

No, Lord. A sigh escaped his lips. He went back and kneeled beside her, taking her hand. "You should have told me."

"I am sorry," she said, her head hung.

"IF you need divine intervention, there is no god more powerful than the invisible God."

She looked at him doubtfully. "How can you be so sure?"

"How can you doubt?" He asked, releasing her and spreading his arms wide. "He is omnipotent. He sits in the heavens with the whole earth as a footstool. He set the hours for sunrise and sunset and has never once been late. He exists outside of time, yet controls times and seasons. He made my one-hundred-year-old great-grandfather and his barren, ninety-year-old wife, parents. And what about me?" He asked, placing a hand on his bare chest. "He transformed me from a hopeless prisoner to Egypt's vizier in a moment."

He let his arms drop to his sides, and continued speaking, "Are you so quick to forget that even when you did not yet know him, he loved you enough to hear your cry, and give you the sign you asked for? Why would he now withhold any good thing from you? He never forsakes us, Asenath, yet he is the only God who gives his own the free will to forsake him."

"And you think by temporarily trying to appease Ra, I forsake him?"

Looking directly into her saddened eyes, he answered. "You cannot serve two masters, Asenath. And the invisible God is a jealous God. He would no sooner bless idolatry than a man would endorse his wife's harlotry."

She recoiled. "Harlotry! I have never—"

"Not against me. But how would you feel if I brought another woman into my bed and made you watch while I took pleasure in her?"

Asenath gasped. "You would not—"

"Never. But how you feel at the thought of that is how the invisible God feels about you appeasing another god."

Asenath crumbled into the bath. "Then He will NEVER forgive me, let alone give me a child."

"Yes, He will." Joseph reached in and took her hands. "We shall fast, and pray, and petition him to forgive us and open your womb."

"Forgive me for the weakness of my faith, but what if he does not? I want you to have children, Beloved, even if you do not have them by me."

"What are you saying?"

She swallowed. "Your father had twelve sons, and only two of those came from your mother."

"And I intend to emulate my father's faith, not his faults."

He held her face in both of his hands, hoping she could see into his soul. "Hear me well when I say this: I would rather die than give myself to another woman, or another God."

He registered the widening of her eyes before releasing her. Rising, he turned away and bowed his head as tears threatened. *Lord, what more can I say?*

The swishing of the water indicated she was emerging from the bath, but he did not turn around. Her wet torso came into view, and then her whole bent frame as she kneeled and placed her head on his feet.

"Forgive me, Beloved."

O my heart! Leaning over, he took her arms and pulled her to her feet. Placing his hands on her shoulders he said, "I love YOU, do you not understand? I can live without children, but please, do not ask me to live without you." *Lord please, forgive. Have mercy.*

Her arms broke out in gooseflesh, as she looked at him, mystified. "I do not even deserve you. Why would I ever leave you?"

"My father never thought my mother would leave him," he said, quietly.

"And you fear my demise might be like hers?"

Yes, but not for the reasons you think. Joseph sighed and took a step back. "It is true she died birthing Benjamin, but there is more to the story." Running his hand over his bald head, he turned away from her slightly, looking at nothing in particular. "My father told me that after she died, they found her father's idols in her tent. And only a few months before then, her father, Laban, had chased my father and his whole family and accused my father of stealing his idols. My father was so indignant, and sure that all in his household served his God with a whole heart, that he had declared the person who stole the idols would die. He had let Laban search the entire camp, but the idols were never found. My father remembers that my mother had never risen to allow her camel to be searched—she had used her time of the month as an excuse.

"The invisible God did not revoke my father's pronouncement, not because he lacked the power to do so but because he not only hates idolatry, he is a just God, and a curse with a cause must stand.

Thus . . . my mother died." He said, his voice breaking, as a tear ran down his cheek.

When he turned to look at her, her face was not only wet, it was ashen.

"I lost my mother to idolatry. I . . . I cannot lose you too."

When she began to shiver, he knew it was not merely due to her being both wet and naked. The fear in her eyes told him the chill within her far exceeded that without. He wrapped his arms around her and held her shaking form silently.

Lord have mercy.

23

The hand that had to labor
For every drop of love
Mistrusts the heart that offers
Love's ocean, freely

***

D awning.
Before the sun had arisen, a rather sober couple found themselves at their garden altar. Were it not for the fire that blazed from the heart of it, it would have been unbearably cold. Not a drop of liquid nor a morsel of food had passed either of their lips, nor would it until dusk. Joseph had not been jesting when he spoke of their praying and fasting. He had made arrangements to have only the most pressing matters of state brought to him at home today. Asenath was grateful for his presence, for she was still uncertain about how to effectively appease an unseen God.

She watched Joseph kneel at the foot of the altar and did the same. When he bowed his face to the ground, she mimicked his gesture, genuinely sorrowful. She listened as his rich voice rose in supplication.

"Most holy and righteous God, we are honored to call upon your name today. Look upon your servants with mercy this day. We have sinned against you and you alone and we plead you forgive us. We repent for the sin of idolatry, and for its root causes: fear, and doubt as to your loving-kindness and your awesome might. Were you to weigh us in the balance, we would fall short. So we ask that out of your tender mercies you forgive us, O Lord . . ."

Forgive me, O Lord, it is I who have sinned, not him.

"And if we may indeed once again find favor in your sight, I make but one request, O Lord. That you, who blessed me in a strange land with a wife who desires to know you, would make her a joyful mother of children. That you would anoint her with the oil of gladness, instead of the garment of sorrow. And give her beauty where she has only seen ashes. God of my *abba* and *saba*, you have shown me that nothing is too hard for you. Show my wife the same, once again. We vow to serve no other gods, and to give you and you alone the glory, both now and forevermore."

His voice drifted off. Only the crackling of the fire could be heard for a few moments, and then she felt his hand lightly rest on her shoulder.

"Do you wish to add anything?" he asked.

She lifted her head and reached for a small bundle beside her. She unwrapped it and showed him its contents. Eyes misty, he inclined his head toward the fire. She rose and threw the ointment and the anklet into the flames. Returning to her knees, she bowed her head and added her words to their prayer of agreement.

"I am deeply sorry, O Lord. Please forgive me for it is I who have sinned. If it pleases you, spare my life, and let it be unto me according to all your servant, my husband, has said."

"So let it be," Joseph said, and she softly echoed him.

"So let it be."

She heard his voice ring loud, in a Hebrew song of praise. Looking at him, she saw his hands were lifted skyward, and she mirrored his gesture, closing her eyes. As he sang, a warm tingle slowly spread from her head down through her entire body. She opened her eyes and glanced around, but saw nothing to explain the sensation. It was incredibly soothing. She felt the heaviness in her heart lifting. *What is this? It feels like . . . liquid peace.* She did not know if there was such a thing. But long after they had left the altar, that warm feeling stayed with her.

The next dawn, Asenath returned to the altar alone, repeating the petition her husband had made on her behalf. This time, she experienced no warmth; contrarily, she felt uneasy. The morning after, the same action produced the same results, more worry and less peace. The fourth morning was no different, and once again, she was at the altar alone.

It was clear by then that Joseph believed the Lord had forgiven them the moment they offered their petition, and so he considered the matter forgotten. For him, everything had returned to normal. But to Asenath, one day of fasting and prayer was too small a price to pay to earn the forgiveness of any deity.

Her husband's forgiveness, she did not doubt receiving. It almost seemed like her misstep and their resulting vulnerability had only brought them closer. They were naked and unashamed before each other, physically and emotionally. They had since rekindled the flames of their love. In fact, if they burned any brighter, she and Joseph would surely be consumed. Asenath had a newfound confidence in her husband's love. The words "*I would rather die than give myself to another woman . . .*" had decimated every sliver of doubt in her. Joseph loved her and would never leave her, of that she was certain. Whether the invisible God would forgive her and grant her heart's desire was another matter altogether. But she did not intend to miss one morning of petitioning him until she got irrefutable evidence to that end. Joseph may have faith in the Lord's mercy, but Asenath had been born to a lineage of priests, and she had never known any god that did not mandate penance for sins. Somewhere deep within her, she was anxiously anticipating the price the invisible God would demand from her.

***

By the twenty-eighth dawn, Asenath had begun to doubt her doubts. And by that afternoon, any uneasiness she had felt at the altar earlier had been completely forgotten. Grinning from ear to ear, she watched her most entertaining student with rapt attention. Patareshnes, the thirty-ninth wife of Pharaoh, could talk the scales off a fish and apparently housed more stories than the palace chronicles.

"A woman will do anything to hide her treasures, especially from a greedy husband," said the slender, flaxen-haired royal.

"I can only imagine," Asenath said.

"Thank the gods for your fortune! Just the other day, Neheb shared that his mother went as far as stitching her jewels into the curtain hems, just so her drunkard of a husband would not trade them for wine!" Patareshnes laughed heartily, her blue eyes watering.

"Surely you jest!"

"Indeed, I do not! How the woman came up with that idea, I shall never know. But the picture of it gives me no end of amusement!"

"It appears necessity births genius!"

"Hear, hear! And the grape never falls far from the vine—Neheb hides things better than a magician!"

"A great skill for the assistant keeper of the royal wives to have. Would Her Magnificence not agree?"

"Invaluable!"

"Blessings of the day to you both," a honeyed voice said.

The two women turned to see Neferubity.

"Perhaps I should return at a less busy time?" the Nubian warrior asked.

"No need," said Patareshnes, rising. "Now that I have talked the ear off Her Eminence, it is time to find another one." She straightened her formfitting *kalasiris* with a heavily bejeweled hand.

"What Her Magnificence means is her lesson is over, so you are not interrupting," Asenath said, smiling. "Please, come in."

Neferubity strode in with her head held high.

"Allow me to present Her Radiance Neferubity, daughter of Panehesy, King of Nubia."

"And this is Her Magnificence Patareshness, thirty-ninth wife of Pharaoh, lord of Egypt—long may he live."

"I am pleased to make Your Magnificence's acquaintance," Neferubity said politely.

"As am I, Your Radiance. Any friend of Asenath's is welcome in my—"

"Blessings of the day upon all, and pardon the intrusion," Aneski interrupted, striding briskly into the chamber. Without waiting for any responses, she fixed her eyes on Asenath. "I am here but a moment to inform you I will no longer be needing your services. I have more important ventures upon which to spend my time."

"I am sorry to hear that, Your Magnificence," Asenath responded.

"No need to be," Aneski answered flippantly.

"That is a striking *usekh*, Aneksi. I am sure I have not seen it on you before," Patareshness said, stepping closer to Aneksi to examine the necklace more closely.

"Indeed, you have not, Patareshness," Aneksi retorted, stepping out of her reach.

"I believe I have," Neferubity said, an unusually stony expression on her face.

"When?" Aneksi asked, a startled look on her face.

"Our chambers are across from each other. We crossed paths in the hallway earlier," Neferubity answered.

"I had not realized," Aneksi said coolly.

"So I gather. That is a turquoise, is it not? Where might one get such a stunning piece of jewelry?" the Nubian princess asked.

"One might not. It is one of a kind."

"A gift?" Patareshness asked, ever-eager for gossip.

"Not that it is any of your concern, but yes. Obviously Pharaoh, lord of Egypt—long may he live—considers me worthy of it, since he gifted it to me."

"Then your womanly arsenal surely boasts some secret weapons! Inclined to share?"

"Secret weapons? Nonsense! I have nothing to hide. But enough of this inquisition. I have a beauty regimen to complete and no time to waste. I merely came to dismiss Asenath in person as a courtesy. You may carry on as you were before I interrupted."

Dismiss me? Someone awakened on the arrogant side of her bed today. "How generous of Your Magnificence," Asenath said evenly.

As Aneski hurried out of the chamber, Patareshness said, "I do believe Aneksi may have sprouted horns on that empty head of hers!"

The reactions to such a bold insult were immediate:

Asenath inadvertently snorted, clamping a hand over her mouth.

Neferubity gasped, her jaw slackening as she fixed wide, brown eyes on the brazen royal.

"Do not look at me so. I have known her since childhood," Patareshness said, eyeing Neferubity. Shifting her gaze back and forth between the two sun-kissed beauties, she continued. "We are distantly related on my father's side, not that I am inclined to noise that fact about. Unless I am mistaken, which I am not, tonight is her night with His Divine Magnificence. I fail to see why that is newsworthy; we all have at least three nights with him yearly. If anyone has something to boast about, it is the woman who holds the record for the most nights with His Divine Magnificence in the same year," she said, thrice-rolling her wrist while giving an exaggerated bow.

"Impressive!" Asenath said.

"You flatter me. On that note, I bid you both blessings of the day!"

"And to you as well. I look forward to seeing you next week," Asenath said, turning to find Neferubity's bronze brow deeply furrowed. "Care to share what troubles you?"

"I cannot profess fondness for the redhead."

"Aneksi? She probably just had a rough night; she is harmless."

"Take it from a warrior—there is no such thing as a harmless woman."

"A valid point! But do not take offense with her on my account. I certainly did not. Pray tell, to what do I owe the pleasure of your presence here?"

"I came to inform you about an unexpected visit I received from the captain of the king's guard yesterday. He came to speak with me about a strategy for schooling the royal children on swordsmanship. I was wondering if you knew where he would get an idea like that," she said, her dark brown eyes gleaming.

"Me? What do I know about swordplay? I am but the humble wife of our vizier," Asenath teased.

"Indeed!"

"In all seriousness, I am thrilled at your news. No doubt you will have those children fighting better than the king's guards in no time!"

Neferubity's expression sobered. "I am really here to extend my profound gratitude."

"Then you are speaking to the wrong person. I merely mentioned the idea and thought nothing more of it. It is my husband you should thank."

"Then please, let His Eminence know that I am in his debt. If there is ever anything I can do for either of you, do not hesitate to ask."

"He will receive your message, but I know he will say you owe us nothing. All I ask is that you return those pampered children to their mothers in one piece!"

"I shall keep that in mind. There is something else that occupies my thoughts at the moment; might be something, might be nothing, but—"

"Pardon the intrusion, Your Eminence. His Eminence asked that this be delivered to you," said a guard bearing a scroll.

As Asenath read the missive, she could not stop the smile that brightened her face. "Thank you, tell His Eminence his message is well received." The guard bowed and exited the chamber.

"Good news?"

"It appears our illustrious vizier has just invited me to a garden dinner tonight."

"Heavens! You are the envy of all of us loveless women."

She is unhappy. "Forgive me, I did not mean to flaunt—"

"No need to apologize. Pharaoh may not have called me to his chamber yet, but I assure you, I consider that a cause for joy! I hope he never does! But enough about me. What shall you wear tonight?"

"I have hardly even given it a thought."

"May I suggest your emerald *kalasiris*, it brings out your eyes."

Asenath was astonished. "How could you even know that? I have probably not worn that in—"

"A fortnight and five days."

What? "I see you are a sorcerer pretending to be a warrior."

Neferubity's laughter rang like the tinkling of tiny bells. "If only. I merely have the eye of an eagle, and the memory of an elephant. 'Tis a gift, and a curse."

"Remind me never to make an enemy of you."

"As long as you remember to relay my gratitude to your husband tonight, sometime before you lose yourself in his charms."

"Lest I forget—you started to mention something earlier, before the interruption."

"Another time, perhaps. You go, and be sure to hold on tightly to that man of yours."

"Such is the beauty of his love: I hold no fears of ever losing it. Not in sickness or soundness, luxury or lack, storm or shine. Nothing but death could ever part us."

"Then may the number of your matrimonial years exceed that of Pharaoh's wives!"

"So be it! Blessings of the evening to you, Neferubity," Asenath said with a smile and a dip of her head.

Neferubity returned the gesture with the slightest of bows. "To you as well, Asenath." The Nubian exited the chamber with the effortless stealth of a cat. Left alone to speculate about what the night held in store, Asenath hummed the notes to the lover's tune and did a short sequence of *Raqs Baladi* footwork.

***

Asenath was almost at the end of the long hallway in the west wing of her home when she noticed little bursts of color on the gleaming floor. Purple iris petals formed a bright pathway leading up to the door of the grandest hall in her home. *A formal dining invitation and dinner in our official feasting chambers? This is going to be a special night indeed.* Asenath was glad she had taken Neferubity's advice to take extra care with her attire this evening. Pausing for a moment to fill her lungs with the fragrant air, she adjusted her *usekh*, and nodded to the attending guards. They pushed open the double doors, after which she took three steps in and froze. The sight before her was utterly unexpected.

Their formal dining chamber was gone. In its place was an enchanting, beautifully lit indoor garden. Bouquets of flowers hung from censors in every corner of the hall. Strategically positioned lamps made a circle of lights on the floor, giving the room a refreshing warmth that contrasted the weather outdoors. And in the heart of the ring of light, was an intimate place setting for two, beside which stood her beloved husband, looking even more handsome than the night they first met. Asenath strode toward him slowly, unable to restrain her broad smile.

***

Joseph watched his smiling wife walk toward him, his heart speeding up with her every step closer. She was beautiful at any given moment, but tonight she was glowing. Parted down the middle, her hair cascaded like a waterfall of curls from the top of her head to the small of her back. Her emerald attire clung to her every curve. The amber stone in her *usekh* matched her perfectly lined eyes, but more than that, it warmed his heart. She could have adorned herself with any other jewel, yet she had chosen to wear that one—his gift to her on her eighteenth birthday.

"You steal the very breath from my being, my purple iris."

"As you do, the words from my mouth, Beloved."

Joseph cupped her face and kissed her lips softly. Only when he gestured toward their seating did she notice it had been arranged such that they reclined side by side, rather than across from each other. Instead of the feast being between them, it was spread out in two halves: Egyptian delicacies beside her, and Hebrew appetizers beside him. Gracefully lowering herself onto the animal skin rug, she leaned back onto the plush cushions and watched her husband do the same.

"Beloved, this is . . . breathtaking. To what do I owe the pleasure?"

"To the mysterious manner of a man with a mesmerizing maiden."

"Mesmerizing?"

"Utterly."

"Hmm, is that all?"

"No, I wanted you to know you are immensely loved. Nothing you can do will ever make me love you less. You need do nothing to earn my favor, for I would never withhold anything in my power to give you. And though I may do things to demonstrate my love more, I cannot actually love you more, for you have all of my heart, yesterday, today and for all our tomorrows."

"O Beloved, I love you too, absolutely. I never tire of hearing you profess your love for me, but I am curious. What inspired all of this?"

"A truth I want you to ponder long after tonight: if I, an imperfect man, feel this way, how much more does a perfect God love you?"

Asenath was silent, letting his words and the truth in them sink in.

Joseph picked up his goblet and raised it. "To the love of my life."

"To the love of MY life," Asenath echoed, raising her glass.

They took sips of the sweet wine, and then Joseph raised a hand and snapped his fingers. Seemingly out of thin air, servers emerged to dish out their meal, as the room was filled with the soft melody of strings being strummed skillfully. Asenath searched out the source of the sound and picked out a lone harpist in the far corner of the room, behind a sheer curtain. Joseph had thought of everything.

"I do not know about you, but I am famished. I was so occupied I missed the afternoon meal." Joseph said, digging into a moist piece of roasted duck.

"Whatever with?" Asenath asked, scooping a spoonful of roasted vegetables.

"A riddle of all things."

"A riddle?"

"Masqueraded as an anonymous letter that mysteriously made its way to my desk late this afternoon."

"Have you solved this riddle?"

"No. And I may not have given it a second thought were it not for a dream I had this morning. In fact, wanting to tell you about it was how I noticed your absence from beside me this dawn. Based on a foreboding that has lingered all day, I have a feeling the dream and the riddle are connected to each other."

"Tell me more," Asenath said, putting her utensil down.

"This evening is not supposed to be about work, or me. But you."

"Well, I, the guest of honor, would like to hear about these mysteries. Details, if you please."

"Well, you could stop by my receiving chambers tomorrow, and take a look at that puzzle of a letter for yourself . . . "

Asenath clapped her hands gleefully.

"And in that case, I will share the dream, on one condition."

"Name it."

"You keep eating."

Asenath picked up a steaming bowl of lentil and vegetable soup and stuffed three large spoonfuls into her mouth. Cheeks bulging, she chewed, her eyes fixed upon him in eager anticipation.

24

Foolish
Many think it
To pen a hopeless dream
Only faith perceives what it is:
Wisdom

***

A mused.

Joseph's hearty laughter filled the room. "A more eager or attentive audience no storyteller could hope to find in nine lifetimes!"

My overstuffed, vigorously moving mouth must make for quite a comical sight, Asenath thought. Cupping her left ear, she kept on chewing, her lips far too occupied with keeping morsels contained to break into anything more than a faint smile.

Dropping his utensil, Joseph cleared his throat. He took a sip of wine, before launching into a recounting of his latest vision of the night. "It was a still, starry night and I found myself on the banks of the Nile, when suddenly, a strange being emerged from the dark waters. It had the head of an enormous cobra, with an upper body formed like man's except it appeared to be covered in golden, fishlike scales. What resembled an eagle's wings sprouted from its back, but while the right wing had white feathers, the left had black ones. I could hardly decide if the creature was flying or floating, for its lower half was submerged beneath the river. Much to my alarm, it began to move abruptly from side to side."

Intriguing. Asenath's left brow involuntarily raised itself as she reached for a moist piece of roasted duck.

She noticed her husband watching her chew it, before he asked. "Tasty?"

"See for yourself," she said, picking up another piece and holding it up to his face. His lips took it from her fingers, without breaking their eye contact.

After chewing briefly, he said, "Very tasty."

"Go on."

"I fear I have lost my train of thought."

Asenath chuckled. "The being; shaking from side to side?"

"Yes! Furiously. Its left wing flapped as it floated to the left; then the right wing flapped, and it sailed in the opposite direction. Suddenly, it swung out both arms and they began to vibrate. They shook so hard that the golden scales fell off, revealing the left arm was made of copper, and the right formed from gleaming, precious stones. Without warning, this unearthly creature swung its right arm inward, wrapped its copper fingers around its own serpentine neck and began to choke itself!"

"What?"

"Believe me, I was as bewildered as you are, especially when the snakelike eyes bulged out of its pointed cobra head. But then the jeweled right arm swung toward its neck, grabbed the copper wrist and began to twist it. The creature fought itself for a few moments, then I heard a loud crack, and the copper hand hung limply off a broken wrist. Now saved, the serpent head turned a forked tongue and struck its own left arm."

"I cannot fault it in that regard. What happened to the poisoned arm?"

"It exploded into an innumerable amount of tiny copper fragments that fell into the river. The right arm reached for the now armless left shoulder and held it as the creature dove into the waters. I thought that was all, but momentarily, it sprang back up, hissing furiously, a new left arm in place as sparkling as the right one. It spread out both wings, which now boasted purely white feathers, and flew into the dark sky," Joseph ended, reaching for another bite of the roast duck.

"Most mysterious. What does it mean?"

He swallowed before answering. "No meaning has come to mind, but I suspect an internal power struggle of sorts."

"A secret *you* cannot reveal?"

He smiled. "I never claimed I was the revealer of secrets. His Divine Magnificence did."

"Valid point."

"The Lord will reveal it in his time. But enough about other matters. Let us talk about you."

"What about me?"

"I have something for you. But before I give it, I need you to answer me one question."

"Ask anything."

"You can take your time, but tell me, what would you name your firstborn?"

Firstborn? Asenath's heart stopped. "You jest, surely."

"I do not," He said, softly.

Asenath dropped her utensil. "You choose this moment to remind me of my shame?"

"No! Never. I merely hoped to ignite your faith."

"How so?" she asked, crossing her arms over her chest.

"As the stars in the sky and the sand of the shore, so shall your seed be."

"What the invisible God said to your great-grandfather, Abraham."

"While he was still *Abram*, and childless, no less."

She lowered her arms and crossed her legs, fully facing him. "You have my ears."

He imitated her posture, so they were face to face, then he took both her hands in his. "The Lord gave Abram a picture of his future. One he would see whether he looked up or down, and no matter where he found himself, so that his faith would not waver in the face of a mountain of doubt. I want you to have such a picture. A faith vision; written in plain sight." Releasing her right hand, he snapped his fingers, and a servant approached with a cloth-covered dish and set it beside him. He lifted the cloth to reveal a small scroll and a reed pen.

She looked from the scroll to her husband. "You want me to write the answer to your question."

He smiled. "Precisely."

She picked up the blank parchment and held it silently, her head bowed. Raising teary eyes to his, she asked, "Do you really think the Lord would give me such a gift as to be a mother?"

Without a moment's hesitation, he answered. "I do."

"How can you be so confident?"

"Because the Lord is unchanging, and His loving-kindness is to a thousand generations. If I carry the blessing of my forefathers, then you possess the promise of their wives. As He empowered Sarah, Rebecca, and Rachel to be fruitful and multiply, so will He empower you."

Picking up the reed pen, she dipped it in ink, and then looked at him hesitantly.

He inclined his head.

She bit her bottom lip.

"Tell me," he said.

"I do not know whether to write a boy's name or a girl's."

Joseph laughed. "Write both."

"Egyptian or Hebrew?"

"Good question. What do you think?"

"Hebrew."

"Why?"

"I want our children to have the faith of their father, and their forefathers."

Joseph smiled. "As long as they have your wit, beauty, and grace."

Beaming, Asenath said, "Then I think, Natanya? For a girl."

"'*Gift of God*.' Befitting. And a boy?"

"The son that makes me forget my shame? . . . Manasseh."

"Manasseh. I like that even better."

"Because you want a son, correct?"

"Not just that," he said, his face sobering as a distant look filled his eyes. "You are not the only one who carries a sorrow sooner forgotten."

His brothers' betrayal.

Replacing her pen in its ink jar, Asenath took his hand in hers. "Do you wish to speak about them?"

"When nothing good can be said, it is best to remain silent."

She squeezed his hand reassuringly before letting it go. Retrieving her pen, she wrote on the papyrus. The room was silent, save for the soft sound of music. When she was done, she lifted the parchment and turned it facing Joseph. He smiled.

"As you have written, so let it be."

She raised her goblet, "To the Lord causing us both to forget."

Raising his chalice, her husband echoed her toast, "To forgetting."

Asenath laid her goblet aside and fixed her gaze on Joseph. "Beloved . . . "

He looked at her, trying to read her mysterious expression. She leaned in, the curve of her chin almost resting on the crook of his neck, and whispered three words: "Clear the room." Leaning back, she took in the rapid succession of emotions on his face: Surprise. Delight. Desire.

Not waiting to be told a second time, he clapped his hands and ordered. "Leave us, all of you. No one is to enter this chamber until we exit it." Once the last servant exited, Joseph turned to his wife, "As Her Eminence ordered."

"Excellent. Now, if His Eminence would be so kind as to hand me his tunic."

Joseph sat up and shed his outer garment, leaving only a small shendyt around his waist. Picking up a single purple iris petal, she began brushing it in whimsical arches, tracing the defined muscles on his torso from his chest down to his abdomen. And there, as softly as a feather's landing, she placed a kiss.

She heard him suck in a breath.

Raising her eyes to meet his, she unclasped the single strap on her *kalasiris*, and let the fabric fall off her torso. Right as he leaned in toward her, the chamber doors burst open.

Asenath gasped. She was not sure which was more forceful; the doors slamming against the walls or her husband, crushing her chest against his, and flinging his arms protectively around her bare torso.

"Who DARES enter against my command?" Joseph yelled.

"Forgive the intrusion, Your Eminence," said Wadjenes, keeping his head bowed low. "Your presence is requested immediately. There has been an attempt on His Divine Magnificence's life."

Someone attempted to kill Pharaoh?

She felt her husband's arms stiffen around her, even as he gave his next order. "Saddle my steed."

Wadjenes left immediately, and Joseph released her. Before she could refasten her garment, he was dressed.

"I am coming with you," she said, pushing herself to her knees.

"No. The palace will be on high alert—it is best you stay," he said in a quelling tone. Offering a hand, he pulled her to her feet, and said more softly. "I hope to find you in my chamber when I return—so I can finish what you started." He winked, turned around, and ran for the doors.

She smiled. *He may be a dedicated servant of the invisible God, and the vizier of all Egypt, but my husband is, first and foremost, a man.*

***

Egypt's vizier entered the royal bedchamber to discover a bare-chested Akhenaten in a flying rage, kneeling over a pale, disheveled Aneksi. She was lying on her right side, clutching the left side of her chest and gasping. Her body was covered in sweat and her ripped raiment barely hid her nakedness.

"Tell me who gave you this instrument of destruction, or I WILL KILL YOU MYSELF!" Pharaoh roared, waving her *usekh* in his clenched fist.

Grim-faced, the captain of the king's guard stood behind the lord of Egypt.

"Life, prosperity, and health, Your Divine Magnificence!" Joseph greeted him, rushing to kneel by his side.

"You DARE bid me life, prosperity, and health when you let this treacherous serpent in to poison me?" he rose, glaring at Joseph.

Before the shocked vizier could respond, Potiphar said, "Your Divine Magnificence, the guards were given strict orders to search all visitors to your chamber thoroughly. They assured us she was unarmed."

"Then hang them all for ACUTE INCOMPETENCE!" Pharaoh bellowed.

"Forgive us, Your Divine Magnificence," the befuddled Joseph pleaded. "May I ask how she concealed poison on her person?"

"In this!" Pharaoh responded, flinging the necklace at Joseph, who examined it briefly before handing it to Potiphar.

"This was specially designed. Definitely the work of an expert jeweler," Potiphar observed.

"Then find out who made it! Better still, get her to confess!" Pharaoh ordered, pointing at the dying woman. Turning to Joseph, he added, "Surely the most astute diviner in all of Egypt has an answer to this mystery?"

"Perhaps I can help," a deep voice rumbled. Three pairs of eyes turned to see Akhom standing at the doors.

"You?" Pharaoh said. "You know something we do not?"

Striding confidently into the extravagant chamber, he glanced at Aneksi. "I know women. She could not have come up with a scheme so cunning on her own."

"Is stating the obvious your attempt at assisting?" Pharaoh snapped.

"No, Your Divine Magnificence," Pharaoh's half brother answered while standing over Aneksi. Joseph watched Akhom's eyes search her form. When her eyes locked with his, she struggled to raise a feeble arm toward him. Seemingly unmoved, Akhom turned away, and continued casually. "Instead of trying to get a confession out of a dying traitor, we should be searching her things and questioning those closest to her. We need to find clues as to the brains behind this nefarious incident."

Joseph saw Aneksi's eyes widen at Akhom's comment. Her mouth opened as though she was trying to speak, but no words came out. Then she gasped and went still.

"You have spoken well, Akhom," Pharaoh said.

"Indeed," Joseph said, observing Aneksi intently. "Whatever secrets she held, she has taken to the afterlife."

Potiphar said to Pharaoh, "I shall have her things searched immediately."

"See to it personally! The competence of your guards leaves much to be desired!" Pharaoh ordered.

"Yes, Your Divine Magnificence," Potiphar said, departing hastily.

"Metjen should know best who her closest companions were, Your Divine Magnificence," Joseph stated.

"If I am not mistaken, Metjen may be indisposed. Sudden illness this afternoon," Akhom said nonchalantly.

Metjen took ill? Why have I not heard about this? Joseph wondered.

"Then send for . . ." Pharaoh hesitated. Waving his hands impatiently, he asked, "What is the name of his right hand?"

"Neheb. I shall see to it, Your Divine Magnificence," Joseph said with a bow.

Akhom raised his hand, as though trying to stop Joseph. "Your Eminence, if I may, I think His Divine Magnificence needs your presence and your wisdom by his side, now more than ever. Allow me," he said, turning to head for the door without waiting for a response.

Joseph watched him leave, an uneasiness wrapping itself around him. Before he could question the feeling, Pharaoh's voice thundered.

"Get this godforsaken wretch OUT OF MY SIGHT!" The lord of Egypt was gesturing toward Aneksi's swiftly cooling corpse, his face twisted with disgust.

"GUARDS!" Joseph yelled. Two guards appeared instantly. "Take her to the morticians," he ordered.

The guards quickly removed Aneksi's remains while Joseph silently offered a brief plea: *Help me, O Lord. Let the perpetrators of this evil fall into the pit they have dug and grant Pharaoh your great peace.*

"She ought to be fed to the vultures!" Pharaoh said, spitting in disgust. "As surely as Pharaoh lives, the man behind this treason will be given a taste of his own medicine!"

Joseph looked at Pharaoh with all the earnestness he could muster. "I will not rest until he is caught, Your Divine Magnificence; I give you my word."

Pharaoh grunted.

Undeterred, Joseph continued, "His Divine Magnificence is to be commended for escaping such meticulously crafted treachery."

"Pharaoh is no mere man; he cannot be easily fooled," he said, puffing up his chest.

"Perhaps His Divine Magnificence will deign to share details of his prowess," Joseph hinted, hoping to get more insight into the situation.

"The witch was not herself. An aggressive lover playing coy? Pharaoh was immediately suspicious. And then she, who usually wants her man in his most alert state, was insisting Pharaoh first partake in some wine. Since she appeared to be taking more than the typical amount of time to refill the royal goblet, with her back turned no less, Pharaoh stealthily strode up to her and leaned over her shoulder, only to catch her in the very act of pouring her venom into the wine! The serpent had the nerve to say it was merely a potion to enhance Pharaoh's performance. As though Pharaoh, who has fathered twelve dozen children, needs any such enhancement!"

Joseph cleared his throat loudly to smother a chuckle rising. "Perish the thought!" he said.

"And any who conceive it! Naturally Pharaoh saw through her. Ripping the house of poison off her neck, he forced every last drop of the tainted drink down her lying throat."

What a wretched end. She was probably nothing more than a pitiful political pawn.

***

Several moments later, Joseph and Akhom stood side by side, observing the exchange between Pharaoh and Neheb. Neheb had implied, in not so many words, that the late Aneksi had a lover. For a man he claimed not to know, Neheb was giving a lot of details. Too many. And without pause. His answers seemed rehearsed. Joseph was thinking he ought to question the man alone when Potiphar joined them. The captain of the king's guard was stone-faced.

"Life, prosperity, and health, Your Divine Magnificence," he said with a bow.

"You have returned in time. The assistant keeper of my wives was just informing us that my treasonous late wife was also an adulteress. In which case her lover is the man we are after."

"Can you identify this man?" Potiphar asked Neheb.

"No, my lord. I merely came to the conclusion based on noticing her return from a few midnight excursions and her receiving a higher than average amount of luxurious gifts."

"And did you report your suspicions to Metjen, or anyone else?" Joseph asked, wondering why he did not, if he was speaking the truth.

Neheb's eyes shifted. "No, Your Eminence, I did not dare to make such an accusation against Her Magnificence, with no evidence."

"I believe Captain Potiphar went in search of the same," Pharaoh said pointedly.

All eyes turned to Potiphar.

"My search was fruitful, Your Divine Magnificence. Neheb, you may leave us." Potiphar said, holding his tongue until the assistant keeper of the royal wives had exited. Then, indicating a scroll in his hand, he said, "We discovered this missive strategically concealed in Her Magnificence's chamber."

A hidden missive? It must hold some answers! Joseph thought as Potiphar strode to Pharaoh and handed him the letter. Joseph, extremely curious, was eager to find out the contents of the letter. He watched Pharaoh closely.

The lord of Egypt read silently. His jaw clenched as he lifted a steely gaze directly at his vizier.

"Why does this treasonous communication bear the seal of the ring Pharaoh personally placed on *your* finger?"

Completely taken aback, Joseph asked, "What?"

Pharaoh stretched the letter toward him. He reached for the parchment and read words that nearly stopped his heart.

Beloved Aneksi,

I had this usekh custom-made for you because a rare jewel deserves a rare jewel. Wear it as a symbol of my affection. And know this: within it lies the power to change our future. Guard it with your life until the opportune time. It will not be long before all of Egypt celebrates our love in the open, as much as we do in secret. Meet me at our haunt tomorrow at midnight.

Affectionately yours,

Joseph

A paralyzing chill crept up his spine. *This cannot be! Lord, no. Not another betrayal!*

"It may not bear your name, but I demand to know: why does it bear *your* seal?" Pharaoh asked, in a frighteningly soft tone.

"I . . . I do not know, Your Divine Magnificence," Joseph said simply. He felt like the air had been sucked out of him.

"I thought you were the revealer, and not the concealer, of secrets."

"I hide nothing, Your Divine Magnificence."

"In that case, can you at least enlighten Pharaoh as to whom this *Joseph* might be?"

Joseph lifted his eyes to the man whose order catapulted him from the prison to the palace in one moment, fully aware the sovereign could reverse the command. "I am he."

Akhenaten, clearly dazed by Joseph's admission, was momentarily speechless. His jaw slackened. He blinked twice, then slammed his mouth shut as his features hardened. "You?" he asked. "You . . . in whom Pharaoh placed the utmost trust and the future of Egypt . . . you dare betray *me*?" he growled through clenched teeth.

Joseph stood as one frozen, the sound of his furiously pounding heart drowning everything else out.

"Have you nothing to say, *Joseph*?" Pharaoh asked menacingly.

Have mercy, O Lord, for you are a just God. Let my righteousness come forth like the dawn, my innocence rise like the noonday sun. He lifted his eyes to Pharaoh once more and said softly, "May the will of the Lord be done."

The vein in Pharaoh's temple appeared close to bursting. With an entirely crimson face, he thundered, "I AM THE LORD, and my will shall indeed be done!"

25

Eyes that laugh at life's puzzles
Are yet to see one:
The riddle of death

***

Disquietude.

That was the state that enveloped Asenath the moment she awakened to find herself alone in her husband's bed. *He did not come home.* Given his last statement to her the evening before, she was certain a band of wild horses would not have kept him from returning. *The happenings at the palace must have taken some unexpected turns.* She lay on the passel of purple petals with which she had decorated his sheets last night, contemplating the best manner in which to worm her way into the center of the intrigue, when she heard Merit's voice.

"Blessings of the morn, Your Eminence," her handmaiden said from Joseph's antechamber.

"And to you, Merit. What is it?"

"Wadjenes presently awaits an audience with Her Eminence."

The day has barely dawned! "At this hour?"

"He said he must speak with you the moment you awaken."

Something is wrong. "Help me dress then. Make haste," she said, waving her hands.

Moments later, Asenath walked into Joseph's receiving chamber. Merit shadowed her. Standing there, looking like a shadow of himself, was Wadjenes. Asenath's heart skipped a beat. *Something is gravely wrong.*

"Blessings of the morn, Your Eminence," he said, bowing deeply.

"And to you Wadjenes. Is that a missive from His Eminence?" she asked, eyeing the parchment in his hand.

"No," he answered.

"Then what is it? And where is His Eminence?"

"I implore Her Eminence to be seated."

What has happened to Beloved?

"Wadjenes, I do not appreciate one dancing about the river. What is it?" she demanded, her heightening alarm shortening her temper.

"Forgive me, Your Eminence." The steward walked up to her, missive outstretched. "I am asked by Captain Potiphar to deliver this to Her Eminence myself, and extend his deepest sympathies."

Sympathies?! Asenath grabbed the parchment. "Bring the light closer," she ordered a nearby servant carrying a lamp. The servant did as bid. Asenath began to read.

To Her Eminence, Asenath, wife of His Eminence, Zaphnath-Paaneah, vizier of Egypt

I am deeply saddened to inform Your Eminence that by order of Pharaoh, lord of Egypt—long may he live, His Eminence, Zaphnath-Paaneah, vizier of Egypt, has been arrested on charges of treason—

Treason?!

—there being found irrefutable evidence implicating him in a failed attempt to extinguish the life of His Divine Magnificence.

"No!" Asenath whispered, her heart palpitating as she continued reading.

Unless, by the mouth of at least two witnesses, he is proven innocent, he will be executed—

Executed? She felt the room move.

"Your Eminence!" Merit's panicked voice sounded as though it was far away. As the parchment fell to the ground, Asenath felt arms around her, steadying her, and easing her into a chair. Trying to steady her panicked breaths, she held her hand out toward the fallen scroll, snapping her fingers twice. Merit hastily retrieved it and handed it to her. She finished the disturbing missive.

—executed at noon, three days hence. Guards will bring you a duplicate of the execution order once His Divine Magnificence seals it.

Your Eminence has my deepest sympathies. Should Your Eminence think of anyone that may be able to testify on your husband's behalf, do not hesitate to send word—day or night.

In the service of His Divine Magnificence,

Potiphar, captain of the king's guard

Lord God of Abraham, Isaac, and Jacob, this cannot be! An overwhelming sense of nausea lodged itself in the midst of Asenath's belly.

"Is all well, Your Eminence?" Merit inquired.

"I require a moment, Merit." Asenath said, placing her head in her hand. *I am to be a widow in three days? No, Lord, no! Why has Beloved been blamed for this? How? They would not arrest anyone without evidence of guilt. What could they possibly have to incriminate him so?* She needed to get answers, and she knew who had them.

She looked at the letter again. "*. . . anyone that may be able to testify on your husband's behalf . . .*" There was only one person she could trust to speak for her husband at this moment. That person, and the one with the answers to her myriad of questions, needed to meet. And they needed to do so discreetly, and immediately. Asenath rose to her feet. "Send for my horse and fetch me a riding cloak. Swiftly, Merit!"

***

"Forgive me for intruding upon your home at this hour, Captain," Asenath said, noting Potiphar's slightly swollen, sleepy face.

"Given the circumstances, I applaud Your Eminence's wisdom. The palace would not welcome Her Eminence's presence at this time, and for that, I am sorry."

"You are too kind, Captain."

"And Your Eminence did not come here merely to pay me a compliment."

"You said if anyone could testify on my husband's behalf, I was to send word, day or night. Am I to take you at your word?"

"I am nothing if not a man of my word. Has Her Eminence found such a person?"

"Yes. Me. And I can testify that my husband is innocent!"

"I do not doubt it, nor do I mean any slight by saying this, but surely Her Eminence is aware that the word of an accused's wife cannot be accepted in his defense?"

"Then I beg you to answer me two questions: First, how are you certain of his innocence? And second, how did anyone possibly ascertain his guilt?"

Potiphar sighed. "Come with me."

Asenath followed him across his spacious, sparsely decorated chamber to a large, scroll-laden ebony writing desk. He seated himself and gestured toward one of the two large chairs across the table from him. "Please, be seated."

Asenath took a spacious but hard seat and met Potiphar's unflinching gaze.

"How much did your husband tell Her Eminence regarding his status before becoming vizier?"

"Every detail."

Potiphar's expression sobered even more than it already was. "Then Her Eminence knows that I made the mistake of sending His Eminence to prison, based on what at the time seemed like irrefutable evidence. It is to this day, my biggest regret. When I walked into His Eminence's office a few days after he became vizier, to beg his forgiveness, I fully expected to be the recipient of justifiable wrath. Imagine my surprise when he not only spared me, but made it clear he bore me no ill feelings. His Eminence stated that any man in my position would have done the same—believed and avenged his wife."

O my beloved.

Shaking his head in awe, Potiphar continued. "If that was not magnanimous enough, when I informed him my wife had hung herself the night before, rather than rejoicing in her death, he grieved for me. Your Eminence's husband alone possesses more righteousness than do all the priests of Egypt, collectively. He indubitably carries divine favor, for my house has never prospered more than when he stewarded it. I do not want to see His Divine Magnificence make the same mistake I did. Therefore, I will do anything in my power to ensure His Eminence does not suffer this injustice a second time."

"Thank you, Captain."

"Do not thank me prematurely. As of now, I am powerless against the evidence. Her Magnificence, Aneksi, tried to poison His Divine Magnificence, with a powder secreted in her necklace."

"No! Aneksi?!"

"Yes. And since the same venom has ushered Her Magnificence into the afterlife, we could get no help from her in uncovering her co-conspirators," Potiphar said, retrieving a scroll from the minute mountain of parchments before him. "Not until this was found concealed in Her Magnificence's chamber."

Asenath took the papyrus and read the words that her husband had supposedly written to Aneksi. She felt her heart stop and had to will herself to resume breathing.

Trying to still her trembling hands, she raised her eyes to Potiphar's. "You are right—this is both damning and irrefutable. Yet as surely as I draw breath, it is false. My husband has emphatically stated he would sooner die than be unfaithful to God, or me. Furthermore, Her Magnificence was my student. I assure you, she did not possess the prowess of mind or penmanship to carry out an affair requiring the exchange of letters."

"Unless Her Eminence can divine who penned this forgery, or summon two witnesses to testify to the identity of that mastermind, it matters not what you and I know."

Then what is it that we do not yet know? She looked at the missive again. "Did you personally retrieve this from Her

261

Magnificence's chamber?"

"Indeed. 'Tis a wonder one of my guards found it—an accident, really. It was stitched in the hem of a curtain. Who ever heard of such a hiding place?"

Patareshnes! "As odd as this might sound, I recently heard a tale of a woman who made use of exactly such a hiding place."

"What an amazing coincidence."

Is it? Or is it a clue in this masterfully murderous plot? Think, Asenath, think. Her mind was a cauldron of confusion. She felt like she was living in a nightmare. *If only this was just a terrible drea— Beloved's dream!*

"What I cannot call coincidental is the fact that His Eminence had a mysterious dream yesterday morning. Though its meaning was withheld from him, I believe it was a foretelling of these treacherous happenings."

"Alas, an already fulfilled dream cannot do us much good."

She sighed. *Potiphar is right. A strange being that tried to kill itself? That is nothing if not a divine ridd—the riddle!* She looked at Potiphar, her heart racing. "There was a letter, a riddle . . . My husband said it was connected to the dream."

"Now that you mention it, His Eminence's last words to me as I bound his hands were, '*A riddle reveals the truth.*' I knew he was giving me a secret message, but I did not know what it meant."

Asenath rose. "He said he left it on his table. I have to—"

"No need. I had all His Eminence's documents confiscated as protocol demands. They are here."

Asenath stood on the tips of her toes as Potiphar searched through documents. *Please, Lord, help.*

"This must be it."

Rushing to his side, she peered over his shoulder and read the most cryptic letter:

To the revealer of secrets

From a perch in a tree, an eagle has seen
Twain meetings and lovers who should never have been
Alas, a head higher than yours may ache
Struck by a ruby, one of many jewels in its bed
Fingers must point when a bruise bleeds

Point them thrice, remembering these truths:
A fiery mane attracts, but it can burn
A hungry hawk will eat its own flesh
A jeweler cannot work with a false right hand

From a grateful eagle

"His Eminence spoke no lie when he declared it a riddle—a more mysterious missive I have not read!" Potiphar said.

"Nor have I. And if indeed it holds the answers to the mystery behind this treason, then it must mean that His Divine Magnificence is the aching head, and Aneksi—"

"The ruby that struck it!" Potiphar finished.

"As well as the fiery mane that burns," Asenath added.

"Fascinating. Who then is this . . . hungry hawk? Or the jeweler? I know no one in the palace with a false right hand," Potiphar said, turning to look at Asenath.

"May I?" she asked, reaching for the parchment.

"Certainly," Potiphar answered, handing it to her.

Asenath strode pensively around the table, and stood facing Potiphar as she thought out loud. "Riddles are poetic; so this may hold a less literal and more symbolic meaning. If Aneksi is one of many jewels in His Divine Magnificence's bed, then the jewels are —"

"The royal wives. So the jeweler would be—"

"Metjen," she said, eyes locked on Potiphar's.

He arched a brow. "I need to question Metjen."

"Wise," Asenath said, looking at the riddle once more. *Why does this state that Metjen has a false right ha—of course!* "May I suggest you question Neheb first?"

"Neheb?"

"Metjen's right hand. The riddle implies Neheb is not to be trusted. I am inclined to agree."

"Why?"

"Because that woman I mentioned, the one that made use of the same ingenious hiding place where the forged letter was found, just so happens to be Neheb's mother."

Potiphar's eyes widened. "Is Her Eminence certain of this?"

"I heard it from Her Magnificence, Patareshnes' lips. Neheb's mother stitched her jewels into a curtain hem, to hide them from his father."

"This is insightfully intriguing. Nonetheless, if Neheb is a conspirator in this scheme, someone put him up to it."

"Which brings us to *the hungry hawk*. I have not the faintest—"

"Pardon me, my Lord," said a male voice outside the chamber, "your carriage awaits."

"I shall exit momentarily," Potiphar said loudly, toward the door. Rising, he shot an apologetic look at Asenath. "Your Eminence, I fear I cannot be absent from my duties on a day like this one. His Divine Magnificence has assigned me the task of unearthing all who participated in this treason, and reporting to him daily. I must go."

"I understand. You have been more than gracious."

"If any new information comes to light, I would rather Her Eminence seek me here, no matter the hour. But, if Your Eminence must come to the palace, inform any who ask that you do so at Captain Potiphar's summons."

"I am truly grateful. If I may be so bold as to ask a favor, may I hold on to this?" she asked, indicating the riddle.

"Certainly. We must do whatever we can to determine who penned that mystery, or this forgery."

"Or better still, both."

"'Tis a bitter irony that the revealer of secrets is himself mystified in this instance. I cannot imagine a moment where His Eminence's powers were needed more."

The revealer of secrets. Asenath smiled. *Beloved always said that title did not belong to him. And the one to whom it belonged was never mystified. It was time to seek the power of the true revealer of secrets.*

"Truer words have never been spoken, Captain."

Potiphar gestured toward the door of his chamber. "Your Eminence." Asenath began walking toward it, Potiphar following closely as he continued. "We are clearly in a race against time in the hunt for the ones who penned both mystery and forgery; so I welcome any, and all, of Her Eminence's future insights. It would be foolish of me to reject an extra pair of eyes in this search, when I cannot boast of the eye of an eagle."

Eye of an eagle . . . Asenath unwittingly froze. *Could it be?* Potiphar's words faded as Asenath's mind raced. *She expressed a debt of gratitude to Beloved, and she did not think Aneksi was harmless. I have to ask her.*

"Your Eminence?"

Asenath turned to Potiphar, who had paused beside her. "Forgive me, Captain. What did you ask?"

"Would Her Eminence like an armed escort back to her villa?"

"Not to my villa. To the royal harem."

Potiphar's wrinkled brow questioned her before he did. "If I may, whom does Her Eminence hope to meet there?"

The singular spark of hope in her heart revealed itself as a small smile on her face. She answered in three words: "A grateful eagle."

***

Asenath entered the grand antechamber of the royal harem, flanked by a guard on each side. It was still morning, but her frayed nerves would have sworn it was midnight. She was hoping to make it to her destination without running into either prying eyes or curious minds. She had made her way across the main hall and was taking a corner to head for the north wing, when she happened upon Neheb.

The false right hand!

"Life, prosperity, and health, Your Eminence," Neheb said, his eyes registering surprise.

"I bid you the same, Neheb."

"'Tis quite a . . . pleasant surprise to see Your Eminence here, today. Is all well?"

The nerve of him, feigning ignorance! "All is well. I merely wish to speak to Her Radiance, Neferubity, about temporarily assuming responsibility for teaching my esteemed students, in my absence."

"How thoughtful. There would otherwise be a sudden vacuum, given the circumstances." Neheb said, a well-manicured finger tapping his temple pensively. "I fear Her Eminence has chosen the wrong day for an audience with Her Radiance."

"How so?"

"It is the day of the earth today; a Nubian festival. Her Radiance left at dawn for the mountains for sacred rites."

No! "When will she return?"

"I believe no later than sunset, tomorrow," Neheb said nonchalantly.

Tomorrow evening? That is the night before the execution! Asenath did not want to show her agitation, especially not in front of one of the parties responsible for Joseph's current plight.

"In that case, I shall leave word with her servant that Her Radiance may send for me upon her return. Thank you, Neheb."

"Certainly, Your Eminence," Neheb said with a bow.

Several minutes later, Asenath departed the royal harem. She hoped the body of her message was clear enough to get Neferubity's attention, yet subtle enough to avoid a spy's:

I wish to request an audience at Your Radiance's earliest convenience to strategize on filling a forthcoming vacuum in the lessons for the royal wives caused by my impending absence. Instructing Their Magnificences can be quite the conundrum with each at a different skill level, but with Your Radiance's mastery of text, penchant for riddles, and eagle's eye, I can think of no one more suited for the position. I would be most grateful for Your Radiance's timely assistance.

Her hope did not assuage her growing concern. Suppose Neferubity decided to extend her retreat, or Neheb underestimated its length? If she could not secure the Nubian princess's help by tomorrow night, it would be too late. *At the very least, I must attempt to send word to Neferubity today.* The challenge was that she did not know Neferubity's exact whereabouts. Surely Potiphar would not object to sending a rider to the mountains in search of the 'grateful eagle.' Even if he was unwilling, she was not. The mountain may not be able to come to her, but she was willing to go to it. She was not sure if present circumstances dictated she needed permission to leave the city, but she was certain she needed an expert guide to navigate the unfamiliar, mountainous terrain. Whatever the case, she needed Potiphar's attention. *I am already within the palace, with an armed escort. It is now or never.*

***

The captain of the king's guard was not in his official chambers. Asenath was informed had left on an "urgent matter regarding Pharaoh's security" and was expected back "sometime in the next several hours." She was undecided about what to do next. She did not necessarily want to leave and return, but waiting indefinitely at a time when every minute mattered would certainly drive her to heights of insanity. She was still standing in the hallway, before Potiphar's chamber doors, when her eyes caught a tall, wiry figure approaching. Recognizing the royal, she bowed.

"Life, peace, and prosperity, Your Radiance."

"And to you," Akhom responded. "It is surprising to find Her Eminence here, given the circumstances. Seeking an audience with the Captain?"

"Yes. Alas, I am told he is seeing to an urgent matter."

"I see. Perhaps I can assist."

"You, Your Radiance?"

"Your Eminence seems astonished. His Reverence Potiphera remains in my good graces. I once told him Your Eminence was welcome to my assistance if the need ever arose. Not only am I a man of my word, I am not one to blame a wife for her husband's treachery."

Asenath felt like she had received a blow to her gut. But she tried not to take it too harshly. The fact remained, in the eyes of the royals, her husband was a traitor until proven otherwise. She had to stay focused on doing just that. "Your Radiance is most gracious, but I could not impose."

"Think nothing of it. I can only imagine what Your Eminence must be feeling at this time. Come, my chambers are a stone's throw away. Her Eminence will be more comfortable there."

"I would hate to miss Captain Potiphar," Asenath said, still rooted to her spot.

"And you shall not." Turning to a guard, he said, "See that you alert my steward, the instant the captain returns." Turning back to Asenath, Akhom smiled, "Shall we?"

Asenath followed, ignoring the disconcerting feeling that crept upon her.

**

Nerves taught, mind frantic, and belly vexed, Asenath picked up the goblet of fruit wine beside her. Not until she drained it did she realize she had eaten nothing all day. She felt nauseous and light-headed. Akhom's opulent receiving chambers were dimly lit, and he had dismissed the servants once refreshments were placed at her side. Asenath selected a small loaf from the tray of assorted meats and breads that had been set beside her. Trying to maintain the eating habits of a lady in a palace, as opposed to those of a beggar on the street, she took a small bite, and glanced up to meet Akhom's dark eyes. Golden chalice held casually, he was looking at her in a manner she imagined dangerously similar to the way she had been eyeing the loaf moments before.

"A lady with a healthy appetite, most refreshing."

Asenath smiled briefly, still chewing.

"Shall I send for anything else?"

She shook her head from side to side, swallowed, and said, "No, thank you, Your Radiance. I cannot linger."

"Yes. The matter for which Your Eminence sought the captain's help. May I ask what that is?"

Asenath did not think it wise to say, "*I need help locating a witness that could testify to my husband's innocence.*" The walls in the palace surely possessed ears, and she was not sure if Akhom would necessarily want to help the man accused of attempting to kill his brother and sovereign.

"I need to visit the mountains today."

"The mountains? Whatever for?"

"The day of the earth. I should have left at dawn for sacred rites but for the present circumstances."

"Is that not a Nubian festival?"

"Indeed. But, I adopted it. Nubian ancestry in my mother's lineage, you see. She valued the tradition," Asenath lied.

"I had no idea."

"Few do. I simply wanted to make the captain aware and obtain permission to leave the city if necessary, with an escort, preferably."

"And Your Eminence would depart even with her husband facing execution?"

"All the more reason to seek divine intervention that he might be spared. My husband is innocent, Your Radiance."

"Says every wife of an accused. I am sorry to serve the bitter truth, but the evidence against Your Eminence's husband says otherwise, and it is irrefutable. While I would not begrudge you a visit to the mountains, Captain Potiphar might not share my sentiment. He has been asked to find all who assisted in this treachery, and Your Eminence's wish to depart the city so suddenly could easily be interpreted as dubious. If I may so boldly advise, unless Your Eminence wishes to return to His Reverence's house a childless widow, your energies are better deployed securing yourself a future."

"I wish no future without my husband."

"An understandable, even admirable sentiment. But a naïve one. Her Eminence is young, intelligent, not yet a mother, and easily one of the loveliest ladies in the palace." He rose and re-seated himself uncomfortably close to her. "If you show yourself willing, any Egyptian royal with half a brain would leap at the chance to husband you."

"I have a husband, Your Radiance."

"One clearly undeserving of a prize like you, Asenath," he said, taking her hand in his and stroking it.

How dare he? Asenath felt a fury fill her. Tearing her hand away from his, she rose. "My husband's character and faith are unquestionable. If anything, it is I who am undeserving of him. And you? If Your Radiance lived a thousand lives, you could NEVER be the man that he is."

Akhom's left eye twitched, and the warmth in his countenance evaporated. Rising, he said, "That he *was*. Perform sacred rites on every mountaintop in the land if you wish, but in three days, neither man nor god will stop your husband from becoming food for the vultures."

Asenath flinched at his cruel words. Before she could utter a response, Akhom turned toward the doors and yelled for the guards.

"Guards, escort this wife of a condemned traitor out of the palace. Ensure that she does not return."

26

Among the living walk the dead
The fatal error of the latter
Was kissing hope
Goodbye

***

Stupefied.

Still reeling from her visit with Akhom, Asenath headed straight for the garden altar upon reaching her villa. Whatever regard the lustful royal may have had for her husband had clearly vanished. She reprimanded herself for even setting foot in his home. Now, she could definitely not so much as grace the palace anytime soon. *To think I asked him for help and lied in the process!* She felt angry and ashamed.

Not bothering to light the wood, Asenath fell face down before the altar. "O Lord my God, have mercy upon my undeserving soul. Forgive me for seeking the help of man, rather than yours. In vain have I done so. Forgive me for relying on my understanding. Forgive me for my falsehood. I thought I could help my husband, but I know nothing. I can do nothing without you, Lord. Your servant, my husband, is blameless before you. Do not let him pay for another's crimes. Do not let them take his life, Lord. His enemies are mocking you Lord, did you not hear the words of His Radiance? He said no god can save my husband, but you are the Almighty. Surely you can deliver him with a mighty arm. Send a wind to blow forth mouths to speak on his behalf. He has said you are the true revealer of secrets, so unveil the hiding places of the guilty. Let them be ensnared in the pit they have dug for your servant.

"I beseech you Lord, I may not deserve him, but I do not want to live without him; he is all I have. If this punishment has come for my sin, Lord, please mete it out to me. Let me be barren all my days. Take my life instead. Banish my memory from the chronicles of time, only spare my beloved. O God of Abraham, Isaac, and Jacob, save my beloved," Asenath prayed, her voice breaking. Giving rein to her sorrow, she wept.

She cried until her well of tears had run dry. She prayed until her river of petitions had stopped flowing. Hours passed, and after multiple attempts, Merit gave up trying to get her mistress to rise and eat, and sat in the grass a short distance away from her, silently sharing her sorrow. The sun was setting when Asenath rose to her knees. Her body felt as though an entire herd of bulls had trampled it. Arms lifted, she sang. A tingling warmth slowly began spreading downwards from her fingertips to her face and all the way to her feet. Her heavy heart felt suddenly light. Her racing thoughts seemed to fade away leaving two words at the forefront of her mind:

Fear not.

Asenath let the words seep into the very fabric of her soul. She had two choices: fear or faith. The former had not helped, the latter could not harm. She would no longer let fear rule her. She would leave the matter in the hands of the Lord, and trust that He was mighty to save.

"Merit, I will eat now."

"Yes, Your Eminence. Shall I serve the meal here?"

Asenath looked at the fading light of the sun and felt serene. "Yes, and have the fire lit." As her dutiful handmaiden bowed and began walking away, Asenath had an impression.

"Wait." For a moment, she struggled with what she felt compelled to do and then yielded. "Return with my writing instruments; and alert Wadjenes to ready a dispatch rider for an urgent missive to Heliopolis."

Several moments later, an empty bowl of venison stew lay beside Asenath. She had her eyes closed and her head against the altar. The words weaving through her mind were the same upon the scroll presently en route to her father:

I thought you should be made aware that my husband was arrested on erroneous charges of treason. He faces the executioner two dawns hence. My faith remains yielded to the will of our Lord, the invisible God.

***

The sound of birds cooing right beside her ear awakened Asenath. Opening her eyes, she straightened her crooked neck, and two doves took flight. She was uncertain whether it was very late or very early in the day. A blanket was draped over her, and her head lay against a cushion, but there was grass beneath her. Clearly, she had fallen asleep in the garden. Scanning the perimeter, she saw Merit, curled on a cloth and cushion, a stone's throw away from her. *Bless her faithful heart.*

She heard a throat clear and looked up to see a tall, masculine frame. Her heart momentarily leaped into her throat.

"Pardon the intrusion, Your Eminence."

"Wadjenes! You gave me a fright! What is it?"

"Forgive me, I come to offer my sympathies."

"They are not yet necessary, Wadjenes." *And hopefully they never will be.*

"Certainly, forgive me, Your Eminence, I . . ." His voice trailed off.

He shifts his feet and wrings his hands. Something is amiss. "What has happened, Wadjenes?"

"I need to beg forgiveness from . . ."

"From whom?"

"From His Eminence."

Asenath's heart skipped a beat. "For what?"

"I did not know it would endanger his life, Your Eminence. I swear upon Ra himself, I would never have agreed to it."

The hairs on the back of her neck rose. "What did you do?"

"I have not been able to sleep all night. His Eminence is the best master I have ever served. He does not deserve—"

"ENOUGH!" Asenath yelled. Wadjenes fell silent. "I demand an answer. What exactly did you do?"

"I was desperately in need of money when I was recruited for this position two years ago, so I agreed to all the terms, including espionage and sporadic meetings, to divulge information."

Espionage?!

"When I last took His Eminence's signet ring to be polished, I allowed it out of my care for a time. I did not realize the details of its use until last night."

To seal the forgery!

"But I swear . . . by the life of Pharaoh and my own life . . . I was not aware that it would ever be used for a treasonous communication or I would never have . . ." Wadjenes' voice broke. "By the mercy of Ra! What have I done?" he asked, falling to his knees and hitting his bald head with his fists repeatedly. "How do I live knowing my hands shed innocent blood?. . . I must beg forgiveness before it is too late."

Asenath tried to find words. *The enemy has been closer than our own kin for two years?!* It was unthinkable.

"Name the man who sent you here as a spy in steward's clothing."

Wadjenes' eyes doubled.

"His name, Wadjenes."

At the mention of his true master's name, Asenath felt a paralyzing chill overtake her.

"Please, let me beg His Eminence's forgiven—"

"Beg?!" Her chill had been replaced by a searing heat. "My husband is to be executed and you, who deserve his fate, wish to beg FORGIVENESS?!" Asenath never thought herself capable of desiring to kill a man with her bare hands until this moment. But even if he were to meet an untimely end, now was not the moment. She needed him alive, and sound enough to testify.

"No, Wadjenes, there is only one thing you *must* do now; and that is accompany me to the captain of the king's guard, before whom you will tell all."

"Yes, Your Eminence," Wadjenes said meekly, his face completely devoid of color.

***

The day had barely dawned, but Joseph was awake. Still awake, to be precise—he had never slept. How could he, when eternal sleep loomed so menacingly close by? Ironically, the chamber he occupied was incomparably more comfortable than the one assigned to him the last time he was imprisoned. He had been a slave then, and he was a noble now, but he would rather have the former sentence than the present one. This was his second dawn in these suffocating quarters, and unless the Lord wrought a mighty deliverance, he had but one more to see. It was unfathomable. Once again, treachery between brethren had set off a series of events that landed him in prison.

He had spent the night on his knees, petitioning the Lord fervently, to reverse the evil wind that had blown his way. To expose the instrument of darkness that framed him. To give courage to whomever that grateful eagle was to step out and speak for him. To give the Lord of Egypt a dream that revealed the truth. He had presented petition after petition for any and everything that came to mind. Then, his many requests had become just one: *Have mercy upon me, O Lord.*

This dawn he repeated his plea, softly. "Have mercy upon me, O Lord. If I have been too proud, or too reliant on my wisdom; too focused on my comfort and the needs of my small family; if I have in any way done anything to displease you, Lord, I beseech you, forgive my wrongs.

"Is your servant, my beloved wife, to become a childless widow, forever regretting her choice to marry me? Lord forbid it! You are the same God who delivered me from this very prison two years ago. You are immutable. Your arms are not too short. Your ears are not deaf. I put my trust in you, O Lord, my salvation. I will not lean on my own understanding . . ."

His ears picked up the sound of footsteps approaching as he continued his earnest prayer.

"Dawn 'til dusk, day and night, your praise will ever be upon my lips, O Lord."

"Visitor for His Eminence!" a guard bellowed.

Potiphar? Joseph thought, rising to his feet. *He must have found the riddle! Who else would come this early?*

A shadow darkened the small, barred window to his chamber.

"I would bid you life, prosperity, and health, but that would be futile given the circumstances. Do you not agree, *Joseph*?"

Akhom! Why is he here? Joseph approached the window. "Why has Your Radiance deigned a visit to a condemned man?"

"Merely to relish the results of two long years of masterful scheming," he answered, his hawklike eyes gleaming.

Stunned speechless, Joseph double blinked.

"Surely you did not imagine I would remain idle while my half-brother so foolishly stained the seat of Egypt's governance with the hind parts of a Hebrew slave?"

Joseph recoiled as though Akhom's blow had been physical.

Akhom clicked his tongue thrice. "To think I so masterfully eliminated your predecessor in order to claim the vizier position, only to have a prisoner swoop in and steal it."

He orchestrated the death of his father's cousin two years ago! Suddenly both Joseph's mysterious dream about the serpent attacking itself, and the line from the riddle about a hawk eating its own flesh, made sense. *He is the hungry hawk!*

The royal gave a self-satisfied smile. "No matter, I have righted that egregious wrong. Now, you will not begrudge me savoring the fruits of such tireless, thankless labor, will you, Hebrew?"

A blinding rage rose within Joseph. Maintaining a calm facade, he said, "I am amazed His Radiance is not presently celebrating after all his hard work."

Akhom chuckled deeply. "Patience is a virtue. There shall be plenty of merrymaking when I, a pure-blooded royal son of Egyptian soil, am paraded as her rightful vizier. Undoubtedly, I shall become Pharaoh in due time, but my coronation as vizier will suffice for now. It is unfortunate you will not live to see the joyous occasion," he said with feigned sorrow. "I shall save a seat for your grieving widow; she looked quite comfortable on my cushions yesterday. And her skin, soft as butter."

Joseph's hands curled into fists by his side. "You LIE!"

"Ask her yourself if she deigns to visit you," he replied with an infuriatingly unruffled smile.

He is a liar, here to rub salt into your fresh wounds. Do not give him the satisfaction. "I would not order festive garments just yet, Akhom," he cautioned the heartless royal.

"Why ever not?" Akhom asked, an amused expression on his bony face.

"Because if I know my brilliant wife well, and I do, she is occupied with ensuring your victory is temporary," Joseph said more confidently than he felt.

Akhom's smile faded slightly. "One night here and already you lose your senses? I expected more from one supposedly so wise," he said.

"And I expected more from a supposed master schemer than to allow his clandestine meeting with his brother's wife to be witnessed," Joseph quipped, recalling the 'grateful eagle,' had witnessed *lovers who should never have been.*

Akhom's left eye twitched.

Having ruffled the conniving royal's feathers, Joseph continued. "You may buy your allies, but I earn mine. While you waste time in here, they are hard at work turning the tide against you."

Akhom's calm tone belied his now stony face. "I hate to destroy your delusions, but a hundred allies could no sooner turn my brother's heart against me than they could ever again turn it in your favor."

"Perhaps not," Joseph said, his gaze unflinching, "but one God —my God—can."

***

After the morning's shocking visit, Joseph had paced, prayed and pondered himself to a state of exhaustion. By evening, his tired eyes had shut, but his racing mind had relentlessly painted a plethora of haunting pictures. Until the slam of heavy metal doors opening slapped the sleep out of his eyes.

"Visitor for His Eminence!" *Please let it be the face of a friend and not a foe.*

The face that peered into the barred window bore signs of exhaustion, but it could not be more welcome.

Joseph's eyes misted, as his chest tightened. "You came . . ."

"I would have battled the entire host of Hades to see you tonight, Beloved."

"I do not doubt it. But I was uncertain if that murderous schemer would somehow prevent you from coming."

"You know the one who ensnared you?!"

"He was here this very dawn; flaunting his victory in my face! He made so bold as to admit responsibility for the death of the last vizier—his father's cousin!"

"No! I cannot believe I was foolish enough to ever ask that black-hearted beast for help!"

She asked him for help? "So it is true?"

"What?"

"You were in his home?"

"His official receiving chambers. I originally went to ask Captain Potiphar for assistance, but he was not there. His Radiance met me waiting and offered to help."

"What happened?"

"While I was waiting in His Radiance's chambers, I ate some bread—I was famished to a near faint. My visit was a waste of time otherwise. Once I knew he had only selfish intentions, I left."

Selfish intentions? "Did he lay a hand on you?"

He saw her swallow.

"He . . . grasped my hand for a moment, but I pulled it away. He indirectly said I would be more than welcome as an additional wife, after you . . ." She fell silent.

"Are executed?"

"Bite your tongue, Beloved! I told that selfish snake he could NEVER be the man you are. I am only sorry I ever believed he wanted to help!"

"Why would you even go with him?"

"For you. I wanted Potiphar's help getting to the mountains to find Neferubity to speak for you."

"Neferubity? How could she speak for me?"

"She is the '*grateful eagle.*'"

What? "I would never have guessed!"

"The Lord helped me to piece it together from certain things she had said. I went to seek her and discovered she had left for a retreat in the mountains and was not expected back until sunset today. I left word for her, but in order to leave nothing to chance, I thought I should send word to the mountains or even go there myself . . . I would never . . ." Asenath's voice trailed off, as a lone tear rolled down her cheek.

I have been a fool. "I know . . . Forgive me, my purple iris, please," Joseph begged, standing as close to the window as he could. "Akhom used your presence in his chamber as a weapon against me, and I . . . It is obvious he twisted the truth to inspire the worst images in my mind . . ." He kicked the door angrily. "I wish I could wring his neck with my bare hands . . ." he said, raising his hands and arching his fingers as if choking an invisible enemy.

A brief burst of laughter surfaced from Asenath.

"What could possibly be amusing about this?" Joseph asked, dropping his hands.

Wiping her tear-stained cheek, she laughed again. "The irony. I felt exactly the same way yesterday, except it was Wadjenes's head I sought to separate from his body."

"My steward?"

"Correction: Akhom's spy, who has been masquerading as your steward for two years."

"It cannot be!"

"By his own admission, he gave His Radiance your signet ring. He has testified the same to Potiphar already, but the law demands —"

"Two witnesses. More so; for a steward's word cannot stand against a royal's."

"Precisely."

Joseph let his head fall into his hands, a heavy sigh escaping his lips. "So I am to be betrayed again and again until my last breath."

"Never by me, Beloved. I swear it." Flinging her arms up in the air, Asenath paced in front of the chamber door. "I do not care what protocol demands, I am going in search of Neferubity. She is a royal, her testimony can get you—"

"No!" Joseph said, catapulting himself to the window again. "I will not let my wife also become an enemy of the palace. Nor can I allow you to endanger your life."

Asenath stopped and looked at Joseph, eyes brimming with fresh tears. "But what is my life without yours?"

O my heart. Lord have mercy! Letting out a slow, long breath, he answered her gut-wrenching question. "Whatever God makes it to be. But I need you to give me your word that you will not journey to the mountains."

"You have my word," Asenath whispered, tears silently rolling down her cheeks.

Joseph sighed and bowed his head. "I am sorry marrying me has caused you so much pain."

"Hush, Beloved. It is I who am sorry; clearly I have brought the Lord's wrath upon us. It is I who deserves to die, not you."

"No!" Joseph exclaimed, reaching through the window. "Give me your hands, Asenath." She did, and he stared directly into her tearful eyes. "Listen to me. My predicament is not your doing. An evil one has done this. Never, ever, ever think this your doing—no matter how this ends. The Lord is God, my life is in his hands. We must trust that His will shall be done."

Joseph heard the guard in the hallway clear his throat. "Your Eminence, it is time."

No, please. Do not make her leave.

As though privy to his silent plea, she cradled his face in her hand. "*Ani ohev otkha*, Joseph *ben* Jacob," she said in Hebrew, uttering the three little words that universally expressed love. "You are the reason I ceased to exist and began to live. I will love you to my last breath."

"As will I, my purple iris," he whispered in a tremulous voice as he placed his hand over hers. *Be strong for her, Joseph.* Clearing his throat, he added. "Having your love has been my greatest joy. And being your husband, my greatest privilege. Today, tomorrow, and always, *ani ohev otkha*." He kissed her palm and let his face linger in her hand, drinking in her familiarly fragrant skin.

The guard cleared his throat again.

Closing his hand around hers, he pulled it away from his face, stretched his arm out of the window, and then opened his palm. Feeling her fingers softly slip away from his was akin to having his heart tear itself from his chest. He watched his heart walk away in slow strides. When she was out of sight, he fell to his knees and wailed, "HAVE MERCY UPON ME, O LORD!"

***

Walking away from her husband for what may be the last time, Asenath could not permit herself to look back. She felt like walls were closing in on her. Unable to see past her tears, she kept taking one shaky step after the other until she exited the prison. The evening sky had already darkened, and cool winter winds whistled.

She was descending a short flight of steps when she missed one, and slipped. Slender but strong arms steadied her.

"Take care, Your Eminence."

"Merit . . ." she said, holding on to her handmaiden lest she dissolve into a puddle of sorrow, "this cannot be the end."

"Your Eminence will make herself sick with worry."

"I must go to the Captain. Perhaps he has elicited a confession from Neheb."

"He would have sent word in that case. He knows time races against His Eminence."

"How can I sit by and do nothing?"

"Your Eminence is warm to the touch. I beseech you, rest an hour. At least eat something. I will dispatch a servant to see if my lord, Captain Potiphar, has any news."

"Very well, but send another to see if Her Radiance has returned."

"Yes, Your Eminence. Please, let us return home."

Too spent to object any further, Asenath let Merit lead her homeward.

27

As heaven's kiss
Breathes life into the earth
So a lost hope found, revives

***

Awakening.
Asenath felt herself being gently rocked back and forth repeatedly.

"Your Eminence . . ."

Merit?

She opened one exhausted eye and let it close again.

"Your Eminence. Rise, PLEASE!"

The urgency in Merit's voice stole the sleep from Asenath's eyes. She sat up and reality came crashing in like the waters of a flood. *How could I have slept when Beloved is hours from execution?* She was in her husband's chamber, fully dressed and still holding on to a tunic of his. It was pitch black outside.

"What hour is it?"

"It is midnight, Your Eminence."

"Midnight?! How could you let me waste such an important evening in slumber?" Asenath snapped, casting the tunic aside and clambering out of the bed.

"I feared interrupting Your Eminence's rest; for the sake of your health."

"This is no time for resting! Is there any word from the captain?"

"No; but someone seeks an audience."

"At this hour? Who?" asked Asenath, rising.

"I am told only to say, 'a grateful eagle.'"

Lord God Almighty! She is here! Chills spread down Asenath's spine. Without another word, she raced out of the room, leaving a perplexed Merit behind.

***

A puffy-faced Potiphar shuffled into his receiving chamber. "Developing a fondness for midnight escapades, Your Eminence?"

"Forgive me; with any fortune, this will be the last one."

Asenath watched him momentarily freeze, as his sleepy, red eyes took in the darker, smaller figure beside her. "Your Radiance!"

"Your witness—at least that is what I am tonight."

"Her Eminence was right?"

"Never doubt a woman's intuition, Captain," Neferubity said.

"Lesson learned," Potiphar said, dipping his head.

Asenath stepped forward. "You have two witnesses now, Captain. Tell me it is not too late."

Potiphar responded by making a beeline for the facts. "The twain meetings Your Radiance witnessed, where were they held? What transpired exactly?"

"The gardens just outside the royal harem. His Radiance, Akhom, gave Neheb a scroll and a bag of money. Neheb departed. Shortly thereafter came Her Magnificence, Aneksi—Ra rest her soul. His Radiance gave her a necklace, and she let him have his way with her, right there on the grassy ground."

Asenath gasped.

Potiphar's eyes narrowed. "Treachery and adultery; against his brother and Pharaoh, no less."

"A hungry hawk will eat his own flesh," Neferubity quoted herself.

"The bitter truth," Asenath said. "Surely His Divine Magnificence cannot deny my husband's innocence any further if he hears this. Do you not agree, Captain?"

"Indeed, but we must present the truth to him without alerting the real traitor. His Radiance is no fool; he obviously has spies everywhere. For all we know, one of the guards outside Pharaoh's chamber may have a bag of Akhom's coins under his bed."

"In which case, he will alert his master if you request an audience at this time," Neferubity said.

"Or arrive with Wadjenes in tow," Asenath added.

"Exactly," Potiphar affirmed both women.

"Which means the audience has to be with only you and I," Neferubity said to Potiphar.

"Except His Divine Magnificence has refused all female company since the incident, and understandably so."

Lord, you have brought us this far. Make a way where there is none. Asenath prayed silently. Musing, Neferubity twirled her small dagger repeatedly between her fingers.

Potiphar paced. "Waiting until Pharaoh awakens would see him in a better mood, that I know."

Asenath said, "But that would only put us all the closer to the noon execu—"

"My Lord, an urgent missive," thundered a male voice from behind the closed doors.

Potiphar raised his hand to indicate silence. Asenath turned and could find Neferubity nowhere. The Nubian had blended into the shadows. Potiphar went to the door briefly and returned with a scroll in hand. Standing close to a lamp, he read silently. Asenath watched a small smile appear on his face.

"What is it?" Neferubity asked, her sudden reappearance as bewildering as her preceding disappearance.

"Does Your Radiance have much skill with role-play?"

"The lateness of the hour must have dulled my hearing. I thought you said '*role-play.*'"

"He did," said Asenath. "And I am very curious why."

"Her Radiance's skillfulness with her hands is proverbial—in the inflicting of injury. But can her hands do the reverse?"

Heal? Asenath wondered, even as Neferubity asked, "Remove an injury?"

"Heal one, to be precise. Or at least, pretend to."

"Pretend? I too am sorely intrigued, Captain, but should we not return to the pressing matters at hand?"

"It is to that very end that I ask my question."

"Then I implore you, dispense with the riddles," Neferubity said, voicing Asenath's exact sentiment.

"It appears we are not the only ones sleepless tonight. His Divine Magnificence has just requested a healer to tend to him as soon as possible. Naturally, after narrowly escaping a poisoning, he objects to any healing potions, so it must be a healer—"

"Of the hands!" Asenath finished.

"Precisely. Not even His Radiance would be inclined to attend to that request at this ungodly hour, but by the morning he might find such a healer, unless . . ."

"You arrive before him," Asenath said, facing Neferubity. She turned to Potiphar, seeking confirmation, and he answered with a smile and a small bow.

"I hate to disappoint, but this is one role for which I am unfit. I do not know a thing about the healing arts."

"But I do. Thanks to my extensive childhood tutelage. And I can teach you enough to play the role," Asenath said.

"In one night?" Neferubity asked, skeptically.

"As gracefully as you have been wielding that dagger? I dare say, in one hour."

Neferubity's face registered surprise. "Then let the lesson begin."

Smiling, Potiphar dipped his head, "Your Radiance, permit me to leave you . . . in good hands."

Both ladies flashed stunning smiles.

The outcome of the next several hours was still uncertain, but for the first time in what felt like an eternity, Asenath sensed the faintest sliver of light at the end of a treacherous tunnel.

***

Dawn found a curious trio outside Pharaoh's chamber.

"Let His Divine Magnificence know the captain of the king's guard is here with a healer of the hands," Potiphar said to one of two muscular, armed men guarding the doors.

The guard eyed the two women standing to Potiphar's right. Neferubity was dressed in her typically skin-flaunting, two-piece attire. Avoiding a neck adornment today, her only pieces of jewelry were the thin gold bands around her head and wrists. Her gravity-defying hair was in its usual updo, save one difference: instead of two thin sticks occupying the lower of her two buns, there was only one thick, cylindrical one. It secretly housed supporting evidence— her rolled up riddle of a letter.

Asenath was dressed in similarly revealing, but more plain attire, with no adornments save a black turban around her head and its matching veil on her face. Keeping her head bowed, she stood a pace behind the Nubian, holding a censer of incense and a plain black cloth.

"Which one is the healer?" the first guard asked.

Asenath saw Neferubity eye him as though he had inquired if water was wet. Throwing herself into her role, Asenath sucked in a sharp breath. Falling to her knees and placing the censer at Neferubity's feet, she waved the black cloth back and forth over it, whispering unintelligibly in the Nubian dialect.

Meanwhile, the Nubian princess closed her eyes and began humming softly, rocking back and forth on the balls of her feet and making the most delicate movements with her fingers.

Gesturing toward Neferubity, Potiphar answered the confused guard. "I should think Her Greatness's presence speaks for itself."

"Indeed," the now embarrassed guard replied.

"All the same, we are instructed not to allow any strange items in," the second guard said, eyeing Asenath's smoking censer.

Neferubity instantly lashed out. "That is my incense, you half-wit, and it will remain at the door with my assistant, to ward off evil omens!"

"You heard Her Greatness. Only she and I will enter," Potiphar said.

"Very well, Captain, but we must search her," the first guard said.

"I have searched her myself—what little of her remains hidden," Potiphar said pointedly.

"We must ensure His Divine Magnificence will receive her at this hour," the second guard added.

"I shall NOT have these twain towers of ignorance infect my atmosphere with negativity!" Neferubity said in an injured tone. "If His Divine Magnificence is not ready this dawn, you may invite me again after the next day of the earth." Spinning around and backing the guards, she clapped her hands twice, loudly.

Asenath rose hastily and followed the princess, who was storming away.

Racing after them, Potiphar pleaded, "Please forgive their dense insensitivity, Great One." The ladies halted. Eyeing the guards, Potiphar continued in menacing tones, "I will hold you personally responsible should His Divine Magnificence miss this rare ministration, and I will be sure to inform him *exactly* who denied his requested healer entrance!"

The guards exchanged alarmed glances with each other.

"Forgive us, my lord Captain," the first one said. Potiphar silently inclined his head toward Neferubity. She was now grasping at invisible objects above her head and seemingly thrusting them away, as though cleansing the air around her. Had the stakes not been so high, Asenath would have laughed at the Nubian's brilliant role-playing. Instead, she hummed and waved the censer in circular motions before her supposed mistress.

"Forgive us, Great One," the second guard said.

Turning around slowly, Neferubity placed her palms together, raising her elbows, and bowing her head downwards. Then she looked at Potiphar and nodded.

"The doors, NOW!" Potiphar ordered. The guards hastily swung the heavy doors open. Asenath hurried forward, kneeled and placed the censer at the doorpost and waved the black cloth over it thrice. After that, Neferubity walked into the chamber.

Before Potiphar followed her, he turned to the guards. "I will keep watch over His Divine Magnificence's ministration myself. See that no one enters. The great one does NOT take kindly to disturbances."

"Yes, my lord Captain," the guards said, dipping their head.

Watching them enter Pharaoh's chamber, Asenath silently prayed. *Favor them, O Lord.* Then, keeping up appearances, she began rocking back and forth, humming and waving the black cloth.

Several minutes passed uneventfully, when the now weary Asenath noticed a lone figure approaching.

"Blessings of the dawn, Your Radiance," said a guard.

"Is His Divine Magnificence awake? I wish to speak with him."

Akhom! Keeping her unmistakable eyes lowered, Asenath kept her previous activities going with a renewed vigor.

"He is awake, but he has an audience that cannot be interrupted."

"An audience? With whom?" Akhom asked.

"A special healer requested by His Divine Magnificence," the other guard volunteered. "That is her apprentice there."

"Who brought the healer?" Akhom inquired, not deigning to glance at a lowly apprentice.

"Captain Potiphar, Your Radiance. He is overseeing the ministration himself."

"How long have they been in there?"

"Several minutes, Your Radiance."

"I want to be informed the instant they—"

"GUARDS!" a male voice called from inside Pharaoh's chamber. Both guards rushed in. Asenath's pulse picked up pace. Momentarily, one guard emerged.

"His Divine Magnificence will see Your Radiance now."

Akhom strode into the chamber.

Now severely nauseous, Asenath momentarily ceased her rocking. Still kneeling, she let herself sit back such that her weight rested on the balls of her feet. She was wondering how much longer she could stay in that position, when Neferubity emerged from the chamber, her unbound hair seated like a mass of dark clouds atop her head. "My work is done! Rise!"

Asenath rose hastily; perhaps too hastily. The walls about her seemed to shift. She was thinking Neferubity had magically duplicated herself, for she saw not two, but four bronze arms reaching toward her, even as her world went completely dark.

***

The surroundings Asenath opened her eyes to were luxurious, but unfamiliar. The rays of the sun streaming in from a high, latticed window felt warm on her skin. That warmth registered two things in Asenath's mind: save for her unbound head, she was still wearing her revealing disguise, and morning had definitely passed. *Noon. The execution!*

She sat straight up in the strange bed, swiveled her legs out of it, and rose to her feet. The room moved again, and she fell backwards into a seated position on the bed. Soft hands attached to powerful arms steadied her.

"Rest easy, my friend, the battle is over," Neferubity said gently.

"My husband?"

"Outside, visiting with the chief palace physician."

"Physician? Did they—is he wounded? I must see my husband!" Asenath said, rising again, more carefully.

"Then look no further," a familiar baritone voice said from the chamber doors.

Asenath took one look at the smiling face she thought she may never again see, and her feet willed themselves into a sprint. "Beloved!" She flung herself into his arms and he lifted her off the ground in an emotional, extended embrace. Her tears fell unbidden. Leaning back, she let her eyes search his face. "My beloved."

He cupped her face in his hands, "Weep no more, my purple iris; for the Lord has turned our mourning into dancing."

Thank you, Lord. Laughing and crying, she flung her arms around him once again. Then she eased back just far enough to begin planting kisses all over his face, as the room echoed with the strong, soothing sound of his laughter. When she finally pulled back to drink in his face once more, he took her hand in his and began leading her toward the bed.

Neferubity rose and started making her way toward the door they had just vacated. When they met in the center of the room, Joseph paused and turned to the princess.

"Your Radiance need not leave."

"On the contrary, the beauty of this moment requires no witness, though I am honored to have seen it."

"Your Radiance has our eternal gratitude," Joseph said, bowing.

Taking the royal's hand in hers, Asenath said, "Thank you, my friend; now it is I who owes you."

"Send me an invitation to your next celebration, and I shall consider the debt paid." As the Nubian exited, the reunited couple sat side by side on the bed.

"I have so much to tell you," Joseph said, placing his arm around her shoulder.

"I want to hear every detail," Asenath replied, laying her head on his shoulder.

"And you will, when we get home."

"I can hardly believe you are here." Suddenly aware of her unfamiliar surroundings, she pulled away. "Where are we anyway?"

"The infirmary at the royal harem."

"I do not understand. Why?"

"You fainted earlier, and being feverish, Neferubity brought you here, and sent for the physician. I am particularly glad she did, given his diagnosis."

Asenath's heart skipped a beat. "Diagnosis?"

"Have you been feeling ill a while?"

"Just nauseous and tired, but I have neither been eating nor sleeping well in the past few days. How could I?"

"That is all about to change; not only will you be sleeping soundly, you will be eating double portions starting tonight."

"Are you trying to earn me more curves, husband?"

"I do not need to," Joseph said, placing a hand on her belly. "Manasseh, will see to that himself."

Manasseh? "This is not the moment for jesting, Beloved."

"No, indeed. It is a moment for rejoicing. For today I was gifted with both the blessing of freedom and the promise of fatherhood."

What? "Are you saying what I think you are saying?" Asenath asked, eyes wide.

"Yes, mother of my unborn child."

Impossible! As though in a trance, Asenath whispered, "I am to be a mother?"

"In less than eight months, if the physician's estimate proves exact."

"How?"

"How? Surely Your Eminence knew our passionate nights would attract consequences?" Joseph said, his eyes twinkling mischievously.

"Do not tease! I am at a loss for words. This is . . . it is . . ."

"A doing of the Lord and a marvelous one."

"I, Asenath, am with child?"

291

"You have been with child for over a month. Do you realize what that means?"

"The invisible God is indubitably the Almighty God. He can make a way where there is none!"

"Undoubtedly, but the timing of your conception reveals much more. Was it not just over a month ago that we spent the day at the altar in fasting and prayer after your return from Heliopolis?"

And then we spent that night together . . .

"O Lord, my God," Asenath said, falling to her knees as she realized the undeniable truth: the Lord not only forgave her, he answered their prayer from the very first day they had prayed in agreement. "Is the rejected daughter of Potiphera to be a joyful mother?" she asked, tears streaming down her face.

"Yes," Joseph answered, joining her on the plush animal skin and encircling her with his arms. "And she gets to deliver the thrilling news to her father this very afternoon."

Asenath raised a puzzled face to her husband's smiling one. "Explain."

"Your father awaits us at home. Along with Heqaib."

My missive! "Truly?"

"Indeed. They came thinking to mourn with a widow, but the Lord has caused that they shall instead rejoice with a mother-to-be."

"Blessed am I among women."

"It is I who am blessed. For I, who thought to never see another sunrise, will get to see three suns rise each morn: one at dawn, the others as you open your eyes."

She felt his warm hand cradle her face, then his lips kiss hers tenderly, and she could not hold back her tears. As their sweet kiss ended, she rested her head on his chest and let him hold her. And when she had expended her emotions, she looked up at him and said, "Take me home."

He rose first, then helped her to her feet. She let him wrap a moderately thick bed linen around her shoulders, before he took her hand and began leading her out at a deliberately leisurely pace. Strolling through the spacious harem hallway, the bejeweled ornaments and murals of deities were lost on them. They had eyes only for each other. They had not walked far before Joseph gave her an admiring smile and looked away. When he repeated the gesture, she spoke.

"What?"

"I am curious as to your . . . fascinating attire."

Asenath smiled and laced her arm around his. "That is *quite* the story; I shall tell you later. Suffice it to say, it was an invaluable loan from Neferubity."

"Was it?" Joseph cleared his throat. "Then His Eminence would greatly appreciate it if Her Eminence forgets to return it, as he would like several opportunities to . . . thoroughly inspect her in it," he said, wiggling his eyebrows.

Asenath gasped. "Your Eminence is shameless!"

"Unapologetically so!" he said, eyes glinting. "Her Radiance did expect us to celebrate."

"I hardly think she was requesting an invitation to that particular kind of celebration."

"You are absolutely right. Clearly, we shall have to undertake *two* celebrations, shall we not?" he asked, smiling from ear to ear.

He wants a feast! "Says the one who does not have to plan a feast."

He raised his right index finger. "A worthy point. Allow me to put forth my strong reasons: one, your family is already here, and two, we have twain miracles of freedom and fertility to celebrate. Furthermore, if those awe-inspiring acts of God are not sufficiently convincing, let me give you a third: the wicked one who wove a web for me has himself been ensnared in it!"

Asenath's feet froze, even as her jaw dropped. Lifting wide eyes to a beaming Joseph, she asked, "He has?"

"Per His Divine Magnificence's order, the noon execution held, with a last-minute change in victim."

What a mighty God we serve! "The Lord is truly a God of justice."

"And a fearsome God, who causes His enemies to be ensnared in the same pits they dig for His children. There is no other explanation for the fact that His Radiance awakened this dawn, preparing to relish my demise, yet by noon he entered the afterlife with a belly full of the very poison with which he had sought to end Pharaoh's life."

"I can neither understand the workings of our God, nor the wickedness of man, Beloved. I still cannot believe Akhom would have murdered his own brother and remorselessly feasted in his tomb."

Joseph's eyes darkened as his voice lowered. "I can. At least he has paid for his treacherous crimes; I know others who never did."

He speaks of his brothers.

The silence was deafening as they walked across the massive antechamber, still holding hands. Seeking to offer comfort, Asenath squeezed his hand and said softly, "Dwell on your joys today, Beloved. The Lord has not only vindicated you, He is making you a father."

Joseph paused and fixed his gaze on her, "Yes, He is!" Throwing his hands in the air, he thundered for any and all to hear. "I am to be a FATHER!"

Asenath giggled at the amused glances that came their way. Suddenly, she felt her husband's arms tighten about her, immediately after which her feet left the ground and the world spun around. As Joseph gently put her back down, he said, "I, a father. And you, the joyful mother of SONS!"

"Sons? Our firstborn is yet in my womb, and even if it is a son, who is to say our second will not be a daughter?"

Smiling ruefully, Joseph answered. "Having twice escaped the sharp blade of brotherhood's double-edged sword, a daughter following a son appeals to me. Nonetheless, should the Lord give us sons, I vow this much: we will love them equally and teach them to love, honor, and defend each other." The fire in his eyes was enough to let Asenath know her husband would keep that vow.

Taking both of his hands in hers, Asenath said, "I would not have it any other way."

"Good. So, we feast?"

Asenath laughed. "We feast; on two conditions."

"For the mother of my child? Anything!"

"First, we make it an intimate gathering—family and faithful friends."

"Done. And second?"

"We honor the two who fiercely fought this battle with us: the captain and the princess."

"I love that we think alike. In fact, I have a special gift in mind for Her Radiance."

"I am intrigued."

"Actually, until I can obtain His Divine Magnificence's consent for it, I would rather not reveal it. Will you trust me?"

Asenath paused and cradled his face. "All the days of my life."

Leaning in, he kissed her, long and strong. Completely oblivious to the world of kohl-lined royal eyes fixed enviously upon them, they basked in their own universe of unadulterated bliss.

PART IV:

THE KEY TO LIBERTY

28

A bed of roses
Flaunts its petals. Hides its thorn.
Lay gently, or bleed

***

SEVEN YEARS LATER (THE SECOND YEAR OF FAMINE)

Howling.

The winds sounded angry on this icy, moonless night. Ominous clouds overcast the sky. Atop a hill, holding onto the rough, broad trunk of a pomegranate tree, Asenath feared she would be hoisted into the violent air at any moment. Even more frightening was the rapidly approaching, gigantic cone of dust that stretched from the land to the sky. It was spinning at a feverish pace and swallowing everything in its path. Doors were torn off their hinges, thick stone roofs caved in, furniture was flung wildly, and buildings were razed to piles of debris. The monstrosity of a whirlwind suddenly began traveling eastward. Her breath caught as she realized what now lay in the direct path of the swirling storm.

No! Lord, not my home! Heart sinking, she knew there was nothing she could do in that moment to save her family. She shut her eyes as a powerful gust of dust enveloped her. Her living anchor shook. She heard what sounded like roots being ripped out of the soil right before she found herself flying toward air-borne debris. "Noooooo!"

She was still screaming when she abruptly awakened, her quivering body drenched in sweat from scalp to soles. Swallowing great gulps of air, she placed a hand over her pounding heart.

297

It was just a dream, Asenath, just a dream. She was in her own bed, the four walls around her solidly in place, and all was quiet. At least, presently. In a matter of hours, their home would be bustling with guests. Asenath thought it best she try to complete her interrupted slumber in readiness for the busy day ahead.

Taking a few deep, calming breaths, she adjusted herself under her plush covers and eventually went back to sleep. But not before an unmistakable uneasiness accosted her like a thief in the night.

***

By mid-morning, Asenath lay on the lush grass in her garden. Eyes lightly closed, she was savoring the warmth of the sun on her skin and silently thanking the invisible God for her many blessings: *Freedom. Faith. Family. Fidelity. Friendshi—*

"*Ima! Ima,* look!" an excited, youthful voice beckoned, interrupting her reverie. She casually opened her eyes and looked in the direction of the call. The sight before her catapulted her to an upright position immediately. Ephraim, her four-year-old son, had climbed up the oak tree that sat in a clearing to the left of their impeccably groomed maze. He was swinging back and forth from a sturdy branch, grinning like a satisfied monkey. Six-year-old Manasseh, self-equipped with his mother's bow and arrows, was poised and ready to shoot at his mark. It was a ring drawn on the stem of the same tree.

Asenath's younger son possessed the uncanny ability to make her feel like she was standing on the edge of a precipice. It was evident from the very day he was born. The Lord had surely graced him to cheat death from birth, and he had grown into a feisty, fearless boy. But his mother would not sit by and silently watch another possible near-death experience unfold.

"Manasseh, hold your fire! Ephraim, come down at once!" she ordered, placing both hands on her slender hips.

"Wonder of wonders. It appears those two inherited your mischievous streak," said a deep voice laced with amusement.

Keeping her eyes on her sons, she heard little feet running up behind her and before she could fully turn around, she was gripped in small but tight hugs. "Aunty Asenath! Aunty Asenath!" Heqaib's three-year-old daughter and nearly-seven-year-old twin sons had her surrounded.

"Sweethearts!" she said, tearing her eyes from Ephraim for the briefest of moments, to place her arms around them all.

"Inyotef! Meriiti!" Manasseh squealed in delight, tossing the bow and arrows and running to greet the freckled-faced twins. Heqaib grinned at Asenath, but walked past her until he stood beneath Ephraim.

"So, little monkey, would you like to come down and play with your friends?"

The lad nodded vigorously.

Heqaib was at his side in three swift moves. He turned his back to the boy and said, "Jump on and hold on." Traditionally still too young to be clad, the naked, chubby-faced boy climbed on his back and clung to his neck. Before Ephraim knew what had happened, he was firmly planted on the ground at his mother's feet. He bowed his almost-bald, olive-skinned head sheepishly.

Asenath noted a few light scratches on his small, unclothed frame, no doubt acquired from his latest adventure. She kept her face stern. "What have I told you, Ephraim?"

"No climbing trees on my own until I grow taller than the iris hedges," he mumbled, his grayish-green eyes lowered.

"So, what have you to say for yourself?"

"I am sorry, *Ima*," he said in Hebrew, wrapping his soft arms around her thighs. Asenath's heart melted. The Hebrew term for mother had since become her favorite moniker. Coupled with her son's warm embrace, it was irresistible.

"I accept your apology," she answered in Hebrew, caressing the singular, bejeweled, sidelock on his otherwise bald head. Switching back to the Egyptian dialect, she added, "Next time, play swords with your brother instead of climbing the tree."

"But I do not like playing swords with Manasseh. He always wins!" the young lad said, matching her lingual transition effortlessly, a scowl furrowing his childishly smooth brow.

Heqaib stifled his laughter with a cough.

Asenath's amber eyes flashed at him briefly. Returning her gaze to her son, she said, "That is only because he is bigger and stronger

—for now. But if you practice, you could become faster and better, and beat him."

"Yes, *Ima,*" Ephraim said, pouting full, pink lips reminiscent of his mother's as his foot went back and forth, tracing an invisible line in the neatly trimmed grass.

"Ha . . . Hia . . . Haaayaa!" The trio looked toward the yelling to see that Manasseh and Inyotef were already sword-fighting. The former was unclad, but the latter wore a white linen *shendyt,* a broad-collared, beaded *usekh,* and bracelets on his wrists and upper arms.

"Now, be a good host, and play with Meriiti," she said to Ephraim, who immediately took off running.

"As for you, do not think I will let you get away with accusing me of passing a mischievous streak on to my sons."

Heqaib laughed. "I have not the faintest idea of that which Her Eminence speaks; she being the embodiment of elegance and whatnot."

Asenath snorted. "Flattery will not soften my revenge."

She felt little fingers tapping her leg gently and looked into large, honey eyes filled with a warm innocence. "Will you tell me a story, Aunty Asenath?"

Little Meresankh was cuteness personified. Almond-brown curls spilled around her perfectly round, fair face. Asenath could not resist picking her up and drinking in the softness of her youthful skin.

"Certainly! How about I tell you all a story after we eat? How does that sound?"

Clapping her hands together, Meresankh broke out in a grin that put dimples in her chubby, rosy cheeks.

Putting the girl gently on the grass, Asenath looked at Heqaib. "Where's our Mother?"

"Where else? Inside, fussing over the meal preparation."

Asenath smiled. "That should keep the kitchen maidens on their toes."

"Hiyaaaaa! I win! I win again! I am the greatest, am I not, *Ima?*" Tall for his age, her ruddy-faced, long-limbed older son stood victoriously, sword pointed at Inyotef. The defeated boy lay frowning on the ground, his sword flung to the floor an arm's length away from him. The triumphant lad looked at his mother, dark brown eyes sparkling with eagerness as he waited for her to affirm his greatness.

Heqaib, trying to hide his amusement, said, "O Manasseh, the mighty warrior! A wise man once said the measure of a man's greatness is not in how many fights he wins, but in how many lives he saves."

Manasseh's thick, dark eyebrows inched closer as he inclined his head. "A wise man?"

"Not just any wise man. The wisest man in all of Egypt."

"*Abba!*" the boy said, flashing pearly-white teeth, his smile the spitting image of his father's.

"Yes, your father!" Heqaib said, now familiar with both Hebrew terms the boys used to refer to their parents.

Asenath chimed in. "See? You should listen to your *abba*. Now, will you show your guest some mercy and let him up?"

"Yes, *Ima*. Come, Inyotef!" he said, reaching down to offer his honey-eyed friend a hand up.

"Now, I am willing to wager there are some sweet treats with your names on them hidden somewhere in the play chamber. Who wants to go and find them?"

"Me! Me!" the childish party of five screamed, each waving a raised hand frantically.

"Run along; Basmat will take you in for your treasure hunt. But do not overindulge your sweet teeth, remember we have a special feast this evening."

The children eagerly followed their plump, cheerful nurse. Asenath watched them briefly before plopping herself back on the grass with a sigh.

Heqaib moved under the shade of the tree, but remained standing.

"Stealing a quiet moment while you can?" he asked.

"Those two can be saints one minute and tyrants the next."

He cleared his throat and gave her a knowing look. "I wonder who those little shapeshifters take after . . ."

In one fluid motion, she rolled over, grabbed her bow and arrow, and aimed it right at his chest. "I would choose my next words carefully if you intend to dine at my table tonight, Captain."

301

Heqaib lifted both hands in mock surrender, a small laugh escaping his lips.

Asenath lowered the weapon, smiling. "It is good to see you laugh, brother."

"It is good to laugh, sister," he said with a small smile that did not reach his eyes. His underlying sadness was not lost on Asenath. It was the unending, ever-present grief of a man bereft.

"We had better go in before that boisterous quintet runs Basmat into the ground."

"You mean go in and dig her out of the ground, because I am certain they have already."

Asenath laughed. The duo started walking toward the house.

"I cannot believe my first born marks his sixth year of life today. I am thrilled to have you all here celebrating with us."

"The children need to be around laughter and happiness," he stated.

"As do you. Family is everything."

"Believe me, I know," he said wistfully. Livening up, he added, "Speaking of family, how is our illustrious vizier these days?"

"My husband is occupied with feeding the nations, as always."

"Do I detect a hint of frustration?"

"Certainly not! Pride, if anything. The wisdom the Lord God gave him is keeping all of us, and multitudes more, alive in this famine and for that, I am grateful. We have just learned to miss him more when he is away and love him harder when he is here. But tonight, he dines with us; and I am not sure who is more excited, my sons or myself!"

Heqaib smiled. "It is safe to say we all are. It will be good to see the savior of Egypt again." Heqaib took a deep breath and let it out. "I know not why, but it always feels so . . . serene here."

"It usually does," Asenath agreed, as the foreboding that took up residence within her after her dream resurfaced.

What could be wrong? She wondered. *I had better check on everyone.*

They were soon indoors and discovered almost everyone was fine, Basmat being the exception. She looked battle worn and especially grateful to see reinforcements. Still, the premonition lingered. But it was soon forgotten in the business of the preparations and by early evening, Asenath felt nothing but excitement.

***

The eminent lady of the villa took in the intimate group gathered in her grand feasting chamber. Seated around a long, thin table, they wined, dined, and conversed with the ease of a close-knit circle. There were two place settings each, at the head and foot of the long table. On the left side of the table's head sat mostly adults, beginning with Asenath and ending with Heqaib. Across from them sat mostly children, beginning with Ephraim, beside whom sat Heqaib's twin sons.

Occupying one of the two seats at the head, and beaming with pride, was the celebrant and guest of honor, Manasseh. He was fully dressed for the first time in honor of attaining the age where clothing became a requirement. The faience-stoned bracelets around his wrists were not a novelty. But a new, white *shendyt* hung from his waist, and new papyrus sandals housed his feet. The broad, bejeweled collar on his shoulders was an early present from his doting grandfather. Asenath took in the vacant seat to Manasseh's left, and her immediate right, and the uneasiness with which she awakened returned. Her husband had not yet appeared, and they were already on the main dish of the night.

"I am surprised His Eminence is yet to make an appearance."

Trying to mask her misgivings, Asenath turned toward the masculine voice that spoke, and looked into the eyes of the well-fed man seated to her immediate left.

"A vizier must expect the unexpected, and so must his family, Father. Notwithstanding, I trust he will appear momentarily."

"I should hope so. After all, the captain of the king's guard has found the time to grace us with his presence," Potiphera said, raising a goblet in mock salute to Potiphar.

From a seat at the foot of the table, the military man dipped his head. "I am not tasked with feeding all of Egypt and the nations that surround her, Your Reverence. Merely overseeing the king's guard, and for that I have the most skillful of assistants," Potiphar said, looking at the dark-skinned beauty beside him.

303

"Assistant? We all know the king's guard is a more formidable force than ever since my membership. They would be a lost lot of pot-bellied, purposeless men without me," Neferubity said, in mock disdain.

"As would your husband," Potiphar admitted, gently brushing her cheek with the back of his hand.

When Neferubity's eyes lowered shyly, Asenath grinned. She never thought she would see the day when her sharp-tongued, warrior of a friend let a man have the last word.

The dark-olive-skinned three-year-old seated to Neferubity's left tried to stifle a giggle, causing Neferubity to wag a plump finger at her.

"I would not test your mother, Benerib, your little brother or sister, is already occupied with doing so."

"Sister!" Benerib said, leaning to kiss Neferubity's protuberant belly, her mass of brown curls nearly hiding her petite face completely.

"Your daughter would have you surrounded with women, Captain." Heqaib said.

"As radiant as these two are? I raise no objections!"

As the room chorused with laughter, Asenath took in the couples' loving glances and her mind drifted down the path of history. It was now nearly seven years ago that those two had been seated next to each other in a feast that featured almost this same group of people. The pair had been co-guests of honor then; a widower and a virgin prize of Pharaoh. No one could have imagined the twists of fate that now saw them as man and wife. They had Joseph to thank for that.

His appreciation gift to the Nubian princess back then had been both incredible and invaluable: liberty to return to her people untainted, bearing a signed treaty of peace between Egypt and Nubia. What her father hoped she would earn with her body, she had received for her brilliance and bravery. Asenath could not have imagined a more perfect present for her friend. Surprisingly, Neferubity had received double honors that festive evening. Captain Potiphar had presented his co-guest of honor with an honorary membership in the king's guard, giving Asenath a glimpse into his enormous admiration for the Nubian. But when Neferubity returned to her people, Asenath thought nothing more of it.

It was a pleasant surprise to all of them when, a year later, she returned to Avaris. Choosing the life of a warrior over that of a princess, she made Potiphar an offer he would have been a fool to refuse: her sword and her skills in active membership in the king's guard. It was not long before mutual admiration and attraction sparked a flame between the two fierce fighters. Four years married and Potiphar still doted on his much younger bride. Asenath derived immense pleasure from teasing her friend about her brief, loveless stay in the royal harem. The warrior couple had fast become her and her husband's closest companions. More so when they too came to pledge allegiance solely to the invisible God, having each admitted to being awed, on multiple occasions, by the character, faith, and miraculous experiences of their eminent friends.

"But I do not want them, Father." The tiny yet commanding voice that spoke drew Asenath's attention two seats to Potiphar's right. There, with a scowl and crossed arms, sat the group's other three-year-old, this one a mirror image of the woman who had died giving her life.

Responding to the girl's defiant declaration, Heqaib said, "Green vegetables will make you grow, daughter. As tall as your Aunty Asenath." When Meresankh's wide eyes locked on Asenath, the amused woman nodded in confirmation. The little girl needed no further urging. She picked up a fresh sprout and shoved it into her tiny mouth. Asenath's heart lurched; watching Semat's daughter and sons grow up without their mother raised mixed emotions. She looked from the child's bright eyes to her father's wistful ones and felt a familiar guilt. If she had not encouraged him to pursue Semat, perhaps he would not know his present grief.

Lord, you spared me the sorrow he bears. The mere imagination of living without my beloved was unbearable. Comfort Heqaib, as only you can. And comfort his children, too.

"*Ima?*" said Manasseh.

Asenath turned to her right. "Yes, *b'ni?*" She answered, using the Hebrew term for 'my son.'

"When do my gifts get presented?"

"After we finish our meal."

The celebrant picked up his half-eaten bowl of lentil soup and swallowed the rest of its contents in one large gulp, after which he displayed the empty dish and released a sound belch.

Laughter filled the air as Asenath frowned at her grinning son.

"Manners, Manasseh! Beg the pardon of your guests."

"I beg your pardon," he said sheepishly.

"And we still have a course of deserts to enjoy, so you will just have to be patient," Asenath added. *Hopefully, your abba will be here by then.*

"Your patience will be well rewarded when you see what else your grandfather brought you," Potiphera said.

"Surely you do not wish to outshine his father in generosity?" said an arresting voice behind Asenath.

"*Abba!*" chorused her sons, leaping out of their seats and throwing their arms around whatever parts of their father they could reach. Joseph patted each of their heads briefly as he addressed the room.

"Life, prosperity and health, to you all. Please pardon my tardiness. I hope you have left some food for this rueful but ravenous vizier."

"I am certain we can scrounge up a crust of dry bread and some moldy cheese for you," Asenath teased, eliciting a chorus of laughter from the adults, as her husband took his seat. Her keenly observant eyes took in the lack of color on his face and the tinge of tension in eyes. Leaning in to brush her lips against his cheek, she asked, "Is all well?"

Joseph hesitated before replying, "All is well," but the look in his eyes belied his words. As surely as she knew her own name, she knew all was not well.

29

Green fields. Blue skies
Glories of nature. Unseen
Blind is the bitter eye

***

Disconcerted.
Before the troubled Asenath could question her husband any further, the sound of three loud thumps filled her left ear and shook their table. She shifted her gaze to see Potiphera's goblet-laden right hand raised.

"A toast to the celebrant is in order. Who better to give it than his eminent father?"

"Toast! Toast! Toast!" chorused the room.

Joseph rose, but rather than raise a goblet, he placed a hand on his son's shiny, sidelock-bearing head. "Manasseh, the one who opened your mother's womb, and caused us to forget our pains, may the Lord our God bless you, and make his face shine upon you, and may all of your days be prosperous and peaceful. May you never know my sorrows, only joys, far exceeding mine," Joseph's voice broke and his eyes misted as he finished by softly saying, "So let it be."

"So let it be," said Asenath, raising her goblet, and glancing around the room to encourage the others to follow suit.

Beginning with Heqaib, all raised their goblets and chorused, "So let it be."

As Joseph took his seat again, Asenath recognized that the look in his eyes held pride with an underlying pain. *Surely, all is not well.* She signaled for the servants to proceed with the final course, a round of specially prepared sweet breads, fruits, and a variety of nuts. The ever-intuitive Merit was already serving Joseph his main dish.

Noting he was rearranging the food before him more than eating it, Asenath announced, "I think the celebrant has exercised enough patience. Let the presentation begin." Turning to her son, she added, "Manasseh, rise to receive your gifts, graciously."

Her firstborn rose and stepped two paces back from the table. He stood in as dignified a manner as he could with his head high and his hands clasped in front of him.

Asenath nodded, and a bearer approached with a small ebony chest. Setting it at Manasseh's feet, he opened it. The boy's eyes widened and he reached in to pull out an exquisitely woven piece of clothing and a pair of papyrus sandals. "There is a whole chest full, *Ima!*"

"Merely six changes of raiment from a proud grandfather to his six-year-old grandson." Potiphera said casually, his eyes twinkling.

"Thank you, grandfather."

As the excited boy replaced the items in the chest, a second servant arrived with an excellently carved, child-sized bow and a quiver full of copper-tipped arrows.

"Now you can shoot with your mother," Heqaib said, smiling.

Asenath flashed an appreciative smile at his thoughtfulness. Intending to speed things along, she had already signaled for the third gift. "You can examine them more closely later, Manasseh, after you receive them all. I wonder what is next," she said, inclining her head to a servant bearing a long, narrow item covered by a white linen cloth. Manasseh pulled the cloth aside to reveal a custom made sword with jewels on its handle. Murmurs rippled round the room.

"You mean to recruit a six-year-old into your ranks already?" Joseph asked, looking at Potiphar.

"Ensnare them young, I always say."

Manasseh was reaching for the sword when his mother leaped to her feet. "Careful, *b'ni*," she said, racing to his side. "You might have to grow into this gift."

"We thought so. Hence the addition," Neferubity chimed in, as the servant who brought the sword pulled out a small replica of the larger weapon with a much shorter, blunter blade.

"I think it is safe to say my grandson is now the most armed and dangerous boy in all Egypt," Potiphera bellowed.

"Not yet," Asenath said, raising her index finger. As Manasseh was presented with yet another gift, she said, "Now he is." Her excited son opened a leather pouch from which he drew out a collection of blank scrolls and a small, reed pen.

Confused whispers traversed the room.

Na'eemah said, "I am no battle expert, but what harm can a scroll inflict?"

"The danger lies not in the scroll itself, but in what may be written upon it." Turning back to her son, she crouched to the floor so she was at his eye level, and said. "Wield your pen wisely, remembering this truth: words can inflict graver wounds than swords."

"Yes, *Ima*."

The joyful mother of sons kissed her firstborn on his shiny, fair-skinned forehead, and said, "Last but not least, your *abba*'s gift."

A smaller chest than the former one was presented before the celebrant. Sitting atop a multicolored fabric were two sets of wide gold bracelets, engraved with hieroglyphs. Manasseh picked one pair up and looked at his father.

Joseph rose and clasped one each on his son's forearms. "These bear the symbols of my authority, as do these," he said, pointing to similar bracelets on his own forearms. "But this . . ." he said, pulling out the fabric beneath and whipping it into its full length to reveal a seamless, long-sleeved tunic, ". . . is a symbol of my paternity, and your ancestry." Helping his son into the multicolored tunic, he pulled out a belt from the bottom of the chest and tied it around his son's waist. "My *abba* gave me one just like it, long, long ago."

"Will you wear yours too, so we can match?" Manasseh asked excitedly.

As Joseph hesitated, Asenath's eyes watered. "Mine is long gone, *b'ni*."

"I want one too," said Ephraim, who had made his way close enough to feel his brother's newest gift.

"No, it is mine, leave it alone!" snapped Manasseh, stepping out of his brother's reach.

"How come he gets to have so many things, and I do not?" Ephraim asked, his reddened, frustrated face upturned toward his father.

Before Joseph could respond, Manasseh did. "Because I am six, and you are just a baby."

"No, I am not! I am four!" Ephraim said, stomping his foot.

"But I am firstborn, and I will always come first!"

"Manasseh!" Joseph scolded. Before he could say anything further to correct his older son, his younger son kicked the quiver of arrows sitting atop the chest of raiment, and it toppled over. Arrows flew haphazardly about the carpeted floor.

"Ephraim, NO!" Joseph said, turning his attention to his younger son.

"Look what you did!" Manasseh said, picking up two fragments of a broken arrow. Turning his reddened face on Ephraim, he hissed, "You spoil everything! I wish you were not my brother!"

"ENOUGH!" Joseph thundered, his eyes ablaze. Grabbing Manasseh by the shoulders, he shook him and said, "You will NEVER say that to your brother again, do you hear me?!"

Eyes wide with fright, Manasseh nodded. Shocked at both her son's and her husband's outbursts, Asenath placed a hand on Joseph's shoulder and whispered, "Beloved, please."

Joseph released his son abruptly and looked at his hands, as though they were a stranger's. They were trembling. His face had lost all color. Without another word, he spun around and exited the room.

Even the fall of a goose feather could have been heard in the chamber.

"Now you can imagine what I face with twin sons. Captain, if I were you, I would earnestly pray for another daughter!" Heqaib said.

A smattering of weak laughter spread across the room. Asenath cast a grateful glance at Heqaib.

"You say that because you have yet to give a daughter away! Talk to me after doing so, and we will see how you feel then," Potiphera said. The laughter was more intense this time.

"Music! And more wine!" the evening's hostess ordered. As the room filled with lively sounds, she crouched down to her sons, put one arm around each and drew them close. In fluent Hebrew, she said, "Your *abba* and I have always said to love each other, have we not?" The boys nodded. Looking at Manasseh, she said, "If you love your brother you will not be boastful of what you have, and you," she continued, turning to Ephraim, "will not be jealous of anything he has." Shifting her gaze back and forth between her sons, she added, "To love is to be kind; in deeds, and in words. Now apologize to each other for your wrongs."

Continuing in Hebrew, the boys addressed each other.

"I am sorry for breaking your arrow, Manasseh."

"And I am sorry for what I said, Ephraim. I did not mean it; I am happy you are my brother." The boys hugged each other.

"Manasseh, remember what we said you would do after you received your gifts?"

"Yes, *Ima*."

Asenath gave a signal, and the chorus of instruments was lowered to only a single harpist. Raising her voice and switching back to the dialect of Egypt, she said, "The celebrant has something to say."

"I wish to express my gratitude for your generosity of heart and . . ." he looked at his mother, and she waved both hands briefly, "heart and hands. Life and . . . Life, prosperity, and health to you all," he said, bowing deeply. As everyone applauded and cheered, Manasseh turned to his mother and added in Hebrew, "I like yours and *abba*'s gifts the best." She bent over and kissed her sweet son's head. Rising, she gave two signals: the first one caused the musicians to play louder, and the second made Merit rush to her side. Speaking only to her handmaiden's hearing, she said, "Have Basmat keep the children occupied, and discreetly request Her Radiance to regale the adults with tales. I shall return shortly." Merit dipped her head and Asenath exited the hall.

Picking up the skirt of her lengthy *kalasiris,* she headed for her husband's chambers as quickly as she could. She met Joseph pacing up and down, beads of perspiration decorating his forehead. He looked disturbingly pale.

"Beloved, I know how averse you are to rivalry among brethren, but I have never seen you like this! You are as one who has beheld a phantom!"

He stopped and looked at her; the sentiment in his eyes both unfamiliar and disturbing. "Not *one* phantom. Ten."

"Ten?" she repeated, arching an elegant brow.

"Ten. Appearing out of my past to plague my present; in flesh and blood."

Asenath's eyes doubled as the meaning of what he said hit her. Her hand involuntarily reached up to her heart. "By the life of Pharaoh . . . it cannot be . . ."

"But it is," he affirmed.

"No . . . they cannot be . . ."

"Yet they are." When the muscle in his lower jaw twitched and he clenched his fist, she identified the strange emotion in his eyes and a chill crept up her spine. It was rage.

"Where are they?" she asked cautiously.

"Where they belong. The dungeons."

Asenath caught her breath. "What . . . What will you do with them?"

"No more than what they intended to do to me," he said evenly, his eyes darkening.

They intended to kill him! Surely they deserve to be severely punished for their crimes, but to kill them, ALL? What manner of man would he become afterward? Will we be able to bear such a husband and father? Will he even be able to stomach himself? The questions racing through her mind were gravely unsettling. She walked to his side and placed her arm on his shoulder. "Beloved, please, sit a moment."

"I cannot," he said, resuming his feverish pacing.

Taking his hand, she tried to lead him toward the couch. "You need to calm yourself, and think—"

"Leave me be, woman!" He shrugged her arm off so aggressively, she stumbled backwards.

Asenath shrank back instinctively, her heart jumping into her throat. Her husband had never so much as raised his voice to her before, but his aggression, now twice displayed, triggered alarm in her. Her breathing quickened as the girl within her panicked at the anticipation of hands striking her womanly face. Not waiting to be issued a second order, Asenath turned and exited the room. Leaning against the wall, she took in a deep breath and let out a shaky one. As the unsettling feeling with which she had awakened blanketed itself around her being, two things settled themselves in her troubled mind:

First, she was going to have to make an excuse for her husband's abrupt exit and conclude hosting the evening alone.

Second, and immediately afterward, she was going to the garden altar, because she did not need a diviner to interpret her disturbing dream. A tempest was coming, fueled by the fury of vengeance, and her family was in the very eye of the storm.

30

A house
Built on the past
Windows to the future,
Shelter in the present. It gives
Neither

***

Absent.

Asenath had not seen her husband for two days. Thoughts of him were at the forefront of her mind, and her petitions. This was not the first time he had been away from home, given the far-reaching nature of his duties. It was, however, the first time she knew without a doubt that he could come home but had chosen to do otherwise.

Two nights ago, she'd had no difficulty making excuses on Joseph's behalf. Especially to those of their guests who had their own homes to which to return. But keeping her resident guests— her family—from plaguing her with questions was no small feat. Mercifully, her father had a three-day assembling of high priests keeping him occupied in the day, and his enthusiastic grandsons keeping him busy at night. Heqaib was at his side during the day, but the widower, knowing his children were in the best of care, took the rare opportunity to spend his nights with old military associates. Na'eemah's curiosity was therefore the most challenging to avoid.

The older woman was not one easily fooled. Should she be given the slightest opportunity, she would undoubtedly ask more questions than the captain of the king's guard interrogating an accused. Asenath had successfully hidden from Na'eemah for the better part of yesterday. But judging by the purposefulness of the motherly woman's approaching strides, it was time to face the music.

"Now, my sunshine, the afternoon meal is over. Basmat is keeping that boisterous brood occupied, and I would like nothing more than a goblet of wine and a game of *senet* with you."

"Is that so?"

"Assuming you have no objections? Surely you have a *senet* board somewhere here?"

"Certainly, Mother, though it will undoubtedly be dust-ridden from lack of use."

"All the more reason to put it to use, then."

Smiling, Asenath signaled a servant and sent her to retrieve the board. There was no use trying to escape the inevitable.

Their game started innocently enough, but no sooner had the older woman gained the upper hand than she began the game she really intended to play.

"Asenath, I have watched you grow from a screaming baby announcing her presence in this world to the beautiful wife, mother, and leader you are now. I know you better than I know my son. And I can tell, not only from your scarcity in the past day but also from the lackluster of your playing, that something other than the *senet* board occupies your thoughts." Na'eemah tossed the paddles and made her next move.

Asenath made no response, and Na'eemah continued her probing.

"Given your husband's abrupt exit two nights ago, and absence since, I can only assume whatever troubles you also troubles him. I know you are a strong woman, with your own very sound mind, so I will only ask: do you care to tell me what ails you, or do you prefer to carry its burden alone?"

"I do not carry it alone, Mother," Asenath said, making her next move. "I have not ceased to offer prayers to the Most High God."

Na'eemah made a curious face. "That is commendable, my dear; we must all pray. But sharing can also lighten a burden."

Asenath was torn between the desire to keep her husband's affairs private and the desire to unburden herself. Running a hand through her thick tresses, she sighed. "I cannot tell you all. It is a most delicate matter, but I will share what I can. Even what I do share must be kept in the strictest confidence."

"By the life of Pharaoh, I shall take it into the afterlife," Na'eemah vowed.

"Many years ago, a great injustice was done to my husband by persons he called family. He thought never to see them again. But to his great shock, their paths crossed two days ago. Even now, the offending parties sit in the dungeons at his command. But my husband is not himself. I have never seen him as furious as he was when we last spoke."

"These people . . . the wrong they did to your husband, is it worthy of imprisonment?"

Asenath sighed. "It is."

"Then I say they have only received what they deserve."

"For now, but . . ." Asenath fell silent, a frown marring her flawless face.

"Tell me, what is it you fear, truly?"

"I fear he may seek vengeance in the worst possible way, and if he does, live to regret it ever after."

"So you do not think their crime worthy of death?"

"Even if it is, I do not think their deaths should come at his hand." *That would make him no better than them.*

Na'eemah was pensive for a few moments, her *senet* pieces forgotten. "Answer me this then: has it not long been established that your husband is a man of unmatched wisdom?"

"Yes. But his wisdom comes from the invisible God."

"The same one to whom you say you have not ceased to pray, correct?"

"The very same," Asenath affirmed.

Adjusting her ample figure in a plush chair, Na'eemah asked, "Has this God answered any prayer of yours before now?"

"You know He has. Manasseh and Ephraim are evidence of his unmatched power."

"I can know nothing save what you testify about this God. But if he be as powerful as you say, and he has been giving your husband the wisdom that has made him the very savior of all Egypt, surely this God would not cease to instruct him now, when it is most needed. Would he?"

A sudden realization curved Asenath's lips into a smile. *The invisible God can use even those that do not know him to deliver a message to his own.* She heard the message loud and clear:

Trust Me.

She reached over, took Na'eemah's hand, and squeezed it. "Thank you."

"For what, my dear? The musings of an old woman?"

"No. The heart of a mother."

Na'eemah eyes misted, but she tried to mask her emotion by taking a sip from her goblet, and then tossing up her paddles to determine her next move. It was not a very fortunate one. And over the next several minutes, Asenath made a few fortunate tosses and won the game.

"By the mercy of Ra," sulked Na'eemah, "if this is how you show your gratitude, I would hate to be on the receiving end of your rage."

"You? Never!" Asenath said, laughing, as she reached over the board to hug Na'eemah's neck.

***

Joseph's house had retired for the night, but he purposefully made his way to the East wing. Absolutely nothing had gone in his favor for the past two days. His greatest frustration, however, was not being able to share the tiresome happenings with one person: a confidante, friend, partner, counselor, and lover, all merged into one incredible wife.

Asenath would probably have had a witty word at worst, and a simple solution at best, had he not driven her away two nights ago. Alas, he was now lonely when he most needed her companionship.

This conundrum is of my making, and so must be its remedy. He now stood before the door to his wife's chamber, nervously. He gave a gentle knock, and then eased the door open. Asenath was seated at her desk, scroll in hand, reading by the light of an oil lamp. When he cleared his throat, she looked up, and her amber eyes widened.

She did not expect to see me. The thought only exacerbated his regret.

"May I come in?" he asked tentatively.

She nodded, putting down her scroll.

"What were you reading?"

She smiled, almost sadly, before answering. "The verse you penned on our wedding night."

His insides knotted. *I show her the worst of me, and she holds on to the best of me. What manner of woman is this?* Joseph reached her in a few long strides. He kneeled at her feet, took her hand, and kissed it tenderly. "I behaved like a beast. Forgive me, my purple iris."

He felt her soft hand caress his hairless head, followed by the moist gentleness of her lips kissing it. "I can only imagine the tempest raging inside you, Beloved."

He looked up at her. "Seeing the thing I feared the most manifest itself before my eyes two nights ago was unbearable. That notwithstanding, I was wrong to direct my anger at you."

She cradled his face. "I forgive you, Joseph *ben* Jacob. *Ani ohev otkha.*"

Her tenderness disarmed him, and he sighed with relief.

"You do know, there is another who found himself in the path of your fury."

"Manasseh," Joseph whispered.

Asenath let her silence affirm him.

"I will speak to him; to both our sons. And your family—I owe them an apology for my absence during this visit. I hope they have not given you too difficult a time because of it?"

"No. I am sure they have no misgivings that your apology cannot erase."

"When do they leave?"

"Dawn, the day after tomorrow."

"Then I have a day, thankfully."

Asenath smiled.

Rising, Joseph let his eyes wander over the room aimlessly, as his mind once again fastened itself on the object of his turmoil. The chamber fell silent. It appeared Asenath had opted to keep whatever opinions she held to herself this time. He could not fault her after what happened when she last attempted advising him.

With a slow, soulful sigh, Joseph broke their silence. "If I had not seen them with my own eyes, I would not have believed it possible . . . In the past, I had often wondered how I would feel if I ever saw them again, but even my wildest imagination did not come close to the powerful emotions that overcame me the moment my eyes beheld the ten tormentors of my youth."

"Did they come searching for you?"

"No. The famine drove them in search of grain."

It was Asenath who sighed this time, and the sound expressed relief.

"They did not recognize me. I knew them instantly, but they . . ." His voice broke. "They knew not their own flesh and blood."

"Did you reveal yourself to them?"

And give them the relief of knowing their actions did not cost me my life? "No! Let them lie in the very dungeons that once housed me and think about their sins!"

Asenath was silent for a few moments, but then she asked, "But, Beloved, if you did not reveal yourself, upon what charge are they imprisoned?"

He felt a twinge of guilt. "Espionage."

She gasped.

Joseph turned to face her again, completely conflicted. "Seeing them bowing before me, the very picture of innocence and innocuity when I know their evil hearts, was too much for me! I had to punish them. Everything in me wants them to suffer as I did! But I think of our *abba* . . ." *Yet why should I show mercy to the merciless?* Shaking his head, he said, "I have done what I must. I have put them to the test."

"I see." Asenath said softly. "Testing those whom one has reason to distrust is wise. Of what manner is your test?"

"The kind that punishes my guilty brothers, while letting me once again see the only innocent brother I have."

"Benjamin?"

"Yes. I had the interpreter translate my demand that they send one from among themselves to bring Benjamin here, while the rest of them remain as my prisoners. I said if whomever they choose fails to return with him, then it proves that they are indeed spies!"

Even as he shared his demands, he noticed his wife's increasingly concerned expression. She finally voiced her thoughts. "Beloved, pardon me if I speak out of turn, but I am wondering . . . If truly they came for food, does that not imply that your *abba*, Benjamin, and all the wives and children of your brothers will starve when they do not receive sufficient grain? Surely one brother returning could not carry enough grain for so many mouths, could he?"

No, he could not. Joseph placed his face between his palms and sighed. *How can I punish the innocent along with the guilty?* "The wisdom of the Lord pours forth from your mouth. I shall let nine return and keep one here. Then we shall see if time has lightened the darkness of their hearts."

"I think you have chosen to do the right thing. I know it cannot be easy, and their sins deserve punishment, but I feel it is right."

"I fear what I might have done if I were without you at this moment."

His wife walked up to him and took his large hand in her slender one. "The Lord always knows what, and whom, we need in our darkest hour, Beloved."

"He does. Still, I fear . . . I ask myself, are we cursed?"

"Cursed? In what way?"

"First, my *dodh* Esau hated my *abba* and sought to kill him for supposedly stealing his birthright. Then my brothers hated me for dreams that were not of my making, or perhaps it was for being the recipient of *Abba*'s highest favor. Either way, they sought to kill me. And now I wonder if a generational curse of rivalry among brethren is to divide my sons, too. I cannot bear the thought of my sons becoming as my brethren and I!"

"The Lord forbid it!" Asenath said with an emphatic shake of her head.

The thought of one son feeling about the other, the way he felt about his older brothers, was unbearable. *Forbid it, indeed, Lord. And help me forget. I beg you, for my brothers' words torment me day and night.* He bowed his head, his voice weak with the weight of emotions. "My purple iris, you should have seen them. They stood there and shamelessly told me that one of their brothers was . . . that I was . . . no more." His body began to shake as he forced back the threatening flood of agonizing feelings.

He felt Asenath's arms encircle him, wordlessly. Throwing his arms about her, he crushed her against himself, trying to find a comfort that mysteriously eluded him.

31

The shoulders of boys
Under the burdens of men
Surely sorely sag

***

SEVERAL WEEKS LATER

Scorching.

The weather was oppressively hot. Even standing under the shade of a massive man-made canopy of palm fronds, Asenath's brow still bore beads of sweat. She wiped it as discreetly as she could and attained the desired result: the muscular bearer to her right waved the large goose-feather fan he held back and forth with renewed intensity. Asenath welcomed the resulting gusts of wind that wafted over her. The weather had been the worst part of her newfound translating duties since the famine forced a flood of grain-seeking guests into Egypt. But the scenery more than compensated for it.

Even now, as far as her eyes could see, there were people of every size, shape, and shade. Some sat on camels. Others on donkeys. There were masses more on foot. All of them headed for the imposing group of palatial buildings before which she stood. She tried to imagine what they must think of Egypt, as ones seeing it with fresh eyes.

The palace must seem a spectacular masterpiece of a structure. The pyramids in the distance were certainly awe-inspiring, even to eyes that had beheld them time and again. As for the temple, with its gigantic pylons and partially man, partially horse statues of Ra, it likely appeared grand but strange to those that did not bow to that god.

She heard yelling in the distance and tried to make out the cause of the commotion. An armed man was yelling in a Nubian dialect to clear the way for a woman who was likely nobility. She appeared to be on a carriage borne by four muscular, broad-shouldered, bare-chested men. They wore the skin of animals on their loins, and three gold bands around each of their necks. Each held her carriage up with one hand and held a golden-tipped copper spear in the other. The man in front who was yelling was dressed similarly. The only thing the bearers and the borne had in common was the color of their skin: dark as a shadow, yet it somehow reflected the sun's splendor. Asenath smiled to herself. *That might have been Neferubity, if the river of her life had flowed in a different direction.*

Asenath was deciding whether to end her final shift, at least for the foreseeable future, when her eye caught a movement. A party of bearded men dressed in tunics and shawls, with scarves tied about their heads, was making its way toward her. The men must have heard their native tongue from the translator standing closest to her. He was yelling in Hebrew, "If you understand me, make your way to me!"

When the men stood before the translator, the latter asked the first question that protocol demanded. "From where do you hail?"

"Shalom, my lord. We hail from the land of Canaan."

Canaan! Asenath's heart skipped a beat. Turning her full attention, she searched their faces and tried to count the number in their group.

"You are here to buy grain, correct?" he asked directly.

"Yes, my lord."

Stepping closer, Asenath spoke to the translator in the dialect of Egypt and he, in turn, questioned the leader of the group. "How many in your party?"

"Twelve, my lord."

"From one family?"

"No, we represent three families, my Lord."

It is not them. Asenath felt a twinge of disappointment.

"I see. We shall grant you an audience as one group. Have you any objections?"

"No, my lord, we are grateful for your kindness."

"Follow me." The translator led the men toward the main archway, saying, "You will see His Eminence Zaphnath-Paaneah, vizier of Egypt, briefly. He questions all visitors to our land and gives approval for grain to be sold to them. The audience should not take long." Pausing to eye the visitors, he warned, "Know this: he is a diviner, and the wisest man in all the land. Bow low before him and do not speak until he does."

"A diviner!" said one bewildered visitor to his companion. "Do you think he produces Egypt's grain by sorcery?"

"That would explain a lot. The grass here is as dull and brittle as Canaan's, yet they are swimming in grain!"

Asenath stifled her laughter with a small cough. Joseph would certainly find that story amusing. She could not remember the last time they had laughed together or shared an intimate moment. He was not himself and he had not been for several weeks. Not since he sent nine brothers back, keeping the one called Simeon imprisoned. The longer their absence from Egypt, the greater his absence from his family. Asenath simultaneously ached with him and longed for him, but all she could do was fervently pray for him. She besought the Lord daily to save him from himself. She had also found herself taking on the role of father in addition to being mother to their sons. That dual duty alone was more than enough responsibility for her shoulders to bear. Hence her giving up any duties outside of the home for the foreseeable future. She was going to miss seeing this sea of scintillating sights and sounds, but it was a small price to pay for the security of her home, let alone the happiness of her sons.

***

"*Ima* . . ."

"Yes, *b'ni*?" Asenath said, taking in her older son's sober expression.

"Does *Abba* not love us anymore?" the lanky boy asked.

Completely taken aback by his question, Asenath gasped. "Perish the thought, Manasseh! Your *abba* loves you both, very much indeed."

"But he does not play with us anymore."

"Yes!" his younger brother affirmed, pouting his plump lips.

He does not play with me, either, Asenath thought wistfully. "Your *abba* has a mountain of work these days, so he is very tired when he comes home."

"But why does he have so much work?" Manasseh asked.

How do I explain this? "He is solving a big problem for Pharaoh, lord of Egypt—long may he live."

"What kind of problem?" Ephraim asked, his grayish-green eyes shining with curiosity.

"He is making sure everyone in Egypt has food."

Ephraim's sun-kissed brow furrowed for a moment. "*Abba* is cooking for *everyone* in Egypt?"

Asenath laughed. "No, my little monkey. *Abba* is selling grain to everyone in Egypt. Because there is a famine right now."

"What is a famine?" Ephraim asked, tilting his chubby, shaved head.

"A famine is when there is not enough food in the land. There is no food growing from the ground because there has been no rain for a long, long time."

"Then where does *Abba* get the food he is selling?" her older son asked, crossing his long, lean arms.

"Excellent question. Many years ago, before either of you were born, your *abba*, and all the people working for him, started storing heaps and heaps of grain in very big containers called granaries. They did this because back then, the Lord God made His Divine Magnificence have mysterious dreams but only revealed their meaning to your *abba*, showing him that there would be a seven-year famine after seven years of plentiful harvests. And because your *abba* was the only one who knew the meaning of the dreams, the lord of Egypt put him in charge of everything and everyone, and *abba* made sure all the granaries were full before the famine started. And that is where he gets the grain to sell to everyone here, and people from lands far, far away. That is also why your *abba* is known as the wisest man in all of Egypt!"

The boys simultaneously uttered exclamations of understanding and delight.

"And His Divine Magnificence is very pleased with your *abba*."

After a brief, pensive pause, during which he nibbled the nail of his index finger, Manasseh asked, "But, *Ima*, if he is making everyone happy, then why is he sad?"

It was his mother's turn to be thoughtful. *How can I make them understand the tempest raging in their father's soul? And why should I burden children with loads adults can barely shoulder?* "He just has some bad feelings deep down inside," she said, placing a hand on her chest. "But he will be happy when they go away."

"But when will they go away?" Ephraim asked innocently.

The question of the season, his mother mused. *What if his brothers never return? Will he never become his happy self again?* Asenath had hoped Joseph's brothers were better men now, but that did not seem to be the case. They had thus far abandoned Simeon to rot in prison, just like they had left Joseph to a calamitous fate all those years ago. She wondered what kind of hearts his brothers had—assuming they possessed any at all. What had made them so unfeeling, so unsympathetic, that they would act so cruelly to their own kin?

"When, *Ima*?" Ephraim tugged at the skirt of her *kalasiris* impatiently, bringing her out of her musing.

"I am sorry, *b'ni,* I know not when."

Her sons' faces saddened.

Thinking quickly, she added, "But I know who can take the bad feelings away." *If Beloved will let him,* she added silently.

"Who?" they asked simultaneously, their curious faces fastened on hers.

"The Lord God Almighty. The unseen God that sees all things and knows all things. How about if we all ask him to take away the bad feelings in your *abba*'s heart so he can be happy again? Do you want to do that?"

"Yes!" they chorused, both nodding excitedly, as their matching sidelocks bounced.

"Then I need you to be smart little soldiers and get ready to charge." Asenath made a hollow fist with her right hand and raised it to her lips, making her best imitation of the sound of a horn. "Toooo-rooooo!" Deepening her voice, she barked out orders. "Now, Captain Manasseh and Second Captain Ephraim! Stand up straight! Chest out, chin up!"

The boys obeyed each charge instantly.

Their mother continued. "So you say you want to wage war with some big, bad feelings?"

"Yes!" the eager lads answered in unison.

"Are you sure you are ready?"

"Ready!"

"I cannot hear you, soldiers!"

"READYYYYY!" the brothers yelled with all their might.

"Better! Now, on the count of three, we shall charge to our battle station in the very center of the garden! Do you understand your orders?"

"Yes!" they chorused excitedly.

"That is 'Yes, Commander,' to you!"

"Yes, Commander!"

"Good. Now take your starting positions!"

Manasseh leaned forward on his right leg with his left arm raised and bent at the elbow, poised as though ready to run. Unfortunately, Ephraim, misunderstanding the stance, leaned with both his right leg and right arm forward.

Asenath stifled a giggle, trying to maintain her authoritative character.

"One, two, CHARGE!" she ordered.

"CHAAAARGE!!!" the boys screamed, running as fast as their little legs could carry them.

Asenath took a deep breath and let it out slowly.

She did not know how long she could bear the dual parental duties without herself getting some bad feelings deep down inside. *Today is not the day to give in to discouragement,* she told herself. *It is the day to fight harder. Lord God, grant me strength.*

With that prayer, she took off running after her little soldiers, bellowing, as they had. "CHAAAARGE!!!"

***

Asenath and her sons—with Basmat trailing behind them— were returning from their garden adventure when she sighted her husband's steward, Perneb. *Why is he here and not with Beloved this morning?* The principled, punctual, and very particular Perneb had been Captain Potiphar's recommendation to replace the duplicitous Wadjenes almost seven years ago. Perneb had proven to be a jewel of a steward, with a refreshing sense of sincerity and loyalty.

"Blessings of the morning, Your Eminence, and my lords," he said with a bow.

"And to you also, Perneb," Asenath responded. Turning to her sons, she asked, "What do we say, lads?"

"Blessings of the morning," her sons chorused, dipping their heads slightly.

Facing her husband's steward once more, she said, "I must inquire, what returns you home so early?"

"His Eminence has sent me home with urgent orders to have a meal prepared for some foreign visitors."

"I see. Have you any idea who these visitors are?"

"Yes. Shepherds from Canaan who came to buy grain."

The ones I saw? But why would he host them?

"How many men, exactly?"

"Ten, my lady."

Ten? Could it be?

Before she could think of an appropriate following question, Perneb added, "Actually, counting the one that was just released from incarceration, there will be eleven men dining."

It IS them. ALL of them! Asenath masked her growing excitement with an unbothered tone. "Eleven, I see. And His Eminence wants us to feed these visitors?"

"His Eminence means to dine with them, Your Eminence. At noon."

"*Abba* is coming?" Manasseh asked, eyes brimming with hope.

Asenath gave him a look that said, '*Do not interrupt,*' before turning her attention back to Perneb.

"Has he any special instructions for the meal?"

"Yes. That a selection of Hebrew delicacies be added to the courses, and the visitors be seated separately—they are shepherds," Perneb said, making a disgusted face.

Then Beloved is yet to reveal himself to them. "Naturally, Perneb. I shall have the kitchen prepare accordingly. You may go and see to the men's preparatory needs."

"Yes, Your Eminence," Perneb said with a bow.

As he turned and began briskly walking away, Manasseh resumed his inquiry. "*Abba* is coming, is he not?"

Asenath smiled at her son's enthusiasm. "He is. To feast with some special visitors."

"Can we feast with him too?" asked Manasseh.

"Yes, *Ima*, can we?" seconded Ephraim.

"Not this time, my sons."

"Why not?" Ephraim whined.

"This is a formal feast with foreign visitors. That means your *abba* is working and will not be able to play with you."

The boys' countenances saddened.

"Not to worry, your *abba* and I are sure to throw many more *informal* feasts, and you shall attend them all. But today, I need you to play with each other, and do as Basmat tells you. Will you do that for me?"

"Yes, *Ima*," they both promised.

As her sons followed Basmat to their play chamber, Asenath headed for the kitchen, thoughtfully.

Her husband's brothers had returned—all of them. It was either they had become better men, or the famine had inspired them to at least pretend so. Only the Lord who saw and knew all would know which was the case. In under two hours, her beloved was coming to dine with his brothers. This meal was either going to be a celebration or a catastrophe, but it would certainly be memorable. She may not be able to control the outcome, but there was one thing she could control: the meal would be a feast worthy of Pharaoh himself. After all, questionable or not, those men were her brothers by marriage. She would make sure they knew from entrance to exit that they dined in the house of an incomparable vizier; one whose wisdom was presently preserving every single one of them alive.

A separate table, set for eleven brothers . . . As an idea took shape in her mind, Asenath smiled and hastened her strides. If she was going to bring this notion to life, she had an additional task to complete immediately after instructing the kitchen staff: revisiting the first entry in her husband's journal.

32

The broken heart
Holding its despised
Forever bleeds on its beloved

***

Regal.

Dressed in ceremonial attire, complete with his wig, Joseph entered his formal feasting chamber from a side door and paused, taking in the excellence before him. The feast that had been laid out was one fit for a king.

My wife. Undoubtedly, she had taken the liberty of seeing to the arrangements herself. Her touch was in every detail, from ceiling to floor. *I should have invited her to join us,* he thought ruefully. That oversight was proof that he was not quite himself. He knew he had been distant, and it was partly to avoid subjecting his loved ones to a repeat outburst of his inner turmoil. But today, at least, his eyes had given his heart a reason to hope when they beheld his beloved brother.

He headed for the smallest of the three meticulously-decorated tables in the grandiose chamber. It was laid out in the host's area—the elevated northern section of the hall. As he took his seat, he noticed there was an additional place setting at his table. Before he could question a servant why, the main doors opened. He looked at the entrant and his heart stopped for the briefest moment.

My purple iris.

She glided in with a grace and glory to rival any queen. Her long, sheath *kalasiris* was sleeveless and showed off her figure. A dark, jewel-encrusted concealed her chestnut mane. Gold jewels adorned her wrists and ankles, and the elaborate *usekh* that had been her wedding gift from the lord of Egypt graced her neck. The bottom half of her face bore a sheer, white veil. And he knew why. They were dining with foreign visitors, and not just any, but Hebrew shepherds—a group especially abhorred by Egyptians. He was certain by her uninvited presence she knew they were his brothers, but no other person did. To have entered with an unveiled face would not only be considered insulting to him as vizier, but it would raise suspicion. *She dons her veil to honor me.*

He watched her every step as she crossed the larger and lower section of the hall, heading directly for him. As she ascended the three small steps to the host's area and bowed, he rose to greet her with a formal kiss on each veiled cheek. He lingered long enough to whisper, "You look incandescent. I am delighted to have you here."

"I am pleased to hear it," Asenath said, her bright smile evident beneath her thin veil. They both took their seats and Joseph signaled Perneb, who stood at the main entrance.

At Perneb's order, guards swung open the main doors once more. Eleven men entered the great room, and Asenath observed them closely. They had long, curly, dark hair and thick beards peeping out from under their linen head coverings, which were secured in place with thin sashes. Most of them were graying, some more than others. Their skin showed that they spent a lot of time in the sun. They wore long, belted tunics in various light colors: gray, tan, or white. Brown leather sandals and shepherd's staffs completed their clothing. She was unsure of which brother was whom, except for Benjamin. His youth made him stand out, and his facial features resembled her husband's.

This is what Beloved would look like if he stopped shaving! Asenath thought, with a newfound appreciation for her clean-shaven husband.

Following Perneb across the full length of the large guests' area, the men stood at the foot of the host's section and bowed with their faces to the ground.

"Rise!" Joseph said, communicating through a translator.

As they rose, one of the most silver-haired of the men held up a neatly tied, linen bundle.

"Your servants have brought a humble gift from our land for Your Eminence's delight."

Joseph gestured a signal and Perneb received the bundle and brought it up to his table. The steward unwrapped it to reveal a lovely assortment of Canaan's finest exports: honey, spices, myrrh, pistachio nuts, and almonds.

A thoughtful gift. I wonder which of their wives put this together, Asenath mused.

Evidently, Joseph's mind was on more pressing matters, for he gave the gift only a passing glance before addressing his brothers.

"I am pleased to see you returned to Egypt. Tell me, are your families well?"

"Yes, Your Eminence, your servants are all well," responded the graying brother that was clearly their chosen spokesman.

"And your old father, of whom you spoke, is he well? Is he still alive?"

"Your servant, our father, is alive and in good health, Your Eminence."

Asenath was watching their interaction closely. Joseph's eyes were fixed on Benjamin. "Is this your youngest brother, of whom you spoke?"

The voice of the group put his arm around Benjamin and nudged him a step forward. "He is, Your Eminence."

Asenath could tell her husband was waging an inner war. He looked like an ancient wineskin whose fermented contents threatened to expel themselves at any moment.

"God be gracious to you, my son," her husband said to his younger brother, his voice breaking.

"Thank you, Your Eminence," Benjamin answered, bowing low.

Without another word, Joseph leaped from his seat and hurried out of the hall through the side door. A startled Perneb was about to follow, but Asenath stopped him. "I will see to His Eminence. Order the musicians to play."

As the steward bowed, she hurried after her husband. She heard him weeping loudly even before she entered his chamber. The sound of his anguish made her heart bleed.

Lord have mercy. Wanting to give rein to tears herself, she paused at the entrance for a moment and whispered a prayer: "Grant me the wisdom to know how best to help him, O Lord." Taking a deep breath, she went in.

Her husband was on his knees, bald head bowed into his palms, shaking with sobs. His discarded wig lay upside down on the ground a handbreadth away. She kneeled beside him and silently caressed his bent back, trying to imbue him with comfort. She was otherwise at a loss for what to do. His sobs softened after several minutes, and then he raised his head and spoke.

"You must think me weak, and a fool," he said in a shaky voice.

"Neither, and never, Beloved," she responded, shifting her position so she faced him directly.

"I could not look at Benjamin a moment longer and have him not know me . . . all I want to do in this moment is run and embrace him."

"Then why not do so? I myself thought you ordered this feast to reveal yourself to them."

"Not yet . . ." Joseph sniffed. "I love Benjamin, but . . . I struggle. A part of me wants to see them pay for their sin . . . the other part remembers we are still brethren."

The anguish in his eyes was tearing at Asenath's soul. "You cannot continue this ruse, Beloved. It is destroying you. And I . . . I cannot bear to see you like this," she said, turning away.

He crumbled into a seated position on the floor. "Every time I see them, I remember how I begged them and they just mocked me! Their words torment me until I can think of nothing else! What did I ever do to deserve their hatred? I am their very flesh and blood. How could they hate me so?"

Lord, I have no answer to this agony. Seating herself beside him, she placed a hand on his shoulder. "I have no answers, Beloved. I did not suffer what you did, so I can only try to imagine your anguish. But I need you to think on this: that helpless lad they sold into slavery is no more. You are vizier of all Egypt. No man can raise hand or foot but at your word. Their fate is in *your* hands now. Thus, they have no power over you except that which you give them by dwelling on the memory of their sin."

"But I cannot forget their sin."

"And I cannot make you forget. Yet were it not for that memory, you could not find fault in them today, for they have passed your test. Have they not?"

Joseph was silent for a while. "One of my tests," he said, his eyes darkening. "But I am not convinced. I want to test them further."

Test them further? He means to continue this duplicity? Asenath did not like the thought of that. She folded her hands in her lap and asked, "To what end, Beloved?"

"To know what is in their hearts."

"And if they fail your next test? What then? Do you not see that prolonging this facade will only extend your torment?" Asenath raised herself to a kneeling position and clasped her hands together. "I beg you, either reveal yourself and punish them in a manner befitting their betrayal, or send them back to their families none the wiser. For as long as you remain in this duplicitous state, you are punishing the ones that love you in favor of the ones that wronged you. Your sons need you," she said, leaving unsaid, *I need you!* "They miss their *abba*, and I cannot keep making excuses for your absences." Her voice broke. "I cannot . . ." Raising her hands as though in surrender, she shook her head. "No. I will not let you do that to us anymore."

Joseph looked at her, his swollen, blotchy face bearing a confused expression.

She slowly rose to her feet. "I am taking our sons to Potiphar and Neferubity's for a time; they have been asking to have the lads visit, and I think now is the time. I will tell our sons it is an adventure. They will not grieve for you as much there."

"No!" Joseph said, instantly sitting up. "You cannot leave now . . . I need you," he added, stretching his arm toward her briefly before retracting it.

I am not enough. Her husband's face blurred as her eyes watered. "I cannot eat a meal and pray it quenches your hunger," she said. "Every day, I have gone to the garden to intercede on your behalf; when last did you tarry at the altar yourself?"

His silence spoke volumes.

Blinking back the teardrops that were dangerously close to escaping her eyes, Asenath placed a trembling hand on her husband's drooping shoulder. "No one but the Lord God can still the storm that rages within you. If you do not reach out to him, it will not only consume you, it will destroy us, too." Lifting her hand to her face, she brushed a lone tear aside. "I will see that our sons are settled in before I return."

Her husband raised his teary eyes to her; his mouth opening and shutting wordlessly. She closed her eyes and turned around, heading for the exit. She hesitated at the door and turned back to look at him. Head in his hands, he resembled a statue of sorrow itself.

O my heart. "The Lord be with you, Beloved," she whispered. Then she walked out of his chamber, letting the tears she had been trying to restrain flow freely. She thought her heart would shatter into a thousand irreparable fragments. *O God, why is it so difficult to trust you? I am powerless, and you are omnipotent. I commend him into your hands. He is lost; show him your way. Help him . . . help us, please.*

***

Joseph watched his wife exit, dazed. Her words stung his already bleeding heart. *Have I truly been making my family pay for my brother's sins?* He could not fault Asenath for exercising a maternal instinct to protect her young. *What do I do now?* He was uncertain of the answer, but he knew one thing: it was not sitting on the floor, sorrowing while the feast he had ordered remained suspended. His wife would not cover for his lapse today. He had to rise to the responsibility of the occasion, or make himself out to be a very ungracious host.

Benjamin is in my house, seated at my table, at this very moment. That was enough to focus on for now. He rose and carefully dried his tear-stained face before replacing his wig. His appearance hopefully restored back to its stately order, he returned to the great dining hall. He heard musicians playing from the outside, but once he reentered the chamber, they ceased. He seated himself again and his brothers, who were still standing where he'd left them, bowed low once again.

"Rise and be comfortably seated. You are guests at my table today," he ordered via the translator.

"We are honored, Your Eminence," Judah replied, rising, as his brothers followed suit.

If Perneb was wondering why his master had returned alone, he did not let on. He simply ushered the brothers to their seats. Joseph, who was watching them like a hawk, saw them examine little parchments upon each seat and exchange befuddled glances among themselves. As they took their seats, Joseph wondered what the source of their astonishment was until he realized. They were seated in order of age from Reuben to Benjamin, with Benjamin at the tail of the long, rectangular table such that he was facing Joseph directly.

Another one of my wife's thoughtful touches. As a bittersweet feeling wrapped itself around him, snatches of his brothers' murmurs drifted into his ears.

"How can this be?" Reuben asked.

"This vizier is truly a diviner like none other! If he has so accurately discerned our ages, what prevents him from divining our sins?" Levi asked.

"Be quiet, his translator is but a stone's throw away!" Judah hissed.

Amused, Joseph feigned ignorance of their chatter and waited for them to settle down. Then he raised his silver goblet in his right hand. "Life, prosperity, and health! Let the feasting begin!"

The musicians in the southeast corner of the hall resumed their playing. Belly dancers appeared seemingly out of thin air and began twirling and twisting in time with the drums. The servants who had stood waiting until now, went about dishing out course after course of tantalizing meals, first to their master, and then to his guests.

Having lost his appetite, Joseph shuffled his food around his plate inattentively, his eyes fixed on his brothers. At first, they ate tentatively. But once they realized they were being served food and wine without measure, they relaxed. He focused on Benjamin, delighted to see his beloved brother eating heartily. Since he had no interest in consuming his specially prepared delicacies, he decided to send them to a healthy, deserving appetite.

Signaling Perneb, he ordered, "Have portions from my table given to the youngest man; he can have five times as much food as the others."

Perneb carried out the order swiftly. Joseph saw Benjamin's face light up when his fine foods arrived. His brother looked up at him, but when their eyes met, Benjamin quickly lowered his. Not before Joseph recognized an emotion in his beloved brother's eyes that added salt to the fresh wounds in his own soul: fear. *Why would he not fear me? He knows me not as anything but the terrifying diviner that holds in his mystical hands the fates of himself and his brothers. I have to change that immediately.*

Joseph signaled, and the musicians lowered their enthusiastic playing to a soft melody. Rising, he spread his arms in a magnanimous gesture. "It pleases me to know that you are indeed the eleven brothers of one father. All charges of espionage against you are hereby withdrawn. Be at ease, eat and drink. You may afterward return to your father with as much grain as you can carry."

Judah rose, visibly relieved. "Your servants are most grateful for your kindness, Your Eminence." As he bowed, his ten brothers rose and did the same.

"Let the feasting continue!" Joseph ordered. Immediately, the festivities resumed.

He had just put them at ease for Benjamin's sake; but he did not trust them. They might have come to Simeon's rescue, but he was one of the older ten. Benjamin, on the other hand, was not. Beckoning Perneb, who swiftly came to his side, he quietly issued an order.

"As you did before, return each man's pouch of coins to the mouth of his grain sack."

"They came with double the coin this time, Your Eminence, to repay the previous."

Interesting. "Did you accept it?"

"No. I told them we had received full payment and the coin they found must be a treasure from their god."

"Superb. Now hear me well. Take my goblet after I leave and conceal it in the sack of the youngest man. Make no mistake, it must be the sack of the one currently seated at the head of their table, devouring the delicacies from mine. They will probably set off at dawn. After they have journeyed a while, pursue them. When you catch them, ask why they have been so cruel as to repay my kindness with evil and steal the cup with which I divine. They will protest, undoubtedly, but insist on searching all their sacks and say that the one in whose sack you find the cup must return as my slave; he alone. Employ the utmost discretion, and bring him directly to me upon your return."

"Yes, Your Eminence."

Before the sun sets tomorrow, brothers, I shall know the true hue of your hearts. Joseph did not know what the result of his test would be, but he knew one thing: if their jealousy caused his older brothers to abandon another favored brother to a fearful fate, this time, he would serve justice swiftly and severely.

33

Winds howl. Rains pelt.
In the eye of the storm she soundly sleeps.
Her name? Peace

***

Satiated.

The remnants of a late afternoon assortment of fruits, nuts, and baked goods lay before an overstuffed group comprising of three adults and three children. The lord of the elegant villa rose and cleared his throat. "Young warriors, I propose we adjoin to the courtyard, that I may show you how to disarm your enemy in three precise moves. Does anyone second my proposal?"

"I second!" said Manasseh, leaping to his feet.

"Me too," added Ephraim, mimicking his brother.

"Me three, Father!" Benerib chimed in, her curls bouncing as she jumped up and down.

"Excellent!" Captain Potiphar said, rubbing his hands together in delight. "Now, line up in your ranks, and move out in an orderly fashion, upon the count of three." The children scrambled to their feet.

"One, two, three!"

Girl and boys marched forward all at once, collided with themselves and then proceeded to file out in a rather disorganized manner, much to the amusement of their watching mothers, who sat side by side.

"I would speak falsehood if I termed that anything other than the most disorderly exit I have ever seen," Neferubity said.

Asenath let out the burst of laughter she had been holding in. Wiping her moist eyes, she said, "That should teach the captain not to attempt making warriors out of babes!"

"Him? He is far too happy to have males under his roof to care!"

"Thank you, my friend, for your hospitality; words cannot describe how much it means to me, especially today."

"Do not thank me until they are returned to you unscathed!"

Asenath offered a lackluster smile.

"I gather this has not been a day of fair weather," her observant friend noted.

"It has been a rather stormy one, unfortunately," Asenath admitted. "And there is no sign of the storm abating soon."

"You know I would not hesitate to weather the worst tempest with you, my friend. You need only tell me what is to be done."

"Therein lies my conundrum. Unlike the last time we battled together, I do not know in this case what is to be done. I only know who must undertake the doing of something, lest my family become a casualty of this circumstance."

"The suddenness of your visit and sullenness of your countenance indicate that party is the revealer of secrets."

"Who has chosen instead to be the concealer of a secret; and that choice is wounding him."

One of Neferubity's thick eyebrows arched, but she said nothing.

"Truthfully, it is wounding us all, but I cannot force him to choose otherwise."

Neferubity adjusted her pregnant form atop her heavily cushioned seat, such that her warm eyes now stared directly at Asenath's sad ones. "From what you have taught me, even our Lord gives men the liberty of choice."

"I know, but in this case I wish the Lord would not. I wish he would make my husband do whatever is needful. Neferubity, it was no small grievance that caused his choice, so my heart bleeds for him. Yet simultaneously, my shoulders bleed from bearing the burdensome consequences of his secrecy. I felt like I was drowning under that weight this afternoon, and I had to surface for air."

"Then, my friend, consider my home your sanctuary of reviving winds," Neferubity said, her long arms spread out in an open invitation.

It was not lost on Asenath that her friend had listened without prying and offered comfort. If their positions were reversed, she was uncertain she would have been so gracious. The sincerity in the Nubian's piercing brown eyes melted Asenath's heart, and unstopped the pools of tears that were her own eyes. She leaned into her friend's embrace and let herself cry. She felt Neferubity's soft hands gently massaging her back in comforting motions.

After several moments, Neferubity spoke. "Perhaps you struggle under a weight that is not yours to carry. Should you wish to hand it over to much stronger arms, our altar is yours, tonight, tomorrow, whenever."

Asenath released herself from Neferubity's embrace and looked her friend in the eyes. "Thank you, but perhaps I should go back. I promised my husband I would return as soon as our sons settled in —"

"Then consider them yet unsettled. At least for tonight, agreed?"

Eyes lowered, Asenath was silent. *I do not know what to do, Lord.*

"Asenath, I think more time in calm winds might let you better ride out the storm."

I will do nothing but trust you, Lord. Looking up into Neferubity's flawless, friendly face once again, Asenath said, "Agreed."

"Marvelous, and not a moment too soon." Rubbing her perfectly circular protruded belly, she added, "The warrior within demands nourishment, and will not abide any delays!"

Asenath laughed lightly, as Neferubity called for her handmaiden. "Tell me, what delicacies might you and your sons have a taste for tonight?"

"I assure you Neferubity, whatever the warrior within wants, the warriors without will devour!"

"In that case, we shall sail together as smoothly as a school of fish in the sea!"

As her host turned to instruct her nearby handmaiden, Asenath made a silent plea. *Lord, my family is split apart tonight. Have mercy on us. Restore light to our hearts and laughter to our home.*

***

After so much merrymaking, every occupant of Joseph's household slept soundly that night. Except the insomnolent lord of the seaside villa, who lay on his bed, alone. His heart was devoid of peace and his eyes, bereft of sleep. His mind was a cauldron of words, at the very brim of which swam his brothers'.

You have flaunted Abba's favor in our faces for far too long! . . . Let us kill him and end this once and for all! . . . Let us see what becomes of your dreams now!

Throwing his hands on his head as if that would stop the torturous thoughts, he cried out, "Help me forget, Lord! Ease my anguish!" Slapping his hand on his chest, he wailed, "My heart bleeds, Lord. It still bleeds from the thrusts of an ancient dagger." With a broken voice, he whispered, "How could I not test the ones who wielded it so mercilessly?"

And if they fail your next test? What then? Asenath's words pushed past the tormenting thoughts in his mind. *No one but the Lord God can still the storm raging within you . . . When last did you tarry at the altar yourself?*

He actually could not remember when. Like a jester balancing baubles, he had been overly occupied with trying to balance an endless array of palatial demands, the responsibilities of being a husband and father, and the heavy burden in his soul. But he knew if he continued to carry all three, they would crush him so deeply that the ground upon which he stood would become his grave.

Rising, Joseph snatched a cloak and the nearest torch, and raced out of his chamber. He did not stop running until he reached the garden. As he came upon the clearing in the heart of which stood the altar, he momentarily froze at an unexpected sight: clusters of purple irises bloomed all around the base of the altar.

My wife's handiwork. Has it really been so long since I was here? A sense of shame filled him. Was it not he who had said no one in his household would worship any other gods? Yet, here he was, doing the very thing he had forbidden. The turmoil in his soul had become a god. If his bitter burden was taking all of his attention, and taking the place of his time at the altar, and his time with his family, was it not then an idol?

His wife's words resurfaced. *Every day, I have gone to the garden to intercede on your behalf.*

He should have been the one visiting the altar daily, and with his sons, no less. He set the torch to the wood resting upon the tabular stone surface. As the flames rose, he fell to his knees.

"O Lord God Almighty, God of my father and forefathers, forgive me. Were this my altar alone, its embers would have since been reduced to a pile of ashes. Forgive me, for I have been relying on my wisdom, forgetting that it is foolishness when compared to yours. Without you, I can discern nothing. Help me, Lord. Help me forget; but if I must remember, then take away the sting of my memories that they may wound no more.

"My heart bleeds; it bleeds upon the ones I love. I do not want to lose my family in a bid to save my feelings, Lord. I do not know what to do, but I look to you. You who see the thoughts and intents of all hearts show me the way. Have mercy on me, O God, have mercy . . ."

On and on, Joseph lamented and petitioned with a renewed transparency and fervency. He prayed until words failed him. Heart-wrenching sobs burst forth from him like blood from a severed artery. When his cries were gone, all that was left were groans. He groaned and rocked back and forth on his knees. Finally, when the pain had bled out of his wounded soul, all strength left his body. He fell asleep at the foot of the altar, his head resting against the purple irises.

When he opened his eyes, he was in a painfully familiar, suffocating chamber. His hands and feet were chained and there was a lock on his chains.

Where am I?

It was cold and dark, and a foul odor assaulted his nostrils. He looked up to see a dazzling light shining in from a small window and he shuffled toward it, trying to see what the source of the light was. He saw a gigantic hand from which the light emerged. It was shaped like a man's hand, but multiple times larger. He could barely look at it for its luminosity, but he made out a key in the giant palm, and somehow, he knew. *That key will unlock my chains.*

He tried to reach for it, but the enormous fingers fisted over it. Then the hand turned a quarter-revolution and the index finger uncurled, pointing at his torso. Confused, he looked down at himself. His eyes fell upon a small bronze object attached to a rope around his loins.

Another key! He reached for this key and tried using it to open the lock on his chains, but it did not fit. Suddenly, the light moved, illuminating the dark floor enough for Joseph to discover another surprise. His chain extended all the way to a door in the rear wall of his prison chamber and disappeared under it. He followed it, trying to tug at the chain. As he leaned toward the door, he heard a collective wailing.

I know these voices! The moving light now shone on another window high on the wall, and to the east of the door. It was well above his sights. He looked around and saw a small bench beside the door. He shuffled himself onto its wooden surface and peered through the window.

There, in a chamber similar to, but larger than his, were his ten older brothers. They were huddled together in a circle, and chained to each other. They looked haggard, and starving, as though they had been there for decades. Their heart-breaking cries continued. The brilliant light shifted again, revealing that the chain that bound them all extended from Judah's feet, under the door toward his own feet.

I am chained to them! Joseph realized in shock. He could not get out even if he tried to. The mysterious light shone on a bronze lock in the door to their chamber, and then he saw the hand suddenly appear again. This time, it appeared inside his chamber and the index finger began to write on the wall: *I . . . desire . . . mercy . . . not . . . judgment.*

Mercy, not judgment? The realization of what he must do flooded his formerly confused mind. He took the bronze key and tried it on the door to his brothers' chamber. It unlocked. He shuffled his way to a bewildered Judah and reached for the lock on his chains. Then he inserted the key, turned it, and was rewarded with a singular click. He unbound Judah's stiff hands. One by one, the rest of his brothers were similarly unchained with that bronze key. Then they all followed Joseph into his chamber. Once there, Joseph saw the massive hand open once more, revealing the gold key.

Joseph reached for the coveted key, but since his wrists were still chained, his hand fell short of it. Judah came to his aid, reaching for the gleaming key, and tried it in the lock on Joseph's chains. A welcome click was heard as it unlocked. *I am free!*

Suddenly, the light shifted, temporarily blinding him. He shut his eyes momentarily and felt a pain in his neck. Reopening his eyes, he recognized his lush surroundings.

I slept.

At the foot of the altar.

All night.

Raising his head away from the stones, he massaged his sore neck. Suddenly, a thought slammed itself into his mind. *The ultimate test was set for this morning!* The cool day was already at its brightest, which meant his brothers had surely set off and the test was underway. *I might still stop it if I send a rider after Perneb.* Judging by the height of the sun in the sky, he was most likely too late. He did not know whether his brothers would pass or fail his test, but he now knew exactly what his response must be, regardless.

"Thank you, Lord God of mercy, for showing me your way. Grace me to walk in it this very day." Rising, he brushed leaves and flower petals off his cloak, wrapped it tightly around himself and began making his way back into his villa, purposefully. The hour no longer mattered, for the time was no longer in question. It was time to still the storm.

***

Joseph had just reached his own chamber when a racing servant caught up to him. "Forgive me, Your Eminence, but Perneb awaits at the entrance and asks that I inform you he has returned with the foreign visitors who departed this dawn."

"All of them?"

"Yes, Your Eminence."

This I must see to believe. "I shall join Perneb shortly. You may go."

As the servant hastened away, Joseph entered his chamber and examined himself in his mirror. In this state, he could pass for an unkempt servant in his own home. Quickly shedding his grass-stained garment, he selected the nearest pristine replacement and wore it. Placing his ceremonial wig atop his head, he took in his partially worn kohl eyeliner but told himself, *This will have to do.*

Exiting the chamber hurriedly, he headed for the main entrance, overcome by curiosity. As it came into view, he saw through the fully opened doors that Perneb stood there with the translator from the feast beside him. Before him stood all of Joseph's brothers. Keeping his face stony, the lord of the villa strode briskly and stood in the center of the doorway.

"What is this evil you have done?" he asked sternly, as the interpreter hastily translated. "Do you not know that such a one as I can divine every single one of your deeds?"

Eleven visibly frightened men fell on their faces, lying prostrate before one. Immediately, Joseph saw an image in his mind: eleven sheaves of wheat bowing to one.

My dream. His brothers did not know it, but they were executing an obeisance divinely foretold decades before. *All twelve of us are but pieces in the Lord's senet game.* The knowledge of God's sovereignty, coupled with the understanding of his limitless compassion, was salve upon Joseph's wounded heart. It still bled, but now it was spilling drops of mercy.

He watched Judah cautiously lift his graying head and speak in a completely broken voice. "What shall we say to such a one as His Eminence? How can we claim innocence when God has exposed the sins of your servants? Behold, we all are Your Eminence's slaves."

"God forbid that I should commit such injustice!" Joseph said. "The man in whose hand the cup was found, he alone shall be my servant. The rest of you arise and return to your old father in peace."

Joseph turned around to enter his house again, but the sound of Judah's cry stopped him in his stride.

"O eminent lord, I beseech you!"

Joseph turned to see Judah on his feet.

Dipping his head, Judah continued, "Do not let Your Eminence's anger be kindled against your servant, for you are as Pharaoh himself to us. Pray, permit your servant to speak a word to Your Eminence privately."

Turning to Perneb, Joseph said, "Give me a few moments and then usher them in. I will grant them an audience inside." Lifting a silent plea to the Lord for grace, Joseph walked into his residence, and took a deep breath, trying to compose himself.

Moments later, in the heart of his immaculate antechamber, his brothers once again fell prostrate before him. And Judah resumed his plea. "Your Eminence, before he would give us leave to return to Egypt a second time, your servant, my father, said to us, *'My beloved wife bore me two sons. The first of them is not, surely torn to pieces, for I have never seen him since. And if you take the second one from me, and some evil should befall him, you will bring my hairs down in sorrow to the grave.'"*

Joseph's heart knotted at the thought of his *abba*'s grief, but he stood silently as Judah continued.

"If now I return to your servant, my father, and say the lad is not with us, he will surely die. For his life is bound in the lad's life. And thus, your servants will be responsible for the death of our father." Laying his right hand on his chest, he continued, "Your servant swore to return the lad or bear the blame forever. I beseech Your Eminence, grant us this mercy, though undeserved: let me remain instead of the youth as your slave. And allow the lad and his brothers return to our aged father."

He offers his life for Benjamin's, that Abba too might live! This astonishing gesture was too much for Joseph. "Leave us, all of you!" he yelled in the dialect of Egypt. Every servant within hearing distance vanished as though into thin air.

Forgive me, Lord, for ever withholding mercy. Joseph was trembling from scalp to soles. Reaching a shaky hand to his head, he slowly pulled off his wig.

In his mother tongue, he said, "Brothers, I am Joseph."

He was temporarily uncertain whether they had understood him, for not a single one of them moved or uttered a word.

"It is I, Joseph, who stands before you," he emphasized. "Pray tell me, does my father live?"

He watched their heads slowly lift and saw expressions ranging from utter confusion to shocked disbelief on his brothers' bearded faces. Still, they remained on their knees, speechless. The chamber was deathly silent.

"Do you not hear me speak to you in Hebrew? I am Joseph, I live. Rise!"

They began to rise, slowly, visibly shaking. He could imagine what the older ones were thinking. If truly it was the brother they betrayed that now stood before them, then their fate was no longer in question: they were dead men standing.

Joseph stepped closer to them. "Fear not, brothers. I will do you no harm."

Benjamin was the first to speak. "Is it really you, brother?"

O my Benjamin. Stretching his arms out wide, a misty-eyed Joseph said, "It is I, brother, it is I." In the blink of an eye, Benjamin closed the distance between them and flung himself into his long-lost brother's arms. Joseph heard the deafening cry before he realized the one voicing it was himself.

34

***

Peaceful.

Contrary to her state of mind when she departed, Asenath was returning to her luxurious home feeling serene. She knew her newfound peace resulted less from her being a pampered guest for a night, and more from her beginning the day at her friend's altar. For there, she had relinquished the burden she knew herself incapable of bearing. The day was still young, and she was not sure what awaited her inside, but that uncertainty bore no anxiety with it.

She was ascending the stairs toward the main entrance when a loud wail sent a paralyzing chill up her spine.

Who weeps? Another voice joined the wailing. *What is happening?*

The absence of guards flanking the grand doors was not lost on her. Then she noticed the doors were slightly ajar. Gently pushing against one ebony door, Asenath carefully leaned in and caught her breath.

Bald head bared and face awash with tears, Joseph was embracing one of his brothers, while the others stood staring at them with varying degrees of astonishment registered on their faces.

He revealed himself! Rooted to her spot, Asenath stared on.

Then the brother that had spoken for the group at the feast fell to his knees, weeping violently, as the rest became similarly floored by the mighty wave of emotions. Slowly, Joseph released his equally wet-faced, smiling brother.

Benjamin!

Benjamin turned to the brother who had kneeled first, the spokesman of the group, and said, "Judah, can you believe the Lord's mercy? My brother lives!"

So that is Judah!

Still on his knees, Judah crawled forward to bow at Joseph's feet.

"Forgive them all, brother. It is I who deserve to be your slave, for it was I who accepted silver in exchange for my flesh and blood. It is I who deafened my ears to the cries of your tortured soul, and I have been cursed ever since. Not until I buried my first son, and then my second, did I understand the anguish my sin brought upon *Abba*. I took the light from his eyes. I stole your freedom. It is right that mine be taken from me for the rest of my days."

"This is not a moment for justice, but for mercy, Judah. And I . . . I forgive you," Joseph said, bending low to help an awe-struck Judah up on his feet, and then throw his arms around him.

Embraced in undeserved mercy, Judah let out a spine-chilling lament.

Asenath put a hand to her fluttering heart and released a slow, silent breath.

Once Judah's cries had subsided, Joseph pulled back. Then he wiped both of Judah's wet cheeks dry, and kissed each one, saying, "You are forgiven." Stepping forward, he gave a sweeping gesture that encompassed the rest of his brothers and said, "I forgive you, all."

"How can you forgive us when we did nothing to stop your enslavement?" one of the oldest brothers asked.

Joseph smiled. "Because it may have been your hands that sold me into slavery, but it was the Lord's plans that brought me to Egypt. The God of our fathers arranged it back then, for such a time as this. Brothers, this famine has lasted two years, but I assure you, there are yet five more years of lack to come. Our God sent me ahead of you all, that I might preserve you alive. That the family of his servant, our *abba*, would be saved from starvation."

Joseph spread his arms wide. "Do you not see? If I had not come and we all perished, how could the Lord's promise to multiply the seed of our forefather Abraham into a great nation be upheld?"

Lord God of mercy, your ways are too wonderful for comprehension. Asenath was in awe of both what was transpiring and the fact that she was witnessing it. One by one, the brothers rose from their feet and surrounded her husband in a group embrace. Joseph began to laugh and cry simultaneously from their midst. Asenath could no longer see him, but what he said next was loud, clear, and utterly incredible: "You must all return to Canaan at once. Bring *Abba* to Egypt, along with and all of your wives, sons, daughters, even your sheep!"

"Bring everyone here?" she heard Benjamin ask, as the others stepped back in shock, opening up the ring of brethren.

"Yes! Everyone!" Joseph said, laughing, as he spun around in the heart of his brotherly circle. When he stopped, he faced Judah. "The Lord has made me like a father to Pharaoh. No man lifts hand or foot in Egypt but at *my* word. You shall live in the best of Egypt's lands and I shall provide for you all. Go, tell *Abba* of all the glory your eyes have seen, and bring him to me."

You are reuniting the whole family, Lord? Asenath looked at the circle of brethren, tears silently falling down her face. She suddenly felt like one intruding on a sacred moment. Stepping back through the narrowly open door, she gently pulled it shut and let them be. Slowly making her way to the servant's entrance, she felt like shouting, dancing, and weeping all at the same time. Indubitably, she and her beloved would have a tearful reunion of their own tonight; and she could hardly wait. It was fortunate their sons were away, for she wanted no interruptions this night.

Catching her own line of thought, Asenath shook her head at the incredibility of it all. By this time yesterday, the tempest that threatened to destroy her family raged fiercely, with no signs of abating. Yet the Lord had required nothing but her trust to still it. She was immeasurably grateful she had entrusted the situation to the invisible God. Who else could have done the impossible *overnight*? The sight she had just witnessed may have felt like a dream, but it was real, concrete evidence of one incredible truth: the storm was over.

A FEW WEEKS LATER

The reddish-orange hues splashed across Goshen's vast skies were awe-inspiring. Nevertheless, it was not the striking sunset, but the scenery beneath it that took Asenath's breath away. Under her sandaled feet, thick grass stretched out endlessly, like a divine rug. How the grass here remained green in the heart of a famine was inexplicable, but it left no doubt about Goshen being the very best and most fertile land in Egypt.

A stone's throw before her, standing tall upon his chariot, was her beloved; the wind whipping at his tunic. Behind her was the horse-drawn, covered carriage that had conveyed herself and her sons from Avaris. One above the other, her son's faces resembled twain floating heads, peering out of the partition in the carriage's animal skin flaps. The lads were curious about the sight looming before them, and impatiently anticipating the moment their *Ima* would let them descend. Asenath did not begrudge them their curiosity, for descending upon them like a small army were all of her husband's relatives.

The air was filled with the bleating of several herds of goats and flocks of sheep. There were men leading scores of heavily laden donkeys. Others driving a plethora of Egyptian wagons filled with women and little children. The impressive collection of wagons had been a gift from Pharaoh upon learning that Joseph's family would be joining him. As the exodus drew nearer, they spread out to the left and the right in what was reminiscent of a parade.

"What is happening, *Ima*?" Ephraim asked.

"It looks like they are forming a line," Asenath answered.

"Why, *Ima*?"

"I know not, my little monkey. Let us be patient; we will find out soon enough."

When some of the cavalcade went past them on either side, Asenath peered around her carriage, and smiled. *They are surrounding us.* Returning to her former position, she smiled at the two pairs of arched brows awaiting.

354

"It is not a line, but a circle. They are encircling us."

She swept the scene from left to right and counted six wagons before them. *If a similar number lie behind us, they must have grouped according to the family of each brother.*

As the wagons halted around them, one made its way forward and towards Joseph. All of this time, Judah, who had been sent ahead to prepare the way for the rest of the travelers, had been on a horse next to Joseph's chariot. Now, he nudged his horse forward, toward the wagon that was presently halted not too far from them. Then, from the folds of his tunic, he unearthed a somewhat twisted wind instrument, and sounded a long, loud note. The men leading each caravan, whom Asenath now identified as Joseph's brothers by virtue of the two closest to her, descended and each stood before his caravan. Judah raised the wagon flap before him, and a man resembling a younger version of himself leaped out of the tent. Both he and Judah then assisted a wiry old man out of the tent. Judging by the scantiness of the gray locks that hung from beneath his head covering, there was more hair in his long, silver beard than there was upon his head. Judah handed him a cane, which he leaned heavily upon. His age and stature left Asenath no doubt as to his identity. *Abba Jacob.*

***

Joseph had been patiently standing in his chariot, watching his entire family literally surround him. But when his eyes fell upon his now aged *abba* descending from a wagon, he could no longer remain composed. Like a boy who had been awaiting his father's return from a protracted voyage, he yelled at the top of his voice, "*Abba!*" and ran toward Jacob.

The patriarch had barely limped two steps away from his caravan before Joseph reached him. The once-lost son fell upon his *abba*, flinging his arms about the frail old man. Realizing he had not given his father a chance to even look at him, he stepped back for a moment and stood directly before Jacob.

He saw Jacob's timeworn eyes roam all over his face. Letting his cane fall to the floor, the aged man reached two weathered hands towards his son. Joseph felt their roughness run over his forehead, and outline his facial features. Finally, his father cradled his chin in both hands.

"*B'ni* . . . My beloved son, Joseph, lives," he said, as his eyes watered.

"Yes, *Abba*, I live," Joseph said, not bothering to stop the tears pouring down his cheeks.

"I held your bloody tunic in my arms, convinced a wild beast had devoured you and I would go to my grave grieving. Lo, my eyes have beheld my son, in the land of the living. Now I may die in peace."

"Not today, *Abba*, not today!" Joseph said, laughing and crying, as he drew his father into his embrace. He felt the old man's arms grip him with surprising strength. And there, in the arms of his father, every last trace of pain buried deep in his soul faded away. *Thank you, Lord God of my fathers, for restoring my family to me —my entire family!*

Letting his father go, he turned around and his eyes caught Asenath's. He waved her over. "*Abba*, I want you to meet my three reasons for rising each dawn."

Turning back, he saw his sons race ahead of their mother, who walked elegantly, but swiftly, behind them. As his sons reached him, he positioned them on his right and left.

"My firstborn, Manasseh, and my second son, Ephraim," he said, laying a hand on each one's head, respectively.

"The Lord bless you, my little ones," Jacob said, squinting. As his stance wavered, Joseph picked up the discarded cane and handed it back to his father.

"Are you really *Abba's abba*?" Ephraim asked in fluent Hebrew.

Jacob laughed, "Yes, I am your *saba*, Israel, *ben* Isaac, *ben* Abraham."

He called himself a different name. "Israel, *Abba*?" Joseph inquired.

"The Lord has seen fit to change my name, *b'ni*."

From a name that means 'Supplanter,' to one that means 'Let God prevail.' "How wonderful, *Abba*. The Lord has indeed prevailed. And he has also seen fit to gift me a jewel of inestimable worth," Joseph said as he placed his arm around his misty-eyed, smiling wife. "*Abba*, this is my greatest treasure, a devoted daughter of our Lord, my wife, Asenath."

***

Asenath's heart had been singing as she watched the interaction between her husband, his father, and his sons, but now, at Joseph's praise, it was dancing. She took to her knees, bowed her head, and spoke in Hebrew. "Blessings of the Lord be upon you, *Abba* Israel."

"And upon you, *biti*," Israel said, using the Hebrew term for 'my daughter,' which warmed Asenath's heart even more than his gentle touch on her head. Rising, she looked directly into his eyes. "It is a joy beyond measure to have you here, *Abba*. Your son is God's gift not only to me, but to all of Egypt."

Israel took both her hands in his cane-free one, and said, "I myself have been a stranger in a foreign land, so I know he would not be who he is if you had not loved him and cared for him. Blessed is he indeed to have such a wife, and one who has borne such strong, handsome sons!"

Joseph's laughter rang, as it had not in a long time. At the sound of it, Asenath tingled from her head to her toes.

Releasing Asenath's hands, Israel cradled Joseph's face and said simply, "*B'ni.*" Then, with tears streaming down his face, he lifted his hand skyward and cried out, "Bless the Lord, O my soul, and all that is within me praise his name."

Lowering his hand to lean heavily on his cane, he slowly began descending to the ground. Joseph assisted him to a kneeling position and kneeled beside him. Cane laid down once more, the glad grandfather lifted both hands up, and prayed, "Blessed be the Lord God Almighty! God of my fathers! For he has done a thing too wonderful for my understanding! I imagined my son dead, but now my eyes behold not only him, but his sons as well. Bless the Lord, O my soul. Let everything that draws breath praise him!"

Joseph lifted his hands and joined his father in praising God. Asenath followed, as though it was the most natural thing in the world to do.

Like ripples spreading out from a stone dropped in the sea, one after the other, his brothers kneeled, and so did their wives, their sons and their wives, too. In what seemed like a mere moment, there were over seventy pairs of hands lifted skyward, in praise of the Almighty God.

Bless the Lord, O my soul. Asenath prayed silently, her hands raised. *He has set the solitary in a family. You have restored my husband's family back to him, larger and more united than ever before. You have made him savior and king, in his own family. And what a family; they are a veritable village! And they are my family too—my village!*

Instantly, the words of her own childhood declaration resurfaced. '*I will have a village, Mother!*' and her skin broke out in gooseflesh.

Lord God, how are you so mindful as to grant the long-forgotten desire of a once-pagan girl? Bowing her face to the ground, Asenath began to weep.

She felt small hands encircle her.

"*Ima*, do not cry."

She looked up at her second son's concerned face and hugged his small frame.

"These are tears of joy, my sweet. *Ima* is so very happy." She kissed him and said, "Now sing praises with your *abba*; go on."

As Ephraim edged closer to his father and his high-pitched voice contrasted with Joseph's deep tone, Asenath's heart melted. She looked at her sons kneeling beside their *abba*, who himself kneeled beside his *abba*. Three generations side by side, lifting their voices and hands to their heavenly *abba*. A large lump wedged itself in her throbbing throat, and she could neither sing nor speak past it. It was all she could do simply to lift her hands up and let the tears of joy fall down. The air was filled with the sweet symphony of united voices, worshiping in song.

As the family of Israel ended their melodic psalm, their patriarch shouted, "Let all say, 'Bless the Lord, O my soul, for his mercy endures forever!'"

As one, the village of voices echoed Israel's, "Bless the Lord, O my soul, for his mercy endures forever!"

There was a moment of utter stillness, and then, like a sudden rainfall in the desert, an abundance of words showered down upon Asenath's mind. It was as though her soul were reciting a psalm for the hearing of only her creator. As verse after verse flowed forth, Asenath made a decision. This very night, at her earliest opportunity she would pour out the praise dancing in her soul upon a parchment, letter after letter, line upon line, that she might for the rest of her days, remember how she felt in the moment she finally became the queen of a divinely orchestrated village.

35

The sea of mercy
Drowns the ashes of wrongs
Burned in the flames of love

***

Blissful.

Wife and husband had slept embraced in each other's arms. It was the sweet sleep of lovers with joyful hearts and peaceful minds. Asenath wished they could just stay in that blissful state forever. When at last she awakened, it was to discover she was still in her husband's bed, but he was not. The dimness of the room suggested the day had not fully dawned.

Where is he? She wondered, stretching her unclad self beneath the thick, warm sheets.

A throat cleared.

She sat up. *Merit? In Beloved's chamber, at this hour?*

"Blessings of the morn, Your Eminence."

Still in high spirits, Asenath teased, "The morn is yet to dawn, Merit."

Tilting her head shyly, Merit smiled, "Blessings of the dawn, then?"

Asenath laughed. "What brings you *here* so early? And where is my husband?"

"His Eminence asks that Her Eminence meet him in the garden this morn as soon as possible."

"Then fetch me a *kalasiris*, forthwith." Merit gestured toward the couch to her right, and Asenath saw a garment of hers, neatly laid out beside a bejeweled cloak. She raised an eyebrow. "This

361

one?"

"I thought it might pair well with His Eminence's attire, Your Eminence."

What finery is Joseph wearing? More importantly, what is he up to?

Merit's instincts had never proven wrong before. "In that case, bring me my favorite *usekh*."

"And an adornment for your hair?"

A mysterious morning adventure in the garden, is it? Beloved is not the only one who can be adventurous. Asenath smiled. "I hope your hands are skilled in weaving, Merit. As I have an unusual adornment in mind."

***

Joseph stood in the garden, quietly watching the flames dancing on his altar. Their red, yellow, and orange colors blended together seamlessly, and they moved as though in time to an invisible rhythm. *Perhaps the Lord plays a song only they can hear.* The thought drew a smile. Soft footsteps approached. His pulse quickened in anticipation. He turned around and his heart skipped.

My purple iris. She looked as beautiful as she did when he first saw her, if not more so. The *usekh* her mother once owned graced her elegant neck, and her body was adorned in the same white *kalasiris* she wore the night they became one flesh. Except it hugged her curves a little more tightly now than it had then.

Wife of my youth. Her glorious mass of curls was crowned with a most unusual, intricate wreath of fresh, purple irises.

Mother of my sons. The soft morning breeze caused both her chestnut tresses and the skirt of her garment to join the dance of the flames.

My gift from God. She sauntered with long, elegant strides until she stood a handbreadth from him. Her full lips spread into a half-smile. He suddenly found himself tongue-tied. Fortunately, she did not share his fate.

"Someone is overly dressed for a stroll about the gardens, would you not agree?"

He grinned. "'Tis a good thing we are not here for strolling."

"No? I would never have guessed it!" she teased.

Smiling, Joseph reached out and brushed a pair of straying curls out of her face and then he cradled her chin and lifted it. He held her eyes with his for a moment, letting his eyes speak first, before kissing her tenderly. His lips lingered, savoring hers. When their kiss ended, he looked lovingly into her eyes and said, "Blessings of the morn, my purple iris."

"And to you, Beloved."

"You are wondering why we are here."

"Not at this moment," she said, giving him a knowing look.

Joseph laughed. "I love you!"

"Tell me something I do not know," she said, wiggling her eyebrows.

"Your beauty this dawn is breathtaking."

"I was advised to keep up with my handsome husband's impeccable style."

"My thanks to Merit. I am feeling ceremonious, and for good reasons. Actually, I would like you to perform a unique ceremony with me, here and now," Joseph said, leaning down and retrieving a worn leather pouch leaning against the altar.

"You have my full attention."

"Do you recall my dream from the night before I revealed myself to my brothers?"

"Mercy above judgment?"

Joseph smiled. "Precisely. I was thinking about how in that dream I could not break free from the prison until I freed my brothers. Since I was not a physical prisoner when I dreamed it, I understood that holding onto the memory of their wrongdoings against me was keeping me captive on the inside."

Glancing at the pouch, he said, "My journals. These parchments hold a record of the wrongs done to me by my brothers and others. And I wish to hold on to them no longer."

He noticed both of her brows leap toward her hairline, but she said nothing, so he continued.

"The Lord has reunited my family and expanded it beyond my wildest imagination. My *abba* gets to watch me be an *abba*. My sons have another *saba*. They now have eleven men to call '*Dohd*,' and I want them to grow up knowing and loving those uncles. That will not happen unless we forget the past and start anew, being kind and merciful to one another, as the Lord is kind and merciful to us. When I think about the future, I envision the family of my birth and the family of my blessing, blended into one big family."

"A family of love, united by the God of love," a watery-eyed Asenath said.

"I could not have said it better. To that end, I have chosen to burn these—save for my family tree." He said, pulling out his journals. "Will the eminent lady be so kind as to join my journal-burning ceremony?"

Asenath wiped a lone tear, smiled, and replied, "I would be honored."

One by one, they drew out each roll of papyrus and threw it in the flames. Then they stood side by side, arms around each other, and watched the parchments burn.

Taking his eyes from the flames to his wife's face, he said, "There's something else I wanted to say before our brief ceremony ends."

"Tell me," she said, turning to face him, and wrapping her arms about his waist.

"I want us, together, to start a new collection of journals. And I want you to write the first entry."

"Me?" Asenath asked, surprised. "What would I write about?"

"The same thing we will write about from this day onwards: verses and tales about the wondrous mercies the Lord has shown us and our family."

A broad smile lit up her face. Releasing him, she raised a hand, "Wait here, Beloved, do not take one step." She turned and began heading for the house.

"Where are you going?" he asked, delightfully curious.

She yelled over her shoulder, "Do not move! I shall return in a moment."

Picking up the skirt of her *kalasiris*, she raced out of sight.

There is never a dull moment with this mysterious, marvelous wife of mine. Thank you, Lord, for gifting her to me.

***

Asenath half skipped and half ran, her heart filled with joy. What human mind could have foreseen that she would pen a psalm the very night before Joseph would request one? She found her most recent literary work exactly where she had left it: on her writing desk. She hastily retrieved it and returned to the garden.

Joseph was standing right where she had left him, his arms crossed in front of his broad chest, a puzzled expression on his face. Without a word, she held the scroll out to him.

"What is this?"

"If you approve, the first entry in our new journals."

His expression changed to show surprise. Reaching for the scroll, he read it silently while Asenath shifted from side to side, musing.

He wants verses and tales. She knew the potency of her verse may be questioned, but there was one tale that would indubitably evidence the Lord's mercies. Getting permission to tell it was another matter altogether.

When Joseph looked up from the parchment, his eyes were moist, and he blinked rapidly. In a breathy voice, he said, "I approve, absolutely."

Yes! Asenath beamed.

His face expressing utter amazement, her husband asked, "When did you write this?"

"As soon as our sons and I returned last night—before you returned."

"I think I ought to let you do the writing henceforth!"

"Speaking of which, I do recall you saying verses *and* tales of mercies. I shall leave the next verses up to you, if you let me write a tale."

"Why would I ever stop you?"

"Because it will contain some of what we have just burned."

Joseph's brows furrowed. "Explain. Please."

Asenath took a deep breath. "I know of no better tale to evidence the Lord's loving-kindness than our stories. Think on this: I grew up a prisoner of my predestined future. Until recently, you were a prisoner of your harrowing past. Yet we stand here, both free, by the mercy of the Lord. Even so, the path to that freedom was a painful one. Especially for you. But to recount our story without the pain would defeat the purpose. For no one could ever truly appreciate the miracle of our joys, without understanding the misery of our sorrows."

"Including my betrayal."

"And your soul-stirring, wholehearted forgiving of it."

"Which was the key to my freedom."

"Precisely. The mercy of the Lord has been doubly showered upon us: the force of forgiveness liberated you, and the strength of love liberated me."

Her husband looked intrigued. "How so?"

"Your love for me opened my heart to the invisible God's incredible love and embracing his love only enabled me to love you more. I am still in awe that an omnipotent, omniscient, perfect God chooses to love imperfect mortals who can do nothing to deserve his loving-kindness. But by so doing, he has shown us the right way to love each other. Ours is a three-way romance; it supersedes the typical love solely between man and wife. I believe that is what makes ours such a compelling love story."

Joseph smiled. "A divine one."

"Precisely."

"So my wife means to pen a romantic tale?"

Asenath grinned. "Ultimately."

"Have you a title for it?"

"Two wrestle in my mind, already."

"And they are?"

"To be revealed upon completion of the story, naturally."

Joseph rolled his eyes. "I should have foreseen that response. Let me pose a different inquiry: who do you hope will read your tale?"

Good question. Asenath pondered it for a few moments. "No particular person comes to mind at the moment. But I imagine that if we stumble across others struggling under the sorrows that once held us bound, our tale might help them find the path to freedom. Even if it were but one such person, would that not make it worth telling?"

"Absolutely."

"Truly? You will allow me to pen it, then?"

"If it is half as moving as this verse," Joseph said, waving her rolled scroll, "I look forward to reading every word."

"*Ani ohev otkha,* Joseph, *ben* Israel, husband of my youth, father of my sons, and savior of Egypt."

"I know you love me, and that knowledge fires every fragment of my being, every moment of every day."

Asenath lifted her face to his and he gently closed the gap between their lips. Arm in arm, they savored the sweet sincerity of their kiss. In the heart of the garden where their love first bloomed, they stood. The record of the past, a pile of ashes before them. The hope of the future, a flame of fire within them. And in Joseph's hand, Asenath's heart poured out in droplets of ink upon a papyrus:

Bless the Lord, O my soul
For his ways are perfect
And his paths wondrous
He ends a matter before it is begun
Yet he has neither end nor beginning

Bless the Lord, O my soul
For he sets the lonely in a family
One as great as a village
He takes their sorrow and makes it joy
And turns their mourning into dancing

Bless the Lord, O my soul
For he teaches the hard heart to love
And the bitter heart to forgive
He takes a stranger and calls her daughter

My ears had heard of his wonders
And now my eyes have seen them
Too wonderful for comprehension
Too marvelous for elocution

Bless the Lord, O my soul
Among the gods there is none comparable
To the invisible God, who does impossible things
Who beholds all, but cannot be beheld

Who fathoms all, but cannot be fathomed

Great is the Lord indeed
He is worthy of all praise
And great is his loving-kindness
Even unto endless generations

Bless the Lord, O my soul
Let his praises ring from our lips
And the lips of our children
And their children, for all time

~ Asenath, wife of Joseph ben Israel, ben Isaac, ben Abraham—friend of the invisible God

EPILOGUE

Falsehoods. Betrayals. Wrongs, great and small
"How many times must one forgive?"
Hark! The answer of heaven:
"Seventy times seven"
Let this truth resound:
Bitterness binds;
Forgiveness
Sets one
Free

***

TEN YEARS LATER

Musing.

Asenath thoughtfully studied her reflection in the spotless, bronze-framed mirror before her. *Perhaps a grander usekh? Then again, that depends on where we are going.*

"Blessings of the evening, *Ima*," her fourteen-year-old son said, striding into her chamber, casually.

"And to you, *b'ni*," she said, looking up at the lad many had termed the taller, masculine version of herself.

"You seem especially excited this evening, *Ima*. May I ask why?"

"Your *abba* is taking me out for the anniversary of our wedding."

"Wait, I could have sworn that it was not for five more days."

"You are correct, Ephraim. But your *abba* has a unique habit of starting our anniversary celebrations early, and making them mysteriously adventurous. That is one habit of his for which your *Ima* has no objections!"

"Of course. First Manasseh's starry-eyed sighs, and now your romantic saga. Where can a lad go to find persons not afflicted with love sickness?"

"I am delighted to say, I know not! What I do know is that your brother has had eyes only for Benerib since you were but babes, and now that she is finally beginning to return the sentiment, you can hardly begrudge him his happiness."

"Please, *Ima*. You mean, begrudge you and your best friend your happiness."

"Neferubity is more than just my best friend; we are as sisters before the Lord. If our children decide in the future to marry, we could hardly complain," Asenath said playfully.

"And by that, you mean breaking out *sistrumsas* and tambourines."

Asenath laughed. "Might I suggest, since you cannot escape the lovesick, that you join us? Benerib's little sister is equally stunning."

"Even the blind can see that, *Ima*, but no, thank you. I would rather not play second string to my brother in yet another realm." Ephraim's voice had a hard edge to it.

Turning around, Asenath strode to her couch, seated herself, and patted the vacant cushion beside her. Accepting her wordless invitation, Ephraim occupied it.

"What troubles you, my sweet?"

"It is just . . . sometimes Manasseh makes me want to grind my teeth."

"You are brothers and close ones; it is to be expected."

"But he gets everything so easily. It is as though the heavens favor him and frown upon me."

"You are referring to the archery tournament."

"Yes. I practiced for months! He was hardly even interested. He only entered at the last minute because Benerib said she would love to watch!"

"Second place is very praiseworthy, Ephraim."

"Not when I was aiming for first place, *Ima*. I wanted one thing, one place where I am not in the shadow of my brother, but no, he had to have that too."

"Being firstborn, your brother has received many gifts before you, but you have equally many, if not better, gifts. It is true, life seems to throw more challenges your way—even your birth was a battle. But I have come to learn that the ones with tougher battles build greater strength and win grander victories." She said, planting a kiss on his cheek. "Now, as for this incident, I do not think Manasseh knows how much the tournament meant to you, do you?"

Ephraim shook his head.

"Did you speak with your *abba* about how you feel?"

"*Abba* would never understand. *Dohd* Judah worships the ground he walks upon. None of his brothers ever dispute with him; he is as a prince among them. What would he know about feeling inferior to a brother? Or rivaling with one?"

"Far more than you could ever conceive. You have more in common with your *abba* than you think."

"I am not convinced."

"Perhaps a story might persuade you."

"Very well, let us hear it."

"This one you have to read for yourself, *b'ni*. You will find it in the library, in the chest of tales."

"What is it titled?"

"A divine romance."

"Romance? Surely you jest, *Ima*!"

"I would listen to your *ima*, Ephraim. 'Tis quite the tale."

Both of them turned to see Joseph leaning against the door.

"You have read this tale, *Abba*?" Ephraim asked, his disbelief evident.

"Every word. In fact, you could say I have lived it."

Asenath smiled as Ephraim reluctantly gave in. "I suppose I could spend the evening reading. I have nothing more fascinating to do."

"Your enthusiasm warms your *ima*'s heart," Asenath said dryly.

"*Ima*, you know I meant no slight."

"The library is that way," Joseph said, pointing at the door. "Enjoy your evening."

"I can take a hint," Ephraim said. Leaning to kiss Asenath's cheek, he said, "You look resplendent."

As their son exited the chamber, Joseph turned to his wife and said, "He took the words out of my mouth."

"Compliments from son and husband? I am flattered, but also curious. How long were you standing there?"

"Long enough to know he and I will be having a heartfelt conversation soon."

"You are not displeased I suggested he read it?"

"'Tis about time someone did. It has been waiting nearly a decade to be read."

"It seems we did not need to venture far to find a soul struggling with the sorrows we overcame."

"Not far at all. I am shocked he thinks himself inferior. I sometimes see more strength and leadership ability in him than I do in Manasseh."

"Perhaps the Lord has a special story for him, too."

"The future will reveal what the present conceals."

"Indeed."

"Now, is my eminent lady ready to depart?"

"Most certainly, my eminent lord."

"Splendid. It goes without saying, I shall be the envy of every man in sight."

"Where are we going?"

"Her Eminence will just have to wait and see."

Asenath grunted. As they exited her chamber, Joseph said, "You know, it has just occurred to me after all these years, that I never did ask what the other option was."

"Option for?"

"The tale's title."

"Of course!" Asenath said, smiling. "'Prisoners of Fate.'"

Joseph grinned. "Apt. Very apt. I might have chosen that."

"I almost did. But my ultimate choice appealed more, for its timeless nature."

"How so?"

"We ceased being captives years ago, but I like to think our divine romance will never end. Or will it?"

Her husband raised her hand to his lips and kissed it. His eyes never leaving hers, he gave an answer that melted her heart: "Not in life, in death, or beyond."

And so they walked onward regally, the queen of a vast village and her king, so crowned by the mercy of the invisible God.

***

Asenath and her beloved celebrated many more wonderful anniversaries together. Under their loving care, her extended family continued to flourish in the land of Egypt. Her husband enjoyed seven more years with his *abba* restored to his side. Therefore, father and son shared a total of seventeen years together, after that glorious moment in the fields of Goshen, when they were reunited. When Israel lay on his deathbed, he blessed not only Joseph, but all of his twelve sons with unique blessings. Furthermore, he blessed Joseph's sons, placing his right hand upon the younger, thereby giving Ephraim the blessing of the firstborn. And Israel adopted them as his own, bestowing upon his grandsons an inheritance equal that of his sons. And so, Ephraim and Manasseh respectively became the eleventh and twelfth of the twelve tribes that made up the nation of Israel. Indeed, as the Lord had promised their ancestor Abraham, so he did: the Israelites multiplied into a people as numerous as the sand on the shores and the stars in the sky.

For the rest of their lives, Asenath saw that the fatherly blessing their dying *abba*, Israel, had bestowed upon her husband, rang true:

"May the God of your father help you; may the Almighty bless you with the blessings of the heavens above, and blessings of the watery depths below, and blessings of the breasts and womb. May my fatherly blessings on you surpass the blessings of my ancestors, reaching to the heights of the eternal hills. May these blessings rest on the head of Joseph, who is a prince among his brothers." (Genesis 49:25-26)

A prince indeed, he was, and Asenath, his first and only love, for he loved no other woman as long as he lived. And she returned not only his love but also that of the invisible God. Thus they lived ever after, in a divine romance.

THE END

NOTE FROM THE AUTHOR

Dear reader,

Thank you for taking the time to read my debut novel! This book was a dream that died a hundred deaths, but had a hundred and one resurrections, because my Eternal Lover, the one who gives life to dead things, and calls those things that be not as though they were, brought it to life.

The Journey: The idea came to my mind as a three-word impression during a time of devotion: 'Write Joseph's memoirs.' That was April 6th, 2019. I wrote those words down in my prayer journal and thought nothing more of them since I never saw myself as a novelist. Until five weeks later, when I received an unexpected prophecy about my writing abilities—while in a TV audience, no less. Encouraged to obey that three-word instruction, I completed my first draft of the story a few months later. Nonetheless, I had no idea how tumultuous the journey to actually realizing the dream would be. One pandemic, two continents, three and a half years, four story versions, fourteen residences, and several traumas later, it's a book! #NeverGiveUp

The Lesson: Birthing this book took me on a lengthy journey of learning, and choosing, to forgive seemingly unforgivable injustices and life-threatening offenses, over and again. Every time I wanted to cry out for vengeance, I remembered the example Jesus set, when he forgave those responsible for his unjust death, while he yet hung on the cross. Matthew 18:22, which details Jesus teaching his disciples to forgive 'seventy times seven,' inspired the only nonet in this book—the poem that opens the epilogue. Forgiveness was my greatest lesson on this journey, and it truly is the key to freedom. #TheGoldenKey

Fact vs. Fiction: While I did extensive research on Ancient Egypt, and thoroughly studied the biblical story of Joseph, ultimately this is a work of fiction. I'm unashamedly neurodivergent and took imaginative liberties wherever I felt it enhanced my story. For example, my fictitious titles for nobility, *Radiances*, *Magnificences*, etc., and giving colorful gowns to my main character, as I imagine had she access to such vibrant fabric shades as emerald, royal blue, and gold, she would've chosen those. #CreativeLicense

A Plethora of Poems: Poetry plays a pivotal role in my characters' expression of emotion. I say I am a poet first, and a storyteller second, because poetry comes naturally to me. It's also my therapy, especially spoken word poetry, so the fact that this work of fiction is riddled with my original poems is something I make no apologies for! I enjoyed writing Haikus and other short poems to introduce each chapter of this story, and hint at either that chapter's happenings, or the characters' current feelings. If you were not a poetry fan before reading this story, I hope you are now! :) #PoetryIsMyLoveLanguage

Own Voices: Like Asenath, I'm also an African woman who was raised in a patriarchal society. Like Joseph, I'm also an immigrant who has spent years away from family, in a foreign nation. (Except I emigrated willingly!) I chose to write primarily from Asenath's perspective, because I wanted to celebrate the unsung heroine in a popular tale. I gave my Asenath quite a few of my personality traits, including being very introspective and intellectual, a fan of fashion, and a lover of languages and stories. #MeToo

Interpretive Character Names: For those characters not already named in the Bible, I took the time to choose interpretive ancient Egyptian names. For example, naming a mother figure *Na'eemah*, (meaning mother), and a character with a hawklike face, *Akhom*, (meaning eagle). See the reader's guide that opens this book for a glossary of character names and meanings! #Details

Author Goals: I don't know whether this story will appeal to many, but I hope you will see beyond the imperfections of my storytelling and take away two truths:

1. God's love is unconditional, undeserved, undying, and absolutely life-changing. And He freely gives it to all because he SO loves humanity. John 3:16. #GodIsLove

2. True forgiveness is not just divine, it's utterly liberating. But it is very much a choice. Although, if we want to enjoy God's forgiveness, He says, we must also forgive others. Yes, I am painfully aware that is easier said than done. So, dear reader, if you too have suffered grave injustices, I am truly sorry you have

been hurt and I know what that feels like. In the interests of seeing you rise out of your pit of pain, and become the happy and whole person I know God designed you to be, I would encourage you to study Joseph's biblical account found in Genesis 37 - 50, and scriptures about forgiveness. (Matthew 6:14-15, 18:21, Ephesians 4:32, Colossians 3:13, Mark 11:25, Proverbs 10:12, and Isaiah 43:25.) #TheTruthShallSetYouFree

Additionally, I hope this romance provides readers of color with something I never experienced in growing up reading Christian novels: a beauty on the cover with sun-kissed skin a shade similar to mine. #RepresentationMatters

While there are many interpretations of this beloved biblical story, I hope you enjoyed mine. :) I'd love to hear about your favorite parts so please write to me via my website: ifuekoogbomo.com or find me on social media: @inspirologos.

If you'd like to receive updates about my upcoming books, fun bonuses like deleted scenes from *A Divine Romance*, and a poetry performance or two, subscribe to my newsletter/blog. (Details on my website). I look forward to hearing from you!

Passionately committed to inspiring with words,

Ifueko (Pronounced "ee-fw-echo")

ACKNOWLEDGMENTS

An African proverb states, *"It takes a village to raise a child."* Well, it certainly took one to birth this book baby. I would be remiss if I did not give honor to whom it is due.

First, I am immeasurably grateful to my Eternal Lover, and the one to whom I owe body, soul, and spirit, for inspiring me to *"write Joseph's memoirs"* on April 6, 2019, and being my teacher and guide every step of the way. Thank you, Lord, for resurrecting the dream after it died, and for every voice you sent to encourage me along the way. This story would not exist without you, and neither would I.

Additionally, my PROFOUND GRATITUDE goes to the following persons:

My family, especially my mom (and number 1 fan), Christina O. Ogaje, and my sister, Dr. Joy Isa, EdD, for believing in this story, and supporting me tirelessly on the four-year-journey from an idea in my mind to a book on international shelves.

My Christian fiction author friends-turned-sisters, Toni Shiloh, Heidi Chiavaroli, and Jenna Van Mourik, for saying "Yes" to endorsing a debut novel. Your glowing reviews were a heaven-sent salve, healing my wounded aspiring-novelist-soul; and, your permanent validation of this story, imbued me with the courage to keep running until I crossed the publication finish line.

The first Christian fiction author to attest to my potential as a novelist, Jocelyn Green, for spotting and supporting a diamond in the rough.

The man would see this story play out on the big screen, if he had his way, Rev. Nims Obunge, MBE, DL, for endorsing this from the get-go, and always having a listening ear. (We must have tea and chicken sandwiches next time I'm in London!)

The die-hard biblical fiction fan who read a stranger's story in 2021 and emphatically stated it was "captivating," Ebos Aifuobhokhan Nwamu, for endorsing and inspiring me to find an independent window, when traditional doors shut.

My partner-in-design, my sister-celebrator of African history, my *'personal person,'* Ayo Ellen Haynes, for seeing artistic details my tired eyes could no longer see. Every time I look at this gorgeous cover, I recall our intercontinental bookish brainstorming chats, and I smile. *Ese gan.*

Shawn Bolz, for being courageous enough to publicly call forth "a writing anointing" and "novels" from me, an untrained writer who had not yet penned a single novel, and was just an audience member at the TBN *Praise* show taping for his book, *Breakthrough.* (May 15, 2019). Thank you for your prophetic gift; you are a far greater blessing than you know. In my lowest moments on this writing journey, I have replayed your prophetic words, and risen stronger every time. God bless you, sir!

Finally, to everyone else I cannot name, who played a part in the journey to my fiction debut, *A Divine Romance*, thank you! Ultimately, we are all pieces in the invisible God's *senet* game. To Him belongs the victory, and the glory, forevermore.

ABOUT THE AUTHOR

Ifueko Ogbomo is a prize-winning poet, storyteller, voice artist, and sickle cell activist whose life's motto is 'to inspire with words.' A Nigerian immigrant, the United States Citizenship & Immigration Services awarded her the prestigious classification of *Alien of Extraordinary Ability*, for her internationally acclaimed work in the creative and performing arts. A member of the American Christian Fiction Writer's association, she is passionate about sharing the gospel through storytelling and spoken word artistry. Connect with her at ifuekoogbomo.com

MORE FROM THE AUTHOR

Voices of Lament: *Reflections on Brokenness and Hope in a World Longing for Justice.* Edited by Natasha Sistrunk Robinson. Ifueko Ogbomo's poem, *My Utmost Delight*, is chapter 1 of this collaborative, nonfiction book that features essays, liturgies, and poems, from 29 BIPOC Christian women contributors. Published by Revell, 2022.

Poetry & Children's Stories: The author's video collections of spectacular spoken word performances and inspirational children's stories are available on her website: ifuekoogbomo.com